scac

JUN -- 2017

The WANDERING TREE

DANIEL WIMBERLEY

The Wandering Tree
Copyright © 2016 by Daniel Wimberley

All rights reserved. No part of this publication may be reproduced, distributed, or transmitted in any form or by any means, including photocopying, recording, or other electronic or mechanical methods, without the prior written permission of the publisher, except in the case of brief quotations embodied in critical reviews and certain other noncommercial uses permitted by copyright law.

The characters and events in this book are fictitious. Any similarity to real persons, living or dead, is coincidental and not intended by the author.

Design Vault, LLC
www.designvault.net

Title page drawing by Luke Wimberley.

First Edition: May 2016

ISBN: 0692684654
ISBN-13: 978-0692684658

This one's for you, Dad.

PROLOGUE

The hayfield behind my house wasn't always a forgotten place. It was once a perfect elm grove, the sort of pastoral oasis where deer napped in sun dappled shade and doves cooed love songs into a warm breeze.

In the fall of 1937, the acreage was leveled to make room for an enterprise that would never come to fruition. Every bush and creeping vine was ripped from the dirt, every tree toppled and burned in a giant heap.

I say every tree, but if that was entirely true, this story would be short indeed.

When all that remained was a single elm, there came a great hiccup from the belly of progress. Because it wasn't just any tree, you see. It was among the largest ever recorded in Oklahoma, with a diameter of just over eight feet. Local arborists weren't exactly sure how to take it down safely—if in fact it should be taken down at all. And the tree's immense girth wasn't the only problem. Protruding from the dirt at its base, a strange fist of rusted iron drew a flurry of attention from regional scientists. Their curiosity, coupled with the interference of the local historical society, brought construction to an indefinite halt before it could even begin. More than one machine tried and failed to unearth the hunk of space metal—the largest mesosiderite on record, I would one day learn.

The landowner, a middle aged business man by the name of Andre Pruitt, became obsessed with turning a profit from this extraordinary discovery. For two decades, men came on his behalf to excavate the giant meteorite, each with some new fail-proof innovation at his disposal. None were successful.

Over time, the tree was damaged by the careless manning of heavy machinery. Branches were snapped, roots sheared and gouged. Before long, limbs began to lose their leaves out of season; others died altogether. At the time of his passing in 1955, Pruitt had nothing to show for his efforts and so the fuss finally died down. Dirt gradually obscured the mysterious space rock and for a while, it was forgotten.

In 1963, Pruitt's surviving son reported to the Shawnee News Star that the tree, which had miraculously survived, seemed to have wandered significantly across his property over the course of his life. When no one took him seriously, least of all the media, Jorge Pruitt hired a group of engineers to look into the matter. Dubious yet lulled by the prospect of an easy paycheck, these engineers meticulously surveyed the precise location of the tree, chuckling under their breaths all the while. But when they returned the following year to take fresh measurements, Jorge was vindicated. Though it seemed impossible, the tree was without a doubt moving.

With the phenomenon now on the official record, it didn't take long for the scientists to swoop back in. They immediately set to hypothesizing about the hows and whys. In the end, they decided the tree wasn't moving by its own power; the meteorite beneath it was responding—however uniquely—to Earth's constant magnetic power and the tree was simply along for the ride.

Leave it to the experts to sour a sweet mystery.

Nevertheless, Jorge was ecstatic. He must've imagined people flocking from all over, coughing up wads of cash to witness such a sight. But they didn't. Even the locals were content to read about it in the paper, to offer it a quick whistle of amazement over a cup of coffee at the Greasy Spoon. What was there to actually see, after all? A half-dead tree in the middle of a field was hardly worth the trip.

Daunted, Jorge Pruitt washed his hands of the property and moved on with other ventures. The place was gradually forgotten yet again.

And so was the wandering tree.

ONE

In a small town whose boyhood culture stemmed largely from disorganized schoolyard sports, the athletically inept were ripe for rejection, peeled away indiscriminately like patches of molted skin. Brigham Miller seemed to be the exclusive exception to the rule. He wasn't particularly interested in sports, hindered in part by a bad knee. He was gangly with the faintest hint of a moustache. And like me, his economic status was less than pristine. Yet people found him so likeable, so charming, that they chose to overlook these deficiencies just to be around him.

It was baffling and it gave many of us lesser beings hope.

Indeed, Brigham was the envy of every flaccid nerd and geek in school. He hadn't merely sidestepped the cruelty of juvenile ridicule; the very paradigm that kept most of us on the sidelines of life had parted like the Red Sea to grant him passage.

Physical limitations aside, Brigham simply didn't have the attention span for sports. He wasn't much fun on the baseball field, that's for sure—he was sooooo slow. I never told him so but he threw like a little girl and I had literally seen neighborhood toddlers do better at the plate. Brigham was just too preoccupied to keep his eye on the ball. He had a future to plan, I guess, and donning a baseball glove was something he tolerated more than enjoyed.

Don't get me wrong—I mean, if either of us was a millstone around the other's neck, it was certainly me. The fact that Brigham humored my interest in sports at all said something about his character. And if Brigham had been my only friend, I would have considered myself very fortunate.

But he wasn't my only friend; there was also Jeremy Isles. A year older than me, Jeremy was a short, fat Cherokee with wire-framed glasses and a smell about him that most didn't linger to identify. My mom told me once that she thought it was bug spray, considering that his father was an exterminator. If she was right, Mr. Isles needed to consider a different insecticide. Not only did the acrid fumes of his profession follow his son to school—which was a form of social cruelty, in my opinion—I personally was never any less lice-prone for enduring their second-hand miasma. Most of the time this was all bearable, though eating lunch with Jeremy was always a challenge.

What Jeremy lacked in odor-control he more than made up for in intelligence—his IQ was off the charts. Our age difference prevented us from sharing classes, but it was no secret who set the curve in his grade. He breezed through exams with no real thought, absorbed the content of lectures without taking notes. At once, he was every teacher's dream and nightmare. He must've kept them on their toes.

I've known my fair share of smart people; most have managed to rub me the wrong way, flexing those mental muscles at my expense. Jeremy was better than that. He didn't think any less of his intellectual inferiors—that or he just hid his snootiness well—and I found that to be incredibly endearing. He wasn't just book smart, either. He internalized things at a glance that experience alone should teach.

And he remembered *everything*.

Since Jeremy lived across town, he rode the bus home from school. I walked. For many years, our friendship was defined by this, hemmed in by the literal and figurative fences of the public school system, which was our only real common ground. Though we never dug deep, we were content to be buddies. He helped me with homework, I drew pictures for him to hang in his locker. It was an unpretentious arrangement with little lost or gained.

In contrast, Brigham and I were inseparable. We were blood brothers of Lakeview Park, a misnomered quasi-ghetto with no notable view, and certainly no lake. The place was an untidy smudge on the shiny belt buckle of Shawnee's old downtown district. Some called it a trailer park, as if the tin can mobile homes therein got to go home after a day of frolicking in the sun and eating popsicles by the community BBQ grill.

Others called it a trash heap. I won't tell you how that felt, considering what it said about those of us who lived there.

Brigham once called it *the place where dreams come to die* and that assessment has never left me because for many years, the truth of it seemed insurmountable.

The oldest and most decrepit trailer park in town, Lakeview Park was arranged around a horseshoe of pitted gravel which terminated at an asphalt road on both ends. My family lived near the middle of the curve, Brigham's a little off the entrance leg. The span between us was sentineled by a dozen or so Pit Bulls and no less than seven Rottweilers. Ours was a compressed sort of community, cramped in a way that forced relationships where none might exist otherwise.

This was the case for me and Brigham, I think. In the beginning, anyway. For a time, we were like jungle vines, fiercely scrambling—and occasionally grappling—for a solitary ray of sunlight in the canopy. It was a desperate struggle for which

Brigham was far better equipped than me but at least I didn't have to struggle alone. Over time, our friendship grew into something more substantial.

Like many who aspire to do great things, Brigham was motivated by a force greater than public opinion. I'm not sure what that force was, but I suspect that growing up being gawked at and called a cripple probably had a little something to do with it, if inversely. Nevertheless, I admired him. More than any other role model in my life, he was a paragon of humility and goodness. His ability to find happiness in the little things with an eye on greater things was a lantern on my path, casting warm hues upon an otherwise drab landscape.

"Someday, Link," he once told me. "Someday things are gonna be different. You just have to believe it's gonna happen, otherwise it never will."

For a time I even likened myself to Brigham, imagining that I too didn't care what people thought of me. It was an easy claim to make, tossed out there as if merely speaking it would make it so. But it wasn't true and it didn't take much to topple my hasty—and completely wishful—contention.

I sat in the back of the classroom because I would rather go unnoticed than risk being noticed for something embarrassing.

I improved the cosmetics of my shoes with tape and a black marker to belie my inability to buy new ones.

Not that the back of any room actually shielded me from ridicule or that anyone thought me well-to-do for my creative cobblery. But my willingness to be deluded was frank evidence of my true insecurity. Brigham and I simply weren't wired the same way. The thought of another person disliking me for any reason hurt me profoundly. That was me, for what little I was worth.

Still, while our motives veered down different paths, we remained bound by routine. After school we walked the seven blocks to Lakeview Park, where we raided Brigham's kitchen for snacks before his parents got home. He had a garage sale Atari and a wide assortment of games. Only a fraction of them actually worked but we never tired of trying; a few required one person to hold the game cartridge just so in the console while the other played. I had a little crush on Brigham's older sister, Tonya, and for a while she graced us with her company. As we grew older though, and she became more beautiful, we saw less of her. I'm afraid that my incessant drooling over her may have been a contributing factor.

If Brigham's parents grew weary of my constant presence or insatiable appetite, they never complained, oblivious that their kindness would one day be repaid in indescribable disproportion. I didn't see them often but I always got a sense that there was something exceptional about them, much like their son. Their lifestyle hinted that they were gaining on life, that the Millers would one day graduate out of the dump, taking my best friend with them.

I knew that Brigham was destined for greatness and in my heart I knew that I wasn't. That kind of revelation tends to destroy a person, yet for many years I believed that I had slipped by unscathed. I suppose I must've thought that if I was special in any way, maybe this was it.

At the end of the day, I was a nobody with dim prospects. But that was my world. When you've known nothing but poverty, anything else seems either a fantasy or an abstract absurdity. I had my friends and family and that was all that mattered. I was happy.

Left alone I might have been content to stay that way for the rest of my life—and believe me, no one in my little town would've raised an eyebrow. Left alone I might never have known what I was missing.

Then again, left alone there would be no story to tell.

The tangents of our lives can often be traced back to a singular event, a pivot point in time where the future hinged toward a trajectory we weren't at all prepared for. The foothills of my youth are breadcrumbed by painful memories and as hard as I try to navigate them, they rise up like ghosts to haunt me at night. They take me by the hand and whisper things I can't bear to hear. They draw me into the past, back to a time best left forgotten, back to where it all began.

The winter of 1988.

The year everything changed.

TWO

The first day of Christmas break, I woke to my dad standing in the doorway. He was dressed in his Big Smith overalls which meant that he intended to fix something. I knuckled at my eyes, yawning so hard my jaw popped.

"Hey, Dad," I croaked.

"Morning, Kiddo. Get dressed. I need your help."

"With what?"

He cleared his throat and even before he answered I knew my morning was shot. "The car," he said with a hint of apology.

I groaned and let my feet dangle from the side of the bed. "Aw, Dad ... it's Saturday," I complained. "Can't we do it tomorrow? It'd be a perfect excuse to skip church."

My dad didn't reply, but his eyes sparkled with amusement.

"I don't wanna miss church, Link," came a sleepy rebuttal from the upper bunk. "Mrs. Rossin's bringing candy tomorrow."

"It's *Rosslin*, Nicky. Mrs. Rosslin," I chided.

From the kitchen my mom's muffled voice resolved the matter. "They'll be no skipping church, boys!" Ears like a jackrabbit, that woman had.

"Guess you got your answer," my dad said. *It's out of my hands,* his expression seemed to add. "Now hurry up. Let's get this over with."

Complaining would've been wasted on him so I left it at that. If there was one person who enjoyed tinkering with cars less than me, it was my dad. But we couldn't afford a mechanic and good old Midwestern pride prohibited us from hiring one anyway. Unfortunately, my dad was fond of the shotgun approach to maintenance and repair, which often involved breaking one thing at the expense of fixing another. It was a gamble that had never actually paid off. But odds were we'd eventually get lucky and that seemed to keep him going.

On this particular occasion, the plan was to replace the thermostat on my mom's Chrysler LeBaron, an old clunker which had been overheating lately. I wasn't sure if somebody with expertise had provided this diagnosis to my dad or if he had intuited it on his own. Either way I wasn't optimistic. But at the ripe age of twelve, I didn't get a vote.

I heard my grandfather grumbling in his room and was suddenly happy for an excuse to leave. Sharing a wall with that surly codger was no picnic, let me tell you. We'd taken him in two weeks before and I had yet to hear a kind word from him.

Outside, the wind cut through me, carving out a gasp from frosting lungs. From a bent nail in the corrugated porch awning, a battered Marlboro thermometer tittered in the breeze. A thin line of mercury hovered just under twenty-four degrees. In the few seconds it took to traverse the driveway the skin on my face seemed to plasticize into a shell, as if dipped into hot wax. I crawled through the passenger door of my dad's old Ford pickup and waited for the engine to warm up. My dad sipped black coffee from a battered thermos, the kind with a cup for a lid. After a very long five minutes, the choke finally disengaged and we puttered off to the auto parts store.

There was some trivial conversation along the way but mostly I breathed on my hands to keep them warm. My dad looked ahead with determination, no doubt steeling himself for another in a long line of auto-repair failures. His jaw was clenched to keep from shivering and I knew that his fingers had to be throbbing against the steering wheel, despite the thick calluses on his palms. A pair of thick work gloves hung loosely from his coat pocket and I wondered why he didn't put them on. They didn't look particularly warm but surely anything was better than nothing. The vinyl seat was a frozen slab of marble under my rear. By the time we reached the auto store I couldn't feel my lower half anymore.

While my dad went inside, I remained in the truck, fiddling with the tape player to keep my hands busy. The engine idled with sickly coughs and wheezes and I knew it was only a matter of time before it breathed its last. The tape player was an ancient device; its button identifiers had worn away long ago and a mysterious yellow glow traced one of the knobs at night. A Led Zeppelin cassette had been imprisoned in its guts since before the invention of auto-reverse, so I had never heard the other side. Not that it mattered anyway; the tape was so worn out that one song could no longer be differentiated from another.

When my dad eventually returned, the cab had warmed enough that I could almost feel my buttocks again. But then, seconds after we left the parking lot, my dad lit a Pal Mal and cracked the window to vent the sweet smoke. Frigid air rushed in like icy darts and I was frozen all over again.

We stopped at the Handy Dandy and, to my sheer joy, my dad sprung for doughnuts and coffee. The discomfort of the cold was instantly forgotten. This was a rare and wonderful treat. I was sure my dad was stalling and that made absolutely no difference to me.

We sat in a nondescript booth by the magazine rack and sipped our coffee. The tabletop was of burnt orange Formica. The *f*-word was gouged into the surface, exposing pale fibers of particleboard underneath. My dad hastily covered the profanity with the bulk of his keys, as if I had never seen it before. As if he didn't mutter such things under his breath when he got annoyed.

My mom didn't allow me to drink coffee but my dad didn't share her aversion. It was a rite of passage for a growing boy and I liked it fine. With enough cream and sugar, that is. I wasn't an excitable kid so the caffeine didn't affect me much. No more than the pound of sugar in our doughnuts.

Dad took the thermostat out of its box and turned it over in his hands with a dazed sort of curiosity. His examination gave me pause because it seemed to prove what I already suspected: that he had never seen one of these things before and that he wasn't entirely sure what to do with it. I feared we were in for a long morning.

His eyes fell to the price tag on the box and lingered there for a long moment. The corners of his mouth sagged almost indiscernibly and he sighed through his nose. Reaching into his pocket, my dad produced a crumpled sales receipt and squinted at it with a scowl. Another sigh.

"Eat your doughnut," he said through a growing frown. I picked up the speed, though I couldn't help but stretch out the last two bites when, from a rack behind my dad, the risqué cover of an adult magazine stole my attention. There, a beautiful blonde woman wore nothing but high heels and a cleverly placed barcode. My pulse surged and—um, something else may have happened too but that's really none of your business.

"Hurry up, son." Looking up from the receipt, my dad followed my gaze over his shoulder. He shook his head, admonishing my curiosity with a tired snicker.

Oops ... busted.

Rising from the booth, my dad tossed his napkin and empty cup into a nearby receptacle. I mimicked his every move, though my coffee was barely half gone, and followed him past the register to the exit.

"Have a good one," said the cashier.

"You, too," my dad replied. Only he hesitated for a moment at the door, nodding toward the magazine rack. "Might oughta keep the skin mags behind the counter, y'think?" He didn't wait for a response, pushing me out the door with a finger poking into my back like a gun barrel. I expected the cashier to have something wise to crack at this unsolicited advice—which I can assure you would not have ended well for any of us—but a covert glance found him chuckling quite merrily.

To my annoyance, we headed back to the auto parts store instead of returning home. Worse, the cab of the truck was a meat locker again, returning my poor derriere to a state of chapped numbness in a matter of seconds.

"Did you get the wrong part?" I dared to ask. It certainly would not have been the first time yet to acknowledge this was a button one pushed with grave care.

My dad sniffed irritably. "Nah, it's the right one. But he undercharged me five dollars." His eyes were fixed on the road so I'm guessing that he missed my slack-jawed disbelief. Was this a joke? I waited for him to add some clarification but he provided none. He just kept on driving.

"Maybe it was on sale," I suggested.

He considered this thoughtfully, head cocked slightly toward his window. "Maybe, but I doubt it. Man's half blind; probably just hit the wrong key on the register."

Sheesh.

This time I was allowed to accompany my dad inside. The store smelled of old motor oil and axle grease, but at least it was warm. My dad nodded at the clerk behind the counter and plopped his receipt on the counter. The clerk wore coke bottle glasses and had thick greasy sideburns. His dingy shirt was embroidered with the name *Eddie* over a single chest pocket.

"Wrong part again?" he inquired. I did my very best to chew back a smirk but I doubt that I pulled it off.

To my dad's credit, he rolled with the punch. "Too early to say. Think you mighta rang this up wrong though."

Eddie raised an eyebrow and reached for the receipt. "That right?" he mumbled. He poked a few keys on a filthy keyboard and held the receipt up to the monitor. Scratching his head, he whistled between teeth as brown and round as coffee beans. "Well I'll be," he mused. "Sorry about that. Looks like you came out ahead though." He returned the receipt to my dad and poked at the keyboard once more to end his query.

Nodding, my dad shoved the receipt back into his pocket; his hand emerged a second later with his wallet in tow. Eddie waved this off, shaking his head. "No, no. Don't worry about it, now. My mistake."

My dad laid a five dollar bill on the counter. "It's no problem. Fair's fair."

I wonder sometimes if my dad would've gone through all that trouble had I not been with him. He was a different man back then yet the cynic in me questions everything now.

Thanks to an old Chrysler shop manual the casing around the thermostat was easy to locate on the LeBaron. There were only a couple of bolts to remove along with a corroded gasket. My job was to hold the screws and man the flashlight.

Ah, the burden of heavy responsibility!

I kept expecting something to fall into the bowels of the engine, to disappear into one of the million or so crevices hidden down there, because that's how this usually worked. There would be cursing and shame and we'd break something else and spend the rest of the day trying to undo the damage. But somehow it didn't happen like that. We confronted our only hitch, in fact, when I lost one of the stupid screws.

I don't even know how it happened. They were both in my pocket and then one was gone. Just like that. This was my dad's cue to get angry—and rightly so for once—but he didn't. With a patient grunt he wiped his nose on the back of his sleeve, hands trembling from the bitter cold. I felt immensely sorry for him with my own hands snuggled deep in my coat pockets.

"Don't worry about it," he sighed, heading toward the rickety shed. Inside he had coffee cans full of loose bolts, nuts, screws, brackets, you name it. It didn't take him long to find a suitable replacement, though it was a bit longer than the original. In a flash of brilliance he used a hacksaw to bring it down to size before threading it into place. All told, the process took just under an hour. Granted, it was too early to say that we had actually fixed anything but that wasn't the point.

I was impressed with our efficiency, as was my mom. She heated up mugs of hot chocolate for me and Nicky and put on a fresh pot of coffee for my dad.

Smiling with satisfaction, he winked at me. I reciprocated with a grin that I felt all the way down to my toes. Later, me and Nicky settled into the living room to watch cartoons while my parents chatted in the kitchen.

Outside, the wind died down and snowflakes began to fall lazily to the ground.

This is a memory I visit often, like an old friend that I can't bear to break ties with. It's a reminder that life was once a happy affair; but even more, when I dwell on it I can almost believe that if I just hang in there a little longer, life might be happy again one day.

People don't always die at once. Some of us do it a little at a time and as each piece falls away, the living remainder forgets that it used to be something greater.

Maybe I think too much but I remember exactly when I first began to die. I've forgotten a millions cuts and bruises but I don't suppose that I'll ever forget that day. It was an unseasonably warm February afternoon, a brief and exhilarating taste of the coming spring. Fanning across the field behind Lakeview Park, a gentle breeze whispered through the dried grass, drawing sleepy creaks from the branches of the wandering tree. As we had done countless times, Brigham and I lay on our backs in the spidery shadow of its branches staring at the fluffy clouds overhead. Normally we told each other stories here. But not today.

Under different circumstances I might've found it difficult to do anything but smile on a day like that. Yet I felt truly hopeless just then and when the source of your hope begins to waver, even beautiful moments like these can feel ugly. Brigham was talking a hundred miles per hour, a nervous habit which exposed the perilous fragility if not insincerity of his excitement. My mind processed this but had otherwise shut out the world.

Seven miles.

"It has a garage and the lady next door has an above ground pool! And there's this big honkin' tree with a tree house in the backyard—Dad's gonna help me fix it up once we get moved in. We'll be able to see for blocks up there."

It seemed to frustrate Brigham that his ramblings prompted no response from me; eventually he paused to regroup and in that brief moment of silence, his momentum broke. Rolling to his side, my best friend faced me.

"I'm sorry, Link." It was perhaps the best thing he could've said yet it had no effect on me.

Seven miles. That was a good three miles farther than I had ever walked.

"It's fine," I lied. I fought the good fight to keep my voice level but there was a determined tremor rising to the surface. I couldn't look at Brigham so I rolled onto my back. "When are you moving?"

"Tomorrow," he replied in a whisper. "After school."

Talk about short notice. I nodded, the back of my head grinding into a pillow of golden hay. The sting of tears approached and I knew that I would be helpless to control them soon. Closing my eyes, I released a forlorn sigh.

God how I wished those clouds would fall to the ground and just swallow me whole. They were no longer curious shapes or the subjects of meaningless jest; they were idle witnesses to the breaking of my heart.

Seven miles. Six miles farther than my parents would ever knowingly permit me to travel on foot.

"Come on, Link," Brigham pleaded. "It's not like we won't still hang out all the time. We'll just be at a different house. It's a real house, Link."

The faint rustle of movement nearby announced the passing of some small animal, perhaps a field mouse or a grass snake. Probably the former, considering the season. I was too distraught to care.

Contrary to Brigham's reverie, I knew that our season together was coming to an end. My social life—and I use this term loosely, to be clear—had always been governed by a single transcendental law: friendships lived and died at the whims of accessibility. Jeremy was proof of that. Seven miles, a million—not much of a difference really. Tomorrow Brigham would step beyond the invisible edge of my world. The camaraderie that I had grown to rely on would cease to exist except in memory. We would be reduced to schoolyard chums and that was that.

For all his talk, Brigham understood this as much as I did. I wanted to scream at him, to sock him in the jaw for pretending otherwise. How could my best friend so blithely leave me behind?

Brigham sniffled, cleared his throat. "Did I mention there's a creek like three houses down? And I saw a really hot girl across the street too." He smiled desperately, those chocolate eyes bright and glassy. Pleading.

Seven miles.

A small part of me ached to grant him the blessing he so desperately needed and deserved; to celebrate his great escape from the clutches of Lakeview Park. But in the grand sum of my existence this was only a fragment of me—too small and underdeveloped to generate more than a ripple in the pool of my darkening thoughts. I was overwhelmed by sadness and anger. And an unsettling measure of jealousy, to boot.

Since I could remember, the two of us had weaved a future together—best friends taking on the world. Our underprivileged childhoods would be nothing more than sour anecdotes, spots on the tarnish of memory. We had it all planned out, every detail. More than anything else, this was a thread that had bound the frays of our friendship. Our plan, that is. Its abrupt unraveling revealed that while I was no longer a part of the equation, the plan—*our* plan—was no less complete without me in it.

A better friend might've drawn inspiration from Brigham's salvation. Rather, I felt obscenely cleaved from it, like the undesirable crust of a diamond, removed so the rest could shine all the brighter. I felt betrayed.

My selfishness disgusted me yet I found myself at its mercy—which is of course ironic considering that selfishness is by nature indifferent to mercy. Brigham had been my best friend since we were toddlers. Aside from my family, he was one of the few people I had ever cared about. I wanted to tell him this, to speak the words that boys and men alike hesitate to utter: that he was my best friend and I loved him, limp and all. He deserved to hear those words.

I left Brigham lying under the wandering tree and ran to my house, tears blighting out the beauty of the day. Brigham hollered after me and though I heard his voice clearly enough, the words themselves were lost to the wind.

I cried in my room until I fell asleep. I woke once to a motherly caress on my back but I refused to acknowledge it. More than sympathy, I needed to feel through the misery for a while.

There was simply no way to know that the next time I would see Brigham, life would be very different. The world would be a much darker place for us both.

You see, the dying had only just begun.

THREE

I wanted to see the lions. My little brother Nicky wanted to see the monkeys. We flipped a coin and—surprise, surprise—I lost. Inside the primate house, the whoops and shrieks of chimpanzees were alarmingly boisterous. I covered my ears against their piercing chatter but it was no use.

Nicky ran ahead to get a closer look while I hung back near the door, perched lazily on the end of a bench. He forced his way through a small crowd to get a closer look, too young and excited to register the discourtesy of cutting. I people-watched for a while, noticing—not for the first time—the emergent allure of the opposite sex. Nature is not without balance, of course; it graciously provided the stench of urine and animal sweat to counter-weigh my hormones.

At once, there was a collective gasp near the chimp enclosure. Glancing to Nicky's last known whereabouts, my heart skipped a beat. The crowd had stepped back to reveal my little brother, who stood only inches from the cage. Frozen in dismay, Nicky was covered in feces. He wasn't the sole victim but failing to retreat as quickly as his fellow bystanders, he seemed to have gotten the worst of it.

With much hemming and hawing, other poop-speckled patrons scrambled away from the enclosure and toward the exits, women consulting their handbags for tissues, men looking angrily about for someone to dress down. All the while signs warning of such unruly behavior were placarded throughout the building, ignored like shopping mall security guards.

My brother trudged his way back to me, looking downtrodden and disgusted. The front of his shirt might've given Jackson Pollock nightmares, if not an idea or two of the scratch-n-sniff variety.

"Link, look what they did!" Nicky groaned woefully.

I offered a sympathetic smile and tried to breathe through my mouth. "You wanted to see the monkeys, bud."

From the entrance door we heard a sharp gasp. My smile vanished; Nicky's wounded frown deepened, turning fearful.

"Nicholas! What have you done to your shirt!" cried my mom. Her outburst was so shrill that several passersby flinched and faltered in mid-stride. We turned to face her as she approached, cringing under her scorn. My dad walked behind her with an impassive expression.

"The monkeys did it," Nicky squeaked. A tear crawled down his cheek and settled into the perfect dimple of his chin. He glanced furtively to my dad. A tense moment hung in the air as we waited to see how my dad would react.

My knees weakened.

Dropping gently to one knee, my dad wiped the tear from Nicky's cheek. "Son, I think it's time you started using the toilet like the rest of us," he teased, smiling faintly. "Just because your brother waited until he was twelve to potty-train doesn't mean you have to."

I laughed at the jab, enjoying a manic rush of gratitude for my dad. This was the father I loved and adored. Nicky smiled sheepishly and wrinkled his freckled nose, observing: "It smells like when Link's been in the bathroom for a long time."

"No way," I countered. "Dad's got me beat by a long shot." Nicky giggled and I looked to my mom for final approval. I found relief there but no amusement. Her eyes were wide, lips thin and clamped shut like a steel trap.

"They should put up a sign or something," she muttered.

The lions were far less eventful; actually, only one bothered to leave the shade of an artificial rock awning for us to see him and only then for a brief moment. He was old and scarred, likely a reject from the circus or some Vegas sideshow. Yet he was immense and graceful in a way that belied tremendous power.

I remember learning about David and Goliath in Sunday school. Hearing the story for the first time, I imagined a feeble young boy, one not unlike myself. Yet David had fought off lions and bears to protect his flock of sheep, a task that—while heroic— had seemed well within the parentheses of human ability. Seeing this old cat now put David's feats into proper perspective for the first time.

Nicky quickly grew bored and we wandered toward the reptile house. And so went the rest of the trip, plodding from exhibit to exhibit, ogling each imprisoned animal with waning curiosity until our aching feet drove us home.

It was a good day. And after a long lonely summer without Brigham, a much needed reprieve from monotony.

That night, Nicky and I talked softly from our bunks until he fell asleep. He was excited about returning to school in a few weeks, about seeing all his friends. I envied his enthusiasm, though I was also baffled by it. I mean, who looked forward to going to school? Sitting at a stupid desk all day long, trying to stay awake; just counting the days until summer came back around?

Ugh.

Brutus, my neighbor's lively Pit Bull, barked well into the early hours, holding sleep at bay. When I finally went out, I dreamed that lions were hunting me and my little brother, old wizened beasts with paws the size of dinner plates. I wanted to protect Nicky but my arms and legs were bogged down in dream molasses. When one finally attacked, he—well in a way it was actually the truth that grabbed me by the throat, even if it took the form of a lion.

The disheartening truth was that I, Lincoln Chase, was definitely no David.

The front door slammed with a loose metallic clang against the aluminum frame. The whole trailer shook from the impact, jostling something to the floor in the kitchen. When the sickening clap of flesh against flesh reached me, my heart picked up its pace as if preparing to leap out of my chest.

Nicky stirred in the upper bunk, where his body created a sagging profile against the bed springs. Moments later, his soft snoring resumed. I reached frantically under the bed, my fingers wrapping around the hilt of a baseball bat.

I might not have been ready to face a four hundred pound lion but that didn't mean that I was a complete coward. If someone had broken into my house I meant to make him pay for it.

I crept from the bastion of my bedroom and tiptoed into the hall, bat poised with the blissful confidence of a child who has seen his share of ninja movies yet has never been in a real fight. At the end of the hallway, I peeked into the kitchen, which was dimly lit by a naked bulb over the sink. The room was empty, though a broken picture frame lay on the floor near the dinner table. There, the glossy moon face of a nameless aunt smiled up at the ceiling, a shard of glass protruding from one paper cheek.

Abruptly, the floor shook as angry footsteps strode toward the kitchen, toward *me*. Whereas a moment ago I had felt brave I now felt vulnerable; the bat was an awkward burden in my hand rather than any kind of a weapon. I wanted to fight off the intruder—to protect my flock, my family—but in that instant my nerve abandoned me.

Afraid, I scampered back to my bedroom and shut the door, but for a crack. Framed in this sliver, my mom came into view, crying noiselessly. Her face was a twisted mask of fear. She held her hands outstretched, as if to ward off an attack or perhaps in a plea for mercy. My fingers tightened around the bat and for a second, I almost got my nerve back. Honestly—I almost surged right through that door, ready to swing for the fences. Only as my mom's assailant materialized, easing out of the shadows like some kind of demon, my insides turned to stone.

It was the monster. The same monster that my dad had sworn to God would never return, who had in fact left us in peace for months. It was back.

Knobby fingers clutched my mom's upper arm like claws, yanking her close.

"I don't want you ever talking to him again," the monster hissed. "So help me, woman …" He left the threat hanging there, where it permeated the air like an awful stench. The kind man who had wiped tears from my brother's cheek only hours ago was gone. That he could somehow share flesh with this beast confused me, as it always seemed to. It made my stomach churn.

"Finton, you're hurting me," my mom whimpered.

My dad cinched his grip. "Say it, Helen."

"We didn't do anything wrong! He was just asking how we've been and—"

Raising his free hand, my dad stiffened it for a blow. "Say it!" His voice was savage now, an inhuman growl.

Like a tortoise retreating into its shell, my mom tried to cower into herself. "Okay!" she shrieked. "I won't talk to him. What's come over you, Fin? I thought you two were friends."

"Don't you do that, don't you toy with me. Ain't stupid." He released her arm—thank God—and stormed back through the house toward the front door. My poor mom crumpled to the floor with a sob. Outside, the familiar rumble of a pickup truck filled the night, joined in chaos by the barking of dogs.

Opening my bedroom door, I took a tentative step toward my mom. I wanted to comfort her yet while I've never been sure what put a falter in my step, I came to a dead stop. She was on her feet now, reaching for the phone. Stretching the phone cord across the counter to the sink, she peeked nervously through the window.

She was going to call the police, I realized. *Good.*

Her fingers poked frantically at the phone and I started to move again. Only as I counted the digits, it dawned on me that 911 wasn't on her mind.

"Reggie?" she hissed. "He knows."

Back in the shelter of my room, I replaced the bat under the bed, hands trembling like a new butterfly's wings. I remember crying into my pillow then, feeling so alone and confused. Like the catastrophic emergence of a volcano, an existence I wanted no part of was bursting through the ground at my feet. Life as I knew it was crumbling around me and the worst part was that I was too much of a wimp to do anything about it.

FOUR

My mother never wore much makeup. Frankly she didn't need to. She had the kind of natural beauty that demanded little primping. Men noticed her anytime we left the house, which was an endless—and arguably reasonable—source of frustration for my father. This morning she was painted pretty. I couldn't see the bruises but I had no doubt they were there.

Nicky, who was oblivious of last night's incident, set out immediately to dig into his toys. My mother sat quietly at the table, rubbing her cheek absently. Her eyes were tired but otherwise unreadable. The obnoxious clamor of The Price Is Right blasted from my grandfather's room.

I wanted to say something but I wasn't sure what. The events of the previous night were still too shocking to process. If forced to choose a side at that moment, I'd have been at a loss to say who was more wrong.

My mother breathed a melancholy sigh, letting her hand drop from her face. Smiling mechanically now, she pushed a plate of bacon and eggs toward me. I looked in her eyes, expecting to find something telling there but there was nothing. No hint of guilt or deception, nothing.

"Make sure he eats it all this time, hun."

Nodding, I filled a chipped mug with coffee and took the plate.

"Here," my mother offered. She spooned two heaping mounds of sugar into the coffee and gave it a quick stir.

"Thanks," I muttered.

From the living room, Nicky called out to me, "Wanna play trucks, Link?"

"In a little while, babe," my mother responded in my stead. "Your brother's got chores to do first." She ran her fingers through my hair, combing down a cowlick that I had long ago given up on. Her touch made me cringe and I found that I was holding my breath when she finally gave up.

As I made my way down the hall, I heard Nicky drive his toy truck into the kitchen. "Mommy, you look like a princess today!"

She did, I realized. Sans the obligatory dress and tiara, that is, she really did.

I found Grandpa sitting on the edge of his bed, staring at the floor. He was dressed in my dad's old pajamas; the worn cotton was stretched taut like spandex across his substantial frame. His posture was slack, resigned to a pathetic existence here in this little room. Being around him never failed to sadden me.

"You okay, Grandpa?" I asked. I didn't expect a response because I rarely got one, but my pity for him always compelled me to ask anyway. The old man looked up at me sharply, eyes wet and milky. Immediately concerned, I pushed inside.

My grandfather was a proud man, so tears were not something to be taken lightly. His gaze tracked me for a moment, then dropped to the floor again. On the nearby television, Bob Barker introduced today's Showcase Showdown. The volume was cranked to the max, as usual—oppressive in the small space yet comforting in its familiarity.

"I brought your breakfast." I set the plate and coffee mug on a nearby bed stand and turned down the television. "Mom said to eat it all." Grandpa shot me with a worried glance, wringing his arthritic hands. His nose was runny, but he took no notice. When his jaws began to fidget tentatively, I realized that he was working up to saying something. Seconds later, a marbled rasping escaped his lips.

"It's happening again, ain't it?"

I had no idea what to make of that, except that I was pretty sure he wasn't talking about breakfast. "Yup, breakfast again," I said. "We try to do it every day."

Dementia had long ago emasculated my grandfather of his short term memory and, by extension, his grip on the present. Superficial communication was still possible for now. He was perfectly capable of answering closed-ended questions—

Do you need to use the bathroom?

Are you hungry?

Did you just fart, or was that an earthquake?

—that sort of thing.

Once, when the old man was feeling unusually spry, he told me stories from his youth in startling detail, each of which was probably spot on. The past was engrained in him, I suppose. But the daily back and forth, he couldn't quite keep up with that. It was hard for any of us to get used to, yet I can't imagine how frustrating it must've been for Grandpa.

Still, he was a survivor. The old man was a master of improvisation, serving up bits of misdirection and cliché to veil his confusion. At times it felt like we were having a real conversation, like we were both sending and receiving signals on the same wavelength. But these were illusions that couldn't be trusted. The truth was that the old man didn't recognize me—any of us, for that matter. He didn't know where he was, much less how he got there. His mind was a candle nearing the end of its wick; but for a few moments of flickering clarity, his flame was scarcely more than a dim glow.

It dawned on me suddenly that Grandpa was glaring at me, boring into me with unnerving intensity. For a brief moment, his resemblance to my dad surfaced and I blinked in surprise. But then it was gone, mined back into the wrinkles and shadows.

"What is it, Grandpa?" I asked warily.

His gaze cooled at the sound of my voice, falling on the coffee mug. "Gotta sink or swim, son," he muttered with a dazed sort of shrug. He picked up the mug and took a tentative sip. "That's just right. Thank you, Benjamin."

"It's Lincoln, Grandpa. Remember?" Sighing, I turned the volume back up on his television and bolted for the door. "Be back for the plate," I called over my shoulder.

Me and Nicky played trucks for a while, until my mother eventually kicked us out. We spent the rest of the day outside playing catch and hunting bugs in Pruitt Field. I had almost forgotten about the night before, though an impression of the memory simmered in the back of my mind.

Dinner that night was uneventful, though Nicky was the only one with an appetite. I managed to avoid any conversation with my parents for the most part but the tension between them was no less unsettling. It seemed to thicken the air like the charging preamble to a lightning strike. I couldn't wait to get away from them both.

After delivering a plate of food to Grandpa, I drew pictures with Nicky until bed time. My parents talked on the back porch. From my bedroom window, I watched the sun dip behind the wandering tree, listening to the unintelligible exchange of apologies and empty promises.

I thought of the happiness we had once known as a family—before the monster came, that is; before fear of his return became a part of daily life. I wondered who Reggie was and why my mom was calling him.

But mostly, I thought about Brigham; wondering what he was doing just then, wishing that he was still around to talk to. School was about to start up and I couldn't wait to see him. I missed my friend now more than ever because he had a way of making things seem better. And I desperately needed things to be better.

Maybe tomorrow. If not because I deserved it, then by plain old dumb luck; one way or the other, just *maybe* tomorrow would be better.

If only we had stayed home, maybe tomorrow would've been better. This is a thought that haunts me to this very day. If only, life might have taken a very different course for my family. My dad might've landed a well-deserved promotion. Or who knows? My mom might've hit the jackpot on one of her scratch tickets. It's hard to put that kind of what-if to bed, you know? Just when you think you're free of it, there it is again, breathing down your neck again like an annoying roommate.

We were running some errands, my dad and me, that Saturday morning. It was mid August and the mowing season was almost over yet we spent an hour at a small engine salvage yard, looking for a replacement wheel to uncripple our stupid lawnmower. Another half hour at a department store, haggling over something my mom had on lay-away. Finally, twenty-five minutes at a pawn shop where I was asked to stay in the truck.

Things might've been okay if we had gone straight home from there. If only we hadn't stopped for gas. We didn't even need it—the tank was half-full—but the price of unleaded had dropped two cents at the Handy Dandy. A penny saved and all that, my dad just couldn't bring himself to pass it up.

We pulled up to a pump behind a brand new Chevy Suburban with a temporary tag taped to the back window. My dad got the gas pumping and made short work of washing the windshield. Just as always, Led Zeppelin peeked from the tape player, forever taunting me. I wondered absently, as I had done more times than I could possibly count, what was on that other side. What if it was blank? What if all along, that had been the gimmick and no one had gotten around to telling me? That would've been my luck.

I heard the muffled banter of small talk between my dad and the owner of the other truck. I glanced through the window just as my dad rounded the Suburban, out of my line of sight. Slipping our new lawnmower wheel on my pointer finger, I gave it a bored spin. The pump clicked off. Another minute slithered by but my dad was still talking. I didn't mind, though I was eager to get some air circulating; it wasn't scorching outside yet but it was getting hot enough there in the cab of the truck. And for whatever reason my dad was the only person on the face of the planet who could get that dang window to roll down.

Scuffling sounds made their way around the Suburban and though I peered intently through the window, there was nothing to see.

Then I heard the scream. It was a frightened, anguished shriek that was nearly unrecognizable as a man's; a sound that will never leave me, even in my happiest moments.

A split second later my dad returned to the truck, face flushed, chest heaving. He jumped in and started the engine in one fluid motion. In what seemed like mere fragments of a second, the Handy Dandy was reduced to a shrinking image in my side mirror. And then it was gone altogether, obscured by a bend in the road.

I wanted to know what in the world had just happened, why we had just driven off without paying for our gas. Why the pump handle was still protruding from the side of our truck, hose squirming in the wind, skipping against the pavement like a wounded snake. I wanted to know what that terrible scream was all about.

I wanted to know these things and more but couldn't bring myself to ask. Because my dad was clearly afraid and if the answers to these questions were enough to scare my dad, I truly had something to fear as well.

My dad gripped the steering wheel with white-knuckled ferocity, as if it alone kept him from blowing away. His knees bounced a nervous cadence, which was something I often did, but had never seen him do. The truck lurched as we suddenly lost speed and for a second I was afraid that the engine had stalled; but the speedometer began climbing again almost instantly and I realized that my dad's foot had merely slipped off the gas pedal.

It was then that I noticed the blood. His right boot was slick with it, transposing greasy impressions onto the floor mat.

The drive home took ten minutes, during which not a single word was exchanged. In the driveway, my dad threw the truck into park, staring through the bug-spattered windshield at our trailer. A few seconds passed before he turned to look at me. His eyes were wild and when he spoke there was a tremble in his voice that cut right through me.

"Go inside," he said, and as the engine rumbled and the truck rattled beneath me, I realized that he wasn't staying. In a daze, I obeyed. My dad quickly backed out and drove away. I stood there in the gravel lane with one foot ankle-deep in a long-untended pothole, just staring into the distance. Long after the truck vanished I remained, trying for all I was worth to understand.

The sun was high overhead, flaring against the treetops as I ventured inside. Passing Nicky and my mom as they ate baloney sandwiches, I made a beeline for the bathroom.

Where I promptly vomited.

Growing up in a trailer park, I don't remember taking much for granted. At any given time I was lucky to own a few pairs of pants and no more than four shirts—all second-hand from the local

Twice-Is-Nice. As a rule, my shoes were half dead long before I came along to finish them off. And when their soles inevitably cracked or wore through, I lined them with duct tape and the cardboard of cereal boxes.

We weren't a welfare family, in case I haven't mentioned it. Yet my dad's earnings were meager, so when churches and other community outreaches launched their yearly food drives, it was with families like mine in mind. For a few blissful days every year, we ceased to be trailer trash. We were the *unfortunate*; the *needy*. Though it bruised our pride, we gritted our teeth and dug in, gorging on holiday cheer, filling our shriveled humps with charity and goodwill. Because we knew it wouldn't be long before the season blew past us and—just as always—we'd be plain old trailer trash again.

Through it all, despite every upturned nose and gasp of distaste, I never imagined that the Chases actually deserved this lot in life. Because I really thought that we were good people, that we were happy in our own way. We fought tooth and nail to survive, sure, yet there was warmth and solidarity in our home; a sense of family that nothing could stifle.

Do you know what it feels like to be wrong about something like that? God, I hope not.

FIVE

My dad returned home well after dark. When I realized that he was back, I abandoned the seclusion of my bed to wander into the living room. There, he and my mother stood near the couch with their backs to me. While their heated banter had been rowdy enough only moments ago, they now stared at each other in silence. A poignant coldness permeated the space between my parents, chilling the room despite the sweltering summer heat. Against my better judgment, I spoke up.

"Where were you, Dad?" I asked from the doorway. My throat was raw from restless snoring, as well as from throwing up.

My mother jumped at my voice, startled either by its abruptness or the unfamiliar huskiness. Her eyes were bloodshot and swollen, regarding me with a frantic sort of irritation.

"Lincoln, get back to bed," she snapped.

My face must have reflected hurt or shock because a wave of concern seemed to wash over her. "Please, honey," she groaned with a hint of apology. "Everything's fine, okay? Just go on to bed. We can all talk in the morning."

Nodding, I turned to comply.

"Wait," my dad objected. "Let him stay. He can handle it."

I looked back over my shoulder, intrigued but only half invested in the possibility. This was an unexpected turn of events and from the look on my mother's face, it was clear that she was just as surprised as me. Normally, if logic or experience could be relied on, my dad would be in for a tongue-lashing that I'd just as soon skip out on. But not tonight.

"He's just a boy, Fin," was all my mom said.

Funny, I remember feeling more insulted than surprised by that. It wasn't my mother's tactless stating of the obvious that offended me—she was right of course; I was just a boy—but that her tone had lacked any inflection of protectiveness. She wasn't shielding me from the truth; she thought I was too simple to grasp it.

Maybe she was right.

"He's more grown up than you think, Helen," my dad insisted. "Besides, he was there. He deserves an explanation." With that, the debate was over. My dad turned to address me. "Come on over, son."

Exasperated but out of steam, my mother wiped at her puffy eyes with the back of a hand. Like her resolve, her makeup had washed away, exposing a sickly yellow bruise on her cheek. My breath hitched at the sight of it.

Without another word, she left us alone. Outside in the darkness, a punch-drunk June bug tapped against the window, drawn by the glow within. But for its sound, the house was uncomfortably quiet.

My dad steered me to the couch and, once there, gave me a gentle push toward the cushions. I sat dutifully and waited. He moved to sit next to me but at the last second, he changed course and began to pace the room.

"You know I did a bad thing, don't you, Link?"

I nodded, eyes darting to his boots. The blood had been hastily wiped away, leaving behind a rusty smear. "Where did you go?" I asked for the second time.

My dad looked at me for a long moment, eyebrows bunched in contemplation. I'm guessing that his expression was supposed to be stoic but the effect was undermined by his eyes. Deep within them—at a depth I surely wasn't meant to descend—rage and remorse grappled, expanding toward the surface in a swelling geyser. The sight was unbearable yet I was transfixed because it was something that I had never seen before. The transformation between dad and monster, frozen in time.

Send me to bed, I screamed in my mind. But of course, he didn't.

"I went back, Link. I couldn't just leave him there to bleed, so I went back to help him." His faced sagged at the seams, as if physically weighted down by the words he was about to speak. "Only, when I got there I was too chicken to pull in. The sheriff was there with some deputies, an ambulance too."

He ran his hands through close-cropped hair. His eyes were slick marbles, rolling around in search of something—anything—that might scour away the image in his mind. Whatever that image was, whatever he had done? It was tearing him apart and there wasn't a dang thing I could do to help him.

"Dad, what did you do?" I hated myself for asking because I knew that it would hurt him more to relive it out loud. But I had to know. I had to know who *he* was, why *he* was bleeding in the first place. What did it all mean?

My dad gazed into my eyes and seemed to arrive at a decision. "I lost my temper, son. I lost it just for a second and I hurt someone. I think I hurt him bad."

Void of any details, even this watered-down account painted a macabre picture. And as minds tend to do, mine was quick to fill in the gaps with bits of Hollywood blood and gore. Sketchy or not, even a stylized version of the truth was enough to poison the well.

My dad must've known this would happen, I now realize; that vague explanation of his must've been an attempt to nurse along what precious little remained of my naiveté, if only for a bit longer. It was a precious gift, in hindsight. One of his last.

"What's gonna happen now?" I wanted to know. "What're you gonna do?"

Buried in the subtext of this was an entirely different line of questioning, a parallel one that I was too afraid to ask.

Would the monster ever really leave or would he always be there … just waiting?

Would he, like before, show his face when I forgot to wash my cereal bowl?

When Nicky spilled his milk at dinner?

Again a pause and a quick decision. "I know you have a lot of questions, son. I wish I could answer them all but it's complicated. The bottom line is I made a mistake, Lincoln. And I'm gonna have to answer for it. You understand what that means, don't you?"

"Yes, sir." I thought for a moment. "Are you gonna turn yourself in?"

My dad shrugged a single shoulder—tired, noncommittal. "Yeah, I reckon so. If they don't show up by morning, I'll drive on over to the police station and get it over with. No sense dragging things out."

"Will they put you in jail?"

"I reckon they will. For a few days anyway. And when I get out, I expect I'll get sued for some hospital bills."

"Do we have money for that?"

From nowhere, irritation flashed in his eyes and I realized that I had just touched on a subject that my mother had undoubtedly beaten to death earlier. It must've sounded accusatory—maybe even rhetorical—the second time around, coming from me.

"Nope," he replied. "We'll get by, though. I don't want you or your mother worrying about that." The irritation was gone now, revealing endless sorrow.

"Yes, sir," I promised. I could feel my own eyes beginning to sting. Few things tugged at my heartstrings like seeing my dad cry. Dads weren't supposed to do that.

I still had a million questions, but my willingness to ask them had been curbed for the moment. They just weren't worth seeing him hurt like this. Particularly when I knew that no real peace was forthcoming.

"Better get on back to bed now, son."

"Yes, sir." Before I could stand on my own, my dad pulled me bodily from the couch, swallowing me into an embrace unlike any I had ever experienced; it was primal, full of love and regret, of time lost. His fatherly smell warmed me, Old Spice and tobacco, something faintly earthy.

"I'm so sorry, Link," he whispered in my ear. "I just can't believe I did this."

Six

Like many things worth fearing, the police came in the middle of the night. I was already awake when three patrol cars crowded into our driveway, spilling off the gravel lane into the weedy patchwork of our yard. Their lights flickered neon, emblazing my bedroom walls with smears of blue and red. There were no sirens, which only seemed to enhance the eeriness of their arrival; the notorious quiet before the storm.

Awakened by the lights, Nicky climbed off the top bunk and onto mine. His threadbare pajamas generated tiny crackles of static against my woolen blanket. As his hand sought out mine, the severity of his panic felt palpable. He had been told very little of what to expect tonight and I regretted my silent contribution to keeping him in the dark. He deserved better than that.

Car doors flew open. In practiced tandem, a throng of uniformed officers erupted, hands glued to holstered pistols. The butt of a flashlight pounded on our front door, resounding like a cannon ball against the thin aluminum.

Next door, Brutus began to bark.

The whole thing was like an episode of C.O.P.S., minus the hookers and front-yard trampolines. If a shirtless old man had chosen that moment to wobble by on a pink bicycle with a forty-ounce High Life in one hand, I wouldn't have been surprised in the least. But instead, our porch light switched on as my dad stepped into the flickering blast of police strobes.

True to his word, he left without argument or resistance. His hands were squeezed into fists, cuffed tightly behind his back. I knew that he was afraid and I was afraid for him. Nicky and I watched from the bedroom window as my dad was escorted down the driveway. My brother whimpered, cramming against my shoulder to get a better view. We watched in helpless awe as my dad was folded into the maw of a police cruiser. In seconds, the thing had swallowed him whole and disappeared into the night.

Outside, the Lakeview Park community gawked from porches and driveways, drinking beer and enjoying the show. My mother was on the porch now, a tremulous hand cupped over her mouth. One of the officers lingered to talk with her before returning to his cruiser but she barely seemed to register his presence. Brutus's barking had incited a chain reaction and the trailer park was now a riot of canine bedlam.

Once the last cruiser had disappeared around the bend, I opened my bedroom door to rush through the kitchen. My mother was in the living room, sobbing against the front door. I wrapped my arms around her willowy frame, as much for my own comfort as hers. Nicky wasn't far behind, quaking with hiccups of lament.

This was all wrong, everything about it. I mean, things like this weren't supposed to happen in real life. Not to *real* people.

Not to *me*.

Grandpa made a rare appearance outside of his room to investigate the ruckus. Finding us huddled in this spontaneous vigil, the old man was visibly stricken, particularly by my mother's anguish.

"What'd he do, girl?" he barked. "What'd my boy do to you?" This was the first coherent thought that I had heard from him in days, so it caught me off guard. My mother was so startled that she could only gape in response.

"He didn't do anything to her," I answered on her behalf. "Everything's fine, nothing to worry about."

Grandpa's face flushed red and I knew that our usual volley of watered-down platitudes had no place in this moment.

"Ya think I'm stupid, boy?"

I was moved by the pain in his voice because I realized that Grandpa wasn't speaking only of that moment, but in general. Regardless of necessity or circumstances, no man wanted to be treated like a four year old.

"No, Grandpa," I answered. "You're not stupid."

A fat tear wobbled on one of his eyelids yet his cheeks had lost some heat. "Then show some respect and tell me what's goin' on around here."

My mother seemed to collect her wits, yet her grip tightened protectively on me and Nicky. "Do you know who we are?" she asked quietly.

Grandpa furrowed his eyebrows, towering over us like some flustered demigod. "What kind of question is that?" he demanded. "'Course I know who you are."

"I'm sorry, Papa. It's just that—well, you haven't been yourself for a long while. You've been … confused about things."

Leaning against the nearby countertop, my grandfather sighed mightily. The supporting cabinetry creaked in protest. "Ever since my wife died things are—" A fog rolled over his face and then was gone. "Things are hard to keep straight, I guess."

I felt my mother relax. Nicky reached for my hand and held it tight. Poor kid. This was a lot to process in the middle of the night. No one seemed to know what to do next, so we just stood there for a while, tears doing all the talking.

When Grandpa had tolerated his fill, he bellowed, "Well, is somebody gonna tell me what's goin' on, or do I have to make a scene?"

We all rode to the police station together in the morning. Nicky and I sat in the back of the truck so that Grandpa could ride shotgun. From the truck bed, I could see him bickering at my mother; the deep timbre of his voice cut bluntly through the wind, even if the actual words fell apart. His tone seemed especially agitated and I had to wonder if his unexpected stretch of clarity had come to an end.

My mother drove over-cautiously, as if my brother and I were so insubstantial that we might blow out of the back of the truck. As a result, what should've been a ten minute drive dragged into twenty. My hair looked like Tina Turner's by the time we arrived.

Despite my mother's frantic protests, Grandpa was out of the truck and barreling toward the entrance before the truck was even in a parking spot. We did the best we could to keep up but the man walked in strides of dinosaur-like proportion. He was in handcuffs when we finally caught up—not under arrest but restrained for everyone's safety.

This is what happens when you accuse a desk sergeant of kidnapping your boy, we learned.

When things calmed down, we were ushered into a small waiting room that smelled like a wet ashtray. A detective would speak to us when he was available, we were told.

The room contained two long couches, one of which was occupied by a man who lay sprawled with one leg dangling to the floor. Eyes closed and hair matted, he looked to have been there for a while.

Across the room, on the other couch, sat a woman whom I immediately recognized, though I couldn't quite place her. Once I glanced beside her though, my chest swelled with unexpected joy. Only when I saw the look on his face, the joy turned to confusion.

And then, as it dawned on me what Brigham Miller's presence must mean, despair.

Nobody talked at first. The sleeping man began to snore contently, oblivious of the drama unfolding around him, and I kind of wanted to kick him. This whole thing was a mistake; it had to be, didn't it? That Brigham wouldn't look me in the eyes and that my mother was crying again—well, these didn't do much to buttress hope.

My mother approached Mrs. Miller like a dog who knows it'll be kicked but can't help itself. Nicky was completely lost, eyes darting around the room in confusion.

"What're they doing here, Link?" he whispered. "Are they here to help Dad?"

Mrs. Miller shot my mother with a piercing glare, dabbing her nose with a balled-up tissue.

"I'm so sorry, Trisha," my mom said. "Is he hurt badly? Why aren't you at the hospital?"

Mrs. Miller responded with a wet, sob-filled guffaw. Brigham started to cry then but it wasn't until I stole a glance at my mother, whose skin had gone almost transparent, that I finally got it.

Mr. Miller—*Reggie* Miller—was dead.

We had no money to post bail and given the severity of the crime, there was no guarantee that bail would've been granted anyway. So for months my dad remained in jail, waiting. Just waiting for the justice system to get around to him. Criminal proceedings were eventually scheduled, which funneled into a trial. In the event of a conviction, the lead prosecutor was expected to ask for the death penalty.

Talk about a punch to the gut.

Our court-appointed attorney explained that, while my dad's knee-jerk reaction was to accept a plea bargain with the DA—and indeed, such an agreement was likely to bump the death penalty off the table—a trial was more likely to discredit the notion of premeditation. This, the lawyer explained, amounted to the difference between ten to twenty-five years and a life sentence without parole.

My mother kept us home for a while to insulate us both from the trial and the swelling hostility of our peers. We were startled awake more than once by screaming expletives from our neighbors. And once, a rock nearly went through my parent's bedroom window.

My grandfather, who had regressed to his usual state of confusion, couldn't make heads or tails of all the unkind attention. He took to manning the porch with a pellet gun, ready to put a sting on anyone dumb enough to tempt him. I thought it was funny at first but it was actually pretty effective. And it didn't hurt that every moment Grandpa spent outside his bedroom seemed to lift his spirits a little higher. He began eating his meals with us, which became a surprisingly pleasant affair.

As the trial wore on, the official accounting of my father's crime made its way into the public forum. Had I not already been a village pariah, I would surely have become one then. But infamy was the least of my concerns.

You see, like my townsmen, I was hearing the facts for the first time and they were devastating. The things I heard, they stuck with me. I couldn't get them out of my mind, no matter how hard I tried. They were always there in the periphery of my day-to-day routines, just waiting to knock the wind out of me.

The thing my father had done was even more horrific than I could have imagined and I felt filthy for my proximity to it. So while I was allowed to visit my father on occasion, I was open to any excuse for staying home. Our sparse moments together were stiff and awkward; I'm not sure that either of us got any enjoyment out of them.

My father had become gaunt and pale. His eyes were bloodshot, swollen and sagging like a baby bird's. Honestly, the man was hard to look at.

"Relax, Link," he'd say. "It's just me." But I wasn't so sure anymore.

I had a dog once; a sweet German Shepherd whom I loved dearly. And like any self-respecting pet owner, I came to idealize her over all animals, including your average human. This remained the case until the day she chased down and ate a neighborhood cat, right before my eyes. It was an act so disgusting that I nearly upchucked for watching. I'm not sure that I loved her any less for doing what nature had designed her to do, but there's no question that my image of her changed. You see, she had proven capable of something so contrary to my inner likeness of her that it called into question everything else that I held to be true of her.

It was like that with my dad, only exponentially worse. Every single time he had raised his hand to one of us, he had given up a piece of my heart. Now that he had killed a man—the father of my best friend, to boot—there was virtually nothing left of him in me. I couldn't even think of him as my dad anymore, really. He was my father and nothing more, which is to say that he was a guy who had procreated with my mother. End of story.

My understanding of the man had fallen hopelessly out of kilter. The same person who embodied honesty and wisdom shared a body with a monster and as near as I could tell, the monster's appetites had finally outgrown my father.

I saw it so clearly now. A filter had been removed from my eyes, revealing a distorted version of the man I had presumed to know. Parts were exactly as I remembered, while others were completely foreign.

It's just me.

No, I didn't think so. The dad he purported to be died at that gas station along with Reginald Miller.

I have never hated my father for what he did, though I have come dangerously close at times. Rather, I learned to hate myself. I was there after all. And I had done nothing to stop it. I'm not sure what I could've done to stop it, yet that may be the worst part of all—wondering *what if.* What if I had done more than just sit in the truck, twirling a stupid lawnmower wheel on my finger? What if I had actually done something, you know? Anything at all to keep my father from snuffing the life from my best friend's father.

Maybe I was ashamed for no good reason. The thing is though, shame—like fear—can erode a person until nothing is left and reasons don't quite make it into the equation.

That's the way it works, you see; the mind and the heart don't always see eye to eye but the heart is undoubtedly the stronger muscle.

SEVEN

The loss of my father's income ran roughshod over us. As if money hadn't already been tight for the Chase family, we were reduced to pinching the very life from every penny. Supper quietly forfeited the company of side dishes, the phone lost its dial tone. When the LeBaron finally gave up the ghost on my thirteenth birthday, we sold it to a scrap yard for next to nothing. My mother spent the money on a birthday cake and I suppose that I must've felt miserable about it for all of five minutes. The truth was that we couldn't keep two vehicles insured, anyway. The pickup, we needed. The car? Not so much. By then it was more of a burden than an asset.

Other than Jeremy, my classmates continued to avoid me like the plague, and who could blame them? Brigham was one of the most beloved kids in school, so if he didn't want anything to do with me, than neither did anyone else. My own popularity reached an all time low.

Nevertheless, when the last day of school tapped me on the shoulder, I realized that however much I looked forward to being away from my peers, I had absolutely nothing to look forward to for the next few months. The children of Lakeview Park hadn't forgiven me for the sins of my father any more than my schoolmates had. They didn't pick on me, exactly; they basically shunned me, which seemed worse at the time.

I'm not sure why, but Nicky was spared any punishment. I suppose that people must've sensed his innocence as much as they sensed some unresolved guilt in me. Whatever the reason, while Nicky horsed around the park with his friends, I spent my days alone in the shade of the wandering tree, drawing pictures and wishing that I had even the tiniest say in my life.

My father's trial concluded in late July. Sentencing could've been worse but in the mind of an adolescent, eighteen years translated to forever. He was transferred from the Shawnee jail to a permanent cell at the Oklahoma State Penitentiary in McAlester, Oklahoma, close to a hundred miles away.

Incidentally, my father wasn't the only one to vanish from my life. The Millers disappeared into thin air after the trial. There were rumors that the family had left the state but no one could say for sure.

I hoped with all my heart that Brigham might somehow find his way back to happiness, back to the path of greatness he so rightly deserved. Considering what he'd been through, though, it didn't seem likely. Brigham had been the best friend a boy could ever have; to have been rewarded with such cruelty must've been unbearable for him.

I know it was for me.

Yet part of me was relieved when Brigham moved because I knew that I would never again be able to look him in the eye.

Some people collect acquaintances to feel good about themselves, piling relative strangers at their feet like offerings to pacify the god of low self esteem. A choice few don't seem to need any validation at all and their indifference attracts the rest of us with irresistible magnetism. I've always envied that.

Take my little brother, Nicky. Even as a little kid, he must've had more friends than he could count. Yet I'm guessing that he never once wondered why, and I'm downright convinced that he honestly didn't care. He loved people, but the truth was that he could take them or leave them.

Me? Oh, I pitched my tent in a completely different camp. The kind in which so few friendships abounded that one didn't dare to question where they came from, much less why they bothered to stick around. It wasn't that I was so unlikable or that I found my peers to be unlikable. It's just that when given a choice, I invariably chose the known of my own company over the unknown of an acquaintance. As a result, forging friendships became a tricky affair, one that required a rather specific set of circumstances, not to mention a generous splash of serendipity.

I imagine there's a recipe for this sort of thing—

2 sprigs of charisma;
1 pinch of bravado;
1 cup of raw athleticism;
2 heaping tablespoons of good humor;
Mix with others, brown by the city pool;
Serve and enjoy while still young!

—but I couldn't for the life of me nail it down. And the better part of me figured that without the proper ingredients, why even bother trying?

Ah, Darwin would be so disappointed to see that my kind manages to reproduce every day.

I realize that I'm slopping the canvas with some pretty globulous impressions, so let me take a moment to fill in some of the finer details. A few fond moments from my adolescence:

In fourth grade, a girl announced to my homeroom that I was wearing her old shirt. Having only a few, I was stuck wearing it twice a week for the rest of the year.

That same year, I fell asleep en route to a class field trip and spent the day locked on the school bus. No one even noticed that I was missing.

In fifth grade, I got beaten up during an assembly. I walked away with a fat lip and a bloody nose. The other guy? *Harrumph.* Not a scratch on her.

Good times.

I amassed a grand total of two friends over the years leading up to high school, and I kind of figured that I was lucky to pull that off. With Brigham gone now, I was down to just one. And I saw so little of Jeremy in those days that he almost didn't count. Gradually, the ache of loneliness overtook me. It grew and grew like a weed in my heart until it didn't feel like loneliness anymore and my heart didn't feel like a heart anymore. I'm not exactly sure what it felt like but I was grateful to be numb for once.

When allowed, I slept for sixteen, eighteen hours at a time without wondering why I was so tired all the time. Even the waking moments felt a little duller around the edges; true, the few good moments weren't quite as sweet, but neither were the frequent bad ones quite as foul. Living had become a biological process and for a while, that was about the best that I could say for it.

Most summers ease in and out with feathered edges, but that summer seemed to come and go in a single, harrowing nightmare. I'm not really sure how we managed to get through it, honestly. Eventually it was just over and we were still standing. When I came to my senses, I discovered with absolute astonishment that I couldn't wait for classes to resume. I had no expectations of grandeur—school was school, after all—yet it promised a daily dose of normalcy in an otherwise bizarre existence.

In early September, I stepped into the glossy halls of Shawnee Middle School as an eighth grader. Almost at once, the riddles of Pre-Algebra and English confounded me, stumping me at every turn, along with a variety of other academic riddles that I had historically failed to solve. Only this time, I welcomed them. They were sweet mercy.

As always, Nicky was a model student. He excelled in every subject with little or no effort. His teachers were aglow with the joy of teaching him; his peers embraced him with open arms. It was tempting to resent him but I resisted and decided instead to follow his lead. I cracked open my textbooks, committing myself to the drudgeries of homework. I tried to be more outgoing, calling on the ghost of Brigham's witty juju for inspiration.

Despite my best efforts, I remained a nobody. My grades rose from pitiful to the lower side of mediocre and though I did manage to meet a few classmates, I couldn't exactly call any of them friends. If nothing else, I found homework to be an effective distraction from the bleakness of my home life. That alone didn't make the extra effort worthwhile but there's no denying that it helped.

Outside school hours, the gears of organized sports were slowly creaking to life. The football field resounded with the colliding of helmets and the borderline profanity of barking coaches who doubled as history and geography teachers. Lovely young ladies donning cheerleading skirts writhed on the sidelines to the rhythm of music I had never heard before.

I could only look on with open-mouthed envy and trudge home. I wasn't built for team sports, especially football. Slightly below average in height and weight, prone to mild but untimely asthma attacks, I was a benchwarmer waiting to happen. To be fair, I could carry my weight on the baseball field. Of course, that was against Lakeview Park's unpracticed roustabouts. I have no doubt that the kids who trained religiously—I mean the ones who hit the batting cages at dawn and threw fast balls in their backyards until dusk shut them down—could've squashed me like a plump June bug. Still, every boy needs a hobby and baseball was mine.

I hadn't seen Jeremy at all over the summer, adding to my festering boredom. For reasons that would remain unknown for many years, he was never allowed to invite friends over. I eventually learned that his father—the exterminator—had a tendency to bring his work home with him. Literally. He kept all sorts of bugs and rodents as household pets, and he didn't like the world to know it.

Though Jeremy lived well out of bounds, his mother took on the role of after-school chauffeur that year. This was an indisputable act of kindness on her part. The town had written off the Chases, all but this woman and her son. I was eternally grateful, yet how does one thank someone for something like that? Not since Brigham's departure had I enjoyed a single extracurricular conversation with a person who didn't share my DNA. Perhaps out of sheer desperation on my part, my once shallow friendship with Jeremy quickly grew roots. Before long, I felt that everything I had lost in Brigham was rediscovered in Jeremy. Maybe I was seeing things as I needed them to be rather than as they actually were, but it really didn't matter. I needed someone. Jeremy and his mother stepped up when no one else would and I'll always be grateful for that.

Over the summer, Jeremy had done some changing. His once-portly mantle had burned off, exposing a chiseled core of hard muscle. Puberty could only take so much credit. Jeremy had earned this transformation, working out and dieting with militant resolve. He tried to explain the science behind his success— something about muscle confusion and simple versus complex carbohydrates—but like most things that Jeremy understood innately, it went right over my head. Whatever the means, its effectiveness was honed to an unbelievable point. Reconciling Jeremy with the pudgy kid I had known only months before was very nearly impossible. He even worked out a solution to his odor problem, one that I could understand: cologne. It's amazing what that stuff can cover up, though one can easily overdo it.

We spent a few afternoons a week taking turns pitching and batting in Pruitt Field. Nicky played catcher, though he rarely lived up to the title. Bless his little heart—he was more like a ball boy on a tennis court than a catcher. Me? I could throw okay, and I guess my hitting was on par with that of most boys my age. Which is to say that I was extraordinarily ordinary.

Jeremy was good. Very good. He could hit just about anything I could throw at him, but it was his pitching that was truly exceptional. With him on the mound, I was lucky to hit one out of ten.

When Jeremy eventually confided in me that he was gunning for tryouts in the spring, I wasn't at all surprised. I told him that the team would be stupid not to snatch him up, and I meant it. He asked me to try out with him, and I declined. He didn't press the issue because he'd only been going through the motions by asking, anyway. We never discussed my financial standing because it was a common theme that needed no explanation, and moaning about it wasn't likely to change anything. The cost of uniforms alone was a firm barrier to entry for me and Jeremy knew this well. More to the point, we both knew that my chances of making the team were slim at best.

I secretly hoped that Jeremy wouldn't make the cut. It isn't easy to admit something so slimy but I knew that if he made the team, I could forget all these afternoons and weekends with his undivided attention. He'd be swept up in a tornado of team practices and away games, summer training camps and jock parties. On the other hand, I imagined that by practicing with him, I was playing a small role in his remarkable metamorphosis. So part of me was eager to share the glory as those who had once looked down on Jeremy now looked upon him with awe.

Like Brigham, Jeremy had the potential for greatness. And if the planets managed to align perfectly for even a moment, it stood to reason that I might just hitch a ride on his coattails. In other words, I rewarded his selfless friendship with misguided greed.

I didn't have any classes with Jeremy, since he was a year ahead of me. Other than a little hallway interaction between classes, I saw little of him at school. Lunch was the sole exception. We had a cafeteria routine of sorts. He munched on a bizarre medley of nuts and raw vegetables as I complained about bombing my classes. He feigned a similar predicament and I'd nod sympathetically. I hope he didn't think that I actually bought what he was selling, because that wouldn't speak highly of his perception of my intellect. Either way, I knew that Jeremy was going out on a limb to make me feel better and I appreciated him all the more for the effort.

We practiced baseball a lot during the coming months. On a few occasions, we were able to rustle up some kids around the park to get a game going. Things usually fell apart quickly, though. Invariably, the few players with any talent or gloves were called home for dinner or chores, leaving behind a sad tribe of inept beanpoles who were willing but unable to do more than stand around and yell, "Suuuwiiing, batta-batta-batta, suuuwiiing!"

Nicky's catching improved, though in the absence of a catcher's mitt, my glove was serving double duty. By Thanksgiving the leather was coming apart at the seams. It was too far gone to have re-stitched but half a roll of duct tape held it together nicely. The surface was slippery, which made it difficult to hold the ball for any length of time, but we made do because that's how we lived. You worked with what you had rather than dwelling on what you wished you could have.

Why my mother even bothered to ask what I wanted for Christmas has always been a mystery to me. The things my brother and I asked for—having no idea what they cost or, in the case of Nicky, if they even existed—were almost always out of the question.

Me: A BB gun with a sniper scope.

Nicky: A helicopter.

Me: A freestyle bicycle.

Nicky: A pet octopus.

Me: A samurai sword.

Nicky: A remote controlled dog that pees Kool-Aid.

I wonder now if I was simply obsessing over all the things that I couldn't have, which is a tendency that seems to afflict humans of all walks of life. Nevertheless, when probed on the subject back in 1989, I asked without hesitation for a new baseball glove. It was perhaps the most reasonable present that I had ever asked for, yet the look on my mother's face told me that it was still too much. I wished that I could take it back but it was too late. Worse, I had encouraged Nicky to ask for a catcher's mitt, so my shame was two-fold.

For the next several weeks, my family adorned the trailer with paper snowflakes and other homemade Christmas décor. We hummed carols and decorated the Christmas tree. Nicky and I took turns fetching firewood and the cozy warmth of our woodstove permeated all but the farthest extremities of our home. I felt happier than I had in a long time.

Christmas Eve seemed more festive than in years past, perhaps because it contrasted so distinctly with the gloomy spell we had all been under during the preceding months. Whatever the reason, holiday cheer had its way with the Chase household, filling us each with enchantment and delight.

Just before lunch, a nice lady from the community food bank delivered two heaping bags of pantry goods and a homemade pumpkin pie. I thought about my father then. Did they serve pumpkin pie in prison? Somehow, I doubted it. I hadn't been to visit him in weeks and my mother was no longer pushing me to go—I'm guessing that she couldn't afford the gas anyway. Amidst all the merriment, my heart began to ache for him until my eyes stung. But a boy's mind is a selective organ, prone to forgetfulness that a grownup's would never tolerate. By bedtime, my father was forgotten.

Christmas morning seemed brighter than a summer afternoon. Sunrays poked through uneven gaps in the mini-blinds, splattering the floor in golden puddles. The base of our puny Christmas tree was surrounded by gifts, each wrapped in the same cheap Santa paper. Shortly before Thanksgiving, my mother had taken a second job at a local bakery. With my father out of the equation, we were still hurting and needed the extra income. I felt a little bad knowing how hard my mother was working, realizing that any short-term chance of us regaining a financial foothold had undoubtedly burned up in a *poof* of Christmas presents. Still, as I looked at that worn-out tree, with the needles coming unraveled and a single strand of lights twinkling good morning, I couldn't stop smiling.

I'd like to tell you that I was grateful that we had presents at all, that the love of my family was the most important thing. But that simply wasn't true. My heart did swell with joy, but it was a conditional form, the kind that springs from the absurdity of childish hope. A tissue-thin joy that stood little chance of surviving reality intact.

Not even my grandfather, though confused as always, could fight off the urge to grin. He watched us with an amused hand-on-cheek sense of awe, as if our giddiness was more powerful than the necessity to know who we were just then. I had never seen him smile like that and the sight of it moved me. I wanted to hug his tree trunk of a neck but I resisted, uncertain of his reaction.

Nicky held my hand, something that he rarely did anymore, and gleamed in sleepy anticipation at the presents. There were too many to count but I was only interested in one. One that I had absolutely no business hoping for.

At my mother's go ahead, we ripped into the gifts like a demolition crew. Piles of wrapping paper and bows soon encircled us. There were gleeful shouts as each toy was held overhead for all to see, subdued grumblings when socks and underwear were unearthed in the guise of more glamorous booty. It seemed that I had more gifts than Nicky this year and I wondered why that was. I bit my tongue though, afraid of jinxing my luck. Luck aside, I felt my faith drip dry as the gift pile dwindled until the only remaining parcels were too small or too light to contain a baseball glove. I held fast to my smile but it took enormous energy.

When it was all over, I hugged my mother and grandfather and gave Nicky a gentle clap on the back. I gathered my plunder in an empty box and carried it hastily to my room, where I began to cry. I should've been better prepared. Of course there would be no glove; why had I allowed myself to believe otherwise? The flimsy joy that had felt so real, so buoyant earlier turned to bitterness and I wanted to scream. I was ashamed of my selfishness but I would've traded the whole lot for the one thing my heart longed for.

Before anyone could walk in to witness my pitiful state, I wiped my eyes and returned to the living room to help clean up. I found my mom and grandpa on the couch with Nicky sardined between them. He held in his arms a final wrapped gift, which he held out to me.

"We saved this one for last," he said in a whisper, eyes glistening like root beer candy. I looked at my mother, whose face was awash with maternal pride.

"Go on, babe. Open it."

I tried to swallow but my tongue suddenly felt like a handful of cotton balls. Ripping the paper slowly at a taped corner, I released the odor of new leather. The sweet smell sent my heart sailing. In a frenzy, I freed the glove from a chrysalis of paper and Scotch tape, bouncing up and down on legs made of boneless rubber. I hugged my mother with heartfelt thanks.

She laughed at my zeal but shook her head. "Don't thank me, baby," she said. "Thank your brother."

I released her and turned to Nicky, heart pounding so hard that it pulsed in my ears.

"You?" I asked.

He nodded and clapped his hands. Before I could begin to connect the dots, my little brother wrapped his arms around me and squeezed like the dickens.

"Merry Christmas, Link."

EIGHT

One of the more unpleasant things about growing up poor was having no central heat. One can learn to endure the cold and to prepare for it. You dang sure better respect it because it doesn't get much worse than a long, freezing night without heat. Yet try as I might, I never really got used to Oklahoma's bitter winters. The frigid temperatures, the hellish winds that needled right into my bones. I guess I eventually came to terms with the crazy weather, even the schizophrenic weathermen who bounded from winter weather advisories to tornado warnings to record high temperatures and back again over the course of a single week. And let's not forget the freak ice storms that blew in on the tails of beautiful spring days. I learned to expect the unexpected from the weather gods because that's what you sign up for to live in Oklahoma.

But to be clear, acceptance should not be mistaken for fortitude.

Our primary line of defense against the misery of winter was an old wood stove. While the cast iron beast helped, it also never let you forget what you were up against. With a full belly, the stove heated the living room to sauna-like extremes, yet the warmth tended to putter out just as it reached the bedrooms. It was cheap but terribly inefficient; most winter nights found me and my brother wrapped like burritos in layers of woolen blankets to ward off the chill.

And that was just the beginning.

The thing I hated most was keeping that stupid fire going. Satisfying the neediness of a hungry wood stove was downright exhausting and maintaining a respectable woodpile wasn't any easier. You'd think that growing up in Oklahoma implied a certain reasonable access to trees, and for some people that might've been true. As for my family, trees had the annoying habit of growing on other people's property. Finding and cutting firewood was a constant and formidable chore, one that I had endured for so long that I couldn't imagine a life without it.

Before my father went to prison, we had a routine. Throughout the offseason, we collected and chopped wood to build up a winter reserve. Sometimes we cut down dead trees in the woods, other times we dragged driftwood from the riverbanks. Our favorite haunt, however, belonged to an old farmer and his wife.

The Peterson's pasture measured several hundred acres and adjoined the Pruitt Field at a short rubble stone wall. The property had been on the market since before I was born with nary a nibble. I'm guessing that its close proximity to Lakeview Park probably wasn't much of a selling feature. Worse, the pasture was skirted on three sides by fifty feet of thick pines, oaks and rampant undergrowth.

Back in the twenties the landowners grew soybeans. As was customary, trees had been planted to form a break against the dry summer winds. Nearly seventy years later, the windbreak was terribly overgrown and the soil was only suitable for growing hay. Worse, the tree line crept farther into the pasture every year, squeezing out what little revenue the Petersons could count on. On the rare occasion when cows were brought in to graze, the thick underbrush proved an endless source of burrs and ticks for any animal who ventured near the perimeter.

The Petersons were nice enough to let us cut all we could carry and we were happy to clear underbrush in trade. It wasn't an easy task though. Kindhearted as they were, the Petersons were quick to raise a stink if they felt we had taken more than was earned. As far as I could tell, our efforts didn't even make a dent in the advancing tree line. I have to assume that we made a pretty good dent in the parasite population though, because entire colonies hitched a ride home with us during summer excursions.

Anyway, I had been chopping no less than a rick per week since I could hold an ax, yet it never ceased to amaze me just how quickly the wood pile reduced to ashes in the thick of winter. This was surely a stunt to my otherwise flourishing social life, but it was imperative to our survival. When my father left, it became my responsibility to make sure that the pastime didn't fall by the wayside.

That year I failed. I blew it off at every opportunity, perhaps out of laziness, perhaps out of emotional exhaustion. Either way, the woodpile was depleted to a fraction of a rick before winter even got started.

And so a few days into January, when I would much rather have been breaking in my new ball glove, my mother dragged Nicky and me to the Peterson pasture for wood. It would be a life-altering day, one that I would dwell on for years to come with wonder. And dismay.

Nicky wasn't much use with an ax. He had only recently been allowed to pick one up for the first time and by then his muscles had already settled in for more leisurely duties. My mother had never shown any aversion to my wielding heavy tools, yet she coddled Nicky like a newborn babe until he simply wouldn't tolerate it anymore.

"But your sweet little hands," she'd say. "They'll blister!"

My hands weren't even a consideration.

Nevertheless, what Nicky lacked in brute strength, he made up for in enthusiasm. While I made woodchips, he cleared brush and dragged away fallen limbs. He tied pull ropes and loaded the truck bed, singing radio songs for my entertainment. He didn't complain and he kept a good pace. Though my father's practiced efficiency was sorely missed, my brother and I made a pretty good team.

My mother, on the other hand, was a question mark.

I can't fault her for being inexperienced. She had always been a homebody, a woman who drew comfort from having some measurable distance between her and nature. My father had once stood in that gap, insulating her from the elements just as she had tried to do for Nicky. Those days were gone and I must admit that I felt a swell of pride as my mother dug her toes in and rolled with the punches, because I knew how much they hurt and it took grit to keep taking them. But that isn't really the point, is it? Being willing to step outside of her comfort zone didn't mean that my mother would know what to do once she got there. I wasn't sure if her presence would help or hurt and the best I could do was cross my fingers.

I was working on a small elm tree. Well it seemed small at first, anyway. It was half-dead from Dutch elm disease, branches stripped to a bald sheen by the winds. It seemed so frail, so diminutive, that I expected no resistance.

Boy was I wrong.

Ten minutes in, I was breathing like a steam engine and my mother was quickly losing patience. She wrapped a pull rope around the trailer hitch and eased the truck forward to take out the slack. When gentle tension didn't work fast enough, she gunned the engine as if to rip the tree right out of the ground. The engine stalled in protest but at the last millisecond it coughed and lurched back to life. The tires whirred, scattering dirt and woodchips into the air. At the other end of the rope, the old elm shuddered with a grudging crack.

We were getting close.

I rounded the tree, hacking into the unmarred side with a dozen or so full-bodied *thunks*. Nearby, the truck applied renewed tension but somehow that dying elm stood strong. For a half-dead tree, it was hanging on for dear life.

My mother let off the gas then and the truck sagged into a set of muddy ruts. I stopped to rest too, chest heaving, arms quivering from exertion. Sweat beaded on my skin despite the chill, crawling down my back like foraging beetles. Bless his heart, Nicky brought me a cup of water and I drained it in one pull. He plopped to the ground and began to refill the cup, humming a Bon Jovi song just loud enough to hear.

Behind me, the truck retched and shook and then clunked into reverse. With a creak of springs, it began to back up, slowly approaching with my mother's silhouette bobbing in the filthy rear window. A tiny warning bell clanged in the back of my mind and I took a moment to consider it, wondering what it was that had my hackles suddenly rising.

Abruptly, I got it. I knew what was about to happen, and that it was too late to stop it. Before my lips could even part to form a word of protest, in fact, my mother popped the clutch. With a great roar, the truck sprang forward against the ropes. A frightened, "No!" surged from me but it was like the muttering of a gnat against the great rumble of that engine. The wood my brother had stacked so neatly in the truck bed spilled onto the ground.

Nicky was on his knees at the foot of the tree, crouched just below the ropes with a thermos in one hand and a cup in the other. I screamed for him to move but he merely paused and turned to look at me. He glanced at the spilled wood with an expression of guarded amusement, as if he suspected that some practical joke was in the works. The panic in my expression must've registered with him then because concern slowly wiped away his crooked smile. He tried to get his body in motion, but I knew it was too late.

So I did the only thing that made sense.

I reached out to grab him by the shirt, summoning every ounce of my strength for what I had to do. Just as my fingers found fabric, the telltale snapping of wood announced the moment of truth. One of the pull ropes rustled against my head and I heard it twang with a sudden loss of tension. I felt the tree collapsing then and I threw Nicky with all my might. I felt him lift off the ground as if made of cotton and he seemed to take flight. I released him, hoping to God that I had done enough. There was a sickly tearing sound as the old elm bucked free of its stump. With unbelievable speed and force it grabbed me and together we fell into a blanket of woodchips and dead leaves.

Upon impact with the ground, a pulsing note began to emanate from within me, rising in a vibrating hum like the proud drone of a bagpipe. It seemed to swallow me, detaching from my body and luring what remained of me into soft darkness. I wanted to burrow in, to lose myself in the serenade of that place. I couldn't though. Because just above it, something was calling to me.

It was Nicky, crying. Wailing my name with heartbreaking terror.

The sound of my brother cut through the billowing darkness and I felt death retreat with a silent scowl. My mother screamed then, long and hard, full of woe. The strangeness of that sound dragged me completely back to the surface. I knew that pain would soon overwhelm me, but I didn't care. My brother was okay and that seemed the only thing that mattered.

I remember wondering how I could still be alive. There were moments, in fact, when I wasn't entirely sure that I was. My senses were playing tricks on me, you see. Sound seemed otherworldly and I was completely blind. I should've been in unbearable pain but I felt almost nothing. The only human sensation left seemed to be one of heavy sleepiness. Nicky spoke to me, his voice far away as if whispering from another dimension. I couldn't make sense of the distant words but his tone was frightened. The sound of an engine shrieked and then tapered into silence. Eventually the call of darkness became irresistible and I succumbed to dreamless sleep.

When I awoke later, I had no inkling for the passage of time. The fallen tree was lifting away, casting a blurry silhouette against a cloudless sky. Suspended above me on chains from the bucket of a bulldozer, the tree twisted and turned in a cold breeze. My mother's sobs raged from beyond my line of sight. Someone was kneading my shoulder; I couldn't see who it was, but I'm pretty sure it was Nicky.

Mr. Peterson abandoned his bulldozer and knelt at my side. His face bobbed over mine, backlit and out of focus against a sea of deep blue. "Dear God," he whispered, covering his mouth with a trembling hand. I wanted to know what he saw just then, what it was that had cracked the shell of this hardened farmer. I tried to ask and found that I couldn't. Maybe I was dead after all, because my mouth was eerily unresponsive. Not just my mouth actually— my whole body seemed disconnected from me, as if it was no longer mine to command.

Eventually, the paramedics arrived and began to poke and prod me, grilling me mercilessly with questions that I could scarcely decipher, much less answer. As they examined me, I sensed a shift in their demeanor; sharp wit slipped first into clipped concentration and then resignation. I felt afraid. Terrified, in fact, because if the state of my flesh had these guys worried—men who doted over the sick and dying for a living—I was in serious trouble.

Without the tree to compress my wounds, I was leaking from a dozen or so lacerations. I could sort of feel the blood pulsing from me, dribbling into the soaking tatters of my clothes. Sickly wetness had pooled around me, turning the ground to steaming mud. I was sleepy and I was cold. So cold that I might have frozen solid; so cold that I honestly couldn't imagine ever being warm again.

It was getting harder and harder to breathe. I just wanted to sleep and I wondered if anyone would care if I just stopped trying. Then Nicky rustled my hair, reminding me that I had much to live for.

I managed to move my head a bit. Not much, just enough to glimpse a medic as he fumbled over the ragdoll of a flannel sleeve. My pitching arm had been driven elbow first into the ground like a tent spike. The bones of my forearm had punched through cartilage, skin and dirt before wedging to a halt against something unseen. My hand had nearly been ripped off, hinged backward on a few surviving tendons like the open lid to a mason jar. Somehow, my mediocre pitching arm had miraculously born the immense weight of a fallen tree.

Nicky wasn't critically injured, but that isn't to say that he escaped completely unscathed. He had a nasty gash just above his hairline and one of his ankles had swollen to the size of a grapefruit. These injuries were caused by my tossing him aside rather than by force of the tree. Rather than complain, my little brother clung to me, whimpering hazy syllables of encouragement, blood beading on his dimpled chin and patting to the earth like a rapid metronome.

In some ways, my mother was in the worst shape of us all. She had managed to keep her head long enough to fetch help, bless her heart. But the adrenaline had long burned off, exposing the sort of panic and utter helplessness that only a frightened parent can really grasp. There wasn't a scratch on her but the psychological damage of witnessing the near destruction of her boys—of nearly causing it—proved to be more than she could bear. She wailed until her voice became a gravelly groan, a sound so strange and agitating that few would guess it to be human.

I was a little relieved when she finally passed out, and I'm guessing that I wasn't the only one.

The pain was surprisingly bearable, thanks to the intoxicating magic of shock. More tingling and pressure than anything. From the ambulance, I watched Mr. Peterson reach into the bloody impression that my body had formed in the dirt to retrieve a rock. He brought it to me with an expression of wonder.

"Hard to believe," he mused. "This little thing is the only reason you're still alive right now."

My eyes could barely focus, but they managed to cooperate for a split second. It was long enough to see that I wasn't looking at just any rock. It was rusted and pocked with a distinctly conical profile. I was no expert, but even I knew a space rock when I saw one.

NINE

I had no right to be alive. Forget about that initial moment of impact for a second, the indifferent brutality of gravity—my surviving that was a miracle but that was a given. In the hours and days that followed, any one of a half dozen mortal wounds should've sealed my fate; yet I kept on breathing. Lord was I a mess though. My skull was spider webbed with cracks and contusions. There was some swelling in my brain cavity. Four of my ribs were broken, one of which found its way into a lung and tried like the dickens to drown me in my own blood. My small intestine had become perforated by a gouging branch and infection was a constant danger. And of course, let's not forget about the mutilation of my pitching arm.

I awoke from a medically induced coma the proud new owner of three titanium skull plates and the mother of all headaches. As is the case with any significant head wound, brain damage was a lingering concern. The massive loss of blood didn't put anyone's mind at ease either. For a long while, the state of my mental well being was completely up in the air. It's hard to measure cognitive stability when pain medications are busy mustering up hallucinations and memory loss. It would be nice to holster that as a convenient excuse, by the way. Alas, I can't blame the accident for being an idiot—that's a little something that insurance companies like to call a *pre-existing condition.*

I had been awake for three days before I saw my face for the first time. As startling as it had been to look upon the carnage of my pulverized arm, the damage to my face was far more disturbing. I was so ugly. My nose had been crushed. My front teeth were gone or broken off—every dang one of them, not a single survivor. My upper lip was stitched all the way to my nose, puckered like a poorly remedied cleft palate. My cheeks were black and misshapen. One eye was swollen shut over a fractured orbit, the other a gory patchwork of broken blood vessels. Every inch of my face was shredded, held intact by seam after seam of shiny stitches.

As for my arm, well—you can imagine it was in tough shape. The smaller of my forearm bones was shattered, the larger mushroomed in a series of compact fractures. Many of the bones in my wrist were crushed. A few had disappeared altogether, torn free and left behind to rest in that bloody pasture, no doubt.

Before self-pity could set in, a gaggle of orthopedic wizards converged on me to soothsay over my prognosis. With each declaration, my future inched a little closer to something promising. I would keep my arm, it seemed, even my hand. Countless surgical procedures were on the horizon and I wouldn't be throwing any more curve balls, but I was alive.

And more importantly, so was Nicky.

My doctor, Dr. Grady, was nice. Funny too. As he looked me over for the first time, a single eyebrow seemed to slither halfway up his forehead and hang there like brown caterpillar. "So a little sore throat and cough, huh?" Doped up and caught off guard, I could only stare dumbly up at him. He pretended to make a note in his clipboard, mumbling, "Patient unable to appreciate ironic humor. He probably hates ice cream, too."

I liked him immediately.

"Seriously though," the good doctor said, "there's a lesson to be learned here. Sometimes trees fight back." He seemed a little young to be a physician, but I suppose that his sense of humor might've skewed my perception a bit. He had an animated personality that few adults could pull off, one that—on the surface anyway—didn't quite align with my image of a medical professional.

Adding to my care, a variety of specialists popped in and out of the room throughout my hospital stay—neurologists, plastic surgeons, pulmonologists, otolaryngologists—the best and brightest, the utterly unpronounceable. They pestered me at all hours with redundant tests, which became the hallmark of their disjointed consultations.

You might wonder how we could afford the luxury of such elite medical treatment. You're right to wonder of course, because we couldn't. You see, I had been toting around a little blue Indian card for quite some time. Thus far, this scrap of worn paper had been nothing more than a childish excuse to carry a wallet. But if it was to be believed, I was one-sixteenth Cherokee. Just enough to qualify for free healthcare at any of Cherokee Nation's hospitals; nowhere near enough to appreciate this amazing heritage in any other context. My father used to joke that I probably bled out the Indian with my first bloody nose.

"What was his name?" I would demand.

"Who?"

"Duh, the Indian!"

Yeah, it wasn't very funny back then, either.

Free healthcare was nothing to sneeze at, yet it was a commodity that my family rarely took advantage of. It wasn't that we thought little of our health, just so you understand. The nearest free clinic was a hundred and thirty miles away, farther than we could afford to drive except in extreme circumstances.

I was born in a free clinic, as was Nicky. I have a faded memory of accompanying my mother to the Indian hospital in

Claremore when she developed pneumonia one terrible winter. Other than that, my family did a pretty good job keeping the doctors away. In fact, my personal Indian card had never once proven useful.

Until now.

I'm not saying that things came together without a hitch. Public service can be a slow and creaky machine. Constant communication was needed to grease the wheels and despite the effort, plenty of shuffling around took place in the beginning, with forms and records passing back and forth between doctors and administrators like hot potatoes. My mother was glued to the phone for hours, following up on referrals, dragging unwitting strangers in and tossing others out of the loop as she saw fit. Most of this took place while I was unconscious, so I was spared what must've been a long and tedious spectacle. Eventually though, thanks to my mother's red-faced perseverance, I was admitted to Shawnee Regional Hospital on Cherokee Nation's tab.

I was discharged on day five, following a gauntlet of surgical procedures. Surgical glue was used to repair my punctured lung while my broken ribs were left to heal on their own. My flattened nose and cheeks were neatly reconstructed from a titanium mesh, which would eventually graft to bone and keep me looking somewhat human. To tame the wiles of my toothless grin—or possibly to address a broken mandible—my jaw was wired shut. No bother, really. I didn't feel much like eating or talking in those days. I was sloshed on pain meds most of the time and all I wanted to do was sleep, sleep, sleep.

Though uncomfortable, these remedies were surprisingly bearable. I couldn't say the same for my poor arm. What was once free to high five and toss baseballs was now immobilized in a framework of rods and pins, braced securely against a very sore ribcage, where it would remain for more than a month.

At school—oh yes, even half dead, I wasn't excused from classes for more than a week—I was no less invisible when adorned in metal scaffolding and layers of thick bandages. With the exception of Jeremy and a few teachers, no one appeared to have noticed that I was even absent, much less that I was now back looking like the victim of a sky diving accident. I'm not suggesting that my gruesome brush with death should've engendered popularity with my classmates but I must admit that I expected some sort of reaction. I mean, I'm pretty sure that I was the only kid my age with bridgework, and you'd think the Terminator arm would have been impossible to ignore. Yet still, I managed to slip through the cracks into obscurity. I was a little surprised, but not altogether disappointed. It was a fairly comfortable place to be, after all. Given that I could barely speak, almost nothing was expected of me, aside from merely showing up.

At home, I found it impossible to do more than watch television. If I was on my feet, I was knocking over cereal boxes and making a general nuisance of myself. So I planted my rear in front of our thirteen inch black and white television, with its rabbit ears gnarled like spindly, arthritic fingers and tried to remember what fun was like. Divided between three fuzzy network stations, my afternoons amounted to a few boisterous game shows and a whole lot of soap operas. While Nicky circuited the park with his friends, I cranked the channel knob with utter desperation, hoping for an undiscovered station to burst through the static. Life at home became a window into my grandfather's nightmare and the view was a still life of drab repetition and inescapable loneliness.

Sadly, the misery didn't stop there. For the first few weeks in particular, I endured some of the most traumatic mothering ever. Most of us don't remember the last time our mothers wiped our bottoms and that's precisely as it should be. Alas, I remember it all too well. I'll spare you the details, save for the image of my mother and me crammed into the smallest bathroom in the world. The conflict of my stationary arm with the position of our sink demanded a balancing act, my good arm braced against the bathtub while I struggled to center over the commode.

So there was that mess to clean up. Good times.

I'm not sure who was more scarred by those experiences, which seemed far worse than the terrible accident that preceded them, but I could hardly look my mother in the eye for months.

While I was on the mend, a certain rock was raising some eyebrows at the University of New Mexico, home to a panel of expert meteoriticists. With the passage of each day, my mother became more convinced that the hunk of stony iron might be valuable to some space collector, and why not? Meteorites weren't exactly a common find in our neck of the woods, and it was easy to imagine that a lengthy examination of ours might imply that it was a particularly interesting specimen. Her optimism was contagious. Breaking all the rules of poverty, we began to plan spending sprees founded on what could only be called wishful thinking. We knew better, of course. At least, we should have.

When the official letter finally arrived, my mother looked as if she might cry and it wasn't immediately clear if happiness or despair was affecting her so. According to the experts, ours wasn't just any meteorite; it shared a distinct cosmic fingerprint with another meteorite on record. Apparently Pruitt Rock had once been a much larger body. Long before mankind stepped onto the scene, the meteor had broken apart against the atmosphere and peppered the area like grenades. There were likely hundreds to be found, but for now—excluding a few fragments excised over the years from the still-buried Pruitt Rock—ours was the only one. It was extremely rare and highly sought after. Even a small piece was worth a fortune.

This was all wonderful news. But as my mother's expression had betrayed upon first reading the letter, there was a problem. You see, though we had come to think of it as our own, the meteorite didn't actually belong to us. We had unwittingly pinned our financial salvation to another man's property.

Mr. Peterson, the rightful owner, was a kindhearted soul who recognized the direness of our circumstances. If the value of the meteorite had been marginal, he would surely have given it to us. But it wasn't. And every man's generosity has its limits, especially that of a struggling farmer. He didn't leave us empty handed though. Two weeks after that fateful letter arrived, Mr. Peterson personally delivered a small piece of the meteorite to yours truly. It was a lump the size of a marble with a flat glassy edge. Neatly sliced off the larger rock for microscopic examination, the specimen displayed an otherworldly crosshatched pattern in the iron grain. Mr. Peterson had been kind enough to hang it from a dog tag chain, which fit my neck perfectly. It was beautiful.

Small as it was, this consolation gift was worth a hundred dollars or more. We should've been grateful for the gesture. Mr. Peterson didn't owe us anything, after all. If he had opted to leave us with nothing, he would've been well within his rights. I tried very hard to remember that; really, I did.

But mostly, I stewed.

After four hundred years, my arm was freed from its shackles and bound instead by gauze and plaster. The cast was more uncomfortable in some ways—much itchier, for example—but I could now move my arm at the shoulder, permitting a wide variety of new and wonderful activities: solo bathroom excursions, sleeping on my side, awkward waving—the possibilities were endless. Similarly, the wires were removed from my jaw and for a few days I couldn't hear enough of my own voice. Feeling empowered, I was eager to make myself useful, washing dishes and fetching firewood. I even put in some time at the woodpile, though chopping one-handed proved to be an exercise in futility.

The slow but persistent healing of flesh and bone was exhausting, not only for me but for my family. Nobody likes a whiner, and it turned out that I had a rather unpleasant knack for it. My body ached all the time and for reasons that I can't begin to understand, I was compelled to let everyone know all about it. Moans and groans, dramatic sighs. A sharp rebuke for anyone who didn't pay proper homage to my plight. My mother threatened to rewire my mouth shut on more than one occasion, and I think she might've actually tried it if not for Nicky's constant presence. Yes sir, in terms of shameless grumbling, even my grandfather had nothing on me.

Speaking of my grandfather, poor guy, he stumbled into me outside the bathroom one night and nearly died of fright. Nicky had taken on all grandpa duties, so I had managed to avoid my grandfather for weeks. I wasn't sure what the old man had been told about my condition, if anything, but he was inconsolably distraught by the sight of me that night. My first thought was that he'd taken me for a vengeful mummy—I certainly looked the part—but it didn't take long to see that I was way off. Grandpa wasn't afraid *of* me, he was afraid *for* me.

As the initial shock of our hallway collision faded, he grasped me by the shoulders, abruptly but gently, and cried out, "Benjamin, look at you! Oh Lord, forgive me … what have I done?" He fell into such a woeful state then, sobbing and billowing on his feet like a sail in a turbulent wind, that my mother awoke and came running to his aid. When all other tactics failed to calm him, she fished a pint of Jack Daniels from some hidden stash and sat with him in his room until he sipped himself to sleep.

I knew that this incident was a sign of things to come, and I did the best I could to steel myself. I sometimes lingered in front of the mirror for twenty and thirty minutes at a time, equally fascinated and terrified by the mystique of my own reflection. The person looking back at me might as well have been the Invisible Man, swathed in bleached ribbons to mask his transparency. Because while the face obscured beneath my bandages was naturally opaque, it was still an absolute question mark.

My mother changed my dressings daily at the kitchen table, and though her smile belied indifference with eerie conviction, her eyes were rarely up for the charade. Something terrible awaited me, that much was evident. I was in no hurry to see what caused my mother's iron façade to waver so easily.

Well, that's not really true. As frightening as the prospect was, I suppose that it was just about all I could think about.

On the day when my bandages were removed for good, the face of a complete stranger was revealed. Having never enjoyed an excuse for vanity, I was perhaps more prepared than most to be let down. I had always been a little on the homely side, you see. More plain than unattractive, though I'm told that one can be as bad as the other. Now, I was downright ugly. Ugly to an extreme that nothing could've prepared me for, and I knew that there was no mitigating the effect that it would have on any who dared to lay eyes on me.

I was a quilted obscenity, pink and enflamed with freshly grown scars, skewed and wrinkled by the slight misalignment of stitched flesh. Thanks to the dedication of a few plastic surgeons, my nose was once again recognizable as a nose but it was now an exaggerated feature, swollen and rosy, oddly bulbous like that of an aging alcoholic. The old face of my identity, however unremarkable, seemed gorgeous by comparison. Yet there was no going back to it.

The very thought of becoming someone new—especially something so outlandish, so very revolting—was hard enough to imagine. Accepting that it was my inescapable fate? Well, that was a devastating blow that sent me reeling. Rarely have I cried like I did on that day. I wanted to lie down and die, and that's the awful truth. If my mother and Nicky hadn't been there to comfort me, I might well have finished what that old elm tree started.

For the first few days, Nicky couldn't help but stare at me, his eyes wide and inquisitive. "Does it still hurt?" he'd ask time and again. I loved him too much to be truthful and merely shrugged. There was no remedy for the pain that I was feeling. It festered like a rampant infection in a place so deep within me that no medicine could ever hope to reach it.

While my brother's gaze was open and inoffensive, my mother's stung like pinpricks. The look on her face was distastefully familiar, the same that washed over her in Grandpa's presence. It was a mask of pity and hastily-veiled resentment. Being on the receiving end of such a look from the woman who had given me life carved a wound all of its own. It baffled me as much as it hurt. Nicky managed to look past the scars almost immediately, yet my mother was resigned to dwell on them. How could I hope to make peace with this disfigurement when my own mother couldn't? Would she always see me like this, as another family burden? Only time would tell.

Remember that brand new baseball glove, the coveted Christmas gift that I just couldn't bear to be without? It lay untouched on my dresser with the retail tag still attached, collecting dust like some forgotten talisman. The realization that I would never play ball again saddened me, but only for a second. It was such a small concession, really. Let's face it: I was no Babe Ruth. And besides, though the universe often seemed to have a bone to pick with me, I felt that by offering my life in place of my brother's, I had earned a moment of favor. Despite all the pain and agony wrapped up in that split second decision, there isn't a doubt in my mind that I chose wisely. To this day, I don't see the accident as something that happened indiscriminately to me, you see. It was a transaction of sorts: I had my little brother, the devil his pound of flesh.

I'd do it again in a heartbeat.

TEN

At the outing of my new face, the low profile I had come to appreciate at school suddenly reversed polarity. I was a walking beacon, beckoning attention as if precision built for this singular purpose. People gawked everywhere I went, gasping with open-mouthed revulsion exactly as I had known they would. Not just the students either. My teachers tried to show some decorum, smiling politely and quickly looking away, but their red-cheeked nonchalance wasn't fooling anyone. And who could blame them?

Nevertheless, school became somewhat of a haven. My extra effort over the past year had not been without reward, though the accident had set me back a little. With Jeremy's help, my grades snailed steadily down the alphabet. Along the way, I made a startling discovery.

I could write.

Don't get me wrong, I was no better than my classmates at first. But that I could do it at all was new and struck me as nothing short of supernatural by its strangeness. Whereas I once struggled to differentiate between adjective and adverb, I suddenly understood the subtle power of sentence structure. From thin air it seemed, I conjured the ability to manipulate the tone of a sentence with the deliberate shifting of a single word. Just as my body had been rearranged by trauma, my brain was experiencing a kind of reconfiguration—a less violent one, for sure, but dramatic in its own way. At face value this turn of events seemed a small consolation for all my suffering, yet I sensed that I had stumbled upon something of value, a treasure whose size might be greater than it seemed. This was my Pruitt Rock, I began to suspect. It was my salvation. It would carry me to a better place, if only I could bring myself to be patient.

Patience, unfortunately, was asking a lot in those days. With nothing else to occupy my mind, I was suddenly frantic to unearth that treasure, to expose every facet of its potential. It was all I could think about. I wondered if this was how old Mr. Pruitt had felt, all but frothing at the mouth to get that million dollar rock out of the ground—eyes turned to dollar signs, hands balled into impotent fists with desperation—right up until that terrible moment when the veil of greed fell away and he realized that it was never going to happen. That it had always been impossible.

Was I deluding myself, too? Stranger things have happened to stranger people.

My English teacher began taking an interest in me, less for the quality of my writing than for its unexplainable improvement. This was to be expected, but while it was nice to be noticed for something other than my appearance, I was a little worried that her sudden attention might confuse my other teachers, who conversely had little to gain from raising their expectations. I needn't have worried. They couldn't bear to look at me, much less confine themselves in a room with The Thing to discuss its wasted potential.

Thing still can't solve for xy over square root of z.

Thing bad.

As my writing became more surefooted, I developed a fascination with the elasticity of the English language, which I found could be stretched and bent over itself to create nuance and dimension. The more I practiced, the easier it got. I quickly—and quietly—surpassed my classmates. For the first time in my life I was truly good at something. I was having fun.

Yet despite this welcome gift, and for all my hard-earned angst, I had nothing to say. My prose was well crafted, yet it lacked any real creativity or zeal. My poetry? Oh, it flowed merrily to nowhere, verse after verse stagnating in its own bland juices.

I knew what the problem was, even if my teacher didn't. What modest aspirations I had toyed with as a child had been picked to pieces by the harsh winds of poverty. The future was a black hole to me and all the words in the world couldn't beautify what I could only imagine as emptiness.

I had no hope.

Yet here was a glimmer of something. From nowhere, the universe had thrown me a bone. It was up to me to discover its purpose, to give it a voice. To bridge the gap between my heart and mind, that empty chasm where dreams were meant to abound and characters as real as you or me might one day congregate.

So I did what any aspiring writer should do: I read. The classics, contemporary fiction, essays, romance novels—anything and everything I could get my hands on to fan the tiny flame within me. From Albert Camus to Piers Anthony, Walt Whitman to Stephen King, I left no stone unturned. Thanks to the school library, I was never without something new and different.

Poring through the pages of literary giants, I felt my newfound ability slip into proper perspective: at its best, mine was the tiniest of seedlings, sprouting from the dirt at the feet of towering redwoods. It was more than humbling; it was downright embarrassing.

I should probably have given up. Indeed, it might've been the responsible thing to do, considering that failure was always an option for a Chase. Then again, by my calculations I had very little to lose. I didn't need to be the best. Not yet, anyway. It was enough to have shown some sign of aptitude because for too long I had been completely helpless, a victim of my own inadequacies.

Do you know what that's like, I wonder? To be without a single redeeming quality? To somehow invite the worst of circumstances, just as a wounded animal draws packs of starving dogs from the night? Writing didn't necessarily promise to change any of that, but it was a rare chance to influence my own outcome. Squandering it never even crossed my mind.

Yet as winter politely bowed out—which is to say that it parted on schedule for once, without the usual parting tantrum—and the first buds appeared on the trees, my optimism began to sour. It wasn't immediately apparent what was bothering me, but it didn't take long to develop a loose theory.

As a younger child, spring had been my favorite season. It was easy to get caught up in revival as the world shrugged off the ugly winter like a dead skin, blushing in the deep greens, yellows and pinks of rebirth. But while the colorful display was invigorating to the young at heart, it managed to infect many— including my mother—with the irresistible urge to nest. This was an unfailing phenomenon, one whose presence has never been more evident than it was that year. My mother's annual fascination with domesticity became dangerously entwined with a new and rather shameless compulsion to delegate.

You see, upon my father's imprisonment, the state of our home had begun a lazy drift into neglect. The driveway was littered with potholes; year-old cobwebs hung from the corners like macabre chandeliers; the yard was piled high with fall's windblown leaves. It was as blissful as it was depressing, and it might have gone on forever in a perfect world. But then, a neighborhood kid took notice of our unkempt yard and offered to rake our leaves for five dollars, and my mother—who had been tacitly complicit up to this point—was suddenly awakened to the shamefulness of our laziness. Her reversal couldn't be talked down, yet for all her blustering she couldn't quite bring herself to dirty her own hands. Why, that's what children are for, after all!

Spring was only just stretching its limbs, and I was already growing weary.

Thanks to a certain Lakeview entrepreneur, our well-deserved complacency came to an abrupt end. No more after school naps, no more Saturday morning cartoons. Nothing but busywork as far as the eye could see. I wanted to clobber that stupid jerk with his own rake.

Even as I settled in to stew over my bad luck though, I realized that my consternation was misplaced. Spring was on track to run me into the ground for sure, but when I considered the days beyond, unease wrenched my guts with long, contraction-like cramps. It took those moments of distinct contemplation to realize just how apprehensive I had become, and why.

My classmates gazed through the window banks with faraway expressions, chewing absently on the rubber hats of their number two pencils, and I knew that they were daydreaming of summer bicycle rides around town and icy Cokes by the city pool. Deep in their bones, they ached for the hastening of those carefree days just as I once had.

I was rapidly coming to regard the prospect of summer vacation with dread. My peers would savor each day in leisure, but mine were dog-eared for much more depressing things. Things that weren't at all vacation-like, in fact. Caring for my grandfather, for example. And visiting my dad in prison. Nothing says *vacation* like barbed wire and prison guards, let me tell you. And let's not forget physical therapy, because who doesn't enjoy torturing a still-healing body just to prove that it can survive even more abuse?

So that was it. Other than these tedious outings, I could envision no escape from a long, hot summer trapped at home.

Ugh.

I supposed that on good days I might sit on the back porch and watch the neighborhood kids play ball, but that would lead to dwelling on what it had once felt like to play among them. To smack a fast ball straight down left field into the obscurity of a firefly dusk, believing with childish conviction that all was well with the world. That would give me plenty of opportunity to sulk, at least. I was crippled and a source of local taboo. I felt robbed and incredibly alone.

Yes, I was gearing up for a good old-fashioned pity party and the rest of the world was invited to kiss my rear.

My fourteenth birthday whizzed by so quickly that I barely noticed. I was so focused on what I had lost that it never dawned on me that I might be better off without it. That the best way to become whole again was to seize the day and rebuild.

Naturally, since I wanted nothing to do with summer, the last day of school advanced on me without mercy, stalking me at a run like some grassland predator. When it finally overtook me, I succumbed with a whimper rather than a fight. I walked home that day with a stomach tied in knots, feeling abandoned as if my sanctuary had just spat me out.

I expected nothing good to come of the next few months because good things didn't happen to Lincoln Chase. Terrible circumstances awaited me, I was certain, and the most I could hope for was to survive.

But that wasn't quite how things turned out.

ELEVEN

A person of stronger character might have considered my baseball glove a souvenir of better times. I wanted to light it on fire. Its presence tormented me. Like an unearned dime store Eifel Tower, that stupid glove was a mocking symbol of what would never be, and the sight of it never failed to sting. So without a trace of reluctance, I handed it over to Nicky and bid it good riddance. My brother would put it to far better use than I ever would.

Nicky was popular with the kids in Lakeview Park, which should hardly be a surprise. He had no trouble getting a ball game together at a moment's notice, and every day he became a more proficient player. Watching from the back porch, lazing in the cradle of a rusty folding chair, I soon realized that my little brother was a much more capable player than I had ever been. When that cold reality first sank in, a faint breeze of jealousy began to whisper in my ear. Fortunately, I can be quite deaf when it suits me—

"Take out the trash, Lincoln!"

What's that? A snake stole your cash?

—and the whisper eventually seemed to give up.

Despite all the anxiety I had experienced during the spring, I found an unexpected sense of peace on the sidelines, swelling with pride as my brother inched toward greatness. He still sucked with a catcher's mitt but that kid could pitch. He delivered the ball with remarkable consistency and a fair amount of steam, and not just for his age. His hitting was a little sloppy by comparison but that would improve with time. Once in a while, Nicky blasted a home run with such momentum that my cheeks flushed with envy. I wished Jeremy had been around to see a couple of those; even he would've been impressed.

If these observations alone summed up Nicky on the ball field, I would have considered him a little above average, though prone to occasional moments of brilliance. But as the summer wore on, I realized there was something special going on with Nicky. Something that caused him to outshine the other kids, no matter what he was doing on the field.

What made him exceptional was a spider sense for human dynamics. Those tiny nuances that are all but indiscernible to the rest of us? Nicky read them loud and clear. Nothing escaped his notice. There were no stolen runs with Nicky on the mound. Working a base, he was preparing to cut off a slide long before anyone else knew it was coming. And while he was more or less average at the plate, intuition that bordered on precognition showed my brother just where to put the ball.

He wasn't guessing either. The field was like an extension of him, betraying even the faintest hint of muscle movement as if lined with invisible silk. More importantly, Nicky had the ability to process it all—every feint, every pivoting foot, every non-verbal exchange—in fractions of a second. His body was in motion before anyone else knew what was happening. It was downright mystifying. Honestly, the kid was a joy to watch, and not only because he was my brother.

I might've learned all this sooner had I given Nicky an opportunity to do more than play catcher. I was ashamed to have encumbered his progress for so many years. How long had he crouched behind home plate, biting his tongue for my sake?

Man I loved that kid. The only thing more remarkable than his burgeoning athleticism was his refined sense of loyalty. And it made me smile to see such a selfless creature come to his own, thriving at something that he loved. Something that we both loved.

My mother was pleased too, but with practical reservation. She must've feared just how far Nicky's talent might take him. The day was coming when she would be tasked with coughing up money that didn't exist, and her inevitable failure might well destroy the dreams of a boy who deserved nothing less than the world. It was an impossible situation that didn't bode well for any of us.

In the meantime, Nicky had other problems. My poor brother had reached a sort of Chase age of accountability, though no birthday marked the occasion. One morning during breakfast, my mother observed between sips of coffee, "Son, I think it's time you started earning your keep a little more. Don't you?"

I was a little surprised by this remark because I had been trying awfully hard to do just that. But then, as my face twisted into righteous indignation, I realized that my mother wasn't looking at me.

Nicky smiled knowingly, as if this was something he had been patiently waiting for all along. Oh, that sweet little kid. He didn't have a clue what he was in for. Anyway, just like that—without further discussion—my workload was cut in half. Chores that I had been shackled to for the better part of my life were unceremoniously handed down to my little brother. I couldn't believe my luck.

Obviously this freed up my schedule a bit, which should've been cause for celebration. But while it was tempting to accept my good fortune with abandon, it seemed logical that I was about to step into a new set of accountabilities, just as Nicky had. What kind was a complete mystery to me, though.

I wasn't yet old enough to get a job, so what exactly did my mother have in mind? There was a kid in the neighborhood who mowed lawns for extra money—word on the street was the jerk raked leaves too—but our lawn mower could barely handle our own yard. Throw another lawn or two into the mix and we could kiss our bedraggled machine goodbye. That wouldn't be such a terrible thing if we could afford to replace it, but we couldn't. So what did that leave?

My mother never officially put her plan into words but I don't suppose that she actually needed to. The woman was a master of silent manipulation. Even when her lips were at rest, she never really stopped speaking and her meaning was generally clear. As I considered all the angles of my situation, poking at a bowl of soggy puffed rice cereal, my mother slid a small brochure across the table to me. Her eyebrows arched almost imperceptibly and I felt my smile—one that I hadn't even realized was there— falter. At once, the elation of my newfound freedom sagged. I took the tri-fold in my hands and opened it suspiciously, wondering what sort of torture I had just traded my familiar, albeit tedious, busywork for. Skimming the text for a quick impression, I very nearly choked on my puffed rice. I read it slowly then, considering each word with guarded excitement.

It seemed that the Young Writer's Guild of Oklahoma, an organization whose name meant nothing to me, was hosting a regional writing competition that summer. Cash prizes ranging from fifty to one hundred and fifty dollars were up for grabs and first place winners were guaranteed publication slots in one of several prestigious literary magazines. Second and third place winners would be added to an anthology, which was to be produced by the YWGO and distributed to libraries across the Four State Area.

Following all the good stuff was the fine print, a miniature yet lengthy glob of thou-shalt-nots and nebulous disclaimers. As should be expected of any human child, I ignored all but the basic eligibility requirements, lest I be sent into a bored coma. I was between the ages of twelve and eighteen and a legal resident of the state of Oklahoma. That was enough to get my foot in the door and the rest didn't interest me.

The thought of seeing my work in print was almost as electrifying as it was preposterous, yet I knew that it was the money my mother was interested in. I wasn't sure what baseball uniforms cost but fifty dollars seemed like more than enough. One hundred and fifty was downright excessive and far more than my efforts would ever be worth.

A surge of doubt racked me and I let the pamphlet drop to the table. I didn't stand a chance, did I? It was a pipedream. I looked to my mother for some sign of doubt or confirmation, lips rolled back on themselves. She sipped her coffee primly, arching a single eyebrow. As she rose to leave the table, her mouth curled into a wonderfully mischievous smile. And then she began to hum, as if the matter was concluded. As if my winning was a foregone conclusion and there was simply nothing else to talk about.

Nicky gave me a dumbfounded glance. "What is it?" he wanted to know. Dazed, I could only toss him the brochure.

My mother lit the gas stove and set an old iron skillet on the flame. There was a faint hiss and crackle as a fat dollop of Crisco hit the pan. I closed my eyes and listened, focusing beyond the sizzling, beyond my mother's breathy crooning. Things were unnaturally still. Not a single dog barked, no doors slammed, no engines rumbled. It was like the whole neighborhood—perhaps the whole world—had paused in midstride to spotlight the significance of this moment.

From the hallway, Grandpa's muffled grumbling cut through the sanctity of our silence, breaking my trance so abruptly that I jerked in my seat. "Where's my eggs, girl?" the old man demanded. "Trying to starve me to death?"

I couldn't contain the guffaw that burst forth in that moment. It seemed to erupt from thin air, consuming me in pure joy. My mother believed that I was capable of winning, of being the best at something. And if she believed, why shouldn't I?

At once—in the precise moment when I made up my mind—I was filled with purpose. It was something that I had gone without for far too long and I grabbed for it like my life depended on it.

Competing as a late-blooming almost-ninth grader against seasoned writers—high school honor students, for example—was a long shot at best. Yet in the days that followed, I unconsciously staked Nicky's baseball career on that very outcome, however improbable. To be honest, I think I may have gone a little crazy. The more I indulged my little fantasy, the more convincing it became until it was all but impossible to distinguish from reality. Please don't mistake my delusional mindset for an air of confidence because it was nothing like that. I suppose you might think of it as blind faith, which is a reckless expression of desperation—or even apathy—rather than true self assurance.

On some level I knew that I was tempting fate. Taunting it even. But the reins of common sense had slipped from my fingers and I couldn't bring myself to pick them back up. What was the real downside anyway? If I tried and failed, things would continue on as they always had. The sun would rise and set and life would go right on sucking. But at least there would be one less *what-if* to contend with.

If, on the other hand, I managed to win? Not only would that present a convenient—albeit momentary—resolution to our financial predicament, it might just open a door to that fabled land where anyone could make something of his life.

Even losers like me.

Writers were expected to be eccentric, after all. Weren't they? From what I could tell, they were granted an unusual measure of absolution for their frequent improprieties.

"You remember the weirdo down the street, old what's-his-name? He fetched the newspaper this morning in his skivvies! But, he's one of those writer types, so I guess that explains it."

Novelists were the glamorous face of an otherwise dour industry. Silver-tongued and full of grand ideas, they weren't merely tolerated, they were beloved. Substance abusers, vagabonds, political radicals, fallen playboys—they were eternally bound by their indifference to social mores. The son of a convicted murderer ought to fit right in, don't you think? I figured that my history more or less entitled me to an honorary place among them, or was urinating from the balcony of a crowded opera house a prerequisite to membership?

I told myself these things because I needed to hear them, and I suppose they gave me comfort, to some extent. They weren't lies exactly, just an especially iffy set of conclusions. What I knew—or thought I knew—about life outside of Lakeview Park often proved to be warped, cultivated by Hollywood and the skewed imagination of a sheltered kid. Sadly, it can take years to unlearn the nonsense we teach ourselves.

Despite my selective acknowledgement of reality, I knew that my writing wasn't good enough. Still, even in my midnight fits of self-loathing, I somehow clung to the belief that it could be. With practice and enough brute force, some internal mechanism might clatter into motion and spit out a scrap of brilliance.

Well, at least time was on my side. Submissions were due in seven weeks, which was just shy of a century to a fourteen-year-old. Plenty of time to hone my abilities. Good thing too, because I had absolutely no idea what to submit. Short stories, poetry, essays—they were all fair game in the competition. Yet as always, I struggled for inspiration. Fortunately, for once I knew just what to do.

It was time once again to consult the oracles of my craft.

I needed to read.

TWELVE

Without access to the school library, my hands were tied. I plundered my home of every book I could find. Grandpa reluctantly allowed me to pick through his personal collection but let's face it: there's really only so much inspiration one can draw from Louis L'Amour. Nicky found my father's Dune collection and for all of ten seconds, I thought I was set. They were as thick as phone books though, and I simply didn't have time to grant them the attention they deserved. I needed something more compact. Desperation led me to the storage shed outside, where I found a waterlogged box of Reader's Digest condensed books; my heart sank as they fell apart in my fingers.

Throughout the day my frustration snowballed and by dinnertime, I was on the verge of screaming bloody murder. What was I supposed to do?

"You'll just have to look elsewhere, Lincoln," my mother remarked. "You're not gonna find what you're looking for here. This ain't Walmart."

I started to argue but before I could form a rebuttal, logic suddenly prevailed. The solution couldn't have been more obvious. If only I had been a little less frantic, it might have occurred to me sooner. Unfortunately, the public library closed early on Sundays, so my hands remained tied for the moment.

All that night, impatience pestered me. My imagination knitted countless scenarios together and I was compelled to play each out as I tossed and turned. As dawn broke, my adrenaline retreated like the tide, sucking what little energy I had left out to sea. It wouldn't be long before exhaustion was all that remained of me and I'd have nothing to show for this mental marathon. I crept out of bed while I still could, determined to push through at all costs.

By eight, I was showered and dressed. I inhaled a slice of unbuttered toast on my way to the door, treading lightly to keep from waking the household. My body tingled, both from sleep deprivation and the jitters of newfound adventure. Today was the start of something huge; my first step toward a new life. Now that my body was finally in motion, a little sleep loss didn't stand a chance of interfering. I had a hand on the doorknob when a voice startled me.

"Where you headed so early?"

My head snapped toward the couch, where my mother was lying on her side. She was half covered in a throw blanket, still dressed in her work clothes.

"Oh, um … the Amazon," I quipped. "Doing some piranha fishing this morning. Seen my waders anywhere?"

My mother sat up and gave me a yawning smile. "Smart aleck."

"Mom, it's me … Lincoln. Who's Aleck?"

She smirked. "My mistake. He's the smart one. Smart enough to know piranhas don't bite this early on Mondays, anyway." We both laughed and I was heartened by the look of contentment on her face. We had never really interacted like this. She and Nicky always had a little volley going but it was unusual for us. It was kind of nice, though a little ill-timed.

"You're still dressed from work," I observed. "Did you get home late?"

She groaned. "Yeah, a little after two."

I nodded. Though awake myself, I hadn't even heard her come in. I hated that she was killing herself like this. Despite her best efforts, we were barely squeaking by. It felt like every dollar she earned put us deeper into a hole in the ground. Her paychecks were spent even before she could cash them, and they were never quite enough to buy our way out of that stupid hole. God, I hoped that I could change that someday.

My mother cleared her throat. "Sorry I can't drive you," she muttered, and as she apologized her visage of contentment fell away, revealing weariness. And something else, too. Embarrassment, maybe? In the dimness, it was hard to be sure what I was seeing, but something was definitely there.

With a sigh, she sank back into the cushions and I noticed the bags under her eyes for the first time. Clearly, I wasn't the only one who had suffered a sleepless night. I took a step toward the couch and dropped to one knee.

"It's okay, Mom. Really." I was accustomed to walking everywhere but my mother had never been completely comfortable with it. Particularly in recent days. Every moment that my brother and I were out of her sight, she feared for us and I can't say that I blamed her. I often felt that same sense of panic—a fear that one couldn't really call irrational, given our history.

"It's just that I don't want to leave your brother and grandpa alone—"

"I know, Mom," I assured her. "It's fine." When that didn't suffice to mollify her, I took her hand in mine and gave it a gentle squeeze, adding, "I like to walk, anyway. It helps me think."

"Alright, then. Don't stay gone too long, okay?"

I bounded through the door before she could change her mind. Outside, the morning sun was blinding. A robin took flight at my appearance, trilling angrily down the driveway. I nearly made it off the porch before my mother stopped me a second time. I was beginning to doubt that I'd ever make it out of there.

"Almost forgot," she explained. "This came for you yesterday." Through the doorway, she passed me an envelope. I gave it a glance and scowled.

"Gee, thanks a lot," I grumbled, cramming it into my back pocket

Almost instantly, my mother was on the porch, poking me in the shoulder with a stiff finger. "Don't sass me, young man." Her eyes squinted in the harsh light and began to bounce around my face, leaping from eyes to mouth and back again. She wavered slightly on her feet and as the telltale miasma of her morning breath wafted over me, it was suddenly clear why she couldn't drive me this morning. And it had nothing to do with Nicky or Grandpa. Angrily, I stood there fuming, too baffled to speak.

"You know," she spat. "It wouldn't hurt to write back once in a while." I felt my mouth form a grimace but I held my tongue, waiting for what I knew was coming. My mother appeared to recognize that her reaction must've been disproportionate to my sullenness because she turned away, stepping back inside. She lingered there in the shade of the doorway, but couldn't bring herself to face me. My mother realized that I knew, even if she refused to acknowledge it.

"We're your parents, Lincoln," she said over her shoulder. "The only ones you get. I want you to write back to your father tonight, understand?"

Just over a mile from Lakeview Park, nestled between a small appliance repair shop and an empty antique store, was a conservative brick structure to which I had never given more than a cursory glance. But for the bike rack out front and the book drop near the entrance, I might easily have passed it by. It looked to be newly remodeled, yet the building maintained an unpretentious facade. From the street, the library could easily be mistaken for a rural tag agency, except that it was perhaps a little too tidy to sell the disguise.

So far, inspiring it was not.

Peering through the glass entry door, I could just make out the murky silhouettes of tables and shelves inside. The door was locked, the interior unlit. It remained in this state for more than forty-five minutes with yours truly slumped against the door like a bum, waiting for someone to open up. At nine o'clock sharp when the door was finally unlocked, I was less than half awake. The woman who opened the door admonished me with a cross look but stopped short of any actual rebuke.

Inside, the Shawnee Public Library was much larger than I had guessed. Unlike the cramped sterile closet of books I had grown accustomed to at school, this space was open and warm, neatly organized by rows of tall shelves, each crammed to capacity. There were large tables with DOS computers positioned at the center of the main space, all unoccupied this early in the day. More to my liking, I discovered that comfortable chairs had been crammed into various nooks and corners. If so inclined, a person could curl up for hours and be left in peace to sleep—I mean *read*.

Forget all that tag agency nonsense—I wanted to *live* in this place.

The presence of so many books filled me with such joy, such anticipation, that I could hardly contain myself. I couldn't wait to get to work. There still remained the small matter of a library card however, so I hurried to the circulation desk.

There, I was asked to complete an application, so I did. I was then asked for proof of address, which I didn't have.

Perhaps a phone bill?

A cable bill?

I had neither. The phone had been disconnected shortly after my father went to prison. Cable? Yeah right. I'm sure that we had something at home that would work—maybe an electric bill or an old report card—but it hadn't occurred to me to bring anything like that and the thought of waiting another day was unbearable.

Looking frantically through my wallet, I confirmed that I had nothing useful. It was almost too much. Exhausted and frustrated well beyond my limits, I felt as if I might explode. I was ready to give up—and not without some tears, mind you—when I stumbled across something in my back pocket. It was my father's letter, a little crumpled and still unopened. The envelope was addressed to me, clearly displaying my name and address. My heart threatened to leap from my chest.

Grinning, I handed the envelope to the librarian. Her nametag read *Irene Winters*. The name seemed fitting enough, given her icy demeanor. She took several seconds to peruse it, yet remained unimpressed.

"This doesn't do much to prove you're a taxpaying member of this county, Mister ..." she paused coldly and peered through the lower field of her bifocals at my envelope. "Chase." Her mouth suddenly dropped open a little and she blinked. I saw her gaze shift to the return address field, taking in the Oklahoma State Penitentiary seal, and I barely stifled a groan. A moment later she peered up at me.

"Any relation to *Finton* Chase?" she asked quietly.

I felt my heart drop like a stone. My father was only known for one thing in this town, and it wasn't anything that I wanted to be associated with. I considered lying, but I suspected it was no use.

"Yes, Ma'am," I mumbled. "He's my father." My cheeks were aglow because I knew perfectly well the gasp of disgust that my affirmation was likely to incite. Yet the woman didn't blanch or spontaneously vomit. She took in my tattered clothes, my disfigured face, and handed the letter back to me. Abruptly, she rose from her chair and walked away, leaving me standing alone at the desk.

For a moment, I was too stunned to react. But then I felt tears coming and I knew that I wouldn't be able to stop them. Shoving the letter back into my pocket, I stormed toward the exit. I was humiliated. Worse, my plan for greatness had been stopped cold before it could even start.

I was halfway out the door when I heard her calling after me. "Young man? Where are you going?"

I turned back to the front desk and wiped my eyes. "I didn't take anything," I barked, perhaps a little louder than intended.

"Well, I know that. It's just that—" Mrs. Winters paused in midsentence, befuddled by my tearful state. Her face seemed to thaw a little and she stepped from behind the desk. "Mr. Chase, please come here," she said softly, but firmly. "I haven't given you your card yet."

I left that morning with paperback copies of John Steinbeck's *The Grapes of Wrath* and—on the recommendation of the librarian—*The Native Son*, by Richard Wright.

After lunch I took a nap. Actually, I slept for more than fifteen hours straight, so it was more like going to bed than taking a nap. Too bad, really. I didn't get a chance to write that letter.

I read a lot that summer. More than was probably healthy, if I'm being honest. For the first week or so, I sampled the best seller shelf at random, falling over and over for the misdirection of flashy cover art and jacket teasers. It was amazing how much junk managed to reach best-selling status. I'm not suggesting there weren't some truly great stories mixed in, but finding them was a bit like picking through your grandma's hard candy for that elusive piece that doesn't taste like perfume.

Eventually, I gave up on best sellers and returned to the tried-and-true classics. I was looking for substance, after all—

works built on grit and grime, without all the marketing fluff—because that's what I hoped to one day emulate. Admittedly, these took a little time and patience to fully appreciate but the reward for effort was long lasting.

Mrs. Winters introduced me to a handful that the public school system had recently dropped from its collection. Why were once-revered classics suddenly off limits? I mean, some of the books I encountered at school brimmed with profanity of the highest order—what could possibly be worse than the f-word rearing its ugly face every other sentence?

Well as it turned out, there were far more disturbing things than the expletives I was familiar with. Horrible thinking that dehumanized entire cultures because of their skin color, along with a slew of ugly derogatories that kept the thinking alive. This filth was thrown around in works that were otherwise brilliant. It was disgusting and very confusing.

When pressed on the subject, Mrs. Winters explained that these books were written in a very different era, a time when such language was widely considered to be civilized and without the menace it carries today. She delivered this narrative with an odd, blank expression, which seemed to betray a deep distaste for what must've been a canned response. One that needed revising, to her mind. Leaning in close, she whispered, "Your school means well, Lincoln. But they can't protect future generations from history by hiding it from them." Her eyes were dark and moist. "We can't just pretend it didn't happen."

So mostly to humor Mrs. Winters, I pushed on. I remember fighting my way through *Uncle Tom's Cabin*, by Harriet Stowe. It was slow reading with slang so thick that it might've been a different language. Much of it went over my head, but not all of it. What little I found within my grasp hurt someplace deep within my soul, leaving a scar that was every bit as fleshy and tangible as those visible on my skin. But it was a good scar, the kind that makes a person stronger for having earned it.

There were others, too. *Tom Sawyer* and *Huckleberry Finn* came next. In those, the bitter truth of the times was sugar coated in all sorts of adolescent mischief so that the sting crept in rather than clubbing me over the head. Nevertheless, they got to me. Used with precision rather than flippancy, and in the right context, I supposed that all those ethnic slurs demonstrated just how bizarre and grave social logic could be. And in my discomfort as a reader, empathy for my brethren truly abounded. Perhaps that was the point. I have to believe that, because the alternative—that people who were much smarter than me, world class writers whom I desperately wanted to look up to, were merely well-spoken idiots—was much harder to accept.

Like most kids, my perception of the world began as an extension of my parents', combined with bits of network television, school propaganda and the front page teasers of grocery store tabloids. My immersion into classical literature knocked this homegrown view into disarray. It revealed that the ethnic oppression I had thought of as ancient history—humbly regretted and neatly healed over the course of time—wasn't that ancient at all. Nor was it forgiven. Despite what I had grown up to believe, bigotry remained firmly rooted in the bedrock of this country. It was quieter, for sure. Less blatant? Absolutely. But while fits of disparity were spouted from behind closed doors more often than sundry counters, hate was still very much alive.

This discovery frightened me, tugging hard at the seams of my boyhood naiveté. Innocence isn't meant to last, you see, and mine was quickly coming unraveled. Eventually, I would confront the true state of things, face to face. I knew this, and deep down I think I also knew that I wasn't at all prepared for that moment.

THIRTEEN

A month after I stepped into the public library for the first time, my mother decided that it was time that I learned to drive. I was only fourteen. While the law wasn't exactly forgiving of unlicensed driving, my mother felt that I was up to the challenge and she didn't much care what the law had to say on the subject. What if she was in an accident? Grandpa certainly couldn't be relied on to take her to the hospital. I doubted that the mechanics of operating a motor vehicle would confound him much, but chances were that he'd forget where he was headed and end up drunk behind the laundromat while my mother bled out. I wasn't about to argue with this logic, however slanted it might've been. I mean, why in the world would I?

I got to drive!

For the record, driving wasn't brand new to me. On many occasions—which is to say, roughly five—my father had let me steer the LeBaron while he manned the pedals. So I was kind of an expert already. Of course, that was a long time ago. And I suppose that the leap from steering a car to managing a full-sized truck with a manual transmission was a little steep. It didn't help that our twenty-year-old pickup was riddled with the ailments of old age. Like a grumpy old man, it groaned and popped at its joints and it demanded that one's tongue be held *juuuust* so before falling into compliance. The clutch needed to be pumped twice before it would shift into reverse, for one. And you had to skip from first to third gear because once you got into second the only way back out was to turn off the engine.

Man I hated that truck.

Anyway, just outside city limits there was an old country road that wormed through miles of trees and flood plains. While there were many of these in the area, the woods surrounding this one had been among our firewood picking grounds for as long as I could remember. If you followed it long enough, the gravel would eventually peter out at the edge of an abandoned homestead, which overlooked a small lake. If not for the determination of local fishermen, the road would likely have grown over long before I was born. Its seclusion was ideal for our purposes—no cars or pedestrians, no police. No curbs or fire hydrants.

Good thing too, because I was a serious liability. Well, the few times I managed to take off, anyway.

My fourth lesson turned out to be my last. Kind of a shame too because things were finally starting to click for me. I hit third gear for the first time, which was quite exciting. Still I must've killed the engine twenty times in the first hour. And with every single stall, I had to stop to figure out if I had broken a fundamental rule of shifting or if I had simply neglected to account for our truck being a quirky piece of crap. Fortunately my mom was there to provide all sorts of helpful advice and encouragement.

"You're letting out the clutch too fast. Okay, give it a little gas ... a little more ... perfect ... wait, too much! You got rocks for feet, or what? You gotta pay attention to what you're doing, Lincoln! Are you even listening to blah? I'm trying to blah you blah-ba-de-blah, son. Do you blah-ba-de-blah? Blah!"

All complaints aside though, once I got the pickup going over thirty? Wow. Not even my mother's micromanagement could spoil that overwhelming sense of exhilaration.

Man I loved that truck—I am allowed to change my mind, right?

Commanding thousands of pounds of metal along those weeded ruts, I felt content; strangely empowered like I could leave this town behind and never return. I wondered if other people experienced this sensation too, and if any of them ever gave in to it. Like, if a guy was on his way to work, for example, and on a whim he just drove right past the parking lot and kept on going and going until the pavement turned to sand. I remember wishing that my dad was there with me, in the untainted beauty of that surreal moment. Weird, right? If the next few seconds had played out differently, I might've paused to question where that notion came from.

But right about then, my mother shrieked.

I was so engrossed in the circus act of steering and checking mirrors and manipulating gears that her sudden outburst caught me completely off guard. Startled, I hit the brakes a little too hard, launching myself—and my poor mother—toward the dashboard. If not for our seatbelts, we might've been seriously hurt. The pickup lurched to a halt in the packed gravel, shaking and squeaking on worn springs. The engine sputtered for a second and then went still. I waited for the usual admonishment—

"You gotta push in the clutch before stopping, Lincoln. How many times do I gotta tell you?"

—but it didn't come. I glanced sidelong at my mother and saw that she was locked on my side mirror. I gave it a peek, followed by the rearview. Nothing behind us but empty road.

"What is it, Mom? Did I do something wrong?"

Her gaze pivoted toward the windshield, settling on some fixed point beyond the glass. Her nostrils flared.

"Mom?" I whispered, reaching over to touch her shoulder. "You okay?"

My mother shuddered. "Link, I want you to turn the truck around and head back to the main road." She turned to me quite abruptly then and her face darkened as if a thought had just occurred to her—one that made her angry; angry at me, if I wasn't mistaken. "And keep your eyes on the road," she snapped. "No looking around, hear me?"

I felt my mouth fall agape. What could I possibly have done to put her in this state? I had taken great care to use my mirrors exactly as she taught me. I hadn't driven too fast or ground the gears more than I could help. I hadn't run down any helpless kittens.

"What's going on, Mom? Why are you mad at me?"

She sighed deeply through her nose, hands wringing in her lap. "You didn't do anything wrong, Lincoln, and I'm not mad." She swallowed, forcing a stiff smile. "Just remembered I got something important to do at the house."

Riiiiiight.

My mother was capable of far more convincing deception, and we both knew it. Yet everything about her demeanor insisted that arguing would accomplish nothing. Because you can't argue with fear. And indeed, the more I looked at her, the more convinced I became that fear was at the bottom of this, not anger. So I didn't push it.

"Okay," I said.

I killed the engine twice from a dead stop and then managed to drive ten or fifteen yards toward a break in the tree line. There, I performed a sloppy three-point turnaround, stalling twice more. Gone was the feeling of freedom, the elation. Every mistake put me more on edge until I wanted to rip the steering wheel off and … ugh. Well, let's just say that driving was now the last thing I wanted to do.

My hands were trembling a little by then, so I squeezed them tightly into the grooves of the steering wheel. That seemed to shut them up for a while, though my nerves remained anything but quiet.

As instructed, I worked my way back toward the main road. Yet despite my best efforts to train my gaze forward, my eyes defied me, flickering about without my blessing. My mother's breathing began to grow ragged next to me and I couldn't help but steal a glance at her.

"You sure you're okay?"

She was peering through the passenger window, transfixed, with her forehead resting against the glass. Something out there commanded my mother's undivided attention, yet she still managed to detect my fleeting glance. "Eyes on the road, Lincoln!" she squeaked.

I tried to obey; honest to God, I did. But whether I meant to or not, I managed to catch a glimpse of something beyond the road—something that grabbed me by the spine and shook me for dear life. And in that instant, I must've hit the brakes because we came to a dead stop in a cloud of dust. The engine stalled and there we sat, breathing heavily, the both of us.

"What're you doing, Lincoln?"

I reached for the door handle.

"Son, don't you dare."

But I did dare. I rounded the truck in a trance and plowed through the underbrush lining the road. The thinking part of me— that tiny self-aware mound of soul and heart and gray matter—was barely half in charge by that point. I'm not sure that anyone could've stopped me, short of taking me down.

"Get back here, Lincoln!" my mother cried from the truck, and if I'm not mistaken, her voice was more desperate than angry. "Please, son."

Twenty feet from the road, a corpse lay slumped against the balding trunk of a dead pecan tree. Its mouth hung open in an eternal scream, one so vividly portrayed that I imagined I could hear it, despite the eerie back-road silence.

It was a man. This was evident not by his clothes but in the absence of any. His arms were folded unnaturally behind his back, perhaps bound in place. His head was hinged sideways in a position that no human head was meant to hold, draping a long mane of black hair all the way to the ground. A pair of trousers formed a sodden hump nearby, turned-out pockets blanching against the dirt.

My stomach wrenched and I closed my eyes for a long moment. It wasn't real. It couldn't be real. Yet when I opened my eyes again, the view remained unchanged. Nothing would have pleased me more than to backtrack to the pickup and haul butt out of there. But once again, my body betrayed me. I stepped closer.

Upwind in the truck, there had been no smell. Now as I closed in, the putrid odor of death swooped in to engulf me. Even with my face buried in a shirtsleeve, breathing through my mouth, the stench was only just bearable.

Deeply tanned and bloated, the man's skin was peppered with skittering flies. Deformed shotgun shells lay scattered at his feet and his chest was blotched with gaping holes. Worse, as I watched a beetle crawled from one just as another dove in to take its place. It was almost more than I could bear, triggering a painful gag that doubled me over.

From behind, my mother grabbed a handful of my shirt. "Let's go," she demanded.

But I couldn't. Retching, I stepped even closer until I was at the feet of the dead man. This close, I noticed a withered feather dangling from one temple. It confused me at first but then I understood; the dawning of the truth coursed through me with such intensity that my skin seemed to hum. Someone had forced that plume through his scalp for the sheer sake of mockery. To reduce this human being to some kind of cultural mascot.

The breeze picked up, mercifully diverting some of the smell with it. In the nearby treetops, a blue jay heckled me but I scarcely noticed. I couldn't take my eyes off the man's face. He had died in terror and even now, I can almost swear that I heard an echo of his screams in the wind. Dried up eyes implored me to do something—anything—to take the pain away, to make the death stop.

But I couldn't. Not for him, not for Brigham's dad. Not for anyone. I was useless.

I must admit to feeling enraged by this, by the depths of my impotence. Rage so deep that it seemed to tear me apart on the inside. I wanted to find the person who had done this and hurt him. I wanted to rip him limb from limb with my bare hands. I wanted to watch him bleed into the dirt and beg for mercy.

But then, in the presence of sorrow, the rage began to ebb and when I looked upon this poor man once more, I realized there was really only one thing that I could do for him. I could pluck that stupid feather away and free him from another second of indignity. Yet even as I reached out to snatch it, my mother pulled me back by the shirt with such force that I nearly toppled to my rear.

"Don't you dare, Lincoln."

I tried to shrug her off but she was holding on for dear life. When I ceased to resist, her arms encircled me and her head nestled into the crevice between my shoulder blades. She cried softly into my back, tears burning through the fabric of my shirt.

A weakened thread finally snapped inside me and in that moment, the tattered remains of boyhood fell away like a sheer garment from my eyes. So many things became clear then. Brutal things that I could no longer deny. This was the world I lived in. It was an ugly place, rife with hate and death. And I knew in my broken heart that I would never escape it.

Turning to my mother, I realized that neither of us would be the same again. And by the look on her face, I'm guessing that she knew it, too.

More than anything in the world, I wanted to go home. To curl up in my bed and cry and just let everything out before it all consumed me. But we couldn't just go home. Not yet, anyway.

My mother took the wheel, thank God, and we left in a dazed silence broken only by the crunch of gravel under tires. We called the sheriff's office from the Handy Dandy and a cruiser arrived in minutes. A plump deputy in a taut brown uniform scrawled on a clipboard as my mother described what we had found. I was greatly relieved when she declined to accompany him to the scene, because I couldn't go back there. Nor was I willing to be left behind while she went alone. Especially not here, at the Handy Dandy. A place that was every bit as cursed.

My mother and I didn't eat dinner that night. She boiled hot dogs for Nicky and Grandpa. Per her motherly duty, she made a feeble effort to feed me too, but we both knew that it wasn't going to happen. We had seen something too horrible to wash down with hot dogs. Frankly, if I never ate again, I feared that it would be too soon.

While my mother and Nicky took care of the dishes, I slipped away to watch the news. My timing couldn't have been more perfect, as it turned out. The cheesy, animated intro was just wrapping up as I plopped onto the couch.

First up was a segment devoted to some kind of legal battle surrounding repairs to Interstate 40. Next was a report on city-wide budget cuts, which would likely result in more than twenty administrative layoffs. Then, a realty office was vandalized overnight by a group of amorphous blobs, as captured by the worst security camera ever. Finally, there was a quick story on a local who had caught a three-eyed catfish, and then it was on to sports and weather. Before I knew it, the news was over and some bozo dressed like Abraham Lincoln was bastardizing the Gettysburg Address to sell used cars.

I couldn't believe it.

"Just another dead Indian," my mother spat from the doorway. I wasn't sure how long she'd been standing there but it was clear that her hopes were as dashed as mine. "Wasn't even worth a mention, was he?"

She stalked off before I could think to respond.

FOURTEEN

In the small town of Shawnee, it didn't take much watering for gossip to grow legs. Yet even two days later, no one was talking about an execution that took place in our own backyard. Where was the media? They were either completely oblivious or intentionally sitting on a bombshell, and neither scenario made much sense to me.

Consider this: a couple of years before, an old man died of a stroke in the old IGA parking lot. It was all over the news that same night. I happened to know that my own accident garnered a fair amount of media attention as well, though I made a point to ignore it. And you can't imagine the media storm that surrounded my father's trial. Recently a stray dog birthed a litter of puppies under the mayor's front porch, and wouldn't you know it? Yup, that was news, folks.

Yet a man was murdered and then mutilated in cold blood, and no one had a word to say about it? Come on. It was hard to reach any conclusion other than the obvious: that the people who were supposed to care apparently did not. Given that information tends to flow downhill, I guess that left the rest of us little people in the dark. Elderly ladies kept right on gabbing about the new neighbors, who must be drug dealers because they wore earrings and grew their hair long, and the concerned parents of Shawnee continued to fuss over loud rock-n-roll and the discovery of cigarette butts by the back door, because none of them had the tiniest inkling that a killer might be walking among them.

It was tempting to blame laziness or some other flavor of incompetence because that might've been forgivable on some level. But I was too angry. I thought of all those oppressed blacks I had read about, many of whom had been mocked and beaten and raped—and yes, even murdered—while the law turned a blind eye. As I thought about them, I couldn't help but compare the ugliness that they had long endured to the fate of that poor Indian. The parallels were undeniable, even if the scale was all wrong. And when I considered the very real possibility that injustice of this ilk continued to thrive, even in the here and now? Well, let's just say that it was one of those moments when humanity completely lost its luster.

More and more, my worries turned to Brigham. Oddly, I didn't worry about Jeremy at all; he was Cherokee through and through, but he was also nobody's victim. Brigham wasn't Indian, of course; his skin was the color of milk chocolate. But combined with my image of him as the longsuffering pacifist—a symptom of my guilty conscience, no doubt—Brigham's ethnicity made him just as vulnerable to my mind. Maybe even more so, what did I know?

Oops. Silly me—did I forget to mention that Brigham was black? Sorry about that. I guess it didn't seem particularly meaningful until now. And if you knew him as I once had, you would undoubtedly agree that the color of skin was among the least of his defining qualities. The truth is that Brigham simply wasn't ruled by racial profiles. He transcended them. That's not to say that his ethnicity didn't contribute to his character. I just wouldn't know.

One thing was clear, though; there was much more to Brigham Miller than I had ever realized. Before our falling out, I really thought that I understood all about his daily strife. Because we were both in the thick of it, right? Hogtied by the same socio-economics. But that wasn't entirely true. I now saw that Brigham had been carrying another burden entirely, one that he kept all to himself. A timeless struggle that I'll never experience firsthand and will therefore never truly understand. Realizing this only made me love and respect him all the more. It also terrified me because it meant that upon venturing outside of Lakeview Park, Brigham had entered a very different world than the metropolis of opportunity we had imagined as young kids. One in which skin color was more than a basic descriptor; it was a magnet for unthinkable behavior.

God, I hoped that I was wrong. I believed in Brigham. If anyone was capable of prevailing over hardship, it was him. Yet the odds seemed stacked insurmountably against him. Because if generation after generation of downtrodden minorities had tried and failed to overcome oppression in this country, what chance did Brigham really have on his own?

All that reminiscing over Brigham led me back to the wandering tree. I spent a great deal of time there during that summer, basking in the solitude of its immensity and isolation. Often, I arrived with a novel in hand; I nearly always brought pencil and paper. When I wasn't reading, I was practicing my prose. Mimicking what the greats had done before me, I endeavored to build up a refined sense for what worked and what did not. I toiled over it tirelessly, though on darker days when my emotions felt particularly bruised or chaffed, I shifted to poetry.

For the record, I have never been a fanatic reader of rhyme or verse. Yet composing my own did seem to calm me when nothing else could. There was something soothing about the subtle task of balancing flair and succinctness. Naturally though, since I didn't read anyone else's poetry, I lacked any frame of reference to measure the quality of my work. None of that mattered though. For the first time in my life I was writing from the heart with no ulterior motive.

Those were magical days, despite all the inner turmoil. It was tremendously gratifying to read and write or otherwise daydream in the shade of such a beautiful giant. From that vantage I had a clear view of Lakeview Park, which from a distance took on a rundown returning-to-the-earth sort of charm. Cottontails nibbled on patches of green clover, unabashed, though well within a stone's throw from me. I watched my brother and his friends play ball across the field and I was reminded that life wasn't all bad. On the contrary, it could be quite good.

When inspiration came over me, which was hardly a daily occurrence, it tended to strike like lightning under the majestic wandering tree. Ideas surged into me from thin air, standing my arm hairs on end while I rushed to commit them to paper. A few kept my body tingling well into the night because they just seemed too good to have come from my little pea brain. These were sacred moments during which the meteorite chip around my neck seemed to heat up, adding to the mystique. I sometimes imagined that I could feel Pruitt Rock beneath me, as if the meteorite had been struck just as I had been, and thereby recalibrated to resonate at my precise frequency.

It felt good to be there, curled into the bosom of the wandering tree. To be at peace in a place where my doubts were put to rest. Where I knew for sure that I would always belong, even if the rest of the world rejected me. Given some choice in the matter I might've stayed there forever. But the sun invariably set, sending me home in a reluctant scamper through shin-high grass and invisible clouds of gnats.

Obliging one of my mother's more absurd suggestions, I began reading aloud to my grandfather in the evenings. Initially, I was reluctant to open that can of worms—which is to say that I would rather have wrestled the neighbor's Pit Bull, whose bedside manner was considerably less abrasive. But when the old man caught wind of the conversation—with a hairy ear glued to the wall, no doubt—and expressed a downright giddy interest, I realized that it was too late to back out gracefully. So I gave in to the task, crossing my fingers that at least one of us might get something worthwhile out of it.

My grandfather entered this arrangement with much higher hopes, yet I quickly learned that keeping his interest buoyed was no trivial matter. At even the slightest loss of momentum, Grandpa's eyes glazed over and then fluttered closed. Generally, this was a sure sign that I had lost him for the night. And that I had missed Miami Vice for nothing. Science Fiction had this effect on him, I discovered with dismay, as did other speculative genres that I would later come to adore. And he must've despised literary fiction on pure redneck principle because I'm pretty sure that he never gave one a fair shot.

Perhaps beholden to some geriatric handbook in the sky, my grandfather demanded spy novels and trite, formulaic westerns. I didn't care much for either, but resolved to tolerate them for his sake, figuring that even the ones I disliked might have something to teach.

Alas, this proved to be one of my more idiotic theories.

Over the following weeks, I'm afraid the situation became quite desperate. So desperate, in fact, that I nearly threw in the towel because shooting myself seemed the only other escape from Grandpa's evil font of James Bond and Jesse James wannabes. But then, on a complete whim, I discovered that it wasn't particularly difficult to pass off something of interest to me as one of my grandfather's approved genres, though it was often necessary to apologize for the library's poor classification methods when no actual spying or herding of cattle took place. When the title didn't lend itself to this, I resorted to swapping dust jackets. Dementia isn't completely without a redeeming quality or two, as it turned out. Grandpa bought it every time.

I know, you don't even have to say it. I'm a terrible person.

My conscience nagged me half to death on this point, believe it or not, and I lived in constant fear of discovery. It would've taken very little to bring down that wobbly tower of lies, really. If my mother had ever bothered to quiz Grandpa on our latest adventure, even with a quick, "So what was your favorite part?" my goose would most certainly have been cooked. "Um, that doesn't sound at all like *Patriot Games*, Papa. Come to think of it, that sounds an awful lot like *The Count of Monte Cristo*."

That's not to say that I suddenly repented and turned from my wicked ways, to be clear. If you force a kid to choose between a) endless iterations of the same western, or b) the glittering path of unrighteousness, I dare say that you have robbed that poor child of any real choice. Nevertheless, I exercised this very necessary deceit in moderation because maintaining any kind of deception just plain wore me out.

My grandfather and I worked our way through a book almost every week—sometimes two—with an occasional misfire. I managed to sneak *David Copperfield* under the radar, for example, but Grandpa lost interest in less than five minutes and flipped on the television to watch M.A.S.H. Gotta say, I was kind of with him on that one. Another time I cracked open a brand new Robert Ludlum novel and almost immediately, a certain someone insisted that we had already read it. Not even the copyright date could convince him that he was wrong. In his defense though, the emerging theme was dangerously reminiscent of a recent Mission Impossible episode, not to mention that of just about every other piece of military espionage we had tackled so far.

Aside from these minor hiccups, we managed to establish a fairly enjoyable routine, one that I personally grew to look forward to. My mother sometimes dropped in just to listen while I read, leaning against the door frame with eyes closed and a nostalgic smile. Once, she squeezed in beside me and whispered in my ear that I was "the sweetest boy" and that she was "sooooo proud" of me. Her eyes brimmed with tears that night and for some reason, I'll never forget how they shone in the lamplight, glittering like dewdrops on a face formed of faded pink petals.

Spending so much time together, I suppose my grandfather and I were bound to grow closer. But I honestly didn't expect it to happen as quickly as it did. He was like one of those old dogs you see in pet store windows, the kind who masterfully blends the slightest whimper with a very pathetic and perfectly timed thump of an arthritic tail, knowing that he has precious few seconds to win you over before you move on by.

Only, instead of playing on my sympathy, Grandpa went straight for the funny bone. He set up these long circuitous jokes and then deliberately botched the punch line. He farted and blamed it on a skunk, who he claimed lived in the walls, and who I remarked to be an odd creature, considering that it seemed to make itself most widely known after Grandpa ate a can of chili. He told me about kissing the ugliest girl in school on a dare and how the experience caused him to develop a secret crush that lasted for years, until the day she finally agreed to marry him. It took a minute for me to realize that he was talking about my grandmother, who had indeed been a rather, um … *handsome* woman.

He cracked me up and possibly for the first time since he moved in, I began to see him as a valuable member of the family. No longer the paper-thin human analog that I pretended was my grandfather, but the real thing. The father of my father; a man with nearly eighty years of ups and downs and love and loss under his belt, full of stories and hard-earned experiences.

Grandpa's blue moon flirtations with lucidity revealed a pleasant and often humorous personality, but that's not to say that his usual befuddled state wasn't just as endearing in its own way. The trick was to stick around long enough for fondness to set in. This amounted to roughly three weeks in my case, followed by an intense period of yearning to better understand the man.

There was no instruction book for living with a victim of Dementia, so I considered myself fortunate that Grandpa had a system of tells. And once I figured them out, all those grating eccentricities suddenly took on meaning. It was like learning a second language, minus the flashcards. For example, anytime Grandpa asked where I had been or what took me so long—which he did often and seemingly at random—he was stalling, racking his memory for a meaningful wisp of the present. He wasn't always sure who I was, yet I had become familiar enough for him to realize that he ought to know me. His rare and sporadic victories over forgetfulness were nearly always foreshadowed by a second or two of comfortable silence in place of those meaningless interrogations.

He had little tics, as well. If he used his napkin during a meal, it usually signaled that he didn't like his food. A neglected napkin, or one ignored until his plate was clean, meant that my grandfather was content. This one took a while to figure out, in particular because Grandpa didn't hesitate to share his opinion, however colorful or inflammatory, on much else. Turns out, he was haunted by an irrational fear that he might've specifically requested something that he didn't care for and then forgotten all about it.

Ah, Grandpa. It was pretty hard not to love him once you got to know him.

Speaking of the old fart, I suppose I have him to thank for what happened next. It was his fault after all.

FIFTEEN

One hot afternoon in late July, when the heat was so overpowering that my daily pilgrimage across Pruitt Field was out of the question, and when only the truly insane would dream of playing baseball, boredom drove me and my brother into my grandfather's bedroom where we shamelessly interrupted Lorne Green's *Wild Kingdom* to offer our reading services. For lack of anything else on hand, we settled on a tattered paperback depicting a man on horseback, who overlooked a dusty scrub plain peppered with stampeding steers.

Do I need to describe the sheer, uncontainable excitement that I felt?

Lucky for me Nicky was eager to take the lead, proud to be included in what must've seemed like an exclusive Chase club until that day. Minutes in though, my grandfather became agitated and cut Nicky off with a sharp hiss. My brother gaped as if slapped in the face and for a second, I really thought that he might cry. He would eventually learn not to take offense at these outbursts, but getting to know the old man was a process. Poor Nicky had a long way to go.

"I don't know why we gotta keep reading this thing over and over," my grandfather complained and I thought: *Here, here!* We hadn't, in fact, but I could easily apply that sentiment to the entire genre in good conscience. For all I knew, my grandfather had read it a hundred times; it came from his bookshelf, after all. Turning to me, Grandpa's scowl faltered and then, as if a switch had just been thrown behind those milky blue eyes, it lifted altogether in an instant. Grinning broadly now, he wagged a beefy finger toward the sky. "We need a mystery, Fin. Go fetch us a mystery." Reaching past me, he turned the television back on.

And just like that, we were dismissed.

Nicky stomped into the kitchen and dumped the contents of a puzzle box on the dinner table, a look of betrayal souring his face. I was tempted to join him there. Not that toiling over a puzzle appealed to me in any way but it sure beat the heat. My grandfather's sudden interest in a new, unexplored genre had me pretty excited though. Try as I might, I simply couldn't pass up the opportunity to broaden our reading horizons, not even for a day. So with a great sigh, punctuated by a slight moan with respect to the long hot walk ahead, I ventured headlong into the fiery outdoors for the library.

The heat was absolutely dizzying. It sweltered with such extraordinary fervor that I nearly turned tail at the end of the driveway to crawl back inside, panting like a ragged dog. The news would later report a record high that day of one hundred and fourteen degrees, setting the good people of Shawnee to murmuring about global warming and El Niño for weeks to come. My stupidity prevailed, however. Pounding pavement with sweat dripping off my nose, I struggled to endure the very convincing sensation of dying on my feet. I survived by snatching respite where I could, scampering into the shadows of trees and buildings. During those fleeting moments of relief, I pondered my grandfather's latest Freudian slip.

For quite a while, Grandpa had confused me with *Benjamin*. Who knows, maybe I looked more like a Benjamin than a Lincoln. Nevertheless, this mismatch went on long enough that I eventually ceased to correct him, chalking it up as just another of his many peculiarities. Since the accident though, *Benjamin* had slowly and inexplicably given way to *Fin*, presumably a reference to my father. The transition confused me. True, I looked nothing like my former self, but neither did I look anything like my father. Unless my logic was faulty, Benjamin was more than a sticky name to my grandfather; Benjamin was or had once been a real person. Then again, maybe it was unfair to expect the old man's gibberish to abide by the rules of logic.

My mother was no help on the subject, incidentally.

I considered all this as I walked but I can't say that I reached any sound conclusions. Given the extreme heat, I was probably lucky just to remain conscious. At five past three, I burst into the library, slick with moisture that by all accounts belonged on the inside of my body. The hunk of space metal around my neck, as well as the dog tag chain it was suspended from, stung like a strand of angry yellow jackets, burning a pink line down to my collar bones.

The AC was heavenly. I stood below a ceiling vent in the foyer for ten full minutes before venturing farther inside, stepping away only to drink from a nearby water fountain in the interim.

The place was abuzz with ladies in their twenties and thirties, chasing maniacal toddlers through the stacks with exasperated smiles. Milling around in their midst, a handful of stone-faced senior citizens picked through self-help titles in a way that reminded me of chickens scratching up a barnyard.

Ms. Winters wasn't around, so I approached another lady at the desk. Her eyes widened and then hardened at the sight of me, and I tried very hard to not be offended. I asked for help locating a mystery. In response, the woman gestured toward a large shelf against the back wall. Before I could follow up with another question, she leaned to her side and addressed an elderly man behind me. "Next, please?"

Well, she was efficient. Had to give her that.

The mystery selection was mindboggling. There were true crimes, military crimes, government conspiracies, cheeky whodunits, cozies, legal thrillers, medical mysteries, paranormal mysteries—you name it. Of course, Grandpa was awfully finicky so unless I managed to stumble across a cowboy mystery of some kind, there was a good chance that I was wasting my time.

Alas, I did not find a cowboy mystery. Well, none of the covers were blatant enough to depict a dead cow with a kitchen knife protruding from its back, anyway.

Maybe I had just discovered a niche worth exploiting.

Dark Pastures, by Lincoln Chase.

Sheesh. Anyway, with no other parameters to guide me, I went for something classic: *The Hound of Baskervilles*, by Sir Arthur Conan Doyle, and something more contemporary, to cover my bases: *Presumed Innocent*, by Scott Turow. I took some comfort in knowing that if neither of these panned out, at least there was plenty more to choose from.

Meandering toward the front desk, I dodged a rampaging two-year-old and scanned through the pages of my selections, appreciating the contrast between them and reaffirming that both were promising. As I took my place in line, the small of my back began to tickle where my sweaty shirt was plastered to it like a giant Band-Aid. My hair hung in damp locks against my forehead and every few seconds a bead of sweat seemed to crawl from one of them. I was a hot mess. Hardly the ideal time to encounter the girl of my dreams, but what can I say? The universe is a phenomenally creative jerk.

Her smell got me even before I saw her. Wildflowers and a hint of something nostalgic, some calming spice that I couldn't quite put my finger on. If blue skies and cool spring days had a smell, perhaps. A second later, when I laid eyes on her for the first time, I swear she turned me into Jell-O. I just stood there, statuesque but for a subdued jiggling. There she was, directly ahead of me in line, and I had to assume that even as I was reveling in the sweetness of her fragrance, she was gagging on mine.

She turned slightly then, peeking over her shoulder as if she had just read my mind—or more likely, to pinpoint the source of that sweaty odor—and thereby afforded me a better view of her face. Her features were sprite-like—slightly hooked nose, bright, blue eyes framed by long lashes, a faint band of freckles splayed across the bridge of her nose—a cumulative impression that was attenuated only by a long, flowing ponytail of golden silk. I would later come to think of her as beautiful in the way of planets, which is to say that her overall grandness was regal and immeasurable because of its scale, and because it seemed to whisper that it would always be out of grasp.

I took an involuntary step back, as if the gesture might put some blessed distance between me and my shameful filthiness. Yet my hormones had no respect for shame. They swelled and then raged, flooding my veins with a host of indelicate urges. In my ears, the watery slosh of my pulse flip-flopped and its arrhythmia should've frightened me. But in the heat of the moment, heart failure seemed like the least of my concerns. I was becoming an entirely different kind of hot mess.

Ms. Winters, who must've been tucked away in one of the inner offices earlier, was now at the desk, stamping a book for this lovely girl and chuckling at something one of them had said. Inching closer, I stole a glance to see what the girl was checking out.

Flowers in the Attic. The title rang a bell but it took a second to remember why.

Oh, yeah, I mused. *The infamous incest tale.* Oh, to have been her brother …

Yeah, I know. That felt like too much, even then. I only mention it now to put the absurdity of my mindset in proper context.

"All set, Ivy. Let me know what you think—there's a whole series, you know." Ms. Winters slipped a purple flyer into the paperback and handed it over with a wink.

Ivy. The name was a perfect fit, yet it also struck me as a little muted if not mundane, and therefore unworthy of her.

"Thank you," Ivy replied. Her voice was smiling, sweet like honey.

"You're very welcome," replied the librarian. "See you next week."

Ivy turned toward the door, glancing at me as she passed; eyes of bottomless aqua flickered across the ruin of my face and I felt my breath catch like a train wreck in my throat. Her eyes flinched reflexively and then snapped away, a reaction that I was all too familiar with yet never quite prepared for. My head sagged toward the floor, weighted heavily by self-loathing. Still, I managed a quick peek as she disappeared through the exit.

When she was gone, I felt sick. Sick and weak from humiliation, not to mention the crash of retreating hormones. Never had I hated to be me with such concentrated effort. I wanted to crawl into a deep hole and die, if the worms would even have me.

Ms. Winters beckoned me to approach the desk and I complied in a numb shuffle. Reaching for my books, she fixed me with one of her trademark smiles—amused, but stony. "Pretty girl, huh?" she remarked.

Pretty? On the inside, I scoffed. Sunsets were pretty. Flowers and hummingbirds, dew on spider webs. But just as these things were easy on the eyes, they were also ordinary, whereas I can assure you there was nothing ordinary about that girl.

These were my thoughts as I stared at Mrs. Winters, with mouth agape and dripping drool, no doubt. What I actually said, however, was more along the lines of, "Oh, um … er, uh—" In the end, I shrugged and took another peek at the exit, fixating on the exact spot where the girl's delicate fingers had touched the door handle. Maybe it was silly, but I wished that I could somehow carve off that piece of brushed steel so that I wouldn't have to share it with the rest of the world. Or perhaps to protect it from some skanky loser—yes, like myself—whose sweaty palms might desecrate her handprint.

Thump went the stamp on one of my books. "You know, there's a writing contest coming up. Have you heard about it?"

I nodded absently, wondering if anyone would even notice a disfigured kid hovering suspiciously near the door with a hacksaw.

"You should really consider submitting something, Lincoln."

With a sigh I turned to look at her. "That's the plan."

Her smile brightened as she stamped my other book. "Good! There's a meeting scheduled next weekend, you know."

My eyes narrowed. This was news to me.

"It should be pretty informal, really. Just a little meet-and-greet for our local writers to bounce ideas off each other. And we'll go over the submission guidelines, of course."

"Oh, okay." A pit formed in my stomach and I'm guessing that if I could've recorded its rumblings and then played them back in reverse, I might've heard something like: *fat chance, lady—kids from Lakeview Park don't attend meet-and-greets.* My wardrobe alone would alert security that I didn't belong. Nevertheless, I felt inclined to humor her. "Where's it gonna be?"

"Right here, as a matter of fact." Ms. Winters handed me a purple flyer. "All the information is on this." She smirked knowingly then, as she often did, eyes darting to the exit and back.

"And Mr. Chase," she added. "Some pretty important people are likely to be there too."

"Um, okay …"

Leaning in, she half covered her mouth. "What I mean is you might take some time to comb your hair." She whispered this with an expression that was so kind and genuine that it paralyzed my ability to sense or react to insult. This was a practice dared by very few and pulled off by even fewer. I couldn't help but smile at her finely-honed talent.

On my way out, my blood pressure spiked near the exit. There, a heavyset woman stood vigil over the door and I surmised that her husband was fetching the car. Noticing me, she politely opened the door into the foyer and I couldn't help but notice that her clammy hands were all over the handle. I barely found the sense to say thank you.

I walked in a daze; a scorching, mind-baked trance that stuck with me the entire way home. Even then, it relented only when an idea took form and progressively crowded out the fog by its sheer brilliance.

A twenty minute shower under the coldest water I could stand helped to clear my head even more. When I was finished I toweled away a few hundred heat blisters and applied lotion to the angry patches of sunburn on my face and neck. All the while my brain was frantically knitting, splicing ideas together at their frayed edges and pinning them to a timeline made of thin air. Characters, analogies, subplots.

By dinnertime, I had mapped out my first complete story since school let out. It was, in a word, perfect. Sadly, I was too wiped to actually work on it, or to read for my grandfather. Nicky was still miffed over this afternoon's little incident but my mother graciously volunteered to play stand-in. Exhausted and nursing a dull headache, I collapsed into bed while it was still light outside. I fell asleep to the sound of my mother reading aloud in the next room, her voice a singsong murmuring through the cheap paneling. It felt very womblike and distantly familiar.

Would it be unforgivably trite to say that I slept like a baby?

The next morning, just as the sun was tearing loose from the fiery horizon, I joined Nicky at the woodpile. We had a long way to go in preparation for the coming winter, mostly because my little brother had fallen behind in his duties. My graduation from busywork toward more scholarly pursuits was leaving a mark on the household in the form of forgotten and hastily performed chores. And so far, I had nothing to show for all the trouble I was causing.

Where the woodpile was concerned, I couldn't really fault Nicky. There's an art to processing firewood and my little brother was just getting the hang of it. He didn't need instruction so much as the benefit of time and plenty of hands-on experience. As for me, I still had the knack. Well, sort of. It was a lot like riding a bike, though I suppose my stamina might have grown a little soft over the past couple of months. That was to be expected of course; a pencil is just a tad lighter than an ax, after all.

I left the splitting maul and wedges in Nicky's charge while I took on the miserable task of cutting logs down to size. I'd like to say that my motives for welcoming the heavier lifting were purely selfless but that wasn't really the case. Chopping logs into usable blanks was much more exerting than splitting those blanks into firewood, but it also required a whole lot less precision. Which suited me fine, because I needed something blindly repetitive to occupy my hands as my mind roamed free.

Once I got a rhythm going, it seemed that every satisfying *thunk* of iron into wood drove home a new facet of my story. And as each settled into position, another seemed to bound free from the clutter of my imagination. I swung that ax over and over, sending chips in all directions as I ironed out the kinks in my budding plot. I'm pretty sure that I was grinning like a crazy person, but what can I say? It felt good, cathartic for the body and soul.

Of course, too much of anything is never a good thing. After an hour of hard labor, I was ready to call it a day. In my zeal, I had cut more blanks than Nicky could split in a single morning, so I felt no shame in quitting early. My arms were giving out, anyway. My mind, on the other hand, was just getting warmed up. The mental framework of my composition was filling in nicely and I sensed that I was on to something truly worthwhile. But I had reached a point in the creative process when I needed to see something on paper, some tangible proof that I was on the right track. Ideas aren't worth much until they take some physical form, after all.

Leaving Nicky to tidy up our mess—because when you think about it, that's what little brothers are for—I went inside to gather my notebook and a handful of pencils. Inspiration and determination had entered a state of fusion in me, an event that was producing such enormous energy that I feared I might explode. No matter what, I knew that today wouldn't be just another day of scratching on paper.

The wandering tree was calling and it was all I could do to keep from answering at a dead run.

Pruitt Field seemed shaggier than usual on that day. Someone had done some mowing the previous morning and by the looks of things, he must've thrown in the towel when the heat soared into unfamiliar territory. The tractor stood abandoned halfway down a lane with the cabin door ajar and the mower deck still lowered. Knowing all too well just how treacherous the heat had been, I could hardly blame anyone for having the common sense to skitter inside.

With all that said, Pruitt Field had definitely looked better. Like a bad hairdo, the grass was overgrown in some places and worn to the dirt in others. That it was now shorn neatly at the edges only drew attention to its overall tousled condition. It was like a bad mullet, emerging at a time when there was such a thing as a good one.

Entering the field with this scrutinizing mindset, it dawned on me just how far the wandering tree had traveled over the last couple of years. It was now visibly closer to the north side of the property than the south, which by my meager calculations meant that it was picking up speed. My sense of wonder ballooned at this realization and I wondered if anyone was still tracking its progress.

Unlike yesterday, the sky was slightly overcast, allowing the sun to pop in and out of view every few minutes, yet holding the extreme temperatures at bay. The heat was still pretty intense but with a steady breeze and plenty of shade under the wandering tree, it was bearable.

Settling into my usual spot, surrounded by the whispering of rustling leaves, a strange sensation began to envelop me. Though completely alone, I had the distinct feeling that someone was there with me. Not in a creepy way, as if I was being stalked or even watched. Nor was there anything particularly supernatural about it. Rather, it felt like a sweet friend—the kind you're so at ease with that silence is less of a barrier than a bridge between you—had cuddled up next to me. I wasn't sure what to make of it. Yet even as I tried to dismiss the experience as a byproduct of my overactive imagination, or perhaps a bit of wishful thinking, I was suddenly overwhelmed by the irresistible urge to do something that made absolutely no sense to me.

I needed to pray.

How and for what, I had no idea. Back in the days when my family went to church, I became familiar with something called *The Lord's Prayer*. I had recited it alongside hundreds of strangers on so many occasions, and with such ritualistic monotony, that I came to know it as a lengthy series of syllables as opposed to a meaningful plea to God. When I considered the prayer now, it seemed too generic to satisfy any real purpose. But it was what I had, and beggars couldn't be choosers.

I spoke timidly, voice cracking, stumbling here and there on phrases that had fallen victim to a leaky memory. The words felt empty, like someone else's. Probably because they were.

Afterward, I groaned at my silliness. A breeze gusted and nearby, a lone lily of vibrant yellow seemed to wave hello. Despite the heat—or perhaps because of it—the flower stood tall and pristinely beautiful, yet out of place here. From some cranny in the old elm, a piece of old paper fluttered to the ground and skated across the surface toward me. I snatched it from the air.

High in the sky, an airliner drew a tendril across a patch of blue-gray and then vanished into thicker cloud cover. Closing my eyes, I imagined that I was aboard that plane, headed somewhere beautiful and exotic. I imagined that Ivy was there with me and the mere thought of her made me beam. When I finally opened my eyes a wonderful air of serenity had settled over me. The meteorite pendant around my neck felt warm against my skin. I took a deep breath and picked up a pencil.

And began to write.

SIXTEEN

The day of the meeting, I found myself on Grandpa Duty. My mother took Nicky grocery shopping, leaving me behind to feed the old man. Not that big of a deal, I told myself. I'll just whip something up for lunch and hand it off on my way out the door. It sounded simple enough, yet Grandpa seemed to find great pleasure in nibbling away at any margin for error. The meeting was scheduled for one o'clock and despite substantial efforts to lure my grandfather into the realm of reason, he refused to eat a minute before noon. It was exasperating. Still, it looked like I might just pull it off, right up to the moment when I reached for the doorknob at twelve twenty-five. Which as it turned, out was precisely when Grandpa decided to knock his stupid sandwich onto the floor.

Respectable households don't normally grant the five-second rule to sandwiches that have splattered on the floor in a smear of mustard. While the Chases might not have been respectable by highbrow standards, we did prefer to go through the motions on this particular issue. That put me in a predicament though, because after wasting the last of our bread on the ruin of that baloney sandwich, about the only edible thing left in the house was a package of Ramen noodles.

For the record, a watched pot literally does not boil. Take it from me.

Even at a jog, I arrived late. Naturally—since I remained the universe's favorite punching bag—the meeting got an early start, which exaggerated my ten minutes of tardiness into something closer to twenty. There were no empty chairs when I slipped inside the conference room, so I loitered at the back, cowering nervously against the wall. A few heads turned but thankfully none lingered. It was actually in my favor that I didn't need to squeeze between other attendants to claim a seat, because I was a sweaty mess. My recently combed hair dangled limply against my forehead like wet clumps of yarn.

The meeting was moving along swiftly and when I realized just how much I had already missed, the temptation to slip right back out began to work on me. But I had been spotted and I figured that getting called out as I left would only make an awkward situation that much more unbearable.

It's funny: until that day I hadn't even planned on coming. And looking back, I'm not sure what changed my mind. I had known all along how it was likely to play out, so what exactly was I thinking? I can only say that when I awoke that morning, it just felt right. At some point, I needed to accept that my intuition was schizophrenic and therefore a hopelessly unreliable navigator.

I was dressed in my dad's old Sunday clothes—mine had passed down to Nicky—which proved to be another mistake. I counted fifteen kids, excluding me, ranging from fifth graders to upper classmen, and every one of them wore sensible summer shorts and tee-shirts. My wrinkled slacks and polo shirt, both threadbare and two sizes too large, seemed to cry out for mockery, though to be fair, my casual clothes wouldn't have fared much better. Those were stained and falling apart beyond repair. And they were probably dirty anyway. The frequency of our laundromat visits had a direct relationship with our finances, and lately they were both suffering more than usual.

Near the front of the room, Ms. Winters sat at the end of a long table, hands clasped tightly over a spiral notebook. A panel of four guests—one woman and three men—was seated to her left. Individually, they were the very portrait of scholarship and propriety; as a group, they managed to take on the exclusive stuffiness of a gang of stamp collectors. These were representatives of the Young Writer's Guild of Oklahoma, I presumed, though by the looks of them, they had been born as fifty- to sixty-year-olds and hadn't once enjoyed the company of a kid. One—a short, wrinkled hobbit of a woman who donned spectacles the size of bocce balls—was addressing the room in a shrill voice. Her timbre was so preposterously falsetto that I immediately thought of Monty Python and how a certain silly Frenchman would've threatened to fart in this lady's general direction.

Ms. Winters flashed a tight smile when she saw me and I returned a cringe, both a cry for help and a plea for forgiveness. Her smile flared with amusement and then faded. A second later, she broke eye contact to jot something in her notes and my gaze began to roam in search of Ivy. It didn't take long.

I found her in the front row with arms crossed, golden hair cascading down her back like a shimmering waterfall. I wanted to reach out and touch it, to experience the luxury of its softness between my fingers. At once, as if somehow attuned to—and perhaps agitated by—my gawking attention, Ivy peeked over her shoulder. At the moment when her eyes brushed against mine I felt my heart lurch and my cheeks lit up as if on fire. She looked away instantly with the practiced indifference of a girl who knows that she's beautiful and has yet to decide if it's worth all the attention.

"Alright young writers, I think now would be a good time to split up," the hobbit declared. "Let's count off into groups of five, shall we?" My mouth went dry, but I didn't dare speak up. Thankfully, Ms. Winters interjected on my behalf.

"Oh, I do beg your pardon, Ms. Foster. Perhaps groups of four would be, um—" Her voice wavered slightly, which seemed to defy the ironclad composure I had come to associate with her. "Well, it's just that we have *six*teen participants, so—"

"Do we?" The scholarly guest adjusted her oversized glasses and began to count silently, bouncing a stubby finger in the air over each seat. She spotted me halfway through and her wrinkled mouth formed something that might have been a smile, though the rest of her expression seemed to dispute such a conclusion.

"Ah," she exclaimed, beady little eyes burning holes through me. "I see the problem now." Yup, that was me in a nutshell. "How silly of me, I must've failed to account for your *numerous* time zones. Or perhaps telling time is beyond the scope of public education in your little town?"

Ms. Winters gaped, her expression turning darker than I had ever seen it. An uncomfortable silence began to permeate the room, filling all the voids and bulging into what felt like an impending explosion of outrage. Ms. Foster sensed it too and became noticeably fidgety; I wondered if it had even dawned on the woman that she was grossly outnumbered. Either way, she didn't have it in her to apologize.

"Well," she exclaimed, "let's move on. We don't have all day, do we?" She pointed to someone outside my field of view and I heard a timid: "Um, one?"

The odds were one in four that I would end up in a circle with Ivy; by now you should be able to guess how that worked out for me.

Cripes.

I got stuck next to a long-haired kid whose body odor might've given Jeremy a run for his money, back in his junior high prime. Only, instead of bug spray this guy reeked of unwashed neglect, augmented by the acrid perfume of an overstuffed ashtray. Across from me, a set of twin girls quibbled over the distinction between borrowing and stealing a shirt, given that "you didn't even bother to ask, so don't call it borrowing!" Lastly, there was an overweight kid whom I recognized from school. Ronald something. I knew almost nothing about him, except that he was a couple of years older than me. That and he was constantly picked on at school, though with cowardly restraint, considering that he was big enough to pulverize anyone dumb enough to really push his buttons.

Looking at Ronald, I saw a familiar emptiness, a deep need for something—anything—to hope for and I felt my heart break a little. Despite my personal stake in the competition, part of me wanted this guy to win even more than I wanted to win myself. Because that would feel like sweet justice, even if it wasn't mine.

The purpose of these group sessions—ostensibly, anyway— was to compare our submission ideas, which struck me as a blatant form of sabotage or at the very least, narcissism. Why else would anyone knowingly tip their hand to a group of competitors except to show off? I mean, I got the whole *iron sharpens iron* thing, but this felt like a pretty loose application to me.

Classic loner thinking? Maybe. Probably.

Nevertheless, we dutifully laid our cards on the table one at a time. The twins went first and their concepts were quite good. One read a stanza of her poetry and it was fantastic. The smelly dude's idea for an essay on the legalization of marijuana could've gone either way, I guessed, depending on the strength of his writing. The concept wasn't exactly original but it was definitely a hot topic at the time.

And then we got to Ronald.

Evidently it wasn't enough to merely share his ideas; Ronald needed us to *experience* them in their entirety. Bless his heart, the guy launched into a painfully lively narration of his entire short story—eight excruciating pages—as if this meeting wasn't a meeting at all but the competition itself, and we—the rest of his group—were its esteemed judges.

To his credit, Ronald kept our attention—along with that of half the room. But only as a gory train wreck transfixes a bystander who later wishes that he could've found the strength to look away. The only thing worse than Ronald's character voices—oh yes, he went there—was the story itself. The plot was … oh my. Words simply fail me.

Meet Special Agent in Charge Blaze Thompson and his renowned task force of crack detectives. They're at the forefront of a nationwide hunt for a serial arsonist, whose most recent atrocities include corporate espionage and the subsequent burning down of a cheese factory.

Did I mention that Special Agent Thompson is a mouse?

Yes, that's right. A mouse coordinating a government task force of human detectives, men who have nothing better to do than hunt down a cheese hater. And who are apparently oblivious or completely unconcerned that their fearless leader is a rodent who bounces from crime scene to crime scene in various coat pockets. It was like some spoofed version of Stuart Little, only fraught with so much violence and military jargon that it couldn't possibly have been intended for an audience of children.

You know, sometimes there's just no substitute for the real thing. Strap in, 'cause you're about to enter the one and only mind of Ronald.

Lieutenant Richardson saluted the bad guy with his hand. Suddenly the same hand that recently saluted pulled out a deadly FIM-92 Stinger surface-to-air missile launcher and blew up the man who used to be a bad guy … and was now a pile of dead meat.

Until the bitter end, I held out hope that Ronald was messing with us, that the whole thing was just an elaborate joke. Because if so? Bravo, sir!

But sadly, it was no joke.

Aside from the bizarre storyline, Ronald's writing was fairly on par with most fifth or sixth graders. The problem, of course, was that Ronald was in the eleventh grade. I was just thankful that he hadn't pushed the fifteen page submission limit because there was a limit to how much I could endure with a straight face. I will say this, though: putting himself out there the way he did took a lot of courage. I had to give him that.

When my turn came around, I contributed a barebones synopsis of my work-in-progress but it was clear that no one was actually listening. They were still reeling over Ronald's baffling performance, just as he was desperately trying to extract some validation from their veiled expressions. My feelings weren't hurt in the least by this because I knew that a more favorable setting wouldn't have made any difference. Every once in a while, my charm—if I can even call it that—came to life on paper; but even in the best of circumstances, it amounted to diddly squat in person.

When I was finished, we settled into a long, awkward silence. The other groups were still going strong, yet we had already grown tired of each other. Truth be told, this suited me just fine; I had other things on my mind anyway.

Ivy was seated to my back, which was hardly ideal. I thought about asking one of the twins to trade seats with me but I couldn't come up with a decent excuse. I got by without help, though. Worrying over an invisible thread on my shoulder, I stole furtive glances every chance I could get. If Ivy noticed, she had the decorum to pay me no mind. By the looks of things, her group was thoroughly engaged. Their expressions were animated and inspired, thoughtful. I'm guessing their feedback must've been a little more constructive than ours, especially considering that we had yet to exchange any. And I would be truly surprised if there were any special agent mice or grating character voices happening over there.

Ah, what I wouldn't have given to be sitting near that girl, listening to that sweet voice of hers. Hanging on every syllable.

It bothered me to feel such a strong attraction to someone that I knew nothing about because I knew that it had to be purely physical. But it couldn't be helped. This was unfamiliar territory for me, longing for another person in such a way. My hormones were tying me in knots, and there wasn't a thing I could do about it. Everything about this fascination felt right and imperative, yet distinctly irrational—all at once.

There was something else, too. Behind all the white noise was a fundamental belief that this girl—stranger or not—was meant for me. That there would never be a suitable substitute. This sort of dramatic, self-defeating thinking was part of the teenage condition, I knew, but there was no denying the power it had over me. One thing was certain: if Ivy and I were supposed to be soul mates, fate had a monumental challenge on its hands.

My group was all but forgotten when the stinky kid abruptly leaned into my personal space, reeking to high heaven. His eyebrows jumped into an arch as if seeing me for the very first time. "Whoa, your face is jacked, dude. Were you born like that, or what?"

For a moment, I wondered if he had actually spoken at all or if my imagination was merely getting the best of me. But when I stole a glance at Ronald, the look of pure shock on his face removed all doubt. My blood began to boil. I mean, who says something like that out of the blue? Without any provocation? Mr. Legalize Pot was probably going for some kind of brutal candor, designed more to disarm than offend, but it was a pretty crappy thing to say no matter how you defended it.

My first instinct was to strangle the guy with his own greasy hair. It wouldn't have taken much, either. He was all skin and bones with an Adam's apple the size of a walnut. I could've snapped him like a twig. I kept my cool though, realizing that even a minor scuffle would almost certainly destroy everything that I had been working toward.

With that said, while I was determined to hold my temper, I wasn't about to let this idiot off the hook. Covering my nose with both hands, I replied, "I'm sorry, did you say something? I think my hearing's been compromised by that god-awful smell of yours."

One of the twins snorted, the other gasped. Ronald looked on with green-faced consternation, prepared to throw-up if things happened to escalate. Stinky fixed me with a blank stare that lasted all of five seconds. When I didn't back down, he nodded with a grudging smile. "Touché." Only, because he was a classy guy, his mispronunciation rhymed with a certain feminine product.

After the meeting, Ivy was among the first to leave and I had to wonder if my shameless gawking didn't push her right out the door. I hadn't exactly made plans to talk to her—honestly, what was I supposed to say? *So, how about this weather, huh? What's that? Oh—um, no. I don't live under a bridge ...* —so I didn't necessarily feel deprived of an opportunity to break the ice. But that isn't to say that I didn't feel robbed. There was a craving deep in the marrow of my bones that could only be satisfied by a parting exchange of glances. Just one more split second of eye contact to tide me over for a while, even knowing full well that it would be meaningless to her. This terrible neediness felt sickening, not unlike the aftermath of engorging on too much Halloween candy.

It occurred to me that Ivy might have wandered back into the main library. I wouldn't know because I never got to find out. Ms. Winters beckoned me over before I could bolt for the door and despite my urgency to indulge in behavior that bordered on stalking, I couldn't bring myself to wave her off.

I expected a nasty reprimand for my tardiness, especially considering the disturbance it ultimately caused, but Ms. Winters had nothing like that in mind. In fact, she didn't mention the meeting at all, which I found curious.

Nearby, the YWGO reps were busily packing their briefcases and portfolios, anxious to move on to better pastures, no doubt. Irritation seemed to radiate from their midst and a few of our high school natives were showing signs of an uprising in response. One of them, a junior from one of Shawnee's private schools—as evidenced by his St. Christopher Academy, Class of 1991 tee-shirt—was making a cartoonish show of trying to understand his watch, a look of cross-eyed strain on his face. "You mean the little hand doesn't point north?"

Ms. Winters led me out the door, scowling. "Don't worry about her, Lincoln. That woman's had a bug up her butt since I told her the branch manager took the week off. Like the rest of us are just undereducated secretaries or something. We couldn't *possibly* figure out how to unlock the conference room by ourselves." She pushed her glasses down the saddle of her nose, rubbing at the corners of her eyes. "I swear, if they weren't donors I'd give that pompous midget a piece of my mind."

I must've looked shocked if not merely uncomfortable because Ms. Winters covered her mouth and her cheeks flushed a deep burgundy. Until that moment, I wouldn't have thought it possible, but here was proof that Ms. Winters was in fact completely human. She exhaled slowly between her teeth and it seemed to have a relaxing effect. Her face returned to its usual pallor, softening into a sheepish frown.

"Oh my goodness. I'm sorry about that, Lincoln. It was very unprofessional of me to speak like that in front of you."

I shrugged with an amused smirk. "Midget, huh? Got a problem with little people?"

Ms. Winters groaned and the blush threatened to return. "Okay let's just drop it before I die of embarrassment. Anyway, that's not what I wanted to discuss." In a sudden burst of energy, she began to mole through a huge satchel slung over one shoulder, hands burrowing between magazines and folders and sheafs of dog-eared papers—"I know it's in here somewhere ..."—until finally—"Aha!"—it emerged with a thin paperback. "Have you read this one yet?"

I gave it a quick look. The cover art was muted and unappealing, the emerging hallmark of literary masterpieces. Nothing about it rang a bell, so I shook my head.

"Perfect! Why don't you give it a try? I think you'll like it."

I knew better than to crack open a novel right before bed and I can offer no excuse for abandoning protocol that night. More than most, this book really got its teeth into me; I knew almost immediately that I was in for a long night. By the harsh glow of a penlight, I turned pages in a trance, pausing only to hunt for batteries when the light died. The sun was rising when I finished the last page.

It was spectacular. When Isabelle Holland wrote *The Man Without a Face*, she demonstrated a form of flow and continuity that I could only dream of matching one day. What's more, it felt so relevant, so personalized to me, that it might not have been a novel at all, but an intimate letter addressed solely to Lincoln Chase.

The story was about a boy who wanted so desperately to escape his lot in life that he sought out and befriended the town pariah, a man whose face had been horribly disfigured in a tragic accident. Their relationship was painfully awkward in the beginning, a forced misalignment of generations, but it soon began to bloom. Despite the burden of circumstances—or perhaps because of it—their friendship sweetened and ultimately ripened to a state of unconditional kinship, one that delivered acceptance at a time when neither could find it elsewhere.

The undercurrent of all this didn't merely ripple by, it drew me deep into unfamiliar waters, yet buoyed me safely at the surface. It seemed to confirm a hope that I had been too afraid to embrace: that love—in this case, a mildly scandalous take on platonic love—sees past our cultural and familial eccentricities, our taboos. It truly is blind with no regard for the outward beauty we so openly profess to be lovely.

Maybe I read something into this principle, but it seemed to me that if the rest of it was true, scars shouldn't be any less beautiful than the smoothest skin. Because neither are reliable qualities of the flesh; and both will fade in the end.

I was crying by the end of the book. Not with teary-eyed sniffles but full-blown sobs straight from the heart and I had to bury my face in a fistful of pillow to keep from waking Nicky. Until that night I had unconsciously accepted that I was unlovable. That I didn't deserve companionship because I was ruined. By poverty and hereditary guilt; the enduring Chase curse. By my inescapable ordinariness. The accident wasn't to blame for my ugliness, I believed. It merely put on display what had been hidden within me all along.

Who would've expected that a work of fiction could affect a person so profoundly? Certainly not me yet this one was tremendously empowering. It gave me permission to believe that love wasn't concerned with my stature or the sins of my father any more than it was subject to the laws of physical attraction. Love was—*is*—the heart of grace; it can't be earned because it isn't bound by conditions.

I cried like a baby for the sweet sting of that revelation. And for the fear that always comes with truth, considering that truth changes everything.

SEVENTEEN

A few days before the deadline, I turned in two pieces: a short story and a poem. Both were hand printed on college ruled paper, drafted meticulously in my finest penmanship. I packed them, along with my entry forms, neatly in a manila envelope and walked it to the post office, cradling it from the wind much as a mother shields her baby. All the way there, my stomach spasmed like a clinching fist, perhaps because I knew that once I let go of that envelope there would be no turning back. All discomfort aside though, I couldn't wait to get it over with.

I waited in line for five minutes. The guy directly ahead of me had a mohawk and a skateboard, and I was surprised to see that all eyes were on him rather than me. Even more interesting, he seemed to enjoy it. Rather than look away, he met those wary glances head-on, as if to invite—not challenge, to be clear; his eyes were kind rather than combative—the very small talk that most of us were accustomed to avoiding. Knowing nothing else about the man, I wished that I could be more like him.

Anyway, he bought a book of stamps and in the time it took for me to wonder what a guy with a mohawk and a skateboard would need with a book of stamps—because you know, people with mohawks and skateboards don't mail letters, do they?—my turn came and went. A round woman at the counter made change from my dollar, stamped my envelope and tossed it in a canvas bin. The whole transaction took less than thirty seconds.

Just like that, my fate was sealed.

I expected to feel a huge release of tension with this milestone behind me. I guess that in a way I did; it just wasn't the release I had in mind. The entire trip home was an exercise in mind over matter, struggling to keep from going diarrhea in my pants.

Incidentally—which is to say: let's move on from the subject of diarrhea because nothing good can possibly come from belaboring it—submitting the poem was a bit of an afterthought. For all I knew, it was garbage. But garbage or not, it was special to me. I had stumbled into it just minutes after praying under the wandering tree, and for reasons that I couldn't put my finger on, reading it never ceased to fill me with wonder. I figured there was a small chance that it might have a similar affect on the judges, so I threw it in. More wishful thinking? Probably, but what did I really have to lose? It just made sense to hedge my bets.

Unlike the poem, which could only have been a gift from the wandering tree, my short story represented the culmination of more than two month's preparation. Hundreds of hours devoted to reading and experimentation. Feeling out new techniques and failing miserably, trying again and again until something likable finally squeaked out.

And though I had fleshed out that story immediately after finishing the poem—riding the same wave of inspiration, in fact—producing the story as a whole turned into a process that reached back in time and stretched into a two week obsession. During that period, I wrote, edited, shredded, added to, cut away from, rewrote, scrapped and wrote that story again countless times over. When I finally laid down my pencil, the story had very nearly circled back to my first draft, only polished to a much higher sheen. I suppose that my instincts had been trustworthy from the start, even if my confidence had some catching up to do.

I had every reason to lack confidence though, because nothing had changed. The odds remained against me. I had done my best, to be sure, but who was to say that my best was any good? My family was hardly the ideal focus group, in case you're wondering. They didn't share my passion for the English language; nor were they willing to administer brutal honesty when it was most needed. Their sparse feedback generally went along the lines of, "Wow, that's so great! I wouldn't change a word," followed immediately by something like, "Um, so what exactly does *blithe* mean?"

With good reason, I was teetering on the edge of a breakdown.

And so when a more seasoned writer might've crossed his fingers and moved on to write a best seller, I busied myself with the fantasy of taking it back—all of it—and carrying on as if this dreadful competition hadn't come along to take over my life. Maybe this hinted at my callowness as a competitor. It definitely said a lot about my insecurity as a person, though in my defense, kids my age weren't really meant to shoulder a man's burden. The weight of being tasked with a miracle was proving to be immense, far heavier than I was equipped to handle.

More than anything else—the sickening feeling of defeat, for one—I dreaded the look on my mother's face when she finally saw things as they actually were, when she nodded her head at what she must've always suspected: that her oldest son was a hopeless failure. And knowing that Nicky would ultimately suffer because of my shortcomings just broke my heart even more. I was so tired of being afraid. I couldn't wait for this all to be over.

Even fearing the worst though, I found a small measure of comfort in the meteoric progression of my writing. For the first time, I was moved by my own handiwork and that was no small feat. The elusive bridge from heart to mind had finally revealed itself and it must've been hiding in plain sight all along. The secret wasn't all that sophisticated, as it turned out. It didn't draw from some convoluted train yard of mental circuitry, nor did it need to be teased into the light to appreciate. The trick was simply to dig deep and put myself out there. All of me, without holding back. My hopes and failures, the things that haunted me, things that I cherished. The nuts and bolts that held me in this grotesque shape, for better or worse.

I hoped the judges could bring themselves to recognize that commitment, to look past the sophomoric prose and clumsy plot devices. Because if they could manage that, they might just find a bit of magic in there. A youthful, rebellious variety, to be fair— perhaps a little misguided by the intensity of my desperation—but magic nonetheless with the power to tickle funny bones and tug at heartstrings, if given half a chance. I don't know that I have ever hoped for anything more than I hoped for their favor because it seemed that all I had to offer the world was wrapped up in those fifteen pages.

To reject them was to reject me.

The next two weeks were pure torture. I discovered that even the smallest shred of doubt can thrive when your life is on pause, growing mountainous if pondered for even a moment. And believe me, I had plenty of doubts. They were thick like briars in a patch, dangling amidst the everyday wanderings of my mind. A lone thought had but to venture close for one to latch on. And of course, once doubt had its pesky stickers in me, there was no getting rid of it.

So with the passage of every day, it became more difficult to keep from revisiting my work, second-guessing every decision, every single word. In vain, I reworked my story perhaps another five times, as if it wasn't already too late. I hardly slept at night, and the few hours I managed to wrangle were restless, interrupted by endless sequences of lurid dreams. It was a miserable way to live, if I can call it that.

In terms of day-to-day activity, there wasn't much to do around the Chase homestead, other than cut wood and prepare for the worst. So that's what I did. Mostly, I cut wood because it calmed me, and because Nicky needed the help. But rest assured, whenever the opportunity presented itself, I jumped at the chance to inject a much-needed dose of reality—pessimism, as my mother liked to call it. I wasn't fishing for reinforcement, for the record; I was doing my best to soften a blow that I knew would eventually befall us. Yet despite everything I threw at them, my family remained hopelessly optimistic. At some point baseless confidence starts to feel like delusion, and it was infuriating that my family couldn't bring themselves to acknowledge that.

Just a few weeks before the official end of summer, the winners were finally announced. Of course, I found out days after everyone else. You get pretty used to hanging from the rear end of current events when you don't have cable television or a phone. But that doesn't make it any less aggravating. I'm sure that most of my competitors knew something within hours, if not minutes; but for those of us with no phone? Well, at least one of us learned the news from a poster hanging unceremoniously in the library foyer—at the leisure of happenstance, considering how sporadically I visited the library, lately. If not for the glaring YWGO logo, I might have blown right by the list. But I didn't, thank goodness, and I was also glad for the relative seclusion of the foyer, where I could cry in peace, if it came to that.

And it nearly did.

You see, the problem with over-preparing for anything is that you are, by definition, under-preparing for something else. This was indeed the case with me on that day. I was so steeled to lose that my knees practically buckled when I discovered that I hadn't. My mouth worked like a dying fish as I read the list four times over, expecting my name to disappear or resolve into something else, a close variation of itself, perhaps—*Langston Case, Rankin Champ*—but it didn't. And my name wasn't the only surprise in the winners' circle. The world seemed to blink when I saw, of all people—

"Lincoln Chase!" shouted a voice from inside. Ms. Winters bellowed with such tremendous zeal that she set the foyer glass to rattling in its frames. I imagined that the patrons inside were a little taken aback that a woman who was so notorious for hushing and shushing needed to be reminded that *she* was in a library. The next thing I knew, Ms. Winters was sprinting toward me, closing the ground between us at a pace that was less in form with an aging librarian than a cheetah running down a poor gazelle. I'm not gonna lie—it freaked me out. Even with the glass between us, my arms rose instinctively to shield my face because the glass seemed to disappear in the blur of her momentum. An instant later, the glass door flew open and I was yanked into a fierce embrace that dang near lifted me off my feet. When I was sure that my throat hadn't been torn out by a grassland cat, I gave in to the hug. I even allowed myself a smile, because as far as greetings went, this one was pretty epic.

When we parted, Ms. Winters clasped her hands with a choked giggle—a funny tittering sound like sparrows arguing in a hedge. She tugged me inside toward the circulation desk, prancing as older ladies sometimes do when they're feeling sassy. "I had a feeling, Lincoln!" she sang in a matronly falsetto. "I just knew it." Peeking over her shoulder at me, she beamed. Her smile was incandescent, more brilliant than I had ever seen it, and it warmed my heart.

The spirit of her elation was hard to resist, yet my doubts persisted. "Are you sure this isn't a mistake?" I had to ask. "I mean, the poem—that can't be right, can it?" It seemed too good to be true, and believe me—while stranger things than typos happen every day, a little typo can be plenty damaging all on its own. For example: at the end of fourth grade, I got two A's on my report card—some of my highest marks ever. My parents were so thrilled that they took me out for ice cream. Imagine their dismay—and mine—when a revised report card arrived the next day with D's in place of those beautiful A's.

I haven't had ice cream since.

Okay, that's not true. But my point still stands. It's hard to talk down a cynic with a lifetime of bad experiences in his arsenal. Just saying.

"Oh, it's no mistake, Lincoln. As a matter of fact, I knew the moment I read that poem of yours that nobody else had a chance. Of course, your story would've done just as well, I'm sure, if it hadn't been excluded. That was a spectacular piece of work, Lincoln. I have to ask though, wherever did you get the idea to—"

"Uh, excluded?" My smile had collapsed and concentrated will alone kept it from baring teeth. "Why?"

Ms. Winters crossed her arms, surveying me warily. I maintained a frown, eyes deadpan. We stood at this silent impasse until the librarian realized that I wasn't playing dumb for the fun of it. Her expression pruned then, eyebrows bunching into little knots.

"Oh, my," she muttered, and her tongue *tisk-tisk*ed with disapproval. "Honey, contestants were only allowed a single submission, didn't you know that? Obviously they had to pick one." Ms. Winters sighed, regarding me with a sympathetic yet mildly exasperated shrug. "Honestly, Lincoln. You're lucky they didn't disqualify you altogether."

Funny, I didn't feel so lucky just then. I had spent the better part of a summer slaving over a piece that went directly into someone's trashcan. When I thought of it in those unflattering terms, my legs went boneless. The back of my throat began to burn, and in a split second, I surged into that state of nausea where you wish you could just throw up and get it over with.

I guess that's what I get for ignoring the fine print.

The depth of my despair must've been plainly visible because Ms. Winters placed a willowy hand on my shoulder and offered a gentle squeeze. "Oh, Lincoln. Please don't lose sight of what you've accomplished. There were more than two hundred poetry submissions, did you know that?" I did not. "You beat them all and the truth is that both of your entries were winners. Does it really matter which of them won the judges over?"

She was right as always. It shouldn't matter. But it did because I knew that my entries weren't equal. I practically killed myself writing one while the other seemed to flow up from the ground like a mystical spring. On some level, I was more than half convinced that Pruitt Rock was responsible for that poem, zapping me with a cosmic discharge of brilliance or something. It might be hard to understand, but the credit didn't feel like it was mine to claim. Maybe because I hadn't worked hard enough for it? Who knows. Regardless, the feeling cut me down a notch when I should've been rejoicing.

Looking back, I have to wonder where the ungratefulness came from. I didn't see it that way at the time, but to be clear, that's exactly what it was. Let's review: I had just been handed everything that I asked for—personal validation, bragging rights, a cash prize, a commitment to publication—yet I was pouting over technicalities. If I thought that I had taken the high road—that I had endured all the stress for the sake of my family—I should've known better. My behavior in that moment proved that I was mistaken. Because if my motives had been genuinely selfless, I would've been break-dancing on library tables instead of sulking like a five-year-old.

Still, I wasn't completely oblivious to the value of my fortune. A poem that I had written—scratched out by my hand, regardless of who or what might have inspired it—was going to be published. Wasn't that worth celebrating? A strange warmth came over me at the thought and my breakfast began to settle mercifully back into my stomach. I was going to be a published writer.

Man, did I like the sound of that.

Even as I considered all this, I was trying to work out exactly how Ms. Winters had come to preview my submissions. Not that it bothered me in the least that she had. Her opinion was something that I had come to respect immensely, after all. Yet while her praise filled me with pride, at that moment I was more confused by the logistics of her involvement. My entries had been sent to Oklahoma City, you see, not the Shawnee Library.

"So, did you and the hobbit patch things up?" I wanted to know. "Or did you knock her off to take her place?"

Ms. Winters blanched. "The *hobbit*?"

"Well, it's a little less offensive than *midget*, wouldn't you say? And she did have the look of a woman who was hiding a set of hairy feet."

If you've never seen a librarian turn beet red, by the way, it's worth a look. The transformation is akin to that of a chameleon morphing from pasty white to deep burgundy in a single second. Poor Ms. Winters. She covered her mouth with both hands and squeezed her eyes shut, wagging that silver head in consummate shame. "Oh my," she groaned, and I almost felt bad. "I'm so embarrassed. I don't suppose you'll ever let me live that down, will you?"

"Probably not." I chuckled, patting her on the arm with my best *there, there* look of pity. "But seriously, how did you manage to read my submissions? I mean, you weren't a judge, were you?"

Relieved to change the subject, Ms. Winters bobble-headed a yes-and-no response. "Well, not a judge exactly," she explained. "I volunteered to help pre-screen submissions along with about twenty other readers across the state." Her expression turned mischievous. "And I might have gone out of my way a bit to get my hands on your entries." She flashed a dark yet sheepish smirk, as if she had just confessed a grave sin well past its statute of limitations.

Abruptly, as if remembering something bizarre, Ms. Winters gasped and her voice dropped to a conspiratorial hiss. "Oh, my goodness, Lincoln. You can't *imagine* some of the entries that were turned in."

Ah, but I could. I thought of Ronald and—

"You know what, never mind. Don't even get me started." Returning to her merry self now, Ms. Winters began to bounce on the balls of her feet, hands interlaced tightly at her breast. "This is so exciting, isn't it? Your poem is going to blow everyone away at the banquet, I just know it."

My heart creaked to a halt. Literally—it was like, *Say what?* and my lips began to turn blue. Okay, that's what it felt like, anyway. "Um, what banquet?"

"The awards banquet, of course. You get to read your poem at next week's ceremony in Oklahoma City."

Oh, that was rich. I *get* to? Fantastic. Like it was a dream of mine to stand in front of a few hundred strangers and pee my pants. The room seemed to shift at the thought, as if the floor had come to life and was crawling away with me on its back. Distraught, I stumbled to the nearest chair and collapsed into it, breathing heavily. I felt hot bile creeping back up my throat as I scowled in lament.

Why couldn't I catch a break, just once? Not another cruel joke masquerading as a bonafide blessing but the real thing, with no strings attached? My mind reeled at the potential for mayhem. It seemed exponential, as did the inescapable likelihood of complete humiliation. Unbridled by social boundaries, considering who I was and how I looked, me with a microphone in front of respectable people? Good grief—was it possible to imagine a more probable disaster?

Let's consider a few of the possibilities, shall we?

My larynx could freeze up, forcing me to resort to charades—the scenario has probably happened before, you know; I mean, how else do you imagine the game came to be invented? Worse, what if I experienced a very untimely surge of hormonal magic onstage? You know, with no history book to hide, um …

well you know—*stuff*. And not to be a naysayer, but there was a good chance of me tripping on the way down the aisle, taking down a certain hobbit woman with me. Technically, that would only be half bad, but still. And what if an angry heckler was to recognize my second-hand pants from his—or worse, *her*—retired wardrobe? Can you imagine the sort of nerd mutiny that might incite?

Oh, misery! The possibilities were endless. My mind iterated through them at the speed of fear, and I swear to you that if I thought I could get away with it, I would've called the whole thing off and run home.

Ms. Winters stepped toward me then, concerned yet equally frustrated. "Lincoln, I can't help but wonder how it is that you're so uninformed. We went over all this at the meeting, remember?"

I shrugged. "I was pretty late," I reminded her, kneading my forehead. "Sounds like I may have missed a few things."

Her eyes glazed over for a second as she squeezed the sponge of her memory. There was a subtle flicker of recognition in her eyes and the corners of her mouth began to droop, twitching almost indiscernibly. "Oh, goodness," she muttered. "Well, I wouldn't worry about it, honey. You'll do just fine." She smiled thinly. "Do you own a suit?"

Sigh.

EIGHTEEN

The morning of the banquet arrived under a cloak of gray drizzle. I rolled out of bed with my stomach already in knots. I felt like I hadn't slept a wink, though I must have because Nicky's bunk was empty and I didn't remember him getting up. All night long, it seemed, my mind had dragged me through mazes of mocking crowds when it should've been at rest.

Nicky was already halfway through a bowl of Malt-O-Meal, taking up the whole table like he owned the place with those gangly elbows. My mother was perched against the kitchen counter with a coffee mug at her lips, gazing absently out the window. Her eyes were puffy and by the looks of her she was tired too, though I'm guessing her reasons were different than mine. The crown of what might've been a whiskey bottle peeked from the trash can.

I decided to ignore it.

"Mornin', sleepy head," said Nicky. He showed off a mouthful of oversized, preteen teeth and scooted over to make room for me.

"Hey back." Plopping into a chair, I glanced around for Grandpa's plate. "Is he already eating?" I asked.

"He ate a little early," my mother explained.

While I'm sure this was intended to put my mind at ease, it actually had the reverse effect. My grandfather was a creature of habit, both as a man of the Old School and a victim of dementia. Any sudden break from convention was a cause for concern, in my opinion.

"Everything okay? Is he feeling sick or something?"

"He's fine, Lincoln. Just got hungry earlier than usual, that's all."

I nodded noncommittally, far from convinced but sooooo, so tired. Too tired to pull out the whole story a strand at a time. The truth would just have to wait.

"So are you excited?" Nicky wanted to know.

I groaned. *Excited?* Roller coasters were exciting. Monster truck rallies, ninth innings with bases loaded. What I had in store seemed more like a visit to the gallows as the dishonored guest. "Terrified, actually," I grimaced. "There's gonna be a ton of people there."

"And you have to read your story in front of everyone?"

"No, not the story. Just the poem." Now that I thought about it, things could've been a whole lot worse. My poem was less than three hundred words whereas my short story spanned fifteen pages. Can you imagine how long that would have taken to read aloud? My cheeks flushed when I suddenly realized who *would* be performing that daunting feat. I couldn't help but grin because I knew exactly what was coming.

"Not *just* a poem, Lincoln."

I looked up at my mother. Her expression had turned chiding.

"You have a gift. Don't make light of it."

My mother was like that sometimes. She had zero tolerance for self-deprecation and lately she seemed to detect it where there was actually none. It was getting pretty old, but I let it go. I had enough on my mind without a fruitless argument weighing it down even more.

Nicky stole a glance at my mother and then cleared his throat. "So, um, what're you gonna wear to the banquet, Link?" he asked.

"That's a very good question," my mother chimed in. Her voice—both their voices, actually—seemed louder than necessary. Stiff, too. Sitting in their midst, I suddenly felt like a prop in a bad school play. Naturally, my suspicious nature raised its hackles.

"What's going on with you two? You're acting weird." My voice was full of steel and grit but it was my frazzled nerves doing the talking rather than any real irritation. Suddenly, Grandpa burst through the back door with a wet paper sack bundled under one massive arm.

"'Bout time, woman," he growled. "It's pouring out there." A faint sheen of moisture glistened on his hair and across the peaks of his shoulders, but otherwise he was dry as a bone.

Nicky laughed, observing that, "At least it isn't a hundred degrees out there. It's gotta be twenty degrees cooler than it has been all summer, Grandpa."

Grandpa gave him the stink eye and handed the bag off to my mother, grumbling incoherently under his breath.

"You could've waited in your room," huffed my mother. "Nobody said you had to wait outside."

"Easy for you to say. How 'bout you spend a few years in there and see how you like it?"

That shut her up. For all of a second.

"Fine," she snapped. "Tell you what: you can sleep outside from now on. Problem solved!"

Nicky giggled through a mouthful of breakfast while I looked on in open-mouthed awe. I hadn't seen this kind of grownup exchange—however childish it might've been—since before my father went to prison. It was a little stressful to watch, sure, but it also felt like the old normal. It evoked a sweet sense of nostalgia in me, along with a stab of loss, considering that a household void of parental bickering could scarcely be called a household at all.

My mother groaned, perhaps ashamed but probably just annoyed. "I'm sorry, Papa," she said, though nothing about her tone was particularly apologetic. "Let's just get a cup of coffee in you. You'll feel better in no time." She headed for the coffee pot in a restrained stomp.

Grandpa snorted but stopped short of any real protest. He was choosing his battles this morning, too. Turning to me, he laid a huge hand on my shoulder. "Fin," he said, and then hesitated. A few seconds ticked by and then something happened.

Something amazing.

As I watched, a cloud seemed to drift across my grandfather's face and he blinked hard. "No, that ain't right, is it?" he whispered. Flashing an embarrassed smile, he swallowed and then tried again. "Lincoln. My beautiful grandson, Lincoln." I felt my mouth go dry. It was the first time I could remember him speaking my name and the sound of it brought tears to my eyes. "I'm so proud of you, young man," he crooned, and those milky eyes were lively and full of sparkle. "You're a good kid, putting up with me; you know that?"

My mother laid the paper bag in my lap without a word. Her eyes were soft and warm, touched by Grandpa's lucid sentiment just as I was. She put a hand on his arm, blinking back tears of her own.

The bag contained blue slacks, a white button-down shirt and a pair of charcoal gray dress socks. They looked and felt expensive, if a little damp. There were tags and stickers attached to each bundle and for a moment, I was overwhelmed by that detail alone. These were some of my first new clothes ever, with the exception of socks and underwear—yes, even we had our secondhand limits. Of course, my annual sock allowance consisted of an economy pack—usually five sets of cotton shin-highs squeezed into a plastic sleeve like a fat white sausage—while this pair of Argyles was folded importantly over its own miniature plastic hanger. The price tag was marked through with a black pen but I'm betting it cost more than two economy packs.

"You're a writer now, Lincoln," my mother explained. "Gotta start dressing the part."

It dawned on me then that my mother must have spent the prize money right out from under us, and the wastefulness of this sent my blood into a boil. "Mom, you know we can't afford this." The anger gathering within me demanded harsher words, a more seething tone, yet I fought past the heat of the moment because I had a hunch that I was missing something. My mother was nothing if not frugal, after all. "Tell me it isn't too late to return all this," I pleaded.

My mother guffawed in response, shaking her head as if I was fast approaching the outer limits of absurdity. I looked to my grandfather for clarification; the old man smiled nervously, eyes darting around to avoid mine. It was obvious that I had lost him again. He would be no help now.

"It was on the porch this morning," Nicky whispered, bless him. "Someone knocked and ran."

I managed a quiet, "Oh …" but that was the best that I could muster. Who would have done this, and why?

My mother, the mind reader, finally came to my rescue. "I think it was your librarian friend," she said. Her expression was an oil-and-water blend of gratitude and shame. And if I'm not mistaken, a hint of jealousy.

I thought about her assessment and decided that she was probably right. This did indeed have Ms. Winters written all over it.

"Well?" my mother said. "Are you gonna try them on or what?"

The clothes were a pretty good fit. My father's church shoes were still a little too big but what they lacked in comfort and chic, they made up for in nondescript appeal. Grandpa showed me how to polish them and when we were finished, they gleamed like new.

I was properly tucked and primped, with my hair neatly combed and the peach fuzz freshly shaved from my upper lip. I expected to feel silly, gussied up in clothes that I had never dreamed of owning. Like I was playing dress-up, you know? But I didn't. If anything, I felt transformed. I can't say that I was any less apprehensive about what lay ahead, but I certainly felt more confident in my appearance.

In a few hours, hundreds of strangers from all over the Four States would converge to recognize—in part—something that I had written, something that they deemed worth hearing for themselves. The honor was overwhelming.

With smiles on our faces, the Chases piled into the truck— Nicky sharing lap-space with my grandpa and me—and puttered toward the highway.

Navigating Oklahoma City's congested roadways was a bit like charging a battlefield, only the enemy cut us off and flipped us the bird instead of shooting at us. It was a highly stressful game of hurry-up-and-wait just to end up in the correct lane, not to mention the constant stop-and-go of heavy traffic. It was enough to make me carsick, and Nicky's bony butt cutting off my circulation wasn't any help. By the time we finally exited the freeway onto calmer side streets I felt absolutely green.

The awards ceremony was hosted at an upscale hotel, located in the heart of what would one day be known as Bricktown. As we pulled into the parking garage, I couldn't help but notice that ours was one of a scant few pickup trucks in sight, and probably the only one with more than a hundred thousand miles on it. At my request, we stood in the garage until I felt the world hold still.

Inside, the lobby was bustling. And huge. Fifteen foot ceilings, marble columns and floors. Hallways radiating in all directions. I had never seen anything like it. Hotel personnel herded the masses toward the banquet hall and my family followed in a nervous stampede.

Once there, we waited in line to check in at a registration table. We were each given a program and a name tag that bore the number fourteen on one corner, which turned out to be our table assignment. This was important because there must have been sixty round tables crammed into a room the size of a basketball court. Each was covered by crisp white linen and meticulously set for eight. I heard my mother catch her breath and I could understand why. It truly was a beautiful sight. I turned to check Nicky's reaction but my brother had fallen behind, sidetracked by good old Grandpa, who was making himself comfortable at the wrong table.

After the long, nail-biting drive, it was a huge relief to find table number fourteen and settle in. I did my best to relax, to collect my wits. Meanwhile, my mother *oooh*ed and *aaah*ed over the egg-white china, the ornate flatware. The cut crystal glasses and goblets that shone like jewels. Servers dressed in black tuxedos appeared with appetizers and salads. Grandpa grinned like we had won the lottery and it felt good to see him smile with such abandon.

Minutes later, the ceremony began with the telltale crackle and thump of a microphone coming to life. Monotonous introductions were made, speeches were delivered. Entrees were served. The audience clapped and fell silent when respectively appropriate. I must've unconsciously tuned the whole thing out because I didn't even hear my own introduction. If my mother hadn't been there to squeeze my shoulder, I might've remained in a trance until they gave up on me.

The walk from table fourteen to the small stage was just shy of forty feet, though it was a mile to me with a few hundred strangers watching my every move. Mercifully, I negotiated the clusters of tables without tripping over my feet or toppling any of the dessert carts now making the rounds. Along the way, I heard the usual gasps as onlookers caught their first glimpses of me; but I expected nothing less.

Onstage, a woman with hair like a bruised bowling ball shook my hand while another presented me with an engraved plaque and an envelope containing my winnings. A photographer pounced from the shadows to blind me with her flash—not once, not twice, but three times—and then disappeared into the darkness from whence she came.

"And now, ladies and gentlemen, Mr. Lincoln Chase and his poem, *The Lily*. I'm sure it will move each of you as it did the judges."

Speaking of movements, my guts were churning like a bowl of eels. When compiling a list of potential disasters, apparently I failed to consider the very real possibility of involuntary diarrhea. Oh, boy. This could get interesting.

One of the ladies gave me a gentle nudge toward the lectern and suddenly I was alone in the spotlight. Approaching the mahogany stand, I discovered with dismay that my notes weren't with me. They remained at my table, propped against the rim of my salad plate. And though I gave telekinesis a fair shot, those index cards refused to flutter into my open hands by the power of my mind. Panic swelled and for a brief moment, bolting off stage seemed like the most logical solution. But I couldn't do that. Not with my family watching, so full of pride. So invested in getting me this far. I closed my eyes and took a deep breath. It helped.

I placed my award on the lectern and adjusted the microphone. Taking a quick glance around the room, I found that I could barely swallow. The stage lights made soft silhouettes of my family yet I could still make them out. Their presence calmed me. I considered all that we had been through together, all the strife and sorrow. I felt strangely fortified by those extraordinary experiences, which served to put this brief event into proper perspective. In the grand scheme of this life, my time on this stage—for all my anxiety—was nothing worth sweating over.

It would be inaccurate to say that I became magically at ease in front of all those people. Yet while my stomach still hated me, I did feel more composed. My senses seemed to sharpen, my thoughts slipped into crystalline clarity. I ran through the poem in my mind and realized that I didn't need any notes after all.

I leaned in to the microphone and began to speak—clearly, but with an uncontrollable waver of timidity. I was suddenly grateful for all those hours spent reading aloud to my grandfather. Not only had they refined my diction, they had forced me to make peace with the eeriness of hearing my own voice.

I didn't bother with an introduction, which would've been redundant. I opened directly into my poem, concentrating on taking my time and feeling the words. The stanzas fell from my lips effortlessly, like trickling water. I allowed myself to bask in their serenity without a thought for my listeners, and soon the tremor left my voice.

These weren't merely words committed to memory, I realized. Nor were they mystical extensions of the wandering tree or Pruitt Rock. They were part of me. And reciting them now, despite the venue, didn't feel like an exhibition at all; it felt like a heartfelt confession to the one who had captured my heart, whether or not she was here to witness it.

As I spoke, the low murmurs and clinking of silverware ebbed and eventually ceased. The room seemed to hold its breath so that my voice echoed from every surface. I was alone with the universe, praising the greatest of its creations. It was surreal.

When I was finished, the throw of my voice withered into dead silence. The sudden vacuum of sound in a room so full of people was unnerving. Backlit by stage lights, it was as if the audience had turned to paper cutouts, inanimate and completely void of reaction. Had I done something wrong? Was the microphone even on? Oh, dear God, please don't let my fly be open! Panic took hold of me and it was all I could do to gather my winnings and walk off stage without running.

I was halfway back to my table before the applause began. By then, my cheeks were burning like hot coals and my pace had quickened outside of my control. My mother met me in the aisle with a proud embrace and a fierce kiss on the cheek. Grandpa's eyes were wet, his mouth cupped in a giant arthritic hand. Nicky was clapping for all he was worth, bouncing at the knees the way tweeners do. Glancing down, I confirmed that the barn-door was closed.

All was well with the world. I grinned, victorious, and dropped into my seat.

Eventually, the applause died down and the program resumed. I slumped between my mother and grandfather in a daze, spent. My food remained untouched. And sure enough, those stupid note cards stood on edge against a plate of spring greens, right where I had left them. I flicked them over with a trembling finger, wondering if my nerves would ever fully recover.

Gazing around the room, taking in all the people, I thought: *I can't believe I did it.* If only Jeremy had been there to see it. And Brigham too, though it hurt to think about him.

I saw her then. Ivy was five or six tables away, sandwiched between a handsome couple in their early forties. She wore a simple coral dress with spaghetti straps. Her hair was up and—um, well … she was looking at me rather intensely. She knew, of course. My poem had all but spoken her name, and I had no reason to think that she was stupid. Oddly though, knowing this didn't embarrass me in the least. On the contrary, it seemed to embolden me.

I winked.

The corners of her lips curled up slightly and one ivory cheek formed a faint dimple. She was so beautiful. I could've looked at her all day long, and not even that would've sufficed. But with that said, gazing directly into her eyes like this? Oh man. It threw my heart into a sprint that threatened to put me out.

I felt my grandfather's hand on my shoulder then and I turned to him, panting. His eyes were dry now, but sharp and clear. He was beaming and I just knew that he was about to share something heartwarming, something monumentally profound.

"You gonna eat that?" he whispered, motioning to my salad.

Sigh. "Knock yourself out, Grandpa."

Ronald was at the lectern now. My body began to hum with anticipation and a smile formed on my lips. Part of me hoped for a miracle, but I'll be honest: the rest of me was rooting for another train wreck. I know, I'm horrible.

As he began to read—no, *perform*—his short story, I felt my smile begin to droop and before long, it was hanging open in a full gape. The guy had played us at the meeting. Sure, he introduced us to Special Agent Thompson, and that part of the story remained unchanged as near as I could tell. But he had intentionally withheld the outer framework of his story, which changed the context completely. I listened in awe as Ronald's handiwork unfurled its magnificent wings and I was filled with joy for his wonderful gift. Shame on me for looking down on him.

Ronald's was a story within a story—a pretty fresh concept to my mind—about a frail fourth grader named Timothy, whose encounter with a class bully ends with him locked in a broom closet. Alone all night in that tiny room, the young boy befriends a curious mouse who he names Special Agent Thompson. Timothy passes the night inventing adventures for his little friend, who listens just out of reach under a rack of cleaning supplies.

The inner story, as narrated by the little boy, was just as silly as I remembered. Conversely, the outer story was beautifully written and deeply moving. They were night and day, yet to my bafflement, there was nothing lost between them. The two had been weaved together with expert precision in a fashion that I would never have expected to work. All the details that had struck me as ridiculous before were now cast in a new light: sweet and endearing and distinctly authentic to young Timothy's rowdy imagination.

I marveled at Ronald's effortless transitions from polished omniscience to childlike narrative and back again. I found myself laughing in all the right spots, even while my eyes teared up for the sake of that little boy, abandoned in a dreadful closet.

This was a dark brand of comedy that I had never encountered before. It was sophisticated and layered. It was absolutely hysterical at times yet poignant throughout. And Ronald had somehow managed to squeeze all that into fifteen pages.

The guy was brilliant. How in the world had that gone overlooked?

NINETEEN

A few days after the awards banquet, I knocked on my grandfather's bedroom door with a brand new hardback under my arm. The competition might have run its course, but I hardly needed an excuse to spend time with the old man anymore. All things considered, our reading routine had become the highlight of my day. School would resume in less than two weeks and though I hated to think the worst, I suspected that homework would soon crowd out our time together. Until then, I meant to make the best of it. And that evening I really thought that I had just the ticket.

You see, in weeks past—despite the disparity of our generations—Grandpa and I had finally landed on common literary ground, and his name was John Grisham. We devoured the guy's books like banana bread, which is to say: with enormous gusto and a barely contained urge to finish the whole thing in a single sitting. Naturally, I expected the old man to squeal with girlish delight at the long-awaited arrival of a new release—I mean, I certainly had—but while Grandpa did reward it with an appropriate measure of wide-eyed interest, he also waved it off.

I couldn't believe it.

"Tomorrow maybe?" he offered in apology. "Something I wanna show you tonight." He swallowed then and a look of sadness overtook him as he added, "You know, before I forget."

My expression sagged. Sure, I wondered what all this fuss was about but I was considerably more confounded than curious. I gave a noncommittal shrug and under the circumstances, that was truly the best I could manage.

Reaching under the bowed frame of his bed, my grandfather produced an old shoebox. It was familiar to me, though I had never actually seen inside it. He lifted the lid slowly, reverently, revealing an odd assortment of mementos: old coins, a silver thimble, a bit of red string tied in a circle, faded pictures—you name it. In the midst of them, a thin bundle of letters lay on edge, bound loosely with coarse twine. Grandpa sifted through them, slipping one free with unusually deft fingers. It was heavily worn, yellowed with the patina of many years.

"Ain't much of a poem," he acknowledged, voice wavering just above a whisper. "Never was much of a writer. Not like you."

My mouth turned to sand. Most days Grandpa struggled to recall what he had eaten for lunch, yet this conversation seemed premeditated to me. He must've planned it, and that hinted at … what exactly? I honestly couldn't say. I gazed at the letter in his hands, mystified. The remnants of my frustration began to fall away like dead leaves and I gave Grandpa a nod of encouragement.

As my grandfather began to read, the skin on my arms began to tingle pleasantly. The words he had written so long ago were refreshing in their old-world sincerity. Likewise, his reading of them now was wonderfully unrehearsed. His voice rattled as if through a bag of marbles and I hung on every syllable, mesmerized. John Grisham could wait.

It was a love poem, written for my grandmother during their courtship some sixty years earlier and reclaimed after her passing. The sentiments that my grandfather had put to paper were plain but heart-wrenchingly beautiful. Poetry in its purest form, free from the burden of calculated profundity. Indeed, the truth laid bare rarely needs decoration.

Hearing my grandfather's intimate thoughts from across the decades, seeing the tenderness with which he handled that treasured page, I was overcome with love for him. I felt immensely privileged that he would share something so personal with me, exposing a side of his character that I imagined few had seen.

When Grandpa was finished, he folded the letter and draped it beside him on the bed. His face was a flickering menagerie of emotion; there was the pain of loss, that much was clear. But there were other things too, some more obvious than others. Regret, loneliness. Fear. Gratitude, even.

My heart swelled with compassion for my grandfather, a man who had loved and lost so dearly. I wanted to comfort him, but as they tended to do without a pen in my hand, words failed me. Before I could second-guess the urge, I leaned forward and wrapped my arms around him. This was a first for me, hugging my grandfather, and I more than half expected him to push me away. But he didn't. Powerful hands pulled me into an embrace that all but swallowed me and for a long moment, time seemed to stand still.

"Can't always remember your name, kid," the old man whispered, "but don't let that fool you." He chuckled then and with my ear to his chest, it sounded like a brook gurgling up from a spring. Smiling, I felt the sting of gathering tears. I let them come. Thick fingers tousled my hair and my grandpa said, "You're my son and I love you. Always will."

Have I mentioned how lucky I was to have Ms. Winters at my disposal? Not only did she keep me in constant supply of fresh reading material, her ability to match books with my bipolar whims—not to mention Grandpa's—was uncanny. In the days following the banquet, I visited the library nearly every afternoon—sometimes more than once—in hopes that Ivy and I might fatefully cross paths. I know, you don't have to say it—I wasn't leaving much room for serendipity; but honestly, what else was I supposed to do? Anyway, if Ms. Winters was bothered by my borderline excessive use of the facility, she was kind enough to grin and bear it. But for the record, the woman was nobody's fool.

A week before school resumed, my favorite librarian pulled me aside with a grin that was at once coy and needling. "Guess who came in yesterday?" she teased. "Strolled in not five minutes after you left."

I could've played dumb or even feigned indifference. That's what a cool kid would've done, I'm sure. But let's face it: I wasn't cool. And I was too excited to bother faking it. "Really? What did she check out?"

Ms. Winters snickered, planting loose fists on ample hips. "Now Lincoln, you know I can't tell you that. Patrons are entitled to their privacy."

I felt my smile deflate a little.

"She asked about you, though. I can tell you that much."

Hearing this, my body jolted as if gouged by a cattle prod. The feeling dissipated almost immediately though, and something else crept in to take its place. Something sickly and doubtful, self-loathing.

"Wanted to know who the scarecrow was at the banquet?" I smirked. My mother never let that kind of remark slide, so I'm not exactly sure why I expected Ms. Winters to. Naturally, she didn't. In fact, her eyes flashed so angrily that I really thought she might smack me.

"Don't you dare talk like that," she admonished. There was an unfamiliar seething in her voice, fire in her eyes. "I really hoped you might learn a little something from Justin McLeod but I can see that you haven't."

I was genuinely contrite but also taken aback. "Who?" Sure, the name rang a bell, but it was a distant clang, muffled and detuned by time.

"*The Man Without a Face*, Lincoln. A gentleman who was much worse off than you, if you'll recall."

Sails deflating, I said nothing. She was right. Well, half right. The book had affected me greatly, in fact, completely changing the angle of my outlook. But developing a brand new concept of self doesn't happen overnight. I had a very long way to go.

McLeod had decades of maturity over me, by the way. More importantly though, he had the distinct advantage of being a fictional character. Only a librarian would fail to make these distinctions, and only an old maid would think of holding an adolescent to such an unreasonable standard.

My face must have revealed all because Ms. Winters groaned, laying a tentative hand on my arm. "Oh my goodness. I'm so sorry, Lincoln. That came out harsher than I intended." A hand went to her chest, fingers splaying over the hollow of her throat. "I just wish you could see yourself the way others do. The way *I* do."

I opened my mouth to speak and then clamped it shut, biting off another self-mutilating remark. I was suddenly full of them. They were breeding, multiplying by the second. Even as I struggled to put one out of my head, another appeared in line to take its place.

"It's okay," I finally managed. "Believe me, I get that people are capable of seeing past the way I look. But the thing is, they usually don't."

A pained expression swooped across her brow. "Well, I for one hardly even notice those little scars," she declared. "And I can think of someone else who doesn't seem bothered by them."

"Uh-huh."

Ms. Winters showed me her palms, exasperated. "Well, why else would she be asking questions about you?"

I shrugged, feeling my temperament cool a little. "Guess that depends on what kind of questions she was asking, doesn't it?"

"Good point. Let's see. She wanted to know what school you go to and what grade you're in. And how old you are."

"And you told her all that?" My smile was trying hard to return now but I fought it.

Ms. Winters gave me a guilty cringe. "Well, you know me. Sometimes things sort of slip out before I can stop them. I have these senior moments, I suppose, when I'm inclined to share a little more than I probably should." Ms. Winters was easing back into good form, just as I was. She threw up her hands, the corners of her eyes bunched with amusement. *What can you do?*

I couldn't help but laugh. "Just so I understand," I quipped, "patron privacy is important to you—just not mine. That sound about right?"

"Pretty much." She winked and her tongue formed a tent in the pocket of her cheek. "No such thing as privacy when you're a celebrity, Lincoln. Might as well get used to it."

"Yeah, right." I growled, mostly in jest. "So what exactly *can* you tell me?"

"Hm. Seems like she may have shared an interesting observation or two."

"Dear Lord, you're killing me. What did she say?"

Ms. Winters became infuriatingly blithe, picking absently at her cardigan—standard librarian attire, as near as I could tell—for invisible balls of lint. "Oh, just that you're sweet. And *very* talented."

My ears burned and for a few seconds, I could hear the swoosh of my own pulse. "Huh. And how would she know that?" Like I didn't already know.

"Well, your poem, of course."

Nodding, I fell into silence. The truth was, while this new information filled me with nervous excitement, I didn't have any idea what to do with it. Love was a mystery. And as it turned out, I was a pretty crappy detective.

Ms. Winters glanced at her watch and her gray eyes brightened. "Would you look at that? Break time! Come with me, let's chat. Unless you have somewhere to be?"

I did not.

I followed her to the staff break room, where she fetched two Cokes from an olive-colored refrigerator. We claimed the only couch and settled in to shoot the breeze.

In a writing competition that encompassed four states, what were the odds that two thirds of the first place winners would hail from the same small town? I had no idea. Hadn't even considered it, come to think of it. But Ms. Winters had, and she remained fascinated by the subject. Listening to her prattle on, a warm and fuzzy feeling began to overtake me.

This was a real treat for me, having an adult conversation that didn't center on what was for dinner or how we were going to pay the electric bill. Too, pop was a luxury—especially the name brand stuff, which tasted almost nothing like the cola-flavored Shasta my mother bought on special occasions. And let's not forget that eating or drinking in the library was strictly forbidden. *I could get used to this*, I remember thinking.

Ah, the burden of celebrity.

Sadly, all good things must come to an end. In this case, they began a downward spiral with what must've been intended as a compliment.

"You know, you have your father's eyes," Ms. Winters observed. "Anyone ever tell you that?"

I froze as my stomach performed some kind of round off back handspring. I tried to swallow. "You knew my dad?" My voice cracked, betraying the emotional peril of indulging this conversation.

"You say that like he's dead, Lincoln." Her chuckle was too lighthearted. I let it go but took note. "He was a student of mine," she explained. "A pretty good one, as I recall. A bit of a troublemaker too, but very bright." She looked at me with a mischievous squint, pausing to sip her pop before placing it at her feet. "The troublemakers usually are."

"You were a teacher?"

Her eyebrows rose. "Oh, yes. For many, many years." She chewed her lip wistfully. "You know one of the neat things about teaching in a small town is getting to see your students grow up. If you're really lucky, you get to meet their kids, too."

I thought about this for a moment, swigging my Coke and wincing as it burned down my throat. "Guess you're pretty disappointed with how my dad turned out, huh?"

Ms. Winters clicked her tongue, snatching my hand and sandwiching it between hers. They were cool, slightly moist with condensation from her drink. I didn't pull away.

"Not where you're concerned, Lincoln. Look at you and your brother. You're both good kids. Believe me, I can spot the bad ones a mile away. Finton did just fine."

I didn't know how to respond, so I didn't. I took another pull from my Coke, stifling a burp. My gaze fell to the floor where the abandoned husk of a roly-poly lay nestled in the carpet fibers. Ms. Winters gave my fingers an encouraging squeeze. I liked the motherly feel of her hand in mine. It emboldened me though, when perhaps it shouldn't have. Eventually, I looked up.

"Do you think I'll turn out like him?" I should've known better than to ask a question like that. The problem with fishing for validation is that you never know what you're gonna catch, and it's almost never what you were hoping for.

The smile in her eyes wavered as she considered her response. "Well, if you're asking if I believe that you're doomed to follow in his footsteps, absolutely not. But you could do a lot worse than becoming like your father. He's a kind, intelligent man with a generous heart."

"Um, okay," I said with a bit of steel in my voice. I wanted to ask how she would know but I left it at that. It was me who brought it up but I didn't like where it was going.

Ms. Winters must've sensed my unease—the air seemed thick with it—but she wasn't ready to relent. Not yet. She was on a mission. "Listen to me, Lincoln. I can't even imagine how hard things must have been for you, but you need to understand something. Everybody makes mistakes. Some are greater than others but we all make them. Every single one of us."

I couldn't believe my ears. Was she actually making excuses for my father?

"It's all part of the human condition, Lincoln," she lectured. "People are compelled to judge each other. Sometimes for their accomplishments but usually for their mistakes. We look at a snapshot in time like it's all we need to define a person."

Deep in my gut a knot was taking form. "Maybe that's as it should be," I replied coolly. "Some mistakes are so big that nothing else matters."

Ms. Winters shrugged with a patient sort of frown. "Oh, I don't think so. There's a whole lot of living between our bad decisions. And I'm here to tell you Lincoln, the everyday moments we all take for granted? They matter. They aren't any less significant than the ones people choose to judge us for."

For all her talk about hasty judgments, it seemed to me that Ms. Winters was drawing some pretty loose conclusions about my father, especially considering that she only knew him superficially, as a teacher knows a student. It was tempting to throw that in her face because part of me wanted desperately to lash out. To hurt someone the way I was hurting just then, even if she didn't really deserve it.

Instead, I stood up, releasing her hand. "We've been here a while," I mumbled. "Your break's probably over by now."

Her composure flickered but held its ground. "Now hold on, Lincoln. Please don't be upset. I don't mean to put my nose in your business. It's just that … well, I've come to care about you very much. You're a very special young man. And I have to believe that God brought you into my life for a reason."

The knot was growing, extending to my extremities. What was this? Some sort of weird, misguided intervention? Was she pretending to be my friend for … for what, exactly? To convert me to Christianity? My eyes darted to the door and back.

"I think I better go."

"Just hear me out, okay? I know this is tough to talk about. But you've got to consider the big picture, Lincoln. Your father made a very poor decision, and nothing's gonna change that." Leaning forward, she fixed me in a wide-eyed gaze. "But I'm betting he's made a million good decisions in his life, too. I just don't want you to forget about those. They're still important."

Even angry, I knew that she was at least partly right. But while it was hard to sidestep her logic, the fact remained that Ms. Winters was grossly watering down the truth. The horror of my father's actions couldn't be simplified to a *poor decision*, like splurging on ice cream when the rent still wasn't paid. He had committed the most heinous of sins, and as a result, his family had fallen to the wolves. He left me and my brother fatherless. He left us in the care of a closet alcoholic. He left … me.

He *abandoned* me.

"Why are you defending him?" I cried. I'm not exactly sure when the tears made an entrance, yet here they were. "Don't you understand what he *did*?" Even as I demanded this of her, I realized that I wasn't merely referring to what he had done to Reggie Miller. I was reaching back much farther, remembering that he had been a monster even before.

Ms. Winters stood up abruptly, dismayed. "Oh goodness, Lincoln. I am so sorry! I didn't mean to—" She took a small step forward, toeing her Coke onto its side. Brown fizz began to puddle at her feet.

My head was swimming. Was I really being too hard on my father? Was it so wrong to call him what he was—an abuser? A murderer? I didn't think so, yet my mind was flooding with doubt.

I wanted out of there, away from Ms. Winters and all her pious talk of forgiveness. I wasn't the oppressor, after all. I hadn't hurt anyone. What could she possibly know about my father anyway, other than her skewed impression of him as a schoolboy? He was a stranger to her. To all of us.

Being in that little room with her was suddenly more than I could handle. Ms. Winters said something else in apology, but I was halfway through the door before it left her mouth.

I'd like to tell you that my day got better from there. I wish from the bottom of my heart that it had.

As I rounded the horseshoe of Lakeview Park, still wounded and seething, despite the fifteen minute walk home, I was stunned by the looming of an ambulance in my driveway. The lights were off, as was the siren, yet its stillness was no less foreboding. Crowding the weedy lane with its considerable girth, it affected me like some beast sleeping off a bloody meal. At the sight of it, my breath snagged in my throat. Even as I tried to process the implications of what I was seeing, my feet were already slinging gravel in a mad dash.

Bounding up the porch steps, I heard crying inside. Not yelps of physical pain but the visceral wailing of wounded souls. I hesitated at the half-open door, terrified to go in. God help me, I just didn't want to know what I would find in there.

My mother spotted me through the opening, though, and when our eyes met, I knew at once that the truth was world-shattering. She surged into motion, upending the coffee table in a desperate scramble to reach me. With a guttural cry, she ragdolled me inside, into her frantic embrace. Her face was a shiny ruin of tears and smeared mascara, and it broke my heart to see her so distraught. Beyond us, Nicky was slumped on the couch, heaving sobs into the palms of his hands.

I looked around anxiously but I could do the math. I went numb. Not physically, exactly. My self awareness seemed to detach from the rest of me so that I was trailing a half-second behind the present, like the tail of a comet.

"What happened to him?" an echo of me asked. My mother wailed incoherently in reply, her face buried in the crook of my neck.

A paramedic appeared from the back of the trailer. Seeing me, he approached and introduced himself. I barely heard him at first—didn't even catch his name, in fact—but that's not to say that he didn't have my attention. There was a distinct wariness in his movements that reminded me of an abused dog, and I couldn't help but notice that he hovered just outside of our reach. And if I'm not mistaken, he kept a particularly keen eye on my mother. She smelled like last night's empty bottle and it wasn't hard to imagine that she had become unruly at some point.

"Um, our best guess is that your grandfather had a stroke or some kind of cardiac event," the medic explained. "It's hard to say for sure."

"Is he ... dead?" I asked, still in a latent cloud.

What's-his-name swallowed visibly, grim-faced. "I'm afraid so, son. He was deceased on arrival. I'm truly sorry for your loss."

Looking in his eyes, I got the sense that he had seen more than his fair share of death. But like me—and in spite of his occupation—this guy was nowhere close to making peace with it. I appreciated his sincerity, even if it didn't change a thing.

"We're gonna need to transport him now," he said with a bow of contrition. I'm not sure why, but that cut right through the shock. I felt the numbness burn away in an instant, exposing the sharp grit of reality.

They were taking Grandpa away.

My eyes shot down the hallway toward the old man's room. Just outside the door, another paramedic was trying to wrestle my grandfather onto an oversized stretcher. The trailer shuddered with his effort and a picture fell from its perch on the wall. It struck the floor and shattered, ignored.

There wasn't room for two people to pass in the bottleneck of that hallway, much less an emergency stretcher sized for someone like Grandpa. In life, my grandfather had learned to pivot slightly at the hips to negotiate the passage; even then, it had always been a tight fit. These guys needed a new plan, even if they didn't realize it yet.

It didn't take long for them to reach a similar conclusion and at first I was reassured. But when the stretcher was finally cast aside and the paramedics began to drag my grandfather down the hall by his arms, I was horrified. On some level, I knew there wasn't any alternative but on another, I kept expecting my grandfather to look back at me for help, as if his death wasn't a definitive condition but a phasing out that should allow a few last-minute bouts of animation. And it was incredibly rude to drag the partly-dead around like an old tarp.

Grandpa's enormous shoulders grated against the walls, snicking against grooves in the faux wood paneling like knuckles on a wet washboard. His head lolled with each jostle.

I couldn't watch.

Turning away, I tried to wipe that image from my mind. But it was burned in. My mother was quiet now, reaching out now and then to wipe a tear from my cheek. Her anguish had begun to recede and I was relieved to see some maternal instinct fill the void.

We shuffled over to Nicky, and I honestly couldn't say who was leading who. Dropping to one knee at his feet, I wrapped my arms around my little brother, nestling my forehead into his hair.

My mother squeezed in, kneading his back and crooning in a soft, soothing whisper.

If Nicky registered our presence at all, he didn't show it. He was a vessel in turmoil, heaving and shivering against forces that couldn't be seen. Forces that had always been there with us, the Chase family, hanging back in the shadows until the time was right. I could almost hear them now, rejoicing in our suffering. It made me sick.

In the end, my grandfather was evacuated through the back door, hoisted with grunts and groans onto a waiting gurney. The exhausted paramedics left a trail of fallen pictures and knick-knacks in their wake. There was no sense in reclaiming these; they were tainted now, a mixed bag of keepsake debris whose sentiments were lost to the memory of this terrible, terrible day.

The whole house was tainted, if you asked me. It always had been.

TWENTY

The funeral was unexpectedly crowded. The pews filled shortly after the doors opened at the Byron Hill Funeral Home, leaving any stragglers to pile up at the back. I knew that my mother made some phone calls; I was with her when she camped out at the laundromat payphone, crouched in a folding chair with a handful of quarters. From the tattered pages of an address book, she dialed the numbers of distant relatives—complete strangers to me—and shared the awful news over and over, until only a few quarters remained. These were reserved for the McAlester State Penitentiary, I knew.

I took a walk during that last call, though I doubted my mother would actually get my father on the line. Last I checked inmates didn't have phones in their cells. Anyway, how things snowballed from a few phone calls to a roomful of unfamiliar faces was beyond me.

Grandpa's remains had been cremated. I'd like to tell you that we made this decision in accordance with my grandfather's wishes but the truth is that he never shared his wishes with any of us. Given the exorbitant cost of caskets and burial plots, cremation was the only affordable option. If he was somehow present in spirit, I hoped that Grandpa would forgive our callous practicality.

In place of a casket on the podium, an enlarged photograph of Grandpa rested on an easel, flanked by several potted plants that looked suspiciously like plastic replicas. I couldn't take my eyes off that photo. My grandfather must've been in his early twenties when it was taken. Dressed handsomely in a dark suit, he looked happy; full of boyish mischief, despite the emerging burdens of adulthood. A young man entering his prime. At the risk of sounding ungrateful, I wished that I could've seen that side of him.

A rotund preacher in a ridiculous suit led the ceremony. As near as I could tell, he was a toss-in with the budget funeral package—the best Grandpa's puny Social Security benefits could swing—as opposed to an ordained minister. The man annoyed me even before he said a word, and it only got worse once he opened his smug mouth.

He held a series of note cards, which he consulted frequently. I'm not sure why he bothered. His anecdotal recounting of my grandfather's life, based loosely on details provided by me and my mother, was littered with unnecessary—if not blatantly offensive—hyperbole. Grandpa's brief service in the army as a mechanic, for example, was recast as the heroic adventures of an unsung war hero. The preacher reminisced with an air of easy familiarity, as if he and my grandfather—a man he had never met—had been old friends. It was infuriating.

Everything about the guy rubbed me the wrong way. His greasy comb over. The way certain consonants whistled through the hollows of his tea-colored dentures, like wind gusting at the mouth of a cave. The way he casually leaned on the frail lectern, causing it to bow. I felt a stirring of intense bitterness within and I tried to stifle it. Honest to God, I did. But just as a spider fondles an insect trapped in silk, my emotions were toying with me and there was no fighting them off.

When the sleaze finished his speech, he tossed his notes on the lectern and swaggered to a pew. A middle-aged lady with troweled on makeup and hair like a puffed up lion's mane began to bumble through a dusty hymn on a pipe organ. The clumsiness of her unpracticed—and therefore disrespectful—performance set my insides to smoldering. Every sour note seemed to notch up the heat and before long, I felt that I was going to burst into flame. This whole ceremony had become a blasphemy against my Grandpa.

Something had to be done.

My mother sniffled on my left and I patted her hand instinctively. Next to her, Nicky sat rigidly with his hands curled into tight fists. Their gazes were cold and distant—disgusted too, I realized—just as I knew mine must be. Heedless of my better sense, and before I could think to second-guess myself, I rose and stormed past them to the podium. I snatched the preacher's stupid note cards off the lectern and crumpled them into a single wad. The organ cut off, plunging the room into awkward silence.

I waited for the usual collective gasp over my disfigurement but for once, it didn't come. Apparently, my little tantrum had dulled their senses.

"Some of you knew my grandfather," I began. "Maybe you grew up with him. Maybe you met him once or maybe you came with someone else who knew him." I let my gaze settle on the now uncomfortable preacher. "Maybe you were just counting on some free hors d'oeuvres."

An indignant murmur swept across the room but I didn't care. Well almost. I glanced at my mother to gauge her dismay and was relieved to find none. Her face, while tear-streaked, was serene like wet porcelain. She smiled gently, perhaps relieved that someone was daring to voice what she had been thinking herself.

"I hope you won't mistake my candor for crudeness," I said with somewhat less force. "I mean no disrespect. But whatever your reason for coming, I'd never forgive myself if even one of you walked out of here without hearing something *real* about my grandfather."

I paused then, grasping at memories like elusive fireflies; in the heat of the moment, they were dang hard to catch. And once I had one in hand, it was even harder to put into words. So in the absence of profundity, I turned my attention to the day-to-day moments. Admittedly, they were pretty mundane. But combined, they formed the texture of my grandfather's personality in his final months.

"Grandpa liked his eggs a little runny," I said. There were a few nervous snickers as I considered my next comment. I wanted to keep it light if possible. "He liked the Price Is Right, and he preferred it full blast." A muffled guffaw burst from the second row, and then more silence.

I looked around the room, marveling that I recognized none of these people. "He liked books; almost as much as me." I heard grief creeping into my voice but I pressed on. "John Grisham was a recent favorite, but Grandpa loved cowboys and spies."

The tone of my thoughts began to shift, perhaps derailed by that bittersweet memory. "He woke early every morning wondering where he was and who we were."

Crap. So much for keeping things light.

Fading fast, the levity of moments ago hung in the air like the bloom of a firework. I wanted to focus on the good times, if for no other reason than to blur the bad ones, but it seemed that self-pity had me firmly by the tongue. "I can count on one hand the number of times Grandpa remembered my name."

I was crying now. From the corner of my eye I saw the tear-distorted form of my mother approaching. I thought she was going to steer me off stage like some drunken relative at a wedding reception. I don't suppose that anyone would've have blamed her, least of all me, yet she didn't lead me away. She took my hand, smiling through her own grief, and stood proudly beside me.

"Keep going, honey," she whispered. The comfort of her presence, the strength of her fingers gripping mine—they lifted my spirits. I felt some of the bitterness lose traction.

"But even when he couldn't remember who I was, Grandpa was always kind to me."

"Yes, he was," my mother affirmed.

My breath hitched and I almost lost it. I swallowed, then tried again. "Grandpa liked his coffee black with two heaping teaspoons of sugar. He wrote poems to my grandmother and—" My voice faltered as a thick sob engulfed me, and it was all I could do to catch a breath.

"Papa had the most beautiful singing voice," shared my mother. This was news to me and for some reason, imagining it made me cry even harder. "Like Bing Crosby with a bit of smoke and whiskey," she added. "I swear, he could sing the feathers off a bird."

Someone *uh-huh*ed in agreement.

"He was a cr-crack shot with a p-pellet gun," my brother offered in a breathy stammer. I wiped my eyes to look at him. Standing in the front row, Nicky was alone now, wobbling at the knees like a young fawn. The depth of his vulnerability seemed to trip a switch in me; one moment, I was reminiscing about my grandfather and the next, I was stumbling off the podium, oblivious of onlookers. I grizzlied my little brother off the floor into the protection of my arms and for a moment, everything—the need to know and understand, the chaos of biology and physics, even the slow churning of the universe—seemed to grow still.

A few wordless seconds ticked by and then it all came back to me, punctuated by the self-conscious rustling of fabric-against-fabric. Abruptly, a man whose voice I didn't recognize—a deep, husky baritone—called out from the far side of the room.

"Mannford Chase was the best poker player I ever met. For years, I suspected him of cheating but I could never prove it. Turns out I'm just terrible at cards." A husky laugh, tapering into a nervous cough. "And I think Manny had a nose for sniffing out a bluff." There was a murmur of amused agreement, followed immediately by another tribute.

"Mannford once beat me up over a pack of cigarettes," reported a man whose gravelly voice confirmed that he had indeed done his fair share of smoking. "Then he bought me a beer and a bag of ice. He never was one to hold a grudge for long."

Just like that, the ball was rolling.

The room was suddenly aflutter with testimonials. Most were brief and humorous, a few on the serious side. Each was moving in its own way. What little I knew about my grandfather was rapidly filling in, developing curves and angles where there had previously been empty space. The resulting mosaic honored a man who had been loved and adored, even admired, in life. And knowing that— realizing that my grandfather's life hadn't always been a miserable struggle—soaked right through the pain like a soothing salve. To feel joy like that in a heart so full of sorrow? Wow, what a strange sensation. It was beautiful and paradoxical; it was the last thing I expected from a funeral.

Across the aisle, an obese woman grunted to her feet. "Manny mowed my lawn two summers in a row after my husband passed away," she wheezed. "He wouldn't accept a penny in return. He even paid for the gas."

Just behind me, an elderly woman with long silver hair announced, "Mannford was one big fella, that's for sure. He knocked over my shed back in nineteen seventy five just by leaning on it."

The man next to her—her husband, I presumed— admonished her in a hiss that was just loud enough for us to hear. "Why you gotta bring that up? Thing was barely standing! And he helped build us a new one, didn't he?"

Those of us in earshot chuckled.

"Who are all these people?" Nicky whispered.

Shaking my head in wonder, I looked back to the podium, where my mother stood with a hand over her mouth. She caught my gaze and we both laughed.

An hour after the ceremony concluded, while most of the attendees were still socializing, the Chase family made a polite exit. I got the feeling we were supposed to stick around, but we were too exhausted—or perhaps too uncultured—to give funeral etiquette much consideration. We needed time to heal as a family. To rest and be sad, even angry. To break things and cuss if needed, without an audience present to reinforce what proper grieving was supposed to look like.

Outside the funeral home, cars overflowed the parking lot into neighboring streets, lining the curbs for a block or more in every direction. Everywhere I looked, Texas license plates stared back at me. Though strangers to us, the owners of these vehicles had loved and respected my grandfather. Many had been a part of his life before I was even born. And bless their hearts, they had driven all the way from Texas to honor their old friend.

I was tremendously grateful. And a little envious, if I'm being completely honest. Of their time with Grandpa during the best years of his life.

We drove home in awed silence, a brass urn resting in my lap. I knew perfectly well that the ashes within weren't really my grandpa anymore, but it comforted me to have them as a sacred reminder. At home, I cried some more but the bitterness had fled.

For a while, anyway.

TWENTY ONE

Jeremy's mother dropped him by later that week, the day before school started. Eager to expand on his talent, a muscled-up adolescent had departed for baseball camp a few months earlier. To my dismay, a complete stranger seemed to have returned in his place.

Don't get me wrong, Jeremy still looked like the same old Jeremy. Except for the flesh around his eyes, that is, which sagged in olive folds as if he hadn't slept in days. But baggy eyes could easily be explained by the intense rigors of athletic camp or even a stressful trip home. The real change in him was much more difficult to define, yet impossible to ignore; it shimmered in and out of resolution like a fish floundering in burbling shallows.

There were lingering indicators, though. In and of themselves, they revealed nothing. But in the lulls between shimmers, when it was possible—theoretically, anyway—to forget what I had seen, those unsightly emblems reminded me that all was not as it should be.

Jeremy's gaze, for example—once piercingly and fiercely inquisitive—was now dull, indifferent; sapped dry of any youthful spark as if my old friend was no longer himself but rather a hollowed out approximation of himself. I might've chalked this up to teenage angst if Jeremy had ever been the sort to brood. But brooding was "the hallmark of entitled pansies"—his words, not mine.

I wanted to confront him right away, to put a name—or even a face—to his condition but that wasn't to be. Upon Jeremy's arrival you see, Nicky was all over him like a fly on stink, begging—and I do mean begging, complete with praying hands and a screeching, *"Pleeeeease?"*—for an exhibition of Jeremy's freshly-honed skills. It would be our last brush with freedom before school tied us up for the year, Nicky pleaded, and since Jeremy didn't appear to care either way, the onus was on me to be the hero or the party pooper.

So we plodded onto Pruitt Field, dragging our beaten up gear toward the overgrown ball diamond, whose crude geometry probably resembled a primitive hieroglyph from the air. The Pete Rose die-hards of Lakeview Park must've been glued to their windows that day because they began to trickle on-field mere seconds behind us; within minutes, they were picking teams. My heart sank a little, I'm not gonna lie.

Tossing the ball around with Nicky and Jeremy was one thing, but I was useless for much else. Reluctantly, and perhaps wisely, I bowed out before I could humiliate myself, moseying out to the wandering tree where I could watch from the shade. The ground was mounded here and there by careless meteorite hunters. Someday, I really hoped that I would catch one of them in the act, though I didn't have a clue what I might actually do if that was to happen.

Jeremy's abilities had compounded—that much was obvious right away. He pitched with pinpoint accuracy, striking out the side in no time flat. And when it was his turn at the plate? Good grief, the guy was like a god: nothing had a chance of getting by without his expressed blessing. Even from a distance though, his lack of zeal was hard to miss. He played like some kind of robot, programmed to perform a wide range of specific movements— fluidly and perfectly timed, in all fairness, but without a trace of competitive flair. He might as well have been shucking corn out there or raking leaves. Nicky and his friends were like fumbling toddlers by comparison, but at least they showed some heart.

Something was very wrong with this picture and I suspected that it went beyond exhaustion.

Jeremy and I walked to McDonald's that afternoon, a twenty minute stroll that paraded us past Hembry's Auto Salvage and down a creepy, dumpster-lined alley behind the new Food 4 Less. "Sorry about your grandpa," Jeremy offered along the way. "I had no idea." He glanced at me sidelong, hesitantly. "Not to be callous, but I honestly didn't think you guys were that close."

It was a pretty callous observation, as a matter of fact—however true—but Jeremy's bluntness was rarely meant to be hurtful, so I shrugged. "It was a long summer. A lot happened while you were gone."

His brow rose. "Oh, yeah? Like what?"

For the next several minutes, I brought Jeremy up to speed on the writing competition, describing how it consumed my life for most of the summer, and how it indirectly cultivated an unlikely friendship with my grandfather. Jeremy grunted and *huh*ed now and then, nodding in all the right spots, yet I couldn't shake the feeling that he wasn't really listening. He was half with me at best. Just going through the motions.

We made the rest of the walk in silence, and that was fine by me.

Apparently starved, Jeremy ordered more food than any one person should ever eat without the prospect of winning a substantial prize. "Camp was brutal, man," he lamented. "Can't even remember the last time I had a decent meal. Been dreaming of a fat Double Quarter Pounder all summer."

"So the plan is to eat one for every month you were gone?"

"This is America, buddy," he reminded me. "We don't eat; we binge." He chuckled then, flashing me those dead eyes. The forced, artificial quality of his animation caused me an inward cringe and I had to look away. But at least his wit was still intact, for whatever that was worth.

Anyway, even in America capitalism had its dark side: not everyone could afford to binge. I settled for a cheeseburger and a small order of fries, paying—to the sheer joy of our cashier—with a handful of loose change. We slid into a window booth, which offered drab views of a trash-speckled juniper hedge and a line of cars inching by in the drive-thru lane. Just beyond the parking lot traffic crawled by with fair weather lackadaisy and I realized with melancholy that today was it. My last day to be lazy, to mill around with no particular agenda. It was hard to believe, though I hadn't made up my mind if I was actually upset about it or not.

Just as he had played ball earlier, Jeremy ate with mechanical efficiency. Not the slightest sign of enjoyment or even satisfaction. Bite, chew, swallow. Slurp, swallow. The first burger was gone in less than sixty seconds. Repeat. I gotta say, it was disturbing to watch.

After his second burger, Jeremy's appetite seemed to run out of steam, thank God. "So, how does it feel to be a big time writer?" he wanted to know. "You gonna start growing a moustache and hanging out with the artsy fartsies at the community theater?"

"I doubt they'd have me. What about you? How's it feel to be Shawnee's last great hope for a championship?"

"I'm done with baseball," he muttered, stifling a belch with a fist. For a moment, I thought for sure that I had misheard him because, come on—Jeremy quitting baseball made about as much sense as McDonald's quitting the burger biz. But when I played back the moment in my head, the word *baseball* didn't magically resolve into *lunch*.

The truth is, I was more caught off guard by the flippant delivery of this bombshell than the bombshell itself, given that Jeremy tossed it in my lap without preamble or elaboration. I guess trivializing the news was supposed to water down the shock of it?

Whatever. It didn't work.

Under normal circumstances—when Jeremy wasn't acting like a complete weirdo, that is—I might've held out for the punch line. I mean, he had to be messing with me, right? Jeremy had an odd sense of humor, after all; a sweet tooth for dry sarcasm—the more ironic the better—was as central to his character as Saturday morning cartoons were to mine. Come to think of it, we almost never laughed at the same joke. Nevertheless, he wasn't kidding then; I can tell you that much with certainty.

I laid my cheeseburger down, half-eaten. "What's going on with you, man? Did something happen?"

Jeremy responded with a brief hesitation, followed by a curt shake of the head. Less of a *no* than a *don't ask*. Heeding the warning—no small feat, by the way—I fought down the impulse to sink my teeth in, to bulldog the details out of him. He was supposed to be my friend, to trust me. Yet even after all that we'd been through, Jeremy couldn't bring himself to confide in me. He remained as much a stranger as a companion. It hurt, but I dropped the subject.

Well. Sort of.

"What about college?" I had to ask. "I mean, you were counting on a baseball scholarship, right?"

Jeremy fixed me with a blank expression, head cocked and lips pursed, probably waiting for a polite recant. When none ventured along, his eyebrows mounded dubiously toward the bridge of his nose. "You serious?"

"Well, yeah. I guess." One didn't need to call Lakeview Park home for college to be out of reach. Despite the pronounced gap between our respective financial standings, this was a harsh reality that kept us both in check.

Or so I thought.

Jeremy popped a rogue slice of pickle into his mouth and washed it down with the dregs of his Coke. Clearing his throat, he appraised me with a burst of steely pique. The sudden intensity of his expression—the barely contained animosity in there—froze me in mid-chew of a fry. While it was a relief to see that he was still capable of experiencing human emotion—which more or less proved that he hadn't been cloned by some alien pod creature while away—this was hardly the reaction I was angling for.

"Let's think about it for a second, Link," he suggested, implying of course that I hadn't already been thinking. "I'm sitting on a four point eight GPA." He raked spindly fingers through a scrub of unruly hair. "I've put in time with just about every academic club we have in this little pissant town." His gaze darted out the window and back with unveiled disdain. "Jeez, I've cofounded or captained more than half of them."

Oh, boy. Here we go.

"I have blue ribbons from academic competitions going all the way back to the fifth grade." Jeremy was counting off accomplishments on his fingers now, and I knew that he'd run out of fingers soon enough. "My SAT and ACT scores are the highest in school and I took them as a sophomore." His voice lowered a few decibels—because, you know: wouldn't want anyone to overhear him being a horse's rear. "Did you know I scored a thirty-five on my ACTs?"

Yeah, he might have mentioned that. But the number was meaningless to me in those days. Eventually, I would take the ACTs myself and barely manage a nineteen.

"A thirty-five puts me in the ninety-ninth percentile, nationally. The top hundredth of a percent in the state," Jeremy boasted. "And I have a good shot at a perfect score if I take it again. I mean, I still have a couple of years to get it right."

I had no retort, other than to wad up the congealed heel of my cheeseburger in its wrapper. I didn't care for his tone; it was souring my stomach.

Waving off my silence as if it was a form of rebuttal—as if this conversation was any kind of argument at all, rather than a one-sided hissy fit—Jeremy leaned forward, the tone of his voice narrowing into a laser of concentrated indignation. "I don't need baseball to rescue me, Link. I never did. My whole life, while the other kids were out fooling around?"—myself included, I had to infer—"I was studying my butt off. I've got a free ride to just about any school I want, and believe me: they don't give a crap about how well I throw a stupid baseball."

Wow, I was duly impressed. And I wanted to whip his butt, if I'm being completely honest. At a minimum, I wanted to force feed him that last burger with a pair of salad tongs. Sure, I'd been treated like this plenty of times before—like I was dense or even flat out stupid—but never by Jeremy. Some people are helplessly compelled to flex their cerebral biceps. It gives them a feeling of purpose I suppose, to brandish their genius in the faces of us lesser minds. Jeremy's restraint in this capacity had always been his most endearing quality. That he had chosen to unleash it on me now, however modest the blow, felt like a cheap shot to the gut. The kind that nearly floors you, even as you put on a tough guy face and pretend that you barely felt anything.

Nostrils flaring, I pressed into the curve of my seat back. I knew that Jeremy was troubled, that he was going through something. But in that moment, I didn't care. The guy was deliberately pushing my buttons and it didn't much matter if he thought that I had been pushing his first. "I get it, okay?" I snapped. "You're brilliant and I'm a lazy idiot."

Jeremy glared and then blinked in surprise, cheeks paling noticeably. I don't know, maybe he was developing a split personality and the part of him with the least amount of control— the kinder, more sensible part, apparently—was just catching up to the conversation. Whatever the case, his eyes squeezed shut then, chin dropping to his chest. "God, I'm sorry, Link. I'm just ... I'm just so tired."

Seeing him like that—chagrined, clearly agonizing over something that he wasn't prepared to divulge—pity outweighed my resentment. I felt the anger drain out of me almost at once. It was easy to forget that for all his genius, Jeremy was still human. Just like the rest of us, he made mistakes. More importantly, he was my friend. And I figured that anyone willing to put up with me was entitled to be a jerk once in a while.

"Forget it," I said, and meant it. "I was trying to help, believe it or not. Guess I hit a nerve, huh?"

Jeremy nodded, fingering his straw absently.

An untimely smirk began to pull at my lips. "Anyway, I wouldn't worry about it. This is America, man. We don't play baseball; we watch other guys play it on TV."

A halting snort. "Thanks, that's very patriotic of you to say." Jeremy rubbed his stomach with a groan. "Western culture at its finest, right? No wonder we're all getting fat."

We laughed and for a moment, it felt real. Like old times. Soon, though, the seconds began to pile up and that tiny bit of contentment suffocated under their collective weight.

"Gotta say, man—I really thought you'd take it all the way."

"What, the burgers?"

Ugh. That plastic smile of his was crawling back in place. I did my best to pretend that I didn't notice, but it was no less disheartening. "No, dummy. Baseball."

Jeremy sighed deeply through his nose and I swear I could actually see his good cheer fall like a tattered kite. "Yeah well. Me too," he said in a whisper. When he looked at me then, his eyes were glassy and half-lidded. The third Double Quarter Pounder lay on a plastic tray, untouched, and for a moment Jeremy looked like he might throw up at the sight of it. And it's no wonder. Two Double Quarter Pounders, large fries and a thirty-two ounce Coke would have that affect on most of us. Still, I had a feeling that the Law of Diminishing Returns wasn't the only force at play here.

What exactly had gone on at that baseball camp? It was eating me alive, not knowing. And not only because I felt entitled to know, though I sort of did. It was clear to me that Jeremy wasn't merely bored with baseball, or even jaded by the ruthlessness of peer competition. He was wounded. I wanted so badly to help him, yet I didn't have a clue how.

"The truth is, I never really loved the game the way you did," Jeremy professed, plowing through my thoughts. "I think it was a distraction for me. One of many self-improvement projects that outgrew its usefulness."

On the surface, this revelation almost made sense—Jeremy did hate to see a single ounce of personal potential squandered, after all—but I didn't buy it for a second. You don't become that good at something without loving it. You don't invest hundreds of hours to perfecting an art just for the sake of *improving* yourself. Okay, so maybe baseball wasn't his greatest love anymore—and indeed, maybe it never had been—but it had been a true passion without a doubt. This whole situation—the awkwardness between us, Jeremy's evasiveness, his volatile fuse—it was rapidly wearing me out.

"Well, let's hope Nicky doesn't lose interest anytime soon," I said, returning to what I considered to be more pedestrian conversation. "I'm counting on those major league paychecks to support a lifetime of debauchery." I grinned half-heartedly. "I think he's plateauing, though. He needs one-on-one instruction from someone who knows what he's talking about. Maybe they'll start offering scholarships for that baseball camp."

With no appetite left to speak of, my gaze had drifted to the door. I was about to suggest that we hit the road, yet before the words could reach my mouth, Jeremy was lurching to his feet. Wide-eyed and flustered—possibly angry, I realized—he loomed over me like a crackling storm cloud. My heartbeat picked up its pace. Good Lord, what had I said now?

"Uh, you okay there, buddy? What is it?"

Jeremy had paled, a fine sheen of sweat glistening on his forehead. "Lincoln, you gotta promise me something," he pleaded. No, not pleaded—*demanded*. He was beyond manners, apparently. Again. Only this time, he was barely keeping it together. He was breathing heavily through his nose now and unless my imagination was running away from me, there was an emerging hitch in the rhythm. Clearly, to deny him would be nothing less than problematic.

I shrugged warily.

"Whatever happens," he said, "you gotta keep your brother away from that baseball camp, okay? No matter what."

"Jeremy, what are you talking about? You're kind of freaking me out."

Jeremy clamped his mouth shut, swallowing audibly. The muscles of his jaw began to bulge and striate and I got the sense that he was nearing a breaking point. Whether it be spilling some beans or snapping, it was impossible to tell.

"C'mon," he muttered. "Let's get out of here."

Twenty Two

I turned fifteen and a half a month later, and wouldn't you know it? I got my first job at that very McDonald's. It was an easy walk from school, which was part of its early appeal; but the journey home was long and often painful, with my feet aching like mangled hocks of meat. I was stationed in the back of the restaurant, toasting buns and grilling frozen beef discs with the help of idiot-proof, timed cooking devices. It was hot, monotonous and deeply unsatisfying. Up to the moment when I cashed my first paycheck, I questioned my sanity for sticking around. When I felt that bundle of cash bulging in my pocket though, burning like a slug of hot gold, it all seemed worth it. The horizon seemed to open up on that day, beckoning me forth into a realm of unexplored possibility.

I was a real live consumer! What could I buy first? Seriously, if I hadn't been footing it, I might've ventured into Walmart and blown it all in a few minutes. Fortunately, I came to my senses quickly enough.

With that first paycheck, I bought a very-used garage sale bicycle for less than fifteen bucks. The remainder of my cash— something like seventy dollars—went to my mother. I took great pride in sacrificing it, especially knowing that she would never have asked for it. And it was much needed, too. Grandpa's Social

Security benefits had failed to offset the entire cost of his funeral—no surprise there—so my initial contribution went toward that. My second paycheck covered the remaining debt almost to the dollar.

True, my part-time earnings didn't amount to much—minimum wage was four twenty-five back then, and legally I could only work so many hours because of my age—but we were experts at poverty. The Chases could survive on very little or feast like royalty on just a little more. Within a month, we were getting back on our feet. There was food in the fridge—real food too, not just baloney and half-expired condiments. We finally managed to get the phone turned back on as well, something that we had done without since my father … well, for a really long time. My job might've been unsatisfying but the quality of life that it afforded me was undeniable.

For the first six months, I worked just about every Monday, Wednesday and Friday evening. With no experience in the workforce, this was an adjustment for sure, though not an unbearable one. When I turned sixteen in March, on the other hand, I got a heaping helping of unbearable. My precious Saturdays—and even the occasional Sunday—were gobbled up by the insatiable grill schedule, and there was no talking my way into their return.

Ugh.

My job, combined with a disheartening measure of homework, all but suffocated any opportunity for creative thinking. I was lucky to squeeze in a couple of reading hours during the week, for example, and those were usually snatched up in increments of fifteen minutes, holed up in the McDonald's break room. Nights off were spent at home, treading the mounting tide of homework. Funny: a few years earlier, I would never have guessed that I would waste even a moment trying.

Given the scarcity of my spare time, my literary addictions fell to the tired whims of the school library. As opposed to the public library, that is, whose collection outnumbered the school's by several hundred to one. The quality of the school collection was as dismal as it was thin. Although it hadn't always been obvious to me, it was now hard to overlook that countless works had been plucked from the shelves—for the sake of protecting our delicate little minds, of course—leaving behind a pastel wasteland ruled by The Babysitter's Club and Sweet Valley High. If not for the required reading of my English class, I might have given up reading altogether.

Things weren't all bad, though. There were still a few gems twinkling amidst the kid stuff, even if I did have to dig around for them. And pretty much anything I checked out ended up with grease spattered across its pages, courtesy of a break room that opened directly into the dish room. This seemed like some kind of justice, though against who exactly, and to what end, wasn't clear.

The school library was unexpectedly forgiving of this, incidentally. That or they were simply determined to remain oblivious—it went on far too long to go unnoticed, by my estimation. Either way, those poor ladies must've been used to seeing worse. I mean, let's face it: kids are just gross. I once observed a classmate use a slice of lunchmeat as a bookmark, so it wasn't hard to imagine that a little wear and tear, however persistent, was among the least of the school's concerns. In any case, try returning a greasy book to the public library and see what happens. I'm betting a S.W.A.T. team will beat down your door within the hour.

I befriended some coworkers, though we never actually got together out of uniform. I can't say that I learned much about them as actual people—the blare of fryer timers against the constant sizzle of frozen meat pucks wasn't exactly conducive to deep conversation—but as fellow McGrunts, they were fun and their shenanigans helped to pass the time.

In a way, I was content. I mean, sure—my passion for writing had been placed on indefinite hold, which sucked. Too, I missed Ms. Winters immensely, and it depressed me that I still hadn't managed a single conversation with Ivy. Now that I think about it, I guess my plan for long term happiness was hopelessly unresolved. But hey, I was paying my own way for the first time in my life. And I had a routine, however banal it might've seemed. Things were beginning to feel … I don't know—normal?

And if you asked me, anything *normal* was worth striving for.

Funny thing about fate: you'll never outwit it. I'd caution you not to bother trying, but who listens to me? People devote their entire lives to the cause of influencing fate. We stack the deck, skirt the outer edge of civilized behavior. We demean ourselves. Are we really so desperate to get a leg up on the world? We dream of a winning lottery ticket, a chance meeting with a talent scout, whatever—a single moment of grand fortune that could be relied on to sustain us for life. People kill themselves and sometimes others just to better their chances. Yet for all those efforts, most of us fail. Why do you suppose that is?

Because fate is the booger-flicking middle finger of the universe, that's why. And by now you ought to know how I feel about the universe.

Anyway, I think that I had more or less given up on fate showing any kindness. I was tired of crossing my fingers and being let down, over and over again. One Friday evening in mid-April though, I discovered that fate hadn't yet given up on me.

At times, the McDonald's break room was a stifling sauna, hot and unnaturally humid, packed full of sweaty old men in their skivvies—okay, kidding about that last part. The heat was especially bad during lunch rushes, when the dishwashers cranked away nonstop, billowing steam in great plumes to keep up with demand. It smelled like wet ashtray and scalded grease in there too, which did nothing to engender relaxation. The nonsmokers on crew avoided the break room as an unspoken rule, opting to haunt the restaurant house instead, where it was cool and tidy. My boss professed to have no problem with this in general, yet he branded me the lone exception.

The first time he asked me not to venture out where customers could see me, I laughed nervously, thinking it brazen that a manager would joke like that so freely. While he spoke, the guy combed a tuft of hair growing in the cleft beneath his lower lip. He referenced his reflection in a chrome paper towel dispenser, using a cutoff toothbrush that he apparently kept on hand for this exact purpose. I found the behavior so patently ridiculous that I simply couldn't take him seriously. It took a few talking-tos before I realized that he wasn't just trying to be funny.

"No offense, kid," I remember him explaining, "we're here to sell food, understand? And people aren't gonna wanna eat after seeing that face of yours." I know—classy, right? I won't even pretend that I wasn't offended, but my feelings weren't hurt much because, a) it's hard to respect the opinion of a man who brushes his facial hair with a toothbrush in public, and b) I knew that he was wrong, anyway. Maybe not completely—it would be naive to think there wasn't at least a tiny grain of truth at the heart of his tackiness—but it was hard to believe that a grown man could so easily confuse pity with disgust. Of course, I was an expert on that subject whereas narcissistic a-holes like my boss were by nature a little less discerning.

Even by today's lofty standards, Seth Faraway ranks high among the biggest jerks I've ever known. What made him so exceptional was an unflappable belief that he was better than everyone else. Not because he was older or more experienced, mind you, but because he was singularly devoted to an idea of how things ought to be and therefore *would* be on his watch. Accordingly, even on those days when the break room could be mistaken for the putrid pits of hell, Seth remained firm in his rude misguided convictions. "Suck it up kid," was his smiling mantra. "Better the break room than the alternative, trust me."

Speaking of which, there was *one* other option, even if I dared to entertain it only once.

As a matter of fact, that's how I came to be huddled against the dumpster cage at the far corner of the McDonald's parking lot. There I sulked one fateful Friday afternoon, trying to enjoy the cool spring breeze despite the prevailing rancor of the nearby grease bin.

Good stinking times.

Seth's wishes, however derisive, were the law of the land and I needed this job. So I hid like a good little circus freak, watching a never-ending line of cars snake by in the drive-thru lane with Orwell's *Animal Farm* clamped between my knees.

Under the circumstances, the book was little more than a prop and I wished that I had left it inside. It was my only redeeming bit of homework at the time, yet while I had planned to immerse myself in it, I was too humiliated to relax, much less read. My presence there by the dumpster, secreted away like some homely mistress, felt like a tragic waste of a perfectly good Saturday. But what could I do? I was a young man with few marketable skills.

A red Camaro rounded the curve and as it approached the menu board, I recognized it immediately. It was a vintage model—

never mind the year, I'm not a car buff—lovingly restored with a touch of modern flair. Neon running lights, tinted windows—even the windshield—chrome rims with glimmering spokes. In an agricultural community bustling with farm trucks and old-man sedans, the car wasn't just a thing of beauty; it was a candy-apple monument of Midwestern Americana.

It belonged to a guy named Philip something-or-other, a minor celebrity around town who was beloved by many for his accomplishments on the football field. I had met him once or twice at school, in passing only. Seemed nice enough for a rich jock. Dang cocky, but weren't they all?

Philip's windows were halfway down and a quaking loop of bass tones boomed from within, rumbling across the pavement in pressure waves that tickled my arm hairs, even from fifty feet away. I wondered if he could even hear the music—surely it lost all tone at that level—but decided that it probably didn't matter. The volume was an audible beacon as much as the car was a visual one—blasted for the sake of the deaf, blind or otherwise distracted lest anyone fail to notice the luminary in our midst.

Like I said, cocky.

Philip reached the speaker kiosk and the music dropped a few million decibels. The crown of his head peeked out and I heard him speak. The voice that reached me, though, was an unintelligible smear, not unlike the adult-speak of Charlie Brown land. He idled up to the first window and paid as a Cadillac inched forward to take his place. Up went the stereo again.

That's when I saw it.

Something that got my heart pounding because it was completely unexpected. Unlikely, even. Yet there it was, clear as day.

I jogged toward the drive-thru lane, staying the Cadillac with an open hand. At first, the driver—a somewhat poodle-ish woman in her fifties—recoiled at my approach and locked her doors. I must've been a sight to behold, running up on her car with my sweaty face gnarled up the way it was. She registered my uniform at the last second and smiled with noticeable relief, but the wariness never left her eyes.

Bound tightly by a rubber band, a large roll of cash rocked to and fro against the curb. Calling to me in the friendly way that money does. Snatching it up, I motioned the waiting Cadillac forward with a wave of apology. The driver wagged a few stiff fingers in response, hands otherwise tightly glued to the steering wheel. The way she was looking at me, despite the smile, I had the distinct feeling that she would run me over without much provocation. Uniform aside, I was a bum on her street corner.

I admonished myself—as I often did—to let it go. It was unfair to expect a complete stranger to get over my disfigurement in an instant, especially considering that I wasn't quite there yet myself. And besides—let's be honest, shall we?—I was pretty engaged in my own game of stereotyping. Flashing a thin smile, I turned away.

The wad of cash had considerable heft and as I admired the feel of it, the temptation to just pocket the thing and walk away was almost unbearable. I mean, this was more money than I had ever held in my hands and no one would've been the wiser, right? With the exception of a middle-aged woman who by all appearances just wanted out of there, anyway. Either way, this was a finders keepers world, wasn't it? Except that … I couldn't. Something in me—some stupid force that I had never been able to define—caused me to hesitate, just as it always seemed to.

Approaching Philip's car, I knocked lightly on the back windshield. I was going for nonchalance, but I nearly yelped when my knuckle left a filthy smear on the pristine glass. Even dismayed though, I resisted the urge to wipe it away. I wanted to dispel any lingering impression of vagrancy, after all, not validate it. Nevertheless, I felt the intensity of a disapproving gaze on me and I couldn't help but steal a glance at the Cadillac lady. Her head snapped away toward the brick facade of the building, and I almost laughed when she pretended to whistle.

Fascinating things, bricks.

My knock went unheard, as should've been expected. Scowling, I squeezed into the gap between Philip's car and the building. Not one of my brighter moves, as it turned out. The subsonic frequency of the bass was more focused in that confined space, penetrating deep into my body with every thump. Along with my ears, my bad arm began to ache instantly. Road mapped by the faults of old wounds, those poor bones resonated as if they were about to rattle apart. I saw Philip's silhouette in his side mirror and barked a hello, but his attention was directed inside the car. The pain was suddenly too much.

Retreat!

Backing out, I rerouted around the passenger side where I should've headed to begin with. There, the window was up and the vibrations were much more bearable. I caught a glimpse of my reflection in the tinted glass and groaned. I sported a multi-stained polo shirt and one of those oversized netted caps—you know, the one-size-fits-all variety that only manages to look fitting on truckers and lake fishermen?—both decaled with the iconic double arches. My skin shone with sweat and burger grease. A lump of something—perhaps a glob of special sauce or a soggy bread crumb—clung to my collar, and there was really no telling how long it had been there.

Cripes.

Not that I cared what Philip thought of me; I just hated to think that my beauty sleep had fallen so short. Seeing me, Philip poked his head out the window. His expression was one of mild irritation—startled at first, then blooming with recognition. An unflattering kind of recognition though, to be clear. One that did nothing to blot out irritation, but instead crowded in beside it with an indifferent sigh. The music dropped again, thank God, and the throbbing in my bones finally subsided. Seismographs all over the state of Oklahoma fell still.

Philip gave me a wary chin nod and rolled his window down the rest of the way. Ahead of us, an early model LTD stalled at the pickup window. Its back windshield was cracked, the bumper missing from its mounts. The trunk lid was skewed and bound shut by a bent up clothes hanger, which was twisted against itself in a kinky sort of noose. The starter cranked away like a wet smoker's cough and I tried not to look down on the thing. I'd be lucky to one day own a car at all, so who was I to judge, right? Still, this one clashed with the Camaro like … well, like a busted up Ford LTD clashes with a plush Camaro.

"Hey, uh … Lincoln, right? Didn't know you worked here." I couldn't imagine why he thought that he should, but Philip was undoubtedly an authority on social nuance, whereas I was not. So I smiled and tried to play along.

"Yeah, I'm easy to miss. They like to keep me hidden in the back."

An eyebrow shot up and it seemed to pull at one corner of Philip's mouth until his lips formed a charming yet wickedly crooked smile. No one was impervious to my seasoned wit, it seemed. "Right," he chuckled. "So what's up? There a problem with my order or something?"

"Oh no, nothing like that. You just dropped something back at the kiosk."

The smile drooped a tad. Looking around the interior of his car, Philip made a show of checking that everything was in order. He looked under his visor, patted his shirt pocket. Glanced behind him into the empty back seat. The whole procedure was casual, yet methodical. Oddly rehearsed.

"I don't think so, man. You sure?" He flashed a silly grin and I realized that he was playing dumb. Maybe he performed this little bit for police officers when they pulled him over, which I suspected was a common occurrence. Philip's tinted windshield and running lights weren't strictly legal, you see, even if the rules went largely ignored. And I had my doubts that Philip—or anyone else for that matter—stood a chance of keeping that car under the speed limit for long.

Philip's eyes began to twitch as I contemplated all this and it suddenly dawned on me that he looked nervous. He probably had something on him worth worrying over. A little weed, maybe. A pint of booze under the seat. Who knows? None of my business.

"Check your money, Philip."

He reached into his jacket pocket and, as expected, his hand emerged empty. I saw his face go pale, his mouth fall agape.

"It's okay, I think it's all still here." I squeezed around the hood of the Camaro to hand off the roll of bills. For a long moment, Philip stared at me incredulously and I knew what he was thinking. *This guy must be a few nuggets shy of a Happy Meal.* Believe me, I was thinking the same thing. Eventually though, Philip reached out to accept the money. Leaning in, I happened to glance through his open window, noticing for the first time that he had a passenger. When I saw her, a massive surge of blood pressure swelled into my head, launching it into the air like a rocket, where it exploded and sent brain matter across the parking lot.

Well, that's how it felt anyway.

Because while it could've been anyone in the whole world, the last person I expected to see in there was Ivy. My eyes found hers and locked in place. The rest of the world diffused and somehow blurred into the horizon. God, she was so beautiful.

A voice mumbled nearby, yet strangely distant—as if through a tunnel that stretched from my ears to some point a hundred miles away. "Holy smokes, man," it said, "you saved my life." Blushing now, Ivy broke free of my tractor beam to look at the floor. The stereo was barely audible now but her fingers hovered by her ears as if suspicious of the near silence.

I had been spoken to. I needed to respond, I knew, but it was so hard to think at that moment, looking at her. Flustered, I must've replied something like: "No problem," but I can't be sure. I could just as well have spouted: "Thing love pretty girl!" for all I knew. There was a sharp rustle of paper against paper and I turned to see Philip peeling a note off the roll. The strange novelty of that singular green ink snapped me from my trance. Extending a ten dollar bill between two fingers, Philip grinned. "For you, kind sir. Call it a finder's fee."

I swallowed with difficulty. "Oh, um, that's very nice of you. But I really can't," I muttered, and I hoped that my regret didn't bleed through. "Thanks, anyway."

I should have walked away then. Indeed, it was the socially responsible thing to do; yet try as I might, I couldn't keep my gaze from returning to Ivy. She was a vision, a creature of goddess-like perfection and who knew when I would lay eyes on her again? Whether or not she meant to, the girl had somehow harnessed the power of gravity, pulling me in with inescapable force. Something told me that she was used to this power over the opposite sex, even if she hadn't chosen it.

Philip interrupted my reverie. "Really? Suit yourself, I guess." He followed my gaze to Ivy and back; even from my periphery, the dawning of his offense was hard to miss. The glow of his wholesome persona dimmed and then seemed to blink out. Nearby, the old LTD sputtered and then gave up with a forlorn wheeze and a sudden urge to give it a kick in the tailpipe was almost too much to bear—seriously, who drives a car like that to a drive-thru? With concentrated effort, I turned to give it a glance, if for no reason other than to prove that I was still in control of my own head and neck. Because for a few seconds there, I honestly wasn't so sure.

When I looked back to Philip, I found that crooked smile of his still in place yet the landscape of his demeanor had completely changed. "C'mon, Lincoln," he jeered, and his eyes were suddenly dark and cruel, flashing like wet chips of obsidian. "Everybody knows you need it." The bill dangled from his fingertips, flapping in the wind and I wanted to yank it free so that I could shove it down his throat. Yet even as my cheeks burned hot, I knew exactly whose fault this was.

I stole a final glance at Ivy, whose eyes were now squeezed shut. For whatever it was worth, my cheeks weren't the only ones on fire. To Philip I presented a forced smile that couldn't have been very convincing. I bothered only because I didn't know what else to do; the alternatives seemed likely to escalate out of control.

Suddenly, the bucket of bolts at the pickup window came to life. And if that wasn't proof enough that miracles can happen, it began to shiver forward in a clattering fit. A plume of black exhaust bellowed from its bowels, engulfing me even as it scattered in the breeze.

"Really, Philip. It's fine," I coughed. "Do me a favor, though? Turn the stereo down a little so people can eat in peace, alright?" Then, in a burst of brilliant spite, I remarked: "Looks like your friend could use a break, too."

I walked away without waiting for a response, wishing that I had been given the foresight to call in sick that day.

Well, that could've gone better.

In the nine months since I had last seen Ivy, I must've imagined a thousand chance meetings, each resolving into romance. The McDonald's drive-thru hadn't made the list. So instead of swooning under the power of my trailer park charms, the girl of my dreams had been forced to watch as I humiliated myself like a village idiot. Perhaps more to the point, I had bungled the chance to engage her before she could disappear for another nine months or more.

If only that had been the end of my woes.

Alas, scarcely an hour, later things got a whole lot worse. Wouldn't you know it? A complaint had been lodged against me by an anonymous patron. Seth, who had no patience for things like inalienable rights, didn't bother with an accounting of what I was supposed to have done, much less afford me the opportunity to defend my honor.

I was too shocked to react. This was fortunate for Seth whether he realized it or not because an hour later I was overtaken by a surge of uncontainable rage. And believe me, if Mr. Soul Patch had been within reach at that moment, there's a good chance he might've taken a soggy McRib sandwich to the Adam's apple.

As it was, I left quietly, determined to maintain what little dignity I had left. Not so easy in a goofy uniform. Dang near impossible with a glob of something gross on your collar.

And there was something else, too.

My poor bicycle. It had been vandalized in broad daylight, twenty feet from the front door, and no one had bothered to intervene. Slashed tires sagged on their rims, the seat was MIA. I shuffled home in a daze, amazed that fate could give and take with such fickle abandon.

So ended my lustrous burger-flipping career.

If you're tempted to feel sorry for me though, or if your faith in humanity is wavering, hold on to those horses. Because—if I may lean heavily on a flimsy cliché for a moment—as life closes one door, another tends to open.

TWENTY THREE

If my mother was even remotely disappointed, she hid it well. She must've despaired inwardly, of course. Heaven knows I did. I mean, a full third of our income had just been yanked from under us. Yet my mother administered a sympathetic hug and pecked me on the cheek as if there was nothing at all to worry about.

"Their loss, honey," she said, and I almost believed her. For once, I was grateful for my mother's ability to deceive with so little effort. I needed comfort, after all, not the cold indifference that comes with honesty at a time like that.

Shortly after, I threw the aforementioned fit in my room. It was like the whole world came crashing down on me at once and the injustice of being me was suddenly intolerable. So I did what any self-respecting adolescent would do: I let my inner child take the wheel for a while.

I'm not gonna lie, it wasn't pretty.

I cried. I growled. I ripped the *do not remove under penalty of law* tag from the underside of Nicky's mattress. I brutalized my pillow with closed fists. I squashed a dead roly-poly with my bare fingers.

When I finally ran out of steam, Nicky politely invited me to play cards. We did, and by dinnertime I was more or less feeling my age again.

The following morning, I stopped by the library to return a long overdue book. As had become the norm in recent months, Ms. Winters greeted me with a sharp rebuke for my inconsideration of other patrons. Only this time, she dinged me with a ten cent fine to make sure I got the message. Chastened and ten cents poorer, I assured her that it wouldn't happen again.

The librarian glowered. "I have half a mind to disable your card, you know."

I sighed. "What can I say? I'm glad your mind has a more sensible half to round it out."

Ms. Winters wasn't amused. I offered up news of my unemployment, hoping that it might break some ice, if not garner me a bit of well-earned sympathy. Thankfully, it did seem to soften the woman up a little. She *tisk*ed around a butterscotch candy, pursing her lips in disapproval.

"Well," she declared. "Seemed a bit beneath a young man of your potential anyway."

"Thanks. Too bad potential doesn't pay the bills, huh?"

I browsed the collection for a while, painfully aware that I had absolutely nothing else to do. I suppose I could have gone in search of a new job. Indeed, I probably should have. They were always looking for sackers at Food 4 Less, I knew. But I could scarcely stomach the thought of bagging groceries for customers while they openly gawked at my disfigurement. As it turned out, I needn't have worried.

Stamping my selections for the day—first an oldie followed by a very coveted new release, freshly shelved before my eyes— Ms. Winters appraised me in a squint, eyes poring over me as if noticing for the very first time that I was a fully formed human capable of more than reading and scrawling in notebooks. "How are you at cutting grass?" she wanted to know.

I scoffed. "And you thought flipping burgers was a waste of potential?"

When Ms. Winters didn't so much as blink much less crack a smile, I realized that she was serious. I squirmed. An eyebrow arched over her bifocals, a reminder that her question remained unanswered, and that time would stand still until this was remedied.

"Jeez," I mumbled. "I don't know. Fine, I guess." I considered the question for another second and thought it fair to mention, "Our yard has more weeds than grass though. Honestly, it looks terrible no matter what I do."

Ms. Winters snickered deep in the back of her throat, her mouth slipping into that knowing smile she was so fond of. I doubted that she had any real concept of just how gross a yard could get, but—perhaps wisely—I kept this to myself. Thanks to the unsavory diet of Lakeview's stray animal population and their unruly predilections for doing their business all over my yard, weeds were usually the least of my landscaping problems.

"Well, if you have no aversions to a little manual labor," Ms. Winters was saying, "I may have a good opportunity for you." *Thump*, went her stamp. "Unless you already have plans for the day?"

My eyes widened. "I have none," I assured her. Then, in my best Vincent Price voice—which I now suspect must've sounded more Italian than Transylvanian—I added: "Please, my dear. Tell me more ..."

Later that morning, under the direction of a broken-armed somewhat debonair custodian, I found myself surveying the considerable property of the First Baptist Church. Right away, a field behind the main building had me worried. From a respectable distance, I had seen it used in a variety of capacities over the years—volleyball tournaments, cookouts, Easter-egg hunts, hayrides, carwashes—you name it. Up close it appeared to span an acre, perhaps two or three. Admittedly, my ability to gauge such things lacked any frame of reference, yet I knew that it would take a couple of hours or more all on its own. The task struck me as so daunting, in fact, that I must have subconsciously marginalized the remainder of the campus, which was broken up by all manner of sidewalks, fences and shrubbery.

This was a mistake, of course.

The church owned a riding lawn mower but it had thrown a belt the previous week and was still awaiting repairs. The custodian felt the need to disclose this with a guilty cringe, as if the gall of it ought to be a deal breaker. I couldn't help but laugh. I mean, riding mowers were for golf courses, weren't they? And besides, the prospect of using their push mower was actually a little exciting; the custodian extolled it as a "well-oiled machine" that "purrs like a kitten."

I attacked the dreaded field first. In my favor, it was early in the season, so the grass wasn't particularly tall or thick. The ground on the other hand, was unsettled, rendered spongy by winter's repeated freezes and thaws. Raising the mower deck helped a little but not much. Time and time again, the machine bogged down and stalled in a flurry of dirt. However well-oiled the machine, it had to be wrangled free and restarted just as often as the piece of junk residing in my shed. I won't deny that it looked prettier, though.

When I finally managed to tame the field—which as feared proved to be no small task—I allowed myself a moment of silent gloating, believing that I had all but finished. The custodian supplied tuna sandwiches, green apples and cold water for lunch. I ate ravenously, both hungry and eager to wrap things up. A new Michael Crichton novel lay on my pillow at home and I didn't have to listen hard to hear it calling my name. I could hardly wait to curl up with a cold drink and read until I fell asleep.

I skipped the apple and wolfed down the sandwich. Still chewing my last bite, I surged back into the fray to take on what little remained. An hour later though, it was clear that I had grossly underestimated the scale of *what little remained*. Overlooked in my hasty assessment that morning, small patches of landscape peppered the grounds endlessly—nestled between flower gardens, secreted away in the shadows of outbuildings and hedges, peeking from behind playground structures. Upon finishing one area, the custodian was invariably waiting—with a sympathetic smile that quickly lost its charm—to direct me to another, followed by another. And yet another. And so on.

My hands began to smart from the emergence of blisters and the vibration of the lawn mower, from the repeated dousing of gasoline while fueling the tank. The sun toasted my skin until it stung and the sweat seeping from my pores only served to intensify the sensation. I guess the winter must've softened me, because I considered throwing in the towel several times over. My stamina flagged by the minute, yet the grass kept coming.

I'm happy to report that I did in fact finish the job, though only just. After five hours of mowing and bagging, I turned off the mower with a pained moan. I took a long minute to catch my breath, mentally preparing for the walk home. By then my blood sugar had fallen to dangerous lows and I wasn't entirely sure that I could make the trek on foot.

Just then, the custodian emerged from the church with a glass of water and a giant slab of cornbread, the latter slathered in strawberry jam. Under normal circumstances—that is, when I wasn't on the verge of passing out—the quirky randomness of that cornbread might've earned a wisecrack, or at the very least set me to snickering. In my present condition though, I lit into it with giddy desperation. Oh man, was it ever divine. The sweet jam hit me first, jolting me back to life like an oral defibrillator—those are a thing, right? A moment later, when the starch bloomed in my belly, I became torn between the urge to take a nap or bust out twenty pushups.

The custodian clasped his hands happily and then ventured off to let me eat. I was grateful for the much-needed sustenance, but more than that, I was deliriously pleased to be done. Finally! With each bite, I felt my spirits rise. The walk home didn't seem quite as daunting anymore. And if I hurried, I just might squeeze in a little reading before dinner.

Just as I popped the last bite into my mouth, washing it down with a gulp of cold water, the custodian returned. With a weed eater.

Curse you, Ms. Winters!

Despite no small amount of pouting and brooding, the trimming went pretty quickly. Well, compared to the mowing that preceded it, anyway. But as before, the grass seemed to go on forever and ever. I think that I had literally given up on finishing in this lifetime when all at once—I was done. Just like that. I almost couldn't believe it and I stood there for what seemed like a long time, trembling from exertion as I gazed upon my handiwork. I felt no pride or sense of accomplishment, only relief.

Minutes later, I limped from the maintenance shed toward the main building. The angry pinging and crackling of hot engines grumbled behind me and in that moment, I knew that if I ever heard those sounds again, it would be too soon.

The custodian met me halfway across the parking lot. "Well done, young man. Well done." Grinning, he handed me a grape Shasta followed by a crisp check, folded neatly in half. I pocketed the check with the obligatory *thank you*, wiped the sweat from my face and popped the Shasta.

"I'm very pleased with your work, Mr. Chase," he remarked. "I wonder about your availability next Saturday?" His eyes shot up expectantly.

You might be surprised to learn that grape soda is capable of experiencing fear; I for one was tremendously surprised when a mouthful of the stuff forced its way up through my sinuses and out my nostrils, apparently to escape consumption.

All over town, young ladies swooned; men gaped in awe of my allure.

Chuckling, the custodian—who for all his politeness had yet to introduce himself as anything else—offered me a tissue from his shirt pocket. Noting the pinking of my cheeks and nose, he made a sympathetic hissing noise between his teeth. "Oh, my. Perhaps we can locate some sun screen for you next time. And a hat." More chuckling.

I stood mute and more or less frozen, dribbling purple snot into a wad of tissue. The thought of enduring this nightmare all over again made me want to climb the church steeple and take a nose dive. Give me a stern waterboarding or half a dozen bamboo shoots under the fingernails … but please—no more of this!

Still, the word *no* has never come easy to me. I don't like to let anyone down, I suppose. Nor am I fan of the inevitable ill will created by the word. Looking back, I'm not exactly sure what I feared from human conflict, having endured what I believed to be the very worst that life could throw at a single human being. Oddly though, my perseverance only strengthened my wariness of others, probably because I rarely felt that I could relate to them.

Anyway, heedless of my reservations, I was prepared to make an exception on that day. I did want to live after all, and this job made no promises. The afternoon alone had more than half killed me. By my estimation another like it would almost surely finish me off. So no thank you, Mr. First Baptist. I'll be washing my hair next Saturday. Out of the country.

Stalling, I wiped my face clean and then hazarded another drink. The pop cooperated this time, thank goodness. It was sugary bliss, fizzing a slow burn down the sore parchment of my throat. It felt so good that I nearly fainted; fortunately, the custodian was there to steady me.

All told, I worked for seven hours on the property. The subject of compensation hadn't come up even once, but at that moment it didn't matter. No amount in the world could possibly have been worth it. I would have preferred to gut birds at the chicken plant for seven hours or sack groceries or even—

Whoa. Okay, so maybe my fatigue was getting the better of me. I *really* didn't want to sack groceries.

I used the cleanest of my filthy fingers to tease the check from my back pocket. Unfolding it, I stole a glance at the number written there and in that instant, the grape Shasta slipped from my grasp.

Along with my Saturdays.

TWENTY FOUR

"A hundred dollars for a little yard work? It has to be a mistake." My mother's emotional state teetered somewhere between hopeful and suspicious. And who could blame her? A single day at the First Baptist Church had just yielded more than a week's pay from my former employer. It was wonderful, of course. Yet kind of ... *obscene* in a way. I mean, was this how churches spent the money people dropped in the collection plate? Seemed like a terrible waste to blow a hundred bucks on the lawn.

"It's not a mistake, Mom," I tried to reassure her. "Believe me, I made a point to ask. And I wouldn't call it *a little yard work*."

"There's gotta be a catch, then. They'll expect us to show up for church from now on."

My confidence faltered a little. "I don't think so, Mom," I said, but I wondered if she wasn't right. It took a moment for me to decide how I really felt about the prospect. "Would it really be so bad?" I had to ask. "I mean, don't you miss church at all?"

My mother shot daggers from her eyes and I figured that was as good an answer as any.

Come to think of it, we hadn't stepped foot inside a church since my father's incarceration. The subject was a can of worms that my mother worked tirelessly to keep the lid on even as Nicky and I struggled to pull it off. All introversion aside, I missed the kindness of churchgoing people, and so did Nicky. There weren't many people of faith milling around Lakeview Park; that void was felt in our lives now more than ever.

Actually, to split hairs, there was an elderly catholic lady living in Brigham's old trailer, but it was hard not to discount her. She sat on her porch most days with a rosary in one hand and a Virginia Slim in the other. Anyone polite enough to wave *hello* was rewarded with a pinched glower; a gruff, "Mind your business!" for the few who dared to bid her good morning.

"And they want you to come back next week?" my mother was saying. "Did they even have you fill out an application? I'm sorry, Lincoln, but it sounds awfully fishy to me."

I shrugged, too tired to argue. I could have explained that Ms. Winters had made all the arrangements but something told me that my mother would find fault with that as well, which would then transition to another—possibly more heated—disagreement. And frankly, her disbelief was starting to chafe. It implied that I was either unworthy of the opportunity or too stupid to see that I was being used. Neither scenario stroked my ego.

My joints ached, my skin stung. But I must confess a pleasant burst of satisfaction for having made it through the day, and a hundred dollars richer, to boot. My mother's cynicism couldn't make a dent in that.

For the record, we didn't argue often, my mother and me. On the contrary, we had a tendency to walk away steaming when we probably should've made an effort to clear the air. I suppose we both feared how far an argument might take us if the claws were ever unleashed. There were so many barriers rising between us in those days and the longer we chose to ignore them, the more formidable they seemed. The more distant we became as mother and child.

Her drinking, for one—however discrete—infuriated me. It wasn't about the money wasted on booze, though when I occasionally allowed myself to stew on that, I very nearly blew up in a rain of flesh and hot lava. No, it had nothing to do with her parental irresponsibility. It boiled down to motivation. Her unwillingness to stop revealed that Nicky and I weren't enough to sustain her happiness. That one of us—and I'll let you decide who—perhaps even *drove* her to such behavior. It hurt. Every time I smelled it on her breath, every time the tell-tale clinking of bottle against decanter woke me in the dead of night, I felt betrayed all over again.

As for what was pushing my mother's buttons, it took a long time to put my finger on that. Because whether she realized it or not, I was trying very hard to be a good son. Rarely did I make a move without considering how it would affect her or my little brother. Yet I could do no right lately. My very presence seemed to agitate her. When the truth of why finally dawned on me, I felt physically ill. Because I knew then that nothing I did would ever be right.

My behavior wasn't the problem, you see. Not in terms of the things I said or did, anyway. The culprit was genetics, plain and simple. Every day, my resemblance to Finton Chase sharpened a little more. Not necessarily in the face, of course, but in a million other ways. My father shone through in subtle flickers, some meaningless on their own, others too blatant to overlook. He was in my laugh, the timbre of my voice. The cleft of my chin. The knobs of my knuckles. The way I held my stupid fork.

Apparently, my mother saw this happening long before I did and at some point, she came to resent me for it. Maybe not consciously. Not with the same intensity reserved for the man who had once abused her, but with similar conviction.

I can't help but wonder if she feared me, as well. On some level, anyway. I mean, if I truly was my father's son, then I was worth fearing, right? And likewise, though still young, I wasn't a kid anymore. Puberty combined with years of manual labor on the homestead had filled me out, cutting edges where there used to be curves. My baby fat had turned to iron. I looked like my father in profile, and I—like him—was deceptively strong. Even the weakest of my arms—fully healed but never quite the same—was powerful to a fault, capable of inflicting pain, or worse.

I acknowledged these traits without the faintest conceit because they disgusted me as much as they did my mother. And if that's how I saw myself—as a blurred facsimile of my father with the undeniable potential to hurt others, just as he had—then how must my mother have seen me?

My father had been kind, yet streaked with violence. He made a habit of repressing his anger until it brimmed and demanded an outlet. A victim. I couldn't help but wonder, had he eventually learned to see it coming? Had he felt it growing inside him, out of control, like some kind of parasite? Of my father's many dodgy footsteps, that cycle of violence was the one I most feared stepping in. It was a sinkhole, muddied to its depths with blood and the kind of guilt that doesn't fade. Once in that mire, I knew there would be no escape. Some things simply can't be undone.

Knowing all this, I lived on the edge of my seat. I was afraid of where conflict might lead me yet just as afraid of letting anything fester. True, my fuse had proven to be slow-burning and perhaps longer than most, but I sensed an unfamiliar force building within me. Good or bad, I couldn't say. Whatever it was? I knew instinctively that I didn't stand a chance of containing it.

For a while, my love for reading came to the rescue. No matter how dark my mood, it seemed that I could almost always count on the power of fiction to water down reality. It wasn't uncommon for me to read entire novels in a single sitting, oblivious of the passage of time. Meals were forgotten, my bladder dismissed. Homework neglected. In a way, this became my benchmark for contentment, defined more by the absence of distress than the existence of satisfaction. Kind of pathetic, huh?

Nevertheless, on that evening this was precisely the salvation I craved. Anger is an all-consuming emotion, you see, and I was too spent to maintain it for long. So as always, my mother and I pretended that all was well and went our separate ways—I to read in my room, my mother to set about making dinner. Everything would be fine soon enough.

I don't mean to suggest that reading ever fixed anything or that I didn't lose my temper. I did on occasion, though with deliberate restraint. More often than not though, a well-spun story was just what the doctor ordered to soothe my bruised pride. Given enough time with a good book, the cares of my world would eventually slip into the shadow of another realm, a place where my own grievances ceased to even register. My sense of self was reduced to a thin wisp of familiarity, and that was just fine with me.

But alas, it wasn't meant to be. Not this time, anyway.

I'd been reading for less than half an hour, just getting a feel for the story when my mother rapped on the door and mumbled, "Dinner." Growling under my breath, I slapped my book shut. It was too soon! I needed more time to immerse, to put some distance between me and the impulse to stew or even lash out. I was still flustered; and so was my mother, I had no doubt. Which isn't to say that I actually grasped whatever her problem was; merely that she had a right to get bent out of shape over absolutely nothing if that's how she wanted to live.

From the back porch, I cupped my hands and called Nicky in from the ball field. It was getting dark and as I watched him jog toward the house, I was amazed that his silhouette could have belonged to a grown man. He had changed so dramatically in the last few months that I scarcely recognized him. And I mean that literally. There were times when I noticed him from the corner of my eye and nearly jumped to my feet, thinking: *Who the heck is this dude and what's he doing in my room?*

Gone was the gangly tween, the Chiclet-smiled kid who had worn footie pajamas not so long ago. Side by side, in fact, my little brother was barely a half-inch my inferior. But where I was wiry and jagged at the edges, Nicky was smooth and refined, more athletic. He was beautiful, actually; the perfect blend of Mom and Dad, rounded out so gracefully that—on him—my father's features were more like endearments than stains.

We ate dinner wordlessly—Hamburger Helper, green beans, bread and butter. The bland staples of my youth were finally behind us and thank goodness for that. One could only stomach macaroni and cheese or Ramen noodles or boiled hot dogs for so long before insanity threatened to set in. Scurvy at the very least. As for our new menu and its wonderfully exotic delights, I couldn't get enough of it. Strangely though, while I had been starving half to death earlier, my appetite was now gone. I picked at my food, but I couldn't bring myself to take a bite.

Noting this, Nicky's eyes began to volley between my mother and me, trying for all he was worth to make sense of the tension in the room. Poor kid. Just as he had grown bodily in recent months, his sensitivity to social cues had also hinged to the polar extreme; it didn't take much to freak him out. The weird passive-aggressive feud brewing between my mother and me was bound to raise his hackles but what could I do? Judging from the nervous drumming of his fingers on the table, Nicky wasn't likely to hold out for much longer.

To my surprise, he endured another five minutes before dropping his fork onto his plate and shoving back from the table. The dishes shuddered, water sloshed in our plastic cups. Nicky's chair snagged against a tear in the linoleum and hung there for a long moment, tottering on one leg before righting itself. Even knowing that it was coming, I was still caught off guard by the outburst, by the sheer explosiveness of it.

"What's with you two?" Nicky demanded.

My mother chewed in a trance, oblivious of—or merely disinterested in—the scene unfolding at her dinner table. Naturally, this only heightened Nicky's alarm. Soon enough it would turn to panic.

I knew very well how cruel the human imagination could be, especially for someone like Nicky, whose childhood tended to follow him around like a ghost on a string. Bad things happened in the Chase household. There was no sense in denying it or pretending that life would ever be normal for us. My family—each of us in our own time—had come to accept this, and I doubted that any outsider was truly capable of grasping how taxing that sort of awareness could be. To not think of tragedy in terms of *if* one was going to strike, but rather *when* and *how*. And naturally, *to whom*.

Tired or not, I couldn't abandon my brother to the perfectly rational, yet unfounded, fear that something sinister was upon us. He didn't deserve that. So with a great heave of resolution, I abandoned my sulking to talk Nicky down.

"We're just tired," I sighed. "And a little on the grumpy side, I guess." To further sell my nonchalance, I popped a cold green bean into my mouth, puckering as it squeaked against my teeth. "So, who won today?"

Nicky's eyes hardened. "Don't. Don't do that."

Oops. I guess he didn't appreciate being patronized any more than he liked being left in the dark. My mind flickered back to the night long ago, when my father was arrested. Seems like I made a similar mistake back then, only with my grandfather. Apparently, this had become a pretty arrogant habit of mine—treating members of my family like household pets, that is, as if they lacked the ability to cope with life on their own. As if I and I alone could shoulder reality in all its terrible glory.

Ashamed, I brought Nicky up to speed on my job situation, filling in the back story I had left blank for my mother. It didn't take long. Unlike my mother, you see, Nicky didn't suffer the compulsion to interrupt every few seconds, nor was he determined to nitpick our good fortune to death.

As I relived my belly flop off the fast food high dive, my mother looked on in a faraway gaze, present but only half with us. Her mouth twitched at the mention of Ms. Winters a moment later though, betraying that—despite appearances—she had been listening all along. Yet while I could feel the heat of her disapproval, she didn't comment. She sipped her water and peered out the window, feigning disinterest for reasons that I couldn't begin to understand.

When I was finished, Nicky looked even more confused than before. Still, the fear had left his eyes and that was probably the best I could hope for. I mean, let's face it: I didn't recognize the elephant in the room any more than he did.

"That's great," he said, followed predictably by, "But I feel like I must be missing something." Settling back into his chair, my brother seemed to fold into himself, tanned arms girdling his chest. "I mean, it all worked out in the end, right? Except for your bike."

I gave him a nod and a shrug to match.

"Okay, so what's up with Mom, then? Looks like she swallowed a bug."

I, of course, had no answer to that. Glancing at the woman who had raised me, I was struck by how little I understood her. Normally, talking about her as if she wasn't in the room guaranteed a reaction. But not this time. Maybe she was in rare form or maybe she was half drunk. In either case, while the intensity of her gaze out the window seemed to strengthen, my mother remained otherwise made of stone.

Mischief stirred within me. Along with a distinct tingle of curiosity for what it might accomplish, considering that all else had failed to crack this woman.

"Yes," I agreed. "I think that's exactly what happened. A moth, in fact."

Nicky snickered, eyes widening. "You sure it wasn't a butterfly? I mean, no offense, but would you even know the difference?"

"Ah, I see your point." I scratched my chin, scrunched my eyebrows. "It may have been some kind of beetle, on second thought."

Grudgingly, the corners of my mother's lips were starting to quiver, curling upward a millimeter at a time and I knew that—for all her fighting spirit—we had her on the ropes.

"What, like a stink bug?" *Oh, Nicky. What a perfect setup.*

This was it—the knockout punch. With all the spirit I could muster, I gasped, hands flinging into the air above me. "Now hold on a second there, buddy—are you suggesting that my mother has … *stink bug breath?*" I snatched up my fork and wielded it like a sword. "How dare you, sir! I demand satisfaction!"

Nicky armed himself with a butter knife, struggling to keep a straight face. A glob of margarine dripped off the blade and landed with a wet *plop* in his water cup.

Nicky lost it.

And all at once, my mother lost it too. She was cackling, smiling unabashed, but for the lingering curve of a frown. Soon enough though, even the frown lost its bitter hold. She turned to Nicky with eyes squinted, lips drawn in an odd parody of a scowl, and shook her head, as if to say: "I expected nothing less from him, but *you?*" Nicky was loving it. He clapped his hands and for a long beautiful moment, he laughed so hard that the little boy he used to be shimmered beneath the young man that he had become.

"Eat, will you?" my mother giggled.

Her eyes shifted to mine then, locking in place. My grin faltered. There was a whole lot of mixed emotion swirling behind her visage and I couldn't help but wonder if we would ever get past this … whatever *this* was. The nameless ugliness between us, it obviously ran deep. Far deeper than the petty grievances my mother chose to fixate on, anyway. And I had a hunch that, unless wishful thinking was merely doing its thing, her despair wasn't really about me. Not directly, anyway.

This hunch, as hunches often do without any justification, became more of a surety as the seconds ticked by. It must've emboldened me too, because despite our progress over the last few minutes I must confess a temptation to confront my mother right then and there, to demand not only an end to her mercurial affections but a dang good explanation for them as well. Maybe I figured that with Nicky standing by she would at least pretend to hear me out. But even if I thought that putting my foot down would make the smallest impression on her—and I have to believe that I knew better—I didn't get a chance to try. Because in a split second, my entire thought process was derailed ... by a wink.

The movement was almost imperceptible and on the surface it didn't amount to much, even if it had caught me off guard. Yet as her eyes darted away, its meaning seemed to hang in the air.

Truce, for now.

Something like relief—a diluted version, perhaps; warm and fuzzy but lacking any certainty or closure—enveloped me as I glanced over at my brother, at my mother. We needed more of these moments, I realized. Sure, they took a little energy to put in motion and the effort didn't necessarily assure a positive result. But these were the sort of memories worth storing up. Not all the bickering, the drama that was slowly consuming us. We needed to become a family again and as near as I could tell, this was how it was done. By making memories. By committing daily to share life with the people who mattered as opposed to merely coexisting with them. I'm not exactly sure when or why we stopped trying, but it was clear to me that somewhere along the line, each of us had embraced a solitary existence.

That needed to end.

"You know," I announced, "I just realized that it might not have been a bug after all." Plucking up a green bean, I let it dangle over my plate and crossed my eyes until it hurt. "It might've been one of these, um … lizard tails?"

I felt a light smack on the back of my head and we all laughed.

TWENTY FIVE

The following week, I got a letter from my father. I didn't receive many anymore, so this one came as a small surprise. Since his imprisonment, the stream of our correspondence had trickled from a few letters each week down to a couple per month, and then to one every three or four months.

Nicky continued to send and receive one every week or so, which proved that—among other things—he had a kinder, more forgiving heart than I did. Not that I ever had any doubt.

Knowing very little about prison life, I imagined that my father had little to do but write letters all day, that it should've been nothing of a sacrifice for him to go through the motions on my behalf just as he had for Nicky. Honestly, if I had given him any incentive at all to keep up the routine, I might've been offended that he no longer bothered. But the truth is, if I can bring myself to be brutally honest, I preferred his silence.

Groaning, I sulked all the way to my room and shut myself in. There, reclined on my bed with my father's letter in hand, I was reminded that the space I shared with my brother wasn't much larger than a prison cell. Seriously, no exaggeration. My father had shared the dimensions of his in one of his earliest letters, and if his measurements were accurate, the linear difference between our accommodations was less than a foot in either direction.

Looking back, I can see how a sudden introduction to that tiny space would be a claustrophobic experience for most people, including me. Only, I had grown up in there, so even if it was scarcely large enough to house a set of bunk beds and a single dresser, it was all I knew. And it helped that I wasn't tripping over a toilet or a cellmate. Nicky didn't really count, I should explain, since he preferred to be outdoors and spent almost no time in our room except to sleep and dress.

Anyway, perhaps more to the point, my father was a prisoner. And though I occasionally felt like one, I was not. There was a big world out there. Even if it sometimes felt beyond my reach, there were no physical barriers preventing me from exploring it. I could come and go as I pleased.

So why didn't I? I mean, outside of school and my new Saturday job, I had more free time than ever before. Yet I chose to squander it in the solitude of a room that clearly had been modeled after a prison cell. With my nose buried in a book no less, living vicariously through the adventures of fictional characters instead of daring to experience my own.

Jeez, what was wrong with me?

Well, for one, I was fighting my way through that "life is unfair/nobody understands me" stage of post-pubescent adolescence. It's a miserable time for any teenager to be sure, though—if my mother was to be believed—it's actually much harder on the adults around them, who undoubtedly begin to wonder exactly how serious those child abuse laws are and if the boundaries might be stretched an inch or two given the extenuating circumstances. For my part, I found it difficult to stifle the urge to pout or grumble. About everything. Homework, chores. Bedtime. My inability to quit pouting and grumbling. Nothing was off limits.

Nevertheless, even in my times of deepest, hormonally-conflicted misery, I recognized that I had no legitimate excuse to be complacent, much less a sultry brat. Naturally, I didn't let that stop me. It was my sworn duty as a teenager, after all. Please don't misunderstand—I did make a point to enjoy time with my family whenever the opportunity presented itself. I tried harder than ever before to connect with them, despite my moodiness. I came to think of it as just another affliction to overcome, and more often than not I succeeded.

When I was alone though, it ate me alive.

I moped in my room. I played the woodpile martyr until my hands blistered. I wrote half-hearted stories that were doomed to feed the woodstove. Once or twice, I hiked out to the wandering tree only to bemoan its blatant indifference of me and stomp back home. Likewise, whenever my life felt empty or unjust—which seemed like a daily affair—I didn't stop to consider my father's sad existence, much less acknowledge that things could be much worse for me.

Instead, I thought: *Thanks a lot, Dad.*

Speaking of my father, his letter was fairly short and sweet. Just a trite—and quite belated—*"Happy Birthday, son!"* accompanied by half a page of the same old empty banter:

How's school?

I bet you're taller than me by now.

Have you been following the Red Socks?

Et cetera.

The envelope was filthy, as usual. It probably collected dust in the prison mailroom for weeks before anyone got around to sending it on. They—the prison staff—vetted every piece of my father's mail, and not with any sense of urgency. From the beginning, his letters had been as long as a month out-of-date and most arrived in snaggle-toothed envelopes, resealed with bunched-up strips of scotch tape. Once, Nicky tore open an envelope to find nothing at all inside. It remains a mystery if the letter was found to contain some kind of prohibited content—a plea for files or sharp metal objects, perhaps?—or if someone had simply forgotten to re-stuff the envelope. Either way, I had to wonder if the mail room wasn't staffed by disgruntled prisoners.

Obviously, none of this was my father's fault. His due diligence exceeded mine by far, no matter how I chose to look at it. And I suppose there must've been a time when that made a difference to me. But not anymore.

It wasn't that I hated him, to be clear. Rather, I suffered a profound need to be as estranged from the man as humanly possible, which seemed to demand a certain amount of emotional detachment. I won't pretend to understand the psychology swirling around in my rattled little head. Maybe at heart—beneath the shroud of teenage melodrama—I was still the same little boy who had lost his father and longed for his return. Maybe I always would be.

A *happy birthday* hardly called for a response, but for some reason I figured: what the heck? Actually, I was growing pretty weary of my mother's incessant needling on the subject. "He's your father, Lincoln," she loved to remind me. "He misses you more than you can know." Nice. Go right ahead. Pile it on me, as if I ought to bear any responsibility for my father's emotional state in the pen. Alas, my mother was quite unrelenting and there was really only one way out.

So I grabbed a pencil and paper and went to work.

My letter wasn't much more elaborate than my father's, but it was certainly a step up from my last one, composed many months before under the usual duress from my mother: *"Got your letter. Things are fine here. Well, gotta go."*

Heartwarming stuff, I know.

This time, I described my new lawn gig—the massive property, the pristine lawn equipment. My herculean victory over nature's wiles. The mind-boggling check. I was on a roll when it occurred to me that I wasn't merely providing an innocent telling of events—I was boasting.

Maybe I thought that it would make him proud. Ha! No, I didn't really believe that. I was marking my territory, plain and simple. I wanted the old man to know that I had stepped up to take his place. That *I* was taking care of the family, not him. That *I* was the man of the house now.

I prepared an envelope in neat block print but when it came time to fold the letter, I hesitated. With my better sense finally kicking in, I wadded up the letter and drove it deep into the kitchen trash, where I felt sure that it couldn't be salvaged.

The thought of punishing my father made a pretty satisfying fantasy, I'm not gonna lie. I imagined the look on his face when he suddenly realized how close he had come to destroying the people he was supposed to be providing for, that all the letters in the world would never make up for the damage that he had done. That—if he was lucky—his sons might grow up to be respectable people in spite of him, never because of him.

You know, like he couldn't possibly have reached those conclusions on his own. Like he needed a little pipsqueak like me to spell it out, right? Well, I guess that's the primary appeal of fantasy; it isn't bound by rational thought, much less reality.

Nevertheless, I couldn't do it. Not like that, anyway.

The envelope was ready to go, however. Stamped, even. Sure, I could've tossed it aside for another day when I was ready to write something that wasn't born out of spite. But let's be honest— that wasn't likely to happen for a very long time, if ever. And having wasted the last half hour, I regretted even picking up that stupid pencil because I didn't want to think about my father anymore.

Ugh. I just wanted to be done with all this. With him.

On impulse, I crammed a photocopy of my published poem into the envelope, along with one of the aforementioned short stories—uninspired, written in a single moody pass; it was worthy of scrap or kindling and little else. Before I could change my mind, I sealed the envelope and walked it to the mailbox.

I had done my duty. More importantly, I had bought myself a few months of peace.

TWENTY SIX

When Saturday rolled around again, I was primed for action. The dog next door—bless his mangy little heart—provided an unpleasant yet timely wakeup call just before dawn and upon arousal, I very nearly leapt from my bed. It wasn't exactly excitement spurring me on; more of a primal need to get the day over with, or perhaps simply to take some initiative while I still had my wits about me. Likewise, prudence demanded that I get the earliest start possible if I was going to survive the ordeal. So I lurched to my feet and got in motion.

I didn't bother with a shower. Nor did I eat a proper breakfast, given that my stomach was still more than half asleep. Just a piece of dry toast washed down by a swig of orange juice. I threw a baloney sandwich together and wrapped it in a napkin, stuffing it into a paper sack, along with an apple.

At a quarter to seven, just as the sun was splashing a bruise across the ashen sky, I marched up the steps to the First Baptist Church. The building was locked up tight, the windows unlit. Guess I should've seen that coming, but it is me that we're talking about. Honestly—and I'm stretching the limits of candor by admitting this—until that moment, I had always imagined the church to be a place whose doors were never closed. I mean, with all that Sunday school talk about God's *open door policy*, what was I supposed to think?

The custodian arrived at half past nine to find me snoozing by the maintenance shed. "Goodness, Mr. Chase!" he balked. "I certainly didn't expect to see you this early."

Rubbing my eyes, I scrambled to my feet. "Oh, Mr.—um, Custodian ... I mean—"

"Hampton," he offered with a faint snicker. "Senior, if that matters."

Finally, a name to go with the face! Almost without realizing it, I had begun to think of the man as a parody of the comic book hero, a prosaic character whose only super power was an apologetic smile and an affinity for cleaning dirty bathrooms and changing AC filters.

Never fear, random citizen. The Custodian is on the prowl ...

Yup, I'm an idiot.

"Sorry—Mr. *Hampton*, right." I stretched out a kink in my neck and yawned. "Thought I should get an early start. Hoping to beat the heat, you know?" No point in revealing just how early that start was.

"Call me Clyde, would you? But yes, I see. Makes perfect sense, of course." Looking up with a grunt, the custodian beheld the clear impossibly blue sky and let loose a whistle. In the meantime, I took a moment to appraise him. He was a reedy-framed gentleman in his late sixties, perhaps early seventies. He had the clean cut look of a man who took the time to iron his shirts and polish his shoes before bed, who shaved every morning without fail.

"I expect it will be a scorcher today," he observed. I nodded absently.

Actually, the heat wasn't likely to breach the nineties but we were chasing the leading edge of rising temperatures, that brief feathering of spring into summer in which each day would emerge a little hotter than the previous. And for the record, pushing a steaming mower has a way of adding an exponent to any temperature.

"Mr. Chase," Mr. Hampton—I mean, Clyde—was saying, "while I applaud your eagerness to please, I'm afraid the local noise ordinance prohibits us from getting started before eight o'clock." This was followed by his usual sheepish smile. Not for the first time, I noticed that his diction was crisp and unusually polished, hinting toward an education that seemed at odds with his humble occupation. My curiosity stirred.

As for the noise ordinance, it was news to me. People mowed their lawns if and whenever they felt like it in Lakeview Park, and if there was any opposing force to contend with, it was the harmless—albeit colorful—admonishment of a disgruntled neighbor.

"Why don't we shoot for eight o'clock sharp next week?" the custodian suggested and I quickly agreed. For a hundred dollars, I'd have mowed that lawn at noon or three in the morning and I told him so. Clyde tittered at this. "Well, let's see how your enthusiasm fares in July, when it's over a hundred degrees by breakfast." He had a point, no doubt. On the other hand, it helped boost my spirits that he had such confidence in my long term employment.

Clyde Hampton, who was proving to be a bit of a slow starter, treated me to a cup of coffee and a glazed donut. I could've done without them—the day was getting away from me, after all—but man, did they ever hit the spot.

We sipped our coffee from little Styrofoam cups and Clyde surprised me with news that the riding mower was back in service. I *oooh*ed and *aaah*ed appropriately, but inside I was trembling. Visions of catastrophe tormented me. I took out hedges and garden hoses, gas meters and—in a flash of the truly macabre—a warren of bouncing baby rabbits. Embarrassed, I confessed that I probably knew more about quantum physics than operating a riding mower. And that I wasn't exactly sure what quantum physics was.

If Clyde was at all nonplussed, he hid it well. Rather than belittle my inexperience, in fact, he took great pains to show me the ropes. And as it turned out, there really wasn't much to it. A bit like driving the family truck, though considerably less touchy and without all the tedious shifting. Fast too, with a wide mowing deck that glided smoothly over the uneven terrain. Kind of fun, actually.

Remember that dreaded field behind the church, the one that took me hours to mow only a week before? Yeah, I knocked that sucker out in just over forty minutes and I barely broke a sweat. True, there were some areas on the property that only a push mower could handle; but all things considered, the job was wrapping up much faster than I could've hoped for. By lunch time, I was almost ready to weed eat.

At precisely twelve o'clock, Clyde led me to a covered breezeway where we perched on a set of steps with our lunch bags. Nibbling on sandwiches, we relaxed in the shade and watched cars trickle by. It was a beautiful day. Not exactly the predicted scorcher, thankfully, but instead a little on the windy side and therefore about as close to comfortable as a summer day could get.

Glancing around the property, admiring my progress, a pleasant but unfamiliar feeling began to settle over me. It was a sensation unlike any that I had experienced in my previous employment. Contentment, perhaps? A sense that I was actually accomplishing something? You know, not just racking up hours on a time clock, but making a visible mark on the world.

Clyde and I began to chat about this and that and I was surprised to carry on with such ease. Chattiness wasn't exactly in my nature, as you should know by now. Yet there I sat, shooting the breeze with a man that I hardly knew as if it was second nature.

"So how long have you worked here?" I asked.

"Oh, since I retired in eighty-four." This gave me pause because to my eye he looked too young to have retired that long ago; I did some mental calculation and concluded that I was terrible at math. I moved on.

"Were you a preacher or something?"

Clyde gaped at me for a three-count and then blasted a huge, gut-busting guffaw, slapping the knob of one knee with enough force to drive a nail. He took a series of halting sips from his water thermos, broken up by hacks that nearly resolved into a fit. It was a very dramatic performance.

I looked on with a tight smile, cheeks burning. I couldn't imagine what was so amusing and furthermore, it was the fear of reactions just like this that had always kept me somewhat aloof.

"Forgive me, please," he wheezed, "I'm afraid that hit me directly on the funny bone."

Bewildered and a little humiliated, I could only shrug.

"Well, to answer your question: no, I wasn't a preacher. Actually, I was an accountant for the university," he explained, still snickering—*the university* being Oklahoma Baptist University, just down the street. His gaze lost focus, drifting into the space between past and present. Smiling wistfully now, he cleared his throat. "Strictly speaking, I wasn't employed by the university; I was the sole proprietor of an accounting firm whose sole client was the university."

I didn't pursue this line of questioning because—well, it was accounting for crying out loud. And frankly, the urge to socialize had lost some steam. Like it or not though, I had put this conversation into motion and I now felt obliged to keep it going.

To that end, I wanted to steer us toward more predictable ground, toward a conversation that didn't feel so much like a minefield. Yet—as usual—for all my confidence on paper, I came up empty for anything interesting to say in person.

"So you must like it here a lot then," I remarked. Groaning inwardly, I crammed my mouth with a bite of baloney sandwich, since that was apparently the only thing it was good for.

With a sideways glance, Clyde raised one eyebrow to a near-point. "Yes, of course," he said. "I can't think of a better way to volunteer my time."

I froze in mid-chew. "Um, when you say *volunteer*—do you mean that you don't get paid?"

"Well, I suppose that's a matter of perspective," the custodian replied, crunching into one of those green apples he seemed to favor. His eyebrows bounced provocatively the way my grandfather's had when a book sometimes took an erotic tangent. "I have my own key to the pop machine, you know, and I've been known to put away more than my fair share." He cackled at this, driving a playful elbow into my shoulder as if a good laugh should clear up the matter.

It didn't.

On the contrary, I felt disgusted. How could a single day of my time be worth a hundred dollars when this man worked throughout the week for nothing but soda pop? What remained of my appetite converged into an unpleasant burn at the back of my throat.

The spirit of my dismay must've been plain, though to nail down the precise variation—and certainly the depth—of any emotion required a certain amount of guesswork where I was concerned. Given all the scarring, I mean. A smile was still a smile, for example, but just as one is rendered by a child in crayon, mine was exaggerated and therefore without definitive meaning. Casual interpretation failed to distinguish joy from nervous energy, sarcasm from genuine amusement. Only my family—and perhaps Ms. Winters—could tell the difference, and even they struggled at times. So you can imagine my surprise when Clyde proved to be more discerning than most.

"Please don't make the mistake of pitying me, Mr. Chase," he advised. "No one is twisting my arm. I do this out of gratitude for what the Lord has done in my life and because I believe that my service to this church makes a difference."

I wasn't sure how mopping floors for free made a difference but it seemed like a rude thing to say. Then again, Clyde's arm was out of the cast and in a splint, and—rude or not—I couldn't help but draw attention to it now. Low hanging fruit and all. "Uh, you sure about that? Because it does look a bit like someone got the better of you."

Clyde glanced at his arm and then back at me, chuckling. "Goodness, walked right into that one, didn't I?"

He had. "Seriously, though. Couldn't you just drop some money in the offering plate? I mean, isn't that what people normally do?"

Clyde flashed a cryptic expression, underscored by a deep, thoughtful breath. "Sure, I could do that," he replied. "And you're quite right—that is how many believers show their gratitude. But we're called to be servants as well. The hands and feet of Christ."

This was news to me. I chewed my lip, pondering whether or not to explore this subject further. As it happened, Clyde beat me to the punch. He scratched his head, cleared his throat. "All that aside, I have very little to occupy my time these days."

His eyebrows furrowed and a frown began to take shape. In that moment, there was no denying that conversation had a mind of its own. No amount of caution kept one from straying into deep waters once the current had it.

"My wife went to be with the Lord a long time ago, you see," Clyde said in a voice just over a whisper. "My children have all grown, of course." He looked at me curiously then, head cocked, eyes glassy and narrowing. "You know, I have a grandson about your age. He's fairly involved in sports though, so I don't see much of him."

The custodian clasped his hands in an awkward lattice across his knees, shaking his head slowly. By now, melancholy had completely overtaken the once-cheery man. When his lower lip began to quiver, it seemed that he might cry and I wished that I had kept my fat mouth shut. But somehow, he held it together.

"It may be difficult to understand, young man, but I consider it a great blessing to have something meaningful to wake up for each morning."

I nodded, tears beading at the corners of my own eyes. Not everyone can relate to that kind of loneliness, but I understood it all too well. The same black cloud of purposelessness followed me around, especially now that my grandfather was gone. Sure, I found solace here and there—in books, even busywork—but there remained a feeling of inescapable emptiness. A sense that no matter what I did, my life would amount to nothing. Because something imperative was missing.

In retrospect, I can trace this back to the first time my father ever raised a hand against my mother; in a way, that blow had struck me, too. Not physically, of course—I was a room away— but with inarguable force and lasting effect. So what had begun then as a single prick to the heart was now an unnatural campus of tunnels and caverns, eroded by fear and grief, worn smooth—if not numb—by the cave water of unresolved anger.

Wiping my eyes, I made one more attempt to redirect the conversation. "Guess I'm on borrowed time," I mused with a sniffle, motioning once again to his splinted limb.

If I was embarrassed to be so emotional, I needn't have been. Clyde looked at me—no, not at me ... *through* me—with a weird sort of blank smile. His expression was distant, foggy with the faraway gaze of a man who is immersed in moments past and reluctant to return to the present. Honestly, I could've grown antennae and the guy probably wouldn't have noticed. He remained in this state for so long, in fact, that I strongly considered calling for an ambulance. But the spell did eventually break, and when it did, Clyde sat up straight and cleared his throat like nothing had happened. His eyes were clear now, grayish-blue like stormy seas. He jumped back into the conversation matter-of-factly, as if it hadn't skipped a beat.

"I suppose I never explained that my injury isn't the reason for your employment here," he said. There had been hints toward this affirmation, of course, but until I heard the words spoken aloud, the nag of uncertainty had been a pestering annoyance. It was a relief to finally put that to rest.

"Oh, okay," I muttered. Unsure of what else to say, I finished off my sandwich in silence.

"The truth that is I don't know many who possess a constitution comparable to yours, Mr. Chase. Mine, for one, comes nowhere close. And your predecessors were lazy by comparison."

Cheeks flushing, I snickered. "My predecessors?"

"Oh yes, there were three of them. They were unreliable and quite sloppy. So far, you've outdone them by far."

In the glow of such high praise, words failed me. The best I could manage was to cover the *aw-shucks* smile peeking through my poker face. But even if my lips were veiled, the satisfaction in my eyes couldn't be disguised. Especially not from Clyde, who was nothing if not astute. He clapped me on the shoulder, face lit up by a toothy grin. "I expected nothing less, of course. The lovely Irene Winters spoke very highly of you, and a woman of her pristine pedigree doesn't mince words."

TWENTY SEVEN

On the Sunday before Mother's Day, my brother and I walked to church. My mother declined to accompany or drive us, which was hardly a shock. Yet she let us go without a word of protest and that truly was a welcome surprise. Incidentally, the ninety-five degree temperature outside was also a surprise, though considerably less welcome.

Ignoring Nicky's pleas—in part because that's what older brothers do—we skipped Sunday school. Call me selfish if you will but I needed to ease back into the church experience one step at a time and I simply wasn't ready for any kind of close-quarters peer-to-peer interaction. Furthermore, we were more than fifteen minutes late and sweating like pigs, which pretty much killed any chance of slipping in unnoticed.

So we milled around the reception hall, where coffee and donuts had been laid out on a folding table. People trickled in and out, some nodding hello, others eyeing us with guarded curiosity. Can't say I blamed them; we looked like a couple of ill-costumed hoodlums casing a joint.

The sanctuary of the First Baptist Church might have been described by today's Home Depot hipsters as *transitional*, or perhaps a clash of *midcentury modern* and *minimalism*. Back then, when laymen such as myself were unaware of such distinctions in design, the room was merely striking in its simplicity. It was mostly white, the ceiling vaulted to a height of more than thirty feet and ribbed with straight-grained beams. The pews were of dense white-washed oak, upholstered in plum velvet. It wasn't merely an airy space, it was tranquil with faint dapples of color splaying across the walls from a single bank of tumbled stained glass. Nothing at all like the dated cracker box my parents used to drag us to as children.

The congregation here was massive and getting larger by the second. At first glance, it shivered like a hive, pulsing and undulating as its members greeted each other. But when I forced myself to look closer, faces began to resolve from the mass. Some I recognized. My Oklahoma History teacher first, then a boy from my sixth or seventh grade English class. There was a crotchety old lady who managed the laundromat, then a girl whose school locker had once abutted mine, and so on.

You might expect some familiar faces to help settle my nerves; that was certainly my hope. Unfortunately, my resolve unraveled a little more with each flash of recognition until my poor stomach burned like a bowl of hot ulcers. Anyone I recognized was bound to recognize me as well, you see; and unless they had grown up under a rock, they would know all about the iniquities of my father. They would probably wonder—just as I often did—if the apple didn't fall far from the tree.

Nicky and I squeezed in where we could, which turned out to be in the middle of a row, sandwiched between two elderly couples. They didn't know us from Adam and, um … Adam's little brother. Anyway, this suited me just fine.

The service began at eleven o'clock, marked abruptly by the old-lady pounding of a pipe organ. At the prompting of a man with a little baton we turned to page six-hundred and forty-two of a thick maroon hymnal. Fanning the entire expanse above the choir loft, a peacock tail of gaudy pipework—the sanctuary's only superfluity, as far as I could tell—trumpeted mightily through five flowery verses. The overall effect was stiff and overzealous, a little silly to my ear.

Adding to the silliness, the old man to my left croaked along at the top of his lungs; this might have been only marginally amusing except that he repeatedly mixed up the verses and had to be scolded—quite loudly—by his sprightly wife. Nicky tried to stifle his amusement with a mouthful of knuckles but that barely got him through the first verse. He was beet red and snorting when the song finally ended.

Despite all this, there was a certain sweetness in our midst, a reverence that transcended our foolery. Basking in the softness—calling on it, even—I began to thumb through the hymnbook, which consisted of nearly a thousand pages. The sheer heft of the book was impressive but it had more to offer than cubic density. Some of the songs within dated back to the seventeen hundreds, and when I considered this—that people had prized this same ritual hundreds, possibly even thousands of years ago—I felt a connection to something much greater than myself.

Next came the meet-and-greet—a sixty-second, handshaking rampage during which the tender mood was banished so that non-members could be all but trampled for daring to visit. I'm not gonna lie, it took every ounce of self-control to keep from bolting as that primped horde closed in on me. I looked around frantically, hoping that Ms. Winters might come running to the rescue.

She did not.

Nor did Batman or even my new friend, The Custodian. Like a slab of meat in a piranha feeding frenzy, I was picked nearly to death in a flurry of good intentions. My back was clapped, my shoulders kneaded. Some twenty times over, my badly-healed hand was mangled by men who clearly squeezed billiard balls into little mounds of powder for a living.

It was brutal.

I can't really lump Nicky in with all that suffering, however, because—surprise, surprise—he was completely unfazed. Even as

I shook in my father's old dress shoes, my little brother chatted up our suitors with perfect ease. Lately, it seemed that he was always in his element, but on that day, he shone a little brighter than usual. He was made for this, I realized. Fellowship, that is. Community.

In the middle of the bustle, fringed by the usual surreptitious gawking over my disfigurement, there came a slight tug on my sleeve. If it hadn't been so gentle and therefore utterly out of place, I might have ignored it altogether. Warily, I glanced behind me, expecting something along the lines of a displaced drug pusher or perhaps a runaway toddler.

Seldom have I been so happy to be wrong.

There she was, the girl of my dreams; looking more beautiful than should've been physically possible, given the known limitations of human biology. Eyes drilling into mine without a hint of disgust or conceit, let alone pity. At the sight of her, the blood drained from my face, my knees began to wobble. And despite many years of practice, I suddenly forgot how to breathe.

I have to assume that Ivy was used to this kind of reaction—that or she was briefly stricken deaf and blind—because she endured it with admirable poise. When a lesser lady would almost certainly have made a run for it, Ivy smiled and said *hello*, offering a dainty hand.

For a moment I could only gape. This was the first word Ivy had ever spoken to me and I must admit that I was wholly unprepared for the effect it would have. The world seemed to fade out of synchronicity, leaving just the two of us to share this strange dimension together. I imagined that I could hear the rise and fall of her chest, smell her perfume. Feel the glow of her radiant heat against my skin. I wanted to stay like that forever, even if it was all in my head.

Alas, her loveliness overwhelmed me and I more or less blew the moment. I stared. I panted. Sheesh, I think I might've done some nervous tittering. Not that I ever had to wonder why I was so chronically single, but seriously—it was an affront to humanity that I was even allowed to venture out into public.

"Hello back," I finally managed, though it emerged in a strange, unflattering wheeze. Gingerly, I took her extended hand, painfully aware of the trembling in mine. Her skin was rabbit fur against the grit of my calluses. We shook.

"I'm Ivy," she said, and if I hadn't already been smiling, I most certainly would have then. Her voice was a lone violin; those two words, however prosaic, soared above the toneless rumblings of hundreds in a startling melody.

It was impossible for someone as crude as me to respond in kind, yet I was determined to try. So I dug deep, and—

Suddenly, I felt a flutter in the gray matter as my inner moron made a grab for the bullhorn. "I know," he interjected, and I can't even put into words how much I wanted to wring his little neck. Sadly, it was impossible to strangle him without killing myself in the process. So I did my best to recover. "Sorry, I mean—God, I'm such an idiot ..."

Ivy smirked, then giggled a sharp retort. "I know." She followed this up with a wry sort of wink that sent my stomach into a series of flip-flops. Now, I won't deny that I deserved a good needling, but I had to wonder exactly how something as derisive as mockery could be made to feel so good. I was still pondering this when she gave my hand a parting squeeze; and then—*Poof!*—just like that, she vanished into a barricade of summer dresses and button-up shirts.

Even in her absence though, breathing remained a struggle; I closed my eyes and took a few concentrated breaths, leaning against a pewback for support. It helped some. At Nicky's prodding, I sank into my seat, grinning in a lovesick daze. I think the reverend began his sermon, but I wasn't listening.

"Who was *that*?" Nicky hissed. I turned to look at him and found that his eyes were every bit as wide as mine were half-lidded.

"That, little brother, is the girl I'm gonna marry."

It should come as no surprise that my mother didn't take well to our renewed interest in Christianity. Once upon a time, her obsession with the picture of piety had ruled our lives. To the extent, in fact, that church could be called one of the few absolutes of my early childhood. I can remember finding it easier to connive my way out of school than Sunday services.

Those days were long gone. Incidentally, her views on religion seemed to change shortly after my father stepped out of our lives. This should've been my first clue that—despite appearances—church had been my father's charge all along, not my mother's. With him gone and the family permanently blighted by his handiwork, my mother was done putting on a show. She now openly regarded Christianity as a shameless franchise in which absolution was a commodity to be bought and sold; the church, an upscale crack house where two-faced hypocrites—in her words—"got juiced-up" to judge the rest of us. Based on some experiences that she never bothered to share with me, my mother had decided that all churchgoers lived in duplicity and were therefore untrustworthy.

To some degree I could see where she was coming from—if I held my mouth just so, that is. If I channeled all my energy into being inhumanly objective, I could throw her a halfhearted bone. Assuming I could come up with one, anyway. Long ago organized religion had earned the reputation of a guilt-driven industry; I supposed there was that. And admittedly, there would always be people with a need to trivialize their mistakes by drawing attention to the shortcomings of others. Beyond these admissions though, I couldn't even begin to navigate the tangles of my mother's cynicism.

Seriously—*duplicity*? *Untrustworthiness*? Could she honestly not hear the sour twang of those words coming from *her* of all people? Wow, talk about hypocrisy. It took a great deal of willpower to keep from whacking that low-hanging fruit right off the tree.

Well, no … I suppose that isn't entirely true. It wasn't willpower alone that held me at bay. Because when I thought about my mother—when I really buckled down to imagine life in her shoes—it occurred to me just how terrible it must've been to shoulder the weight of her deceptions. Long before it came unraveled, for example, I'm betting that her infidelity kept her up at all hours, prodding her awake with a start, if and when she managed to nod off. If not from guilt, the constant fear of discovery would've turned my insides to goo, without a doubt.

Even as an adult, I sometimes get caught up in wistful memories of my parents holding hands in church; only now, I can't help but wonder if hidden behind that Mona Lisa smile of hers, my mother was terrified that the whole congregation somehow knew the horrible truth. Had it tormented her? *Thump-thump*ing beneath the floorboards like the imagined heartbeat of Poe's *Tell-Tale Heart*? And who could she have confided in to ease her troubled mind?

Ugh. What a lonely way to live. I hated to think of my mother enduring that kind of emotional trauma, even if she had brought it on herself. I did love her, you know. Despite how I must sound at times.

Be that as it may, while my heart went out to her, I couldn't stomach her bigotry toward Christians. The thing is, not once had I ever felt judged by one for my *heathen* ways. Pitied for my circumstances, absolutely—but never judged. Sure, I was familiar with the stereotypes and I had to believe there were at least a few religious weirdos out there who strived to live up to them. But having never encountered one myself, it didn't seem responsible to draw conclusions from the bent philosophies of my mother.

If anything, her incessant harping made me even more determined that my brother and I should make up our own minds about spiritual matters, sans whatever baggage she felt the need to dump in our laps.

So that's exactly what we did.

I'd like to say that my motives were as pure as Nicky's but I'm rather fond of these pants; I would hate for them to burst into flame. The truth is, despite whatever virtue had inspired me to make a church appearance on that first Sunday, I returned thereafter with Ivy in mind, and little else. I wasn't merely smitten, if you'll pardon the distinction; I was fixated.

Recognizing an opportunity to get closer to her, I mustered the confidence to show up for Sunday school on my second week and then very nearly threw a fit when she wasn't there. More or less in passing, I would eventually learn that Ivy helped fold bulletins while the rest of us were tucked away in Sunday school. As for me, once I walked in I couldn't very well slip away from class unnoticed. It would seem that not even the creator of the universe was above a little bait-and-switch when the mood struck.

Well played, sir. Well played.

Actually, staying turned out to be one of my better life decisions. Bear in mind that I arrived with pretty low expectations, so it didn't take much to impress me. My only frame of reference, you see, was the experience of attending Sunday school as a much younger kid in a very different sort of church; there, I can remember nodding off helplessly as Mrs. Rosslin—a stork-legged lady with shaky hands and a giant beehive on top—dragged four or five of us through page after page of a cheesy workbook, spoon-feeding us answers to pencil in the blanks.

This class was nothing like that.

It didn't hurt that our teacher wasn't a senior citizen, if I'm being candid. In her mid-twenties, Hannah Gray was old enough to bring experience to the table, yet still young enough to remember what it was like to be a teenager. And whether or not that should make a difference to a roomful of raging hormones, it did. She was funny and sincere, approachable in a sisterly way that disarmed all but my most determined anxieties. I liked her at once.

What was more, we didn't toil over meaningless busywork in that classroom. We talked. Well—others talked, I listened. From that first visit, it was clear that our discussions weren't meant to circumvent the minefield of young adulthood; on the contrary, they barged directly into the danger zone with unflinching daring.

Nothing was off limits. The temptation to lie or cheat in school, drug and alcohol abuse. Fighting, smoking. Premarital sex, teen pregnancy. Self mutilation, suicide. All sorts of taboo topics took the stage, few of which were familiar in a church setting without the oversimplification of a *thou-shalt-not*. It gave me hope to know that other kids struggled with everyday life, just as I did. And that they hadn't given up.

Naturally, some of our discussions proved more explosive than others. Not everything resolved into shades of black and white; as you can probably imagine, certain issues had a way of dividing the room. Divorce and homosexuality come to mind. The latter, as a matter of fact, has slipped in and out of national controversy throughout my life; not because it happens to be any more dastardly than the other debaucheries we have come to love and adore—given that sin is sin in the eye of the beholder—but because the measure of its sinfulness is gauged by a self-serving culture in constant flux.

It's funny, though: while controversy proved to be just as polarizing on a smaller scale with us kids, we somehow managed to find common ground; our politicians, on the other hand— refined men and women whose careers centered on their reputed talents for arbitration—remained at each other's throats. Within the context of a Sunday school class—insulated from the pressures of politics and special interest groups, that is, or perhaps merely bound by a stricter moral code—I suppose that we all knew better than to stretch or marginalize the truth for the sake of proving a point. And while it wasn't exactly clear to any of us why things happened the way they did—why God would fill a person with homosexual longings, for one, considering that such attractions sprung from a proclivity described by the Bible as *an abomination*—it was well within our grasp that Jesus's highest command was to love. Not to condemn and certainly not to ostracize.

Hannah gained my hard-earned respect with the otherwise unpopular declaration that it wasn't our job as Christians to educate nonbelievers on right and wrong but rather to show them the unconditional love of Christ. While this ventured against the grain of traditional Southern Baptist doctrine—and indeed, it drew some sharp grumblings from within the church—Hannah proved this point with scripture after indisputable scripture. As believers, we were to build each other up through the accountability of discipleship and to love our neighbors. It was really that simple.

Man, was that ever good news. It still is, actually.

I had only a vague understanding of what discipleship entailed, but I took great comfort in knowing that there would never be an excuse—much less a divine charge—to tear another person down for his or her failures. For me, this was a startling revelation and I wished that my mother had been there to experience it.

Actually, it was dang tempting to hogtie the woman and drag her to class with me because time and time again I saw her prized misconceptions fall apart in that room.

To be fair, it's worth a mention that Christianity didn't necessarily fit me like a glove. I mean, it wasn't a stretch for me to believe that there was a higher power—I think I was born with that knowledge, even if I didn't yet know what to do with it. But if the Bible was our proof of a one-and-only almighty creator? Well, let's just say the jury was still out. The more time I devoted to the Bible though, the more it fascinated me. For the beauty of its stories, the complex interplay of time and culture—of course—but also for its unmatched ability to draw and withstand educated scrutiny over time.

Yet for all its splendor, in those early days the Bible remained nothing more than a book to me—brilliantly composed in my estimation but a book nonetheless. The concept of personal salvation was perhaps outweighed by the intrigue of a louder, more intellectually salient notion: that some five thousand years of comprehensive dogma continued to thrive, despite what I considered to be a pattern of blatant contradiction.

I mean, the human son of God—the same God who scourged the earth for the wickedness of mankind—now wanted us to love our enemies, to turn the other cheek when evildoers wielded their wickedness against *us*.

Um … say again?

Even before Jesus brought forth this new covenant, recorded history seemed to conflict with the character of a just, benevolent God. What about David? You know—the boy shepherd who took down Goliath and was later crowned king? The guy was a peeping Tom, for crying out loud! He watched women while they bathed and when one struck his fancy, he abused his power to lull her into damning infidelity.

Can anyone say *scumbag*?

Come to think of it, he went so far as to send the husband of his mistress off to certain death, yet David was nevertheless championed as *a man after God's own heart.*

What exactly was that supposed to say about God? That He had no regard for the very commandments He so dramatically sent down the mountain? That He provided certain exemptions to those who carved out time to slay giants? It took some concentrated effort to keep an open mind on the subject, because I gotta be honest: what I read didn't paint a pretty picture.

As a budding writer, I had other qualms as well. In particular, the reconciliation of the old and new testaments stuck out like a drunken seam. Not just in terms of disparate ideology but in the conspicuous absence of any literary transition whatsoever. The two halves seemed stitched together in sloppy haste with chronological holes you could drive a truck through. Was it really possible to contain the guts of a leaky plot in such a crude fashion? Well, apparently so.

And it certainly didn't ease my incredulity that the Bible was pieced together from unwritten accounts. Good grief, was I really supposed to buy that a composite of oral histories could endure the passage of countless generations without taking on some modifications? The men who eventually put these accounts to paper clearly did. Of course, they had never dealt with Nicky's exasperating brand of selective hearing when asked to hurry up and take a shower—

"What's that? You want me to shake a flower?"

—and in their infinite wisdom, they had undoubtedly mistaken the early practice of medicine for witchcraft, too. People simply couldn't be trusted to shed the bond between culture and unfounded belief. Nor could they be expected to rise above the prejudices of their upbringings. Or so I rationalized.

Please don't misunderstand—I never doubted the sincerity of their beliefs or anyone else's. I was simply bogged down by a deep-seeded need for unbending logic. I was a teenager, you understand; I thought I knew it all and anything that dared to disrupt that tidy delusion threatened to topple the known universe off its axis.

TWENTY EIGHT

Funny thing: you can choose to nitpick the Bible to pieces but if you take the time to read the teachings of Jesus Christ, they're gonna rub off on you. There's just no way around it.

With only a superficial interest in Christianity, I became a kinder more lighthearted me—if for no other reason than to feel minutely worthy of a certain young lady's attentions. And while I wasn't completely convinced that the Christian depiction of God was spot on, or that Jesus Christ was in fact His son, there was certainly no dismissing the wisdom of Jesus's teachings. As near as I could tell, endeavoring to follow them had no perceivable downside.

Nicky didn't suffer my nagging doubt. He dove in with childlike abandon and never looked back. He had always been a sweet soul but in the months that followed, he careened toward something even more humbling. Where I found ambiguity in God's word, my brother heard a distinct calling. Remarkably, and without the slightest hesitation, he hopped to it.

In the beginning, he signed on for the tried-and-true community outreach programs—food drives, car washes, neighborhood cookouts and the like. These were structured events and therefore ideal for getting his feet wet. But their effectiveness was also softened by flippant participation; volunteers—

particularly the younger ones—often made social events of these ministries, lacking any real burden for the cause they were supporting. Still, while this was frustrating for Nicky, the seasonal nature of such activities kept them few and far between.

When the outreach calendar hit its first lull as summer approached, Nicky spearheaded his own outreach programs—skits at a local nursing home, prayer circles at the hospital ICU. His enthusiasm was hard to ignore, so it came as no surprise when other members of the youth group caught the bug. Before long, the church couldn't keep up with them, which—if you were to ask anyone in church leadership—was a good problem to have. While most boys his age were sneaking peeks at the J.C. Penny lingerie ads, my little brother was actively seeking out opportunities to do for others what they could not do for themselves.

After school on Mondays and Fridays, Nicky tutored a neighborhood kid in Pre Algebra. He read to an elderly blind woman from church on Tuesday and Thursday evenings, much like I had once done for my grandfather. On Saturday mornings, he walked a mile in each direction to collect and shell pecans for a disabled veteran. The remainder of his free time was spent inventing new ways to be selfless.

Watching him carry on with such dedication, my heart swelled until I feared that it might burst. The kid was such a beautiful person. Before too, but now—under the mentorship of Christ—Nicky flourished unlike anyone I had ever known. The completeness of his metamorphosis wasn't just dramatic, it was truly inspiring. And likewise, witnessing firsthand what the love of Jesus Christ could do in a human being affected me greatly. Lately, I felt a stir within every time I looked at Nicky, as if a living thing was nibbling away at all those sickly doubts of mine. It ached constantly, like the healing throb of freshly scrubbed wounds. Not exactly comfortable but neither was it a terrible feeling. Hope is supposed to hurt a little, you know.

Anyway, I couldn't have been more proud to call that kid my brother if he had cured cancer. My mother, on the other hand …

Sigh.

Well, the disgusting truth is that she couldn't stand to look at him. Oh, I'm sure she did her best to play along—at least, that's what I choose to believe—but it was an exercise in futility. Deeply rooted dismay is dang near impossible to mask, you see; even for a seasoned pro like my mother. To her credit, her face betrayed nothing. But her disapproval managed to bleed through in other ways. The too-loud clatter of cookware, the stiff moments of watchful silence. Her clipped tone whenever she bothered to speak. The way she stormed around the house in a subdued stomp, hard enough to rattle the plates, but not quite hard enough to warrant a confrontation. All Nicky's recent efforts to honor her—the notes of encouragement left on the fridge, the Hershey's Kisses left on her pillow before bed—only served to agitate her.

If my feathers were ruffled by her inability to be supportive—and believe me, they were—poor Nicky was crushed by it.

"I don't understand," he once cried. "Why is she like this? Why can't she just be happy for us?"

I had no meaningful answer to this question at the time, when it counted. In the years that followed, however, I did manage to piecemeal a theory together. Of course, like any theory, mine was as likely to be wrong as right. I surmised that Helen Chase was simply a jealous mother. At least where Nicky was concerned. If I was on the right track, she must have resented that Nicky's purity of heart might've stemmed from something other than her parenting. Accordingly, anything spiritual that threatened to overshadow her contributions was surely filed away as proof that the church was conspiring against her, brainwashing Nicky to secretly despise her. No, not just despise—to *abandon* her. To curse her unabsolved sin, just as she imagined Christians were designed to do and then discard her for some magical deity in the clouds.

And as for the many childhood kindnesses we had enjoyed, thanks to the benevolence of Christians—the Christmas presents, the much needed food? These were merely acts of thinly-veiled condescension to her mind. Nothing could convince her otherwise.

Ugh.

If my mother could've set aside her prejudices for even a moment, I feel certain that she would've seen what was so abundantly clear to me and my brother. That the church wasn't filling our heads with contempt for her; the gospel of Jesus Christ wasn't drawing us away.

If anything, it was pushing us home.

Even if all my postulating was on target though, I couldn't really fault my mother. Because it wasn't arrogance that kept her from seeing the truth, you see. It was plain old fear.

Considering how much time I spent in school, it's surprising how little of it stuck with me into adulthood. I'm left with a handful of shallow vignettes that porpoise in and out of memory, months and even years fading in the intervals. A little depressing, I know, but these days I rely more on blurry impressions of my school days than any real recollections. There are a few exceptions, of course.

One in particular comes to mind.

I was almost never late to school; that much I remember well. Punctuality was a high priority for me, rising not from common courtesy but a prevailing sense of anxiety. You see, like any pariah I had learned early on that tardiness drew the unnecessary attention of my classmates—bored, sleep-deprived kids who were otherwise content to ignore me so early in the morning. Yet just a few weeks before the end of my junior year, there came a morning when the universe conspired to put me fifteen minutes behind schedule. Maybe the zipper broke on my pants or the toilet flooded just as I was heading for the door. I honestly can't remember. But while this little detail has long turned to dust, the tumult that it brought about lives on.

The campus was still upon my arrival. Eerily so, like the abandoned set of a long forgotten film. Nicky must've run on ahead, because I hustled across the grounds alone. I remember dew-soaked shoes and flushed cheeks, feeling oddly vulnerable—watched even.

I knew from the occasional bathroom excursion that the main entrance hall was never really empty. Stone-faced administrators were constantly poking around, minding every nook and cranny for some unlucky straggler to terrorize. I headed slightly off the beaten path for the athletic hall, which I expected to be unoccupied at such an hour.

Maybe it was. But alas, the partially-enclosed entryway was not. Propped against the brickwork within, slit-eyed like some kind of ambush predator, Philip was waiting. And he wasn't alone.

Philip was a big guy, but his two pals were bigger. They might've been twins—brothers, at the very least—with their matching caveman brows and blonde crew cuts. Together with Philip, they donned undersized baseball uniforms stretched taut like aerobic leotards, yet they found the gall to snicker at *me*. One of the twins—let's call him Tweedle Dee—made a Frankensteinish grimace as his twin—um, Tweedle Dum?—did the whole, 'Look at me, I'm retarded!' bit. Philip cackled like this was some truly innovative material.

Morons.

Passing through their midst was unavoidable, I realized. But wary or not, I refused to be intimidated. Well, I refused to let on that I was intimidated, anyway. I kept my attention on Philip rather than his buddies, though I didn't dare look any one of them in the eye. Wasn't that supposed to issue a challenge? Eye contact, that is—or did that only apply to bulls and attack dogs? As I approached the door, Phillip leaned in to taunt me with a single, filthy word—one that mischaracterized both my spine and sexuality. More surprised than angry, I stopped in my tracks.

A hundred yards behind me, the athletic bus—identified by a shoddy blue and white paint job—screeched to a halt at the end of the sidewalk. We all turned to look. The bus door accordianed open and the assistant baseball coach—who doubled as my World History teacher—leaned out. Spotting his players, Mr. Briggs called them in with an impatient clap. For a second or two, I really thought everything would be okay, so I gave Philip my back and reached for the door handle. I mean, what kid in his right mind would pick a fight with an adult looking on, right?

Sadly, I must report that rational behavior isn't always a given.

If I as a teenager had anything in common with Michael Jackson—aside from an irreversible familiarity with plastic surgery—it was that I was a lover, not a fighter. I'd say that my track record spoke for itself in that regard, wouldn't you agree?

Okay fine—so I was neither.

But if given a choice, I would've taken a kiss over a knuckle sandwich any day of the week. And so—true to form—when I detected the telltale rustle of fabric behind me, the sharp cutting of air, I didn't have the fighting instinct to duck. Rather, I braced myself for impact.

Philip caught me with a square-knuckled right cross, just behind the ear. It felt like a sledgehammer to the back of the head; the visible world exploded into a field of black, bespeckled with burning spots. In that same instant, while I was still seeing stars, the entryway resounded with a howl. Weak-kneed, I turned and blinked; Philip was nursing a wounded hand in the crook of his armpit, face contorted. Not sure what he expected—skulls are hard, heavy things. Especially mine, which was fortified with titanium plates.

I should've walked away then, of course. That or thrown up my dukes to defend myself. But I did neither. I just stood there like an idiot, too stunned to do anything but wait for whatever came next. And I wasn't the only one in shock. Philip's two friends were equally confounded, glued in place with mouths agape, eyebrows pinned to their buzzed hairlines.

"Dude," Tweedle Dee hissed. "What the heck are you doing?"

Dum nodded in exasperation. "Yeah, Phil. That's messed up! I mean, he's—you know, just *look* at the guy."

Philip flexed an already swelling hand. "Go on, guys. I'll be there in a minute." He popped his neck—for dramatic effect, I must assume, since it was I rather than he who was stiff-necked from a recent clobbering.

Dum sighed. "Let it go, man. The kid can't even defend himself."

"Yeah. He's a cripple or whatever. We got practice, anyway." They inched toward the sidewalk. "Come on, Phil. You're gonna get suspended."

More than the homophobic slur—even more than the sucker punch—the cripple remark got to me. I felt my blood boil and in that brief moment of distraction, my inner idiot once again came out to play.

"Yeah, Philip," it sneered. "Run along. Wouldn't want to get whipped by a *cripple* in front of your friends."

Philip's eyes widened, and unless my imagination was simply hard at work, the campus went from eerily quiet to utterly mute. The birds shushed, the breeze held its breath. Coach Briggs was off the bus now, bulging arms crossed in an agitated tilt, yet even he was silent. He knew what was going on, of course. He just didn't care. The Tweedles shuffled nearby, fidgeting almost noiselessly like livestock before a thunderstorm. It felt like the entire town was watching, waiting to see what would happen.

"Bullies aren't looking for a fight," my grandfather once told me. "They're looking for a victim." I'm inclined now to think he was onto something, because a look of dim uncertainty flickered across Philip's face. I won't lie; some part of me rejoiced.

Even expecting it, I wasn't quite prepared when Shawnee's star quarterback came at me. The guy truly was impressive; he was on me before I registered even the slightest movement. I took a glancing blow to the jaw and the next thing I knew, Philip was heaving me into the air. Just before I left the ground though, blessed muscle memory came to my aid. Throwing my legs wide, I cantilevered them behind me and leaned forward to lower my center of gravity. Philip grunted and I came to rest on my feet again.

Don't be so surprised—you don't share six hundred square feet of trailer house with a little brother and a Hulk Hogan poster without putting in some quality wrestling time. And it didn't hurt that Philip's athletic skill set was apparently limited to ball sports. Why he was so determined to take things to the ground was beyond me, except that his hand must've been throbbing like the dickens from earlier.

As we grappled, it became clear that Philip wasn't looking to settle some kind of a score; he was bent on dominating me. Humiliating me. The realization infuriated me all the more because it was just so senseless. What could anyone hope to gain from bullying a nobody like me? I mean, Philip already had everything—looks, money, popularity, a beautiful car ... the girl of my dreams—yet all that wasn't enough. He had to ... what? Lord over the lower crust, down to the lowly trailer park Thing? It was baffling.

From nowhere, an image fluttered into the caveman corner of my mind. Of this jerk pawing all over Ivy. Kissing her in his stupid car, hands creeping up her shirt. Defiling the girl who helped fold bulletins at church every week—the girl I was meant to spend my life with. Seething now, I sought out his wrists and locked on. They were thick and sinewy, though more gym-swollen than rock hard. A voice inside of me began to whisper and I didn't have it in me to tune it out.

Break him in half, it said. Sufficiently enraged, I allowed myself to squeeze a little harder—enough to restrain him, possibly to hurt a little—but no more.

Philip was busy trying to get me into some kind of leg bar but when his bones began to grind against each other in my grip, I heard him groan softly. The sound sent a shiver through me.

Tear him apart!

I squeezed harder still and yanked Philip to his full height. He lunged at me but my grip stopped him short. The confusion in his eyes was priceless; I'm a little ashamed to admit that I probably grinned.

Mess him up, pleaded that serpent song. *Make him bleed.*

Pinning his arms against his side, I drove Philip hard against the building. His head rebounded off the bricks with a satisfying *thud.*

Make him ugly ... like you.

Philip was afraid now, bug-eyes darting about. Part of me felt sorry for him, but it was a very soft-spoken whisper, drowned out by the louder majority.

Do it—hurt him!

Oh God, how I wanted to ... but I couldn't. I was afraid, you see. Not of Philip, much less his buddies. I was afraid of losing control; of the chain reaction that was sure to ensue if I gave in for even a moment. I knew better than most how abruptly lives could be destroyed by situations like these. I considered my father, wondering if the fateful moment when he had crossed the line felt anything like this. Disturbed by the idea—which was a sickening reminder that I was indeed my father's son—I relaxed my grip a little.

I could've hurt Philip, I knew. With all that adrenaline flowing through me, I had no doubt that I could snap his bones like kindling. Though smaller, I was inarguably the stronger of us; yet a lack of brutality in battle was as good as weakness. It didn't matter that the person I aspired to be had no tolerance for violence and certainly no need to dominate another human being. Given the circumstances, I didn't have the faintest clue what to do. So once again, as if the first time around had done me an ounce of good, I just stood there.

Philip, who was far less conflicted, seized the moment. With arms immobilized, he turned to his next best weapon. It's funny: I saw that shiny forehead of his coming in plenty of time to dodge it, or at the very least position mine to absorb the blow. Yet for reasons that may forever escape words, I didn't want to. The Bible says to turn the other cheek; who's to say I wasn't just following instructions?

I felt the impact on my nose, the blood dribbling forth as if from a leaky faucet. It was unpleasant, I'm not gonna lie. But it was also bearable. I wanted so badly to test my own masculinity, to show this pretty boy what it was like to *really* bleed. I wanted him to rue the day he was born, just as I did routinely.

My body was trembling now, and I can assure you that blood loss had nothing to do with it. This was the moment of truth, I realized. I was toeing the dreaded line beyond which there was surely no return. It slithered at my feet, crooning for me to cross over. *Just a tiny little step*, it whispered. *It's him or you, don't you see?*

Philip butted me again and then again. His forehead was slick with blood, and I was certain that at least some of it was his. Coach Briggs hollered gibberish in the distance; I wished the guy would be a grown up long enough to step in before things spiraled completely out of control. Apparently, that was too much to ask; it was up to me to reason with Philip and that simply wasn't gonna happen.

"I can do this all day," I said. My voice was strange, soft with a parental brand of soothing that sounded nothing short of otherworldly to my ear. The thing is though, I wasn't just talking smack. Scar tissue opens up easily, but it doesn't hurt much. And in the case of my facial bones, the nerve structure was pretty much shot as well. Beneath the grisly patchwork of my face was an unnaturally solid grid of titanium and unfeeling, calcified bone. I would swell up and bruise, for sure; and of course I was already bleeding like a stuck pig. No doubt I would have the mother of all headaches later, but for the moment? My pride was the only thing on the line.

Another wallop and my eyebrow split open. I felt a starburst of bony contact, but little else. I chuckled, full of piss and vinegar and foolish bravado.

"You like that?" Philip needled. His eyes were blinking excessively and it seemed clear that he was hurting himself more than me, even if I looked worse for the wear.

"You can't hurt me, Philip."

Another crack.

Nearby, a tired voice grumbled: "Good Lord." Apparently Coach Briggs was finally within earshot, though he approached in no particular hurry. We might as well have been playing Pat-a-cake for all his disinterest.

I began to squeeze again, still inhibited, and pulled Philip closer to me; there wasn't room for him to inflict any real damage now, but that didn't stop him from trying, over and over.

"You can't hurt me, Philip," I whispered again.

A knee caught me in the groin and the air whooshed from my lungs.

Correction ...

My teeth clamped shut in a pained grimace, revealing that my dental work was bent out of alignment. *Fantastic.* Lesson learned, I pivoted at the hips, using an upper thigh to protect my unmentionables. It was then that Philip decided to call for reinforcements.

"Get this freak off me," he bellowed to his friends, to Coach Briggs.

The Tweedles muttered unintelligibly but Coach Briggs had reached the end of his patience. "What in God's name is wrong with you?" he barked. "Finish that little pipsqueak off and let's get going. You're embarrassing yourself—and me!"

Philip growled and fought against my grip like a dog on a leash, face skewed, eyes tearing up with frustration. "Get off me!" His voice had thickened into the swell of a sob. "Just let go, you ugly freak!"

Believe me, I wanted to. I mean, what else was I supposed to do? I couldn't very well hold him hostage all day. And let's face it: Coach Briggs wasn't exactly out to do me any favors.

"Fine," I said. "But this is over, right?"

Philip glared in response.

Tightening my grip, fingers burrowing into flesh like pilings, I gave him a little taste of what I was actually capable of. "Say it."

"Fine," he yelped. "It's over, okay?"

"Alright then." Releasing Philip, I backed away. Not one of my brighter moves, as it turns out.

Coach Briggs spat on the sidewalk. "You gotta be kidding me, Philip," he jeered. "You're seriously tapping out to this pansy cripple?"

Philip glanced to his coach—a man he clearly wanted to please—then back to me, steeling himself. If he needed an excuse to break truce, here it was. With a shrill war cry, he began to pummel me. He danced and bobbed with startling precision, popping me three times before my mind registered the first hit. The last of these slipped off my chin and clipped me hard in the Adam's apple. The pain was indescribable. Worse, it fueled a fight-or-flight response that overshadowed any need for self control. Of their own accord, my hands formed iron fists and began to rise. It was a shot to the ribs that finally dissolved my resolve. Struggling to breathe, body practically vibrating with pent up rage, I snatched a handful of Philip's baseball jersey and wound up.

Yes, that's it ... just like that.

A final tag to the side of the head and I think I actually sighed with relief. My fist took flight, straight and true.

For once in my life, I didn't hold anything back.

TWENTY NINE

The principal's office was a poorly-lit, foreboding place that reeked of burnt coffee and the sickly miasma of frightened kids. Save for a small reading lamp on his desk, the only illumination came through the doorway. A paddle with large holes drilled in a grid hung from the wall approximately where a window ought to have been. It was peppered by signatures. That inflicting pain under the moral blanket of discipline was something worth celebrating in this inner sanctum unnerved me, and it certainly hemmed in my expectations. Maybe that was the whole point.

I held a bloodied wad of paper towel to my face. The nurse had done her best to clean me up but there are limits to what a person can accomplish with a first aid kit. Or as the nurse had so eloquently put it: "Hell's bells, we ain't equipped for a [GD] train wreck!" My refusal of emergency transport to the hospital didn't improve her demeanor any.

The secretary was now calling my mother, who reserved the final say on such things, but I knew the score—we couldn't afford a trip to the ER, and certainly not a superfluous ambulance ride. My fingers were secretly crossed that my mother would be unreachable. I couldn't face her, looking the way I did—beaten to a bloody pulp, eyes hooded with the shame of it all. Then again, it was long walk home for a person in my condition.

Several of my teeth—the real ones—wobbled in their sockets and my face was cut or mole-hilled in half a dozen places; the worst of these spanned my right eyebrow, which was flayed to the bone and bleeding profusely. Still, the damage was more or less superficial. Relatively speaking, I didn't look any uglier than usual. Just different.

A shadow swept across the room as Principal Donovan, backlit in monstrous silhouette, finally stepped inside. His voice boomed in the confined space.

"Well, Lincoln Chase. Never thought I'd see you in that chair."

Neither did I, but I found it far stranger that he seemed to know me it all. Sure, it was a small school, but Mr. Donovan had never even once made direct eye contact with me in the halls, much less spoken to me. His acknowledgment of me now with such familiarity betrayed that my presence had never really gone unnoticed by him, or anyone else; I had merely been ignored.

I won't tell you how that felt, and I sincerely hope that you never find out.

The principal squeezed behind his desk and plopped into a chair with a grunt. He tossed a thin folder on his desk, eyes deadpan. "What's that they say in the big leagues? Go big or go home?"

I didn't have the slightest idea what they said in the big leagues; my brush with sports had petered out before it could outgrow Pruitt Field, so I could only shrug.

"Point is, you could've started out a little smaller. I mean, Jeezis—Philip Hampton? Kid's got six inches and a good thirty pounds on you." He laughed a dry, asthmatic cackle, but I scarcely noticed—my brain was busy sizzling over that name. *Philip Hampton.* "Far cry from David and Goliath," the principal was saying. "But not by much, and you're lucky—"

"I'm sorry, sir. Did you say *Hampton?*"

Mr. Donovan looked at me over his glasses, frowning sharply at the interruption. "I did."

I swallowed with great difficulty. *Maybe it's a different Hampton*, I thought. But deep down, I knew.

Mr. Donovan watched me curiously for several seconds. "What're you saying, you meant to pick a fight with a different *Philip*?"

I shook my head. "No, it isn't that, it's just ..." Suddenly, the full implication of his phrasing clicked home, snapping me rigid. Before I could think better of it, I shot up from my seat. "Wait a second," I blurted out, perhaps louder than intended. "I didn't pick a fight—"

Mr. Donovan cut me off with a raised hand, smirking playfully.

"Settle down, Lincoln. I was only—"

"But you've got it all wrong—"

"That's enough, now. I'm fully aware—"

"Wait, what did Coach Briggs tell you? Because I—"

"Lincoln, sit down and shut your mouth!" the principal shouted. His eyes narrowed in warning. "Now." The smirk was long gone, along with whatever playfulness had prompted it. Deflated, I obeyed, dropping back into my chair.

"I'm not stupid, you know. Been doing this a long time."

Tearing up with frustration, I let my gaze fall to the floor.

"Matter of fact, I've known Philip his whole life."

Fantastic.

"He's a good kid with a bright future, but I won't deny he's got a wild streak. Starts a lot of fights. 'Course, they don't normally go this far." He paused to scratch his chin, which sounded a bit like an iron file against sand paper. "Seems like a kid from Tecumseh wound up with a mess of stitches last year, but that's about the worst we've seen out of Philip's escapades, until today."

Feeling a little less villainized, and perhaps a little more emboldened by his tone, I straightened in my chair. "It isn't as bad as it looks," I offered with a fat-lipped smile. "I wasn't exactly easy on the eyes to begin with."

Mr. Donovan leaned back, hands clasped across a sizeable midriff. His expression was grim. "Don't get me wrong, Lincoln; I'm sure the next couple of days'll be pretty rough on you, and that's a shame. But the truth is, you're the least of my concerns right now. I mean, Lord knows you've been through worse than this."

I'm not sure how much blood I lost in the fight but all at once, I was hyperaware of a deficit. Dizzy with fatigue, utterly terrified. What exactly had I done?

"He's gonna be okay, right?" I asked, despising the tremor in my voice.

Mr. Donovan sighed through his nose. "Oh, he'll live. I'm no doctor, but it sure looked to me like you busted his jaw. Knocked out a few teeth that I saw, maybe more." He let that percolate for several seconds. "My guess is he'll be eating through a straw for a while."

My body began to tremble. I had hurt someone. No, *hurt* didn't begin to cover it—I had *maimed* someone. And not just anybody, either; Shawnee's great hope, of all people. No point in sugar-coating the despicable truth. Despite everything I had come to believe about my own potential, despite the assurances of those who had entrusted me to walk a different path, I was now standing knee-deep in my father's footsteps. I wanted to curl up in the corner and cry my eyes out.

"Listen to me, Lincoln."

Hunching forward, I buried my face in my hands. The knuckles of my striking hand had mined deep into a swollen blob; the sickly flesh throbbed against my face, hot and strange, and I wondered if it was broken. A terrible sob racked through me, though tears remained mercifully at bay, for the moment.

"I want you to look at me when I'm talking to you, son."

I tried to comply but it was impossible to maintain direct eye contact for more than a second or two. It was like looking at the sun.

"This isn't your fault," he said softly, reasonably.

I felt a tear escape and brushed it away furiously. Was it worse to take all the blame, or none at all? I couldn't decide because neither satisfied my need for balance. "Of course it's my fault," I muttered. "Part of it, anyway."

"What part is that, exactly? We both know you weren't the instigator, and from what I hear, you had more than your fair share of provocation." From this, I surmised that the Tweedles had spoken up as opposed to Coach Briggs. Considering how that man might've spun things, I realized that I was actually pretty lucky. Only, I didn't want to be lucky. I didn't deserve it.

Anger boiled in my belly; a guilty, self-loathing variety that threatened to erupt in a torrent of expletives. "But I punched a kid in the face," I moaned. "As hard as I could."

Mr. Donovan tisked. "What, you think Philip was holding back on you? You were defending yourself, son. And I'd hardly call Philip a kid." He waved a hand dismissively. "Fights happen— comes with the XY chromosomes, like it or not."

"But Mr. Donovan … I—I knew how much I could hurt him." My lower lip began to quiver, another tear fell. "I mean, I *knew* … and I still put everything I had into it." More tears went rogue, cutting paths through a sheen of dried blood. "I just can't believe this is happening."

Mr. Donovan rose from his chair and rounded the desk. Now that he understood the true extent of my culpability, I expected him to take that ridiculous paddle off the wall. Maybe he'd use it to break *my* jaw. I think I wanted him to, in fact, because I had it coming. That would be justice.

He didn't, though. Mr. Donovan laid a hand on my shoulder with the awkwardness of a man who had grown accustomed to a certain amount of separation from the children he ruled over. That he dared to venture out of his element on my behalf should have lent some comfort, and I guess it did help on some small level. But I felt filthy for what I had done and it only made things worse that Mr. Donovan refused to acknowledge my wrongdoing. Why was he coddling me like this? Something wasn't adding up.

"Settle down, now," he said in a voice that reminded me so much of my father's that my heart leapt. "Everything's gonna be just fine."

"I'm okay," I croaked. I wasn't, of course. Far from it.

"Why don't you go on home, son. We'll straighten this all out tomorrow."

"But ..."

"Yes?"

I swallowed. "Aren't you going to suspend me or whatever? Expel me? Something?"

With a tired sigh, Mr. Donovan nodded. "Oh, I'm afraid so. We have a no tolerance policy on fighting here and I take it very seriously. Doesn't matter who starts it. But there's a lot to consider in this case, and the situation is more delicate than you probably realize."

I was afraid to ask, but I did anyway. "What do you mean?"

"Well, I'm guessing you don't already know that Philip's daddy is a fairly prominent attorney. Wouldn't surprise me if he filed a civil suit first thing in the morning."

I clinched my eyes shut, pinching off a tear. I deserved every bit of this, I knew, but ultimately it would be my family that suffered. There was no denying it, now; I truly was my father's son.

"I wouldn't lose too much sleep over it, Lincoln."

I guffawed bitterly.

"I mean it—a lawsuit's no laughing matter but at the end of the day, the Hamptons don't have a case. Not against you, anyway. They'll figure that out soon enough, if they haven't already."

"But if they sue me, I'll need a lawyer, right?"

"Yes, that's probably true."

"We don't have the money for that."

My paper towel was now completely saturated. Blood dribbled uninhibited from underneath it, scuttling down my cheek and collecting on my chin.

Mr. Donovan cleared his throat, shuffling on his feet. "I know, Lincoln." He handed me a clean paper towel and offered a wastebasket for the used one. "Why don't we table the discussion for now, okay? You really need to get that taken care of." He popped his head into the reception area, mumbled something to the secretary and then waited for a response. A moment later, he turned to me.

"Sounds like your mother's on her way," he announced, grinning with unabashed relief.

My tongue turned to sand. Had I really believed there was even a chance that my mother wouldn't come? She'd be crushed, of course.

"Why don't you lie down in the Nurse's station while you wait?" Mr. Donovan suggested. "You look a little pale."

In some ways, the hours following the fight were almost as traumatic as the fight itself. My mother cried all the way to the Indian clinic. Fearful of losing me, grateful that I was alive. Infuriated that anything had been allowed to happen to me. It was a long unsettling drive, to say the least. Thankfully, she was better composed on the return trip, though she stayed tightly latched on my hand the whole time. Every few minutes she gave me a little squeeze and took a deep breath. Even now, I can only imagine the thoughts that were going through her head.

As for me, I remained a mess, albeit a neatly buttoned-up one. My face was pleasantly numb, but I would feel it in the morning. I had twelve stitches along one eyebrow, three on my upper lip, three on one cheek and a few more in my mouth where I couldn't see to count them. My nose was broken and compacted with dried blood but nothing could be done about that. Diddo for the twin shiners, already steeped to a deep purple. And as feared, my head pounded relentlessly. Lastly, let's not forget my precious bridgework, which was in such grave disrepair that I could barely close my mouth around it. The good news was that my hand was only badly sprained, not broken.

I glanced at the gas gauge and cringed to find it hovering just over empty. Our trip to the free clinic in Claremore had just burned through the entire week's gas budget.

"Stop it, Lincoln," came my mother's soft chiding.

"Stop what?"

"Stop worrying. We'll be fine."

This was pure Midwestern posturing; I doubt that she would've phrased things any differently if we were living out of a refrigerator box. The bottom line was that we didn't yet know how much the fight would cost us, even if my mother was unwilling to acknowledge it. And though I knew full well that she was only trying to comfort me, a selfish urge to set her straight managed to get the better of me.

"He's gonna sue us, Mom," I argued.

The cab was silent, save for the squeak of the pickup's tired suspension springs. I hated that I had opened my stupid mouth.

"I know," she eventually whispered. "Probably so." Another squeeze.

I bit my stitched lip in penance.

Ahead of us, the Handy Dandy loomed into view. Even from a quarter mile away, I could make out the pump where Reggie Miller had bled out from his injuries. I tried to fight off the memories—the feral look on my father's face that day, the sound of his bloody boot slipping off the gas pedal; the graphic crime scene imagery released later during the trial, and a dozen more— but they swarmed over me like a plague of locusts to eat me alive.

When my mother let off the gas, it dawned on me with horror that she actually meant to fill up there. An overwhelming panic overtook me, punctuated by a dread so intense that it nearly hoisted me bodily from my seat. "No!" I cried.

Startled, my mother snatched her hand free of mine and shook it as if stung. "Lincoln! What's gotten into you?" Her face was flushed with an expression that wavered between worry and exasperation.

"Not there, Mom," I lamented. "God, anywhere but there." She stared at me for so long that I feared she would drive us right off the road. But then, she abruptly looked away, granting me the faintest of nods. The truck picked up speed and I closed my eyes.

THIRTY

My mother traded shifts with a coworker the next morning to drive me to school. The principal met us at the main entrance with a strained smile, hands clasped stiffly behind his back. He seemed anxious, and that put my nerves even more on edge. He led the way back to his office in long strides, leaving us trailing behind like frightened ducklings.

Once we were all seated, Mr. Donovan announced that he had already spoken to Mr. Hampton—or rather, his attorney. A lawsuit was indeed in the works. Only—thank God—it wouldn't name me; Coach Briggs was in the hot seat, and by extension, so was the school. Mr. Donovan seemed quite flustered by the whole affair.

I felt a little sorry for him.

But then, I remembered that he had never bothered to ask for my side of the story. He had been content to settle for the testimony of bystanders, who wouldn't dream of crossing their beloved coach, even if they'd sell their buddy down the river. Even now, Mr. Donovan wasn't interested in anything that I might offer to round out the truth. I could only deduce that he would rather hear all about it in court.

I had no way of knowing how wrong I was.

Throughout all this, my mother looked on with an expression of baffled relief. The last she had heard, we were about to be sued. Now the burden had been lifted from our shoulders and cast on those of a man she had never heard of. My fault, this time.

In my defense, I hadn't glossed over Coach Briggs's involvement with any intention of protecting the man; I just hadn't seen the point in bringing it up. As far as I could tell, Coach Briggs was just one of many shady characters with the gumption to plunder the privileges of adulthood. That he happened to be accountable for the enrichment of school children hadn't exactly struck me as a cause for alarm; it was just more proof that life wasn't fair. And however unethical the guy might've seemed in my estimation, I had never once thought of his slimy behavior as bordering on unlawfulness.

When the subject of the lawsuit finally petered out, Mr. Donovan turned to address me. My heart lurched. "As for you, Lincoln, I've given the situation a lot of thought. Considering that you weren't the aggressor, I've settled on a three day suspension."

My mother stiffened and I risked a sidelong glance at her. Her dazed expression seemed to blow away like a dried leaf. "Well, I hardly think—"

"Please, Mrs. Chase," Mr. Donovan interjected, hand raised to cut her off. "I understand your frustration, but—" This tactic might have stopped a lesser woman dead in her tracks; my mother swatted it away like a mosquito.

"Absolutely not," she spat. "That is totally unacceptable!"

Mr. Donovan sighed, hands falling limply to his lap.

"My son doesn't deserve to be punished. He didn't start that fight and everybody knows it. If you people had been doing your jobs, it wouldn't have happened in the first place." She crossed her arms and legs with defiant abruptness, her raised foot bouncing in a rapid cadence. My mother smirked then, full of grit and ice. "The Hamptons aren't the only ones with cause for a lawsuit, you know."

"Mom," I whispered. "Maybe it would be best if—" I tried to squeeze in, but she wasn't listening.

"So your golden boy got hit back for once, and now we're supposed to pretend like Lincoln had any choice but to defend himself?"

My cheeks flushed. Okay, so I might've spared my mother the burden of a few more details—like the part where I goaded Philip into finishing what he started with that ill-planned sucker punch.

"Look at him, for God's sake!" my mother demanded.

Mr. Donovan shot me a dry frown, but it wasn't to appraise my condition. I tried to grow a halo. *What? Yesterday it was all Philip's fault, remember?*

My mother was huffing now, cheeks flushed, nostrils flaring. Her eyes flickered to the paddle on the wall and a scowl puckered her lips. I had never seen her so brusque with another adult, and her temperament only festered as the seconds ticked by.

To his credit, Mr. Donovan kept a level head. He seemed to sense that my mother wasn't done ranting yet, that any effort to speak now would only get her going again. And he wasn't wrong; she got her second wind the moment he feinted a retort.

"Think about the message you're sending to the other kids," my mother pleaded. "You're telling them it's better to take a beating—to just give up without a fight—than to stand up for themselves. Well, let me just save you the bother with this one." She gave my shoulder a proud jab. "This young man has been through hell and back; and if you haven't figured it out yet, giving up isn't in his nature. So you go right ahead—you do your worst. But know this …"

Her eyes darkened and a deep crease split her forehead. She leaned forward to point a long finger at the principal, rigid and commanding. The muscles in Mr. Donovan's jaw bulged.

"If you insist on punishing my son for this, you'll only prove that at sixteen, he's already more of a man than you are."

My suspension resolved at one week. However flattering to me, my mother's inflammatory speech only managed to bring out the vindictive bureaucrat in Mr. Donovan. What did I care? A week, a year—I just wanted out of there. I needed time to process all that had happened, and to figure out how I was supposed to move past it. Fortunately, school was down to the last two weeks of classes, which were likely to snail by in a smear of crappy educational movies. I was pretty sure my grades would withstand the blow.

I couldn't stop thinking about Clyde and unless I found a healthier way to occupy my mind, there was a real danger of my poor little brain turning to gelatin. So the following day, I walked to the library. Mrs. Winters was off but I stayed until three-thirty anyway, crannied in the back where nobody could gawk over me. I read a weird yet invigorating novel about a gentleman time traveler. Inspired, I scribbled out a short story on bits of scrap paper. It was crap, but I kind of liked the bones. Later at home, I took another stab with better results. Nicky read the second draft and gushed with praise. I couldn't stop smiling.

I wanted to keep the momentum going, so the next morning I set up under the wandering tree with my writing gear. Someone had been digging for meteorite fragments, which was hardly new, even if it never ceased to annoy me. I smoothed over the holes with the side of a shoe, grumbling under my breath. Only then did the magic overtake me.

The air around me seemed to sing; my mind flooded with new perspective. All my cares turned to vapor and for a while, the world was a beautiful place again.

I quickly mapped out a continuation of the previous day's story and began to bring it to life. Out of practice and bursting with parallel ideas, keeping the plot moving in a straight line proved to be tedious and all-consuming.

It was exactly what I needed to keep my mind off what I knew was coming.

At six-thirty a.m., my alarm clock blared a rude good morning. Nicky stirred in his bunk, ripped a motorcycle fart, then went right back out. I was already wide awake. Actually, I had spent the entire night tossing and turning, thanks to Brutus. The fleabag had barked well into the wee hours, giving it a rest only when the moon finally dropped out of view. You'd think that after all those years I would've learned to tune out the nightly ruckuses of Lakeview Park, as Nicky had done. Then again, you'd think an old dog would know better than to trash talk a celestial body. I guess me and Brutus were both slow learners.

The truth is that I wouldn't have slept much, anyway; I couldn't steer my thoughts away from Clyde Hampton, whose grandson I had maimed. This morning I would have to face him, and the prospect had been nagging at me for days.

Confrontation was something that I dreaded as a rule—as you must know by now—but this went way beyond hashing out a petty disagreement. I had grown to care deeply for the custodian, you see. And what I had done must've sent shockwaves through his entire family. He was a gentle soul who deserved far better than the destructive properties of my friendship.

Considering that we had a phone, I could've saved myself a roundtrip. But the idea didn't feel right. Clyde deserved to hear the truth face-to-face and I would allow no amount of anxiety to rob him of that.

More out of habit than need, I tried to force down a bowl of puffed rice cereal. It was bland stuff that I would forever despise, made worse on that occasion by milk that was on the verge of turning. Halfway through, as the mush turned to hot acid in my stomach, I questioned the wisdom of going through these banal motions. Pretending that everything was fine wouldn't make it so, after all. I dumped the remainder down the drain and hoped to God my mother wouldn't find out.

When the clock read seven-thirty, I headed out the back door.

I cut briskly between the trailers, kicking spray into the air with each determined step. Brutus was asleep next door—finally!—curled against a section of half-shredded carpet, fur glistening with morning dew. *Poor guy,* I thought.

The sound of my footfalls—or perhaps the smell of my sympathy—must've roused him, because the Pit Bull was suddenly on his feet, rushing me in a spasm of bristling fur and yellow teeth. I stumbled back, falling to my rear. Until that moment, down on his level, it had escaped my notice just how huge that dog really was. An absolute monster, I'm telling you. Taller than most Pits but muscle bound and barrel-chested with all the hallmarks of his dominant breed. And as was the nature of such a beast—at least, so it seemed in that moment—Brutus aimed to kill me. He was going to snatch me up in those massive jaws and tear me to shreds. I was too stunned to do more than gape.

Less than three feet away, Brutus jolted to a halt at the end of his chain. He snapped at thin air, whining at his restraints. His fetid breath wafted over me, reeking of carrion and what could only be the bones of missing children.

It was a miracle that I was still alive; yet however grateful I should've been, I was too angry to muster an ounce of gratitude.

"Stupid dog!" I hissed.

Scurrying to my feet, I backed away, shaking. The butt of my pants was soaked through, plastered in grass clippings and something that I chose to believe was mud. I heard muffled cackling behind me and turned to find Nicky framed in the bedroom window, face lit up by a hysterical grin.

"Smooth moves, Ex-Lax!" he jeered. I gave him a sarcastic thumbs-up—you know, because that one never gets old.

Glowering, I pushed across Pruitt Field toward the far tree line, leaving Brutus to guard his pathetic little territory. I needed time to prepare, yet my body was propelled forward by an unrelenting sense of urgency—a primal need to get it all over with before I changed my mind. By the time Food 4 Less bobbed into view, marking the halfway point, I was clipping along at a jog.

What exactly was I supposed to say to Clyde? Ugh. As a would-be writer, it felt like a personal failure whenever words evaded me.

Under the circumstances, there was a very real temptation to stretch the truth a bit. As far as I could tell, it wouldn't take much effort to spin a more palatable reality; I mean, according to Mr. Donovan I was the real victim. But while I had the creativity, I lacked the conviction of a seasoned liar. However ambiguous my face might've been, Clyde Hampton was more discerning than most. And if Nicky was to be believed, I had the worst poker face known to man. No, my chances weren't good. I decided that I'd rather not be pegged a liar on top of everything else.

And let's be honest: maybe I hadn't gone in search of a fight, but neither had I walked away when one reared its ugly head. And as much as I wanted to fault Philip for the whole affair, there was no denying that I too had embraced violence with open arms; if only for a moment.

All I could do was face the music. Even if it led to my unemployment.

The custodian met me with a warm smile. He offered me coffee and a glazed donut. Stomach in knots, I declined.

"You'll regret it later," he warned with a knowing chuckle. I shrugged. The shiny bristles of my stitches must've caught his notice then because his eyes suddenly widened, darting from wound to wound.

"Oh, my goodness," he muttered. "You've been hurt!"

I wanted to spill the beans right then and there, but I froze— riveted in place like a poorly-chiseled bust. Clyde stepped closer for a better look. "For heaven's sake," he breathed, scarcely above a whisper. "Come with me, son."

From his pocket, a large ring of keys appeared. He unlocked the nearest door and ushered me inside. Though I knew the way, I allowed the older man to lead me through the corridors to the kitchen. The grandfatherly smell of aftershave and hair tonic filled his wake, and their sweet familiarity set my heart to aching.

In the kitchen, Clyde rustled through a series of cluttered cabinets until he found a first aid kit. He relieved it of a large gauze pad and handed it over. "Your cheek," he explained. "It's bleeding."

I accepted the gauze and dabbed it against my stitches. It came away blotched with crimson. Clyde was waiting for an explanation, I knew, and the silence between us was soon swelling. This was the ideal time to get everything out in the open, but I hesitated. Once the words were spoken, you understand, there would be no taking them back. Clyde would never see me the same again, no question about that.

Still, it had to be done. So I closed my eyes and swallowed the frog crawling up my throat.

"It was me," I blurted. "I'm the one who—who hurt Philip."

Clyde looked surprised but nodded slightly, the corners of his mouth turning down.

I was trembling now, grasping for the right words. "I didn't mean for it to happen," I pleaded. "I'm so sorry." For all my forethought, this was truly the best I could come up with.

Clyde nodded again, sipped his coffee.

"I'll understand if you decide to fire me."

The custodian laughed at this, his bushy eyebrows merging into a dubious sweep. "Fire you? That's nonsense, Lincoln."

"But I got in a fight at school ..." The relevance of this seemed quite logical at the time. Looking back though, I have to wonder if the old parental 'trouble at school, double trouble at home' decree was crawling blindly through the expanse of my guilty conscience.

Clyde set his coffee on the counter and draped one arm across the other. "Mr. Chase, what happens at school is between you and the school. And as far as I know, it still takes two to tango."

I nodded. "Mr. Donovan says I broke his jaw."

"Yes, indeed you did. And it looks to me like he got some licks in, too."

I groaned, daring a smirk. "You have no idea."

The custodian flashed a smile that slowly faded into melancholy. "Philip is the spitting image of his father, I'm afraid; he's spoiled, selfish and derives far too much pleasure from the humiliation of others." He sighed, shaking his head, and it seemed that he had aged ten years in the last few minutes. "Still," he continued, "he's my grandson and I love him dearly. I hate that he's in pain but ... well, I suppose he'll learn a lesson from this that his mother and father could not—or would not—teach him."

I didn't know what to say, so I said nothing at all. I dabbed at my cheek, which was now dry, and concentrated on holding my emotions at bay. It was a battle that could still go either way, but I was dry-eyed for the moment.

"Philip is a troubled young man, Lincoln. More than most people realize. The only thing he needs more than discipline is Jesus Christ." He tried to laugh, but it emerged as a morose sound that belied deep, festering sadness. "Too bad his parents have deprived him of both." He bit his upper lip, eyes abruptly wet and transient.

"I'm sorry, Clyde. I didn't realize any of that."

The old man waved this off, then shot me a firm glance. "Please don't misunderstand," he said, wagging a finger for emphasis. "I'm not excusing what you did. But nobody's perfect. And I've spent enough time with you to see your true character." Then he smiled and—thank God—it was the real thing again. "So in case you're keeping score, God has already forgiven you. As for me? I have nothing to forgive you for."

THIRTY ONE

By the end of my vaca—um, suspension—I knew exactly what I wanted to do with my life. I just needed to figure out how to make a living churning out stories that no one would ever publish. Of course to maintain inspiration I'd need to take up permanent residence under the wandering tree. Sounded easy enough, except that hoboing around Pruitt Field was probably frowned upon—with no plumbing, there would eventually be a smell. And inclement weather posed a few problems, as well.

Alas, it was back to school with me.

Seeing Philip for the first time that week was a tad awkward. I found him waiting by my locker after first period, hands clasped patiently like he had no particular place to be. What a relief to see the school administration taking his hourly whereabouts more seriously! The Tweedles weren't with him, though another of his friends lingered within earshot by the water fountain.

Smelled like an ambush to me. I considered coming back later but emphatically decided against it; Philip hadn't earned that kind of control over my comings and goings. I approached with caution.

"Hey," he said, and though his lips moved faintly, his mouth remained tightly shut.

"Hey," I replied. My fingers were flexing into fists, I realized. They were ready to rock-n-roll. It was unlikely that Philip would be looking for a fight on his first day back, I knew, but I wasn't willing to bet on it. And I had no intention of taking another beating in any case.

Philip glanced around with a frown and I realized that hallway traffic was piling up on our account; worthy of concern, of course, because an audience could always be relied on to make situations like this worse than they already were. Philip looked back to me, cheeks blooming. This is when a guy like him would normally pull an excuse from his rear to start something—"Heard you were talking smack about me," or something like that. But Philip surprised me with a crooked grin. "Bunch of blood-thirsty piranhas, huh?"

I shrugged warily.

"I wanted to apologize," he said, consonants emerging in a flat lisp. "For what I did, I mean." His cheeks darkened even more. "And for, um … what I called you."

It's hard enough to apologize with the benefit of privacy; it must've been torture with all those people watching. That he made the effort caught me off guard. This was a Philip I would never have guessed existed. Whatever I might've thought about him before that day, and despite the misery he had brought upon us both, he earned a tremendous helping of respect in that moment.

Still, when Philip offered his hand, my certainty faltered. What if this was just an elaborate ruse? And I wasn't the only one hung up on this possibility, for the record; not a single harsh word had been exchanged so far, yet twenty to thirty kids continued to stand by with bated breath. I took a hard look into his eyes and saw what I perceived to be sincerity, and possibly humility. Shame, for sure. It was perhaps my first brush with the notion that people can—and actually do—change, heedless of the cynics among us.

Later in the lunchroom, Philip invited me over to the *cool* table; naturally, I declined. Unaccustomed to hearing the word *no*, he persisted until I finally relented. So, there I sat. Surrounded by the socialites of my class—the *pretty people*, as I had often thought of them—I could barely eat. My nerves crackled like crossed wires each time one of them glanced my way and it took concentrated effort to keep from scampering away when one went so far as to speak to me.

I learned that Coach Briggs had quietly resigned during my absence. Surprisingly, his leaving stirred up very little controversy among the students—teachers were probably a different story. I suspect that most kids were too relieved that he was gone to jinx it with unnecessary questions. A sub took over my World History class and the mood in there was just shy of celebratory.

I never told anyone what I had witnessed, and no one ever asked.

Not that I would know from any personal experience, but Philip's friends agreed that he was a profoundly more light-hearted person with the coach now out of the picture. I had to wonder what kind of torment Coach Briggs had inflicted on the guy.

I would find out one day, of course. Only, by then it would be too late.

We didn't have much in common, Philip and me. For one, he hated reading. He hated writing even more. It was unfortunate for him that being a high school senior demanded a fair amount of both. Beyond this, most of our differences could be chalked up to a basic conflict in upbringing. Waste, for example, was as much a part of his daily routine as scrounging was to mine. He bought soft drinks and tossed them after a few sips; he threw pencils away when they only needed sharpening. I'm betting that if I had taken the time to dig those out of the trash, I could've clad a small house in mustard yellow by the end of the semester.

Not to draw too fine a point on the issue, but I was pretty bewildered—if not disgusted—by Philip's blatant disregard for prudence. I mean, exactly how much money did a person require for it to lose all value like that? It was truly disturbing. Worse, this sort of careless behavior wasn't limited to *things*. Philip went through people in the same way, tossing them aside the moment they ceased to amuse him. Like some Hollywood diva, he used and abused his friends and for the most part, they ate it up. The few who lashed back were branded antagonists and disbanded from the group. It was pretty messed up. I promised that I'd walk if Philip ever treated me like that and he must've taken me seriously, because he never did.

The more I got to know Philip, the more I realized that he wasn't a bad guy; he was a spoiled, misguided kid who wasn't built to sustain a life of stardom. On the rare occasion when he dropped all pretenses, he seemed like the coolest guy in the world—funny, smart, vulnerable. Kind, even. More often than not, though, I just wanted to smack the brat right out of him.

Still, I stuck by him. Something about him struck a chord in me, though I couldn't put my finger on it at the time. Philip was an only child who—like most teenagers—didn't get along with his parents well. He was attention-starved, despite an overabundance of superficial relationships at school. That much I could see plainly. My guess was that he had probably never experienced the ironclad loyalty of an actual friendship—the sort of unconditional bond that can only thrive with no strings attached.

Clyde believed that only Jesus could fill the void in Philip and I didn't necessarily disagree with that assessment; yet I felt compelled to put myself out there in the meantime because everything else in Philip's existence seemed to encourage life on a pedestal. Empty out his wallet and he'd be powerless to entertain himself, much less an entourage. Throw in a season-blowing knee injury and the college recruiters would scatter with the wind, followed by Shawnee's fickle adoration. The guy must've been terrified.

Someone needed to show Philip that he genuinely mattered, that his value transcended his bank account—even his glory on the football field. The problem was that everyone was too busy deifying him, heaping offerings on an altar that was already buckling. They either didn't see or didn't care what it was doing to him.

Well, so be it then. I resolved to be that person.

Of course, I had no idea what the job entailed. I thought it should be enough that I was determined; I would be a light just as Brigham had once been for me. So I put all I had into it, tolerating Philip's unbending sense of entitlement, his mercurial affections. And there were times when I really believed that I was getting through to him. More often than not though, I felt like I was moving a mountain one spoonful at a time.

It was naïve of me—no, it was arrogant—to think that I could make a difference on my own. I see that now.

Just when I was ready to throw up my hands with Philip, he and Jeremy hit it off. It was weird at first, I'm not gonna lie—you know, that whole *worlds colliding* thing—but it didn't take long to warm up to the idea. The timing was perfect, after all. And as much as I had the desire to help Philip, Jeremy had the tools; he wasn't merely older and wiser—already in college, in fact—he understood the pressures of high school athletics firsthand. And it didn't hurt that the two had baseball in common.

Outside of school, they spent a lot of time together—afternoons at the batting cage, evenings at the mall, that sort of thing—and it seemed to do Philip a lot of good. He respected Jeremy in a way that he would never respect me, perhaps because

Jeremy's brilliance spoke louder than my quiet devotion. At times, this stung a little but I learned to focus on the greater good.

As for my own extracurriculars, they remained largely unchanged. Without a car, I was fairly stranded. I couldn't fault the guys for not going out of their way to include me; I mean, who wants to waste away the afternoon playing chauffeur? Actually, if I'm being completely honest, I welcomed the daily reprieve. Being social exhausted me, so it was nice to be alone after school. Solitude had always been important to me. It was familiar—grounding, even—particularly at a time when everything else seemed surreal.

Incidentally, there was no shortage of busywork around the house. You see, the woes of high school were quickly piling up on Nicky—baseball practice, mountains of homework, youth group activities, girls calling every few minutes to say hello.

Sigh. Poor kid.

So it was no surprise that his chores suffered; the only real surprise was that my mother didn't even bring it up. Anyway, Nicky didn't exactly have to beg for help; when I realized what was happening, I offered to take on some of the load and he happily agreed.

It's worth mentioning that my intentions weren't completely noble. The truth is that I missed the catharsis of physical labor. It made me feel stronger, more in control. I could rely on the wandering tree to give me words—inspiration, glimpses into new worlds even—but the intangible wasn't always enough; some frustrations cried out for the woodpile.

THIRTY TWO

When school started in the fall of 1994—my senior year, if you can believe it—I decided to make a serious life change. It was time to get over Ivy. While my heart still fluttered at the thought of her, I was finally seeing the situation clearly—and what I saw was pretty unsettling.

Love at first sight. That's how I justified the unwavering intensity of my crush. Yet over the course of several years, I had blown off countless opportunities to engage Ivy, to nudge reality into eclipse with my little dream world. Not exactly how love was supposed to work.

What the heck was wrong with me?

Blowing off steam with the splitting maul had a way of bringing my anxieties to the surface, no doubt about it. But it was ultimately my fascination with writing fiction that finally exposed the truth about Ivy. Or rather, the paradox of my feelings for her. You see, you can't write a convincing love story based on a long-cultivated obsession; yet that's exactly what I had come to expect out of life. Okay, I should probably clarify that it is possible to write a story like that—but it would be more likely to end with a strangling than a happily ever after.

I was in love with the idea of Ivy, I realized. The fairy tale. Captivated by her beauty to the extent that I created an entire persona around it—in my mind she liked all the things that I liked, hated what I hated. She had all sorts of adorable eccentricities designed to bring a girl of her refinement down to my level. Without even realizing it, I had painted a bizarre alternate reality where it actually made sense for us to be together. Where Ivy was the most perfect lady in the world and yet she was all mine. Who knows, maybe she was everything that I imagined, but the odds weren't good.

And let's face it: a girl like Ivy had no reason to give me the time of day, either way.

Deep down, I must've understood this all along. Maybe I was simply too invested in the fantasy to pick it apart. Meddling with the smoke and mirrors would only spoil the illusion, after all. That or reveal it to be just plain stupid.

Nevertheless, one thing was now inarguable: obsessing over a girl—a relative stranger, at that—was unhealthy. Who am I kidding? It went way beyond unhealthy—it was downright creepy. Nothing good could possibly come of it. My grudging acceptance of this was at once crushing and liberating. Almost instantly, two things happened.

First, other girls suddenly caught my interest. It was like the walls of my romantic tunnel vision were vaporized in a split second. I was surrounded by beautiful young ladies at school, many of whom were quite nice to talk to. Smart witty creatures with long lashes and legs for miles. Not that any were interested in me. Sure, they tolerated me—some even fawned over me in jest— but at the end of the day? I was just *so funny* or *a really good friend. Such a fun lab partner.*

Good Lord, how did I become the new senior class mascot?

Secondly, and tragically, church lost all appeal. Looking back, I can see that it happened in tandem with the shedding of the *old me*—the *me* that ran through rainstorms just to get a glimpse of a childhood crush, only to shy away from actually talking to her.

The *me* that refused to acknowledge that if there really was a god, he either caused or allowed human suffering.

Though I maintained a friendship with Clyde, and still worked for the church as needed, my Sunday attendance became sporadic and then stopped altogether.

That's the problem with buying into religion without a legitimate interest in understanding God, by the way. It becomes a passing phase and nothing more. So like many before and after me, I accepted the very real probability that there was a god—and opted to do nothing about it.

Thanks to Philip, after years of watching from the outside in, I was finally getting a feel for normal high school society. I came in on the low end of the pecking order, understandably. Yet with the exception of Sunday school, this was the closest I had ever come to feeling like a regular kid. No longer the abominable, white-trash freak—even if I had yet to retire the uniform—people treated me like just one of the guys. The same kids who had ignored me for the last twelve years now high-fived me in class, offered me rides home after school. Sure, we were all older and more mature, but I have to acknowledge the joint efforts of Jeremy and Philip; without them, I suspect the rest of high school might've dribbled by in a series of wedgies and wet willies.

It didn't take long to realize that *normal* high school kids were just as messed up as me; they were just better at hiding it. Many maintained split personalities with such skill that I might never have known, had I not routinely come to witness the transitions for myself. Some were model students—rarely tardy, homework always done; they were respectful kids who always remembered to raise their hand before speaking in class. Yet Friday nights unleashed a wild streak in them. They congregated by the river to drink beer and smoke pot around a campfire until they could barely speak in coherent sentences.

This was called partying, I learned, though I don't recall being offered a piece of birthday cake. Not really my scene. Flirting with addiction didn't exactly appeal to my sense of adventure—I didn't need that in common with my mother, thank you very much. The truth was, my aversion went deeper than I could make sense of. The very sight of drugs or alcohol cinched my stomach into knots. And whenever I saw Philip or Jeremy with a beer in hand, my heart swelled with worry.

For this reason, I made an effort to show up whenever invited. Chaperone, babysitter, wingman, designated driver—I was a young man of many hats, determined to earn his keep. And to watch over his friends. Somebody had to be the voice of reason when things like prank calling Principal Donovan or peeing off the dam sounded like a good idea. For the most part, I hung back to observe, venturing into the firelight only when summoned.

Philip quickly gave me cause for concern. The more he drank the more closely he resembled the jerk we all thought he had outgrown. He became snide and generally unpleasant, catcalling the girls and taunting the guys until a fight broke out or he eventually passed out drunk. More than once, I had to drive him home and then walk home myself.

He couldn't be approached about it; not even in the sober hours. Any attempt to do so was met with churlish resistance. "Relax, Lincoln. I'm just blowing off some steam, okay?"

Except that it really wasn't okay, and everyone saw it but him.

In late March, just a few weeks before our senior prom, we nearly lost Philip to alcohol poisoning—something I had never even heard of until then. It was frightening for all the obvious reasons—I mean, my senior class had nearly lost one of its own— but it also revealed our pristine ignorance for all things non-high school. We were months away from graduating and for the first time it dawned on many of us how unprepared we actually were for adulthood. It was a wide world out there, full of wonderful and terrible things. And the day was drawing near when it would be up to each of us to discern between the two for ourselves.

To this day, Brutus remains among the toughest animals I have ever encountered, and he was by far the most feared in Lakeview Park. Once, the old Pit Bull took on two free-roaming Rottweilers who dared to venture into his yard. The grandeur of the ensuing brawl stopped just short of a seismic event, drawing bystanders from a half-mile away. One of the Rotts died on the spot, the other a week later of an infection resulting from his injuries.

The truth is that it would be difficult to put a number to the animals who had died at his feet. Brutus was a finely-tuned killing machine and at times it seemed that he was good for nothing else; but that wasn't really the case.

He was also a hero.

When I was ten years old, a little girl named Darla was almost killed as she rode her bike up and down the lane; a few trailers down from mine, a car struck her on its way out of the park. The driver—not a park resident, apparently—fled and was never identified. Nobody heard or saw a thing. Darla was knocked unconscious with her coat half ripped off, left for dead.

Thankfully Brutus was always watching. Some time after the car sped away he broke his chain to get a closer look. But rather than hasten her death, the Pit curled up against this poor girl to keep her warm. It was cold that day, just above freezing with heavy snow in the forecast. If not for Brutus, she would've died of hypothermia right there on the road.

When Darla's parents came looking for her an hour or more later, Brutus wouldn't let them anywhere near her. Nor were the paramedics allowed to approach when they arrived, which was obviously a problem. Fortunately, the dog's owner—a fifty-something bachelor by the name of Cass Bryant—arrived home from work and was able to talk the dog down before things went any further south.

I remember feeling tremendous guilt on that day, watching the ambulance spirit Darla away. Hours earlier, you see, Darla had been flaunting that new bike of hers outside my living room window—showing off for Nicky, I would one day realize. It shames me to admit that I despised her for this; I hated everything about her because Santa had deemed her worthy of a bicycle and me a deck of playing cards and a second-hand belt. For a long time, I remained convinced that my ugly thoughts had caused her accident. I still wonder about it today, if I'm being honest. In my darkest hours, nothing seems implausible.

Darla suffered a pretty serious head wound along with a broken leg; she spent some time in a coma but eventually awoke to make a full recovery. That little girl had touched the garment of death itself, yet thanks to the hell hound chained up outside my window, she would live to tell the tale.

So in spite of Brutus's violent history, we learned to overlook the incessant barking, even the occasional cat-hunting spree. As a community, we owed him a debt that none of us knew how to pay. Indeed, many tried to reward the beast with treats or chew toys; Brutus ignored these sentiments, recognizing only that there were trespassers to be dealt with.

Over time, the dog became as much a fixture in Lakeview Park as any of its trailer houses, and more so than some of its transitory clientele. His antics could always be relied on to stir things up and when they sometimes strayed into the realm of unlawfulness, those of us with some tenure in the park stepped forward to defend his honor.

The day Brutus died, Lakeview Park didn't merely lose a fixture; we lost a legend. Cass announced the passing of his beloved dog shortly after sunrise with a shrill wail, which trailed into a string of sharp expletives. The outburst snapped me from a deep sleep, sending me stumbling blindly through the unlit house to investigate. Peeking out the kitchen window, I saw Cass cradling the huge animal to his chest—an impressive feat that Brutus would never have allowed in life. When it dawned on me what I was seeing, my breath left me; my brain stalled. A lifeless Brutus didn't belong in this world; it simply didn't make sense and therefore couldn't have been real.

My body abandoned me then, storming out the back door with a mere glimmer of awareness trailing behind it. And then I was at Cass's side, trying to reconcile how I'd gotten there against what was expected of me now that I had arrived. Cass seemed oblivious of my presence, yet even in my own befuddled state, I recognized the paralysis of grief; in my experience, it either robbed a person of his ability to interact with others or knocked the energy to care just out of reach. Either way, I knew better than to take it personally.

Similarly stricken, I had no words of comfort for Cass, so I said nothing. I placed a shaking hand on Brutus's side, more than half expecting—hoping, even—that he would spring back to life, eager to relieve me of my hand. The poor guy's fur was damp and surprisingly coarse, not unlike steel wool. Underneath, his flesh was only slightly warmer than the morning chill; he must've died in the night, I realized. With a stab of guilt, it dawned on me that it must've been Brutus's death—or rather, the silence brought about by it—that had allowed me such a good night's sleep.

Cass looked at me abruptly, as if he could read my thoughts—eyes wild and pleading, mouth stretched in a quivering grimace. He stomped a booted foot in anguish, or perhaps rage— impossible to tell given their tendency to bleed together in times like this. I placed a hand on his shoulder, which was trembling with exertion. I'm not sure where these comforting gestures came from on my part or how they manifested so naturally—lacking the awkwardness that I normally confronted, that is. After all, neither Cass nor Brutus had ever shown me an ounce of affection. Yet I felt a kinship with them now; there was no denying that.

When Cass calmed, we parted company long enough to fetch shovels from our respective sheds. We buried Brutus under a diseased hackberry tree against the property line, which was the best that either of our cramped lots had to offer. Barefoot and still in pajamas, I wasn't much help. But I did try and Cass offered no complaint. It didn't take long anyway, and when the deed was done, Cass shuffled back indoors with a stoic nod.

Approaching the stairs to my own trailer, a tear slipped past my defenses. Then another. By the time my mother met me at the door, I was sobbing. Without a word, she pulled me into an embrace. I didn't expect her to understand, considering that I didn't quite understand, myself.

Somehow though, she did.

That night my mother made me unbelievably proud. When dinner was ready, she asked us to set an extra plate at the table and slipped out the back door before Nicky or I could ask questions. Ten minutes later, she reappeared with a wary and very disheveled Cass in tow. Grinning ear to ear, Nicky offered him a seat and the older man's eyes widened at the feast before him. Fried chicken, mashed potatoes, bread and butter. Sweet tea. A far cry from the canned chili and saltine suppers that he had probably grown used to. He mouthed the letter O, giving us an intimate gander at his only two front teeth, and then quickly covered his mouth.

Before we ate, my mother permitted something that she normally frowned upon, a ritual that Nicky and I had taken for granted as children; we bowed our heads to pray over the food. Nicky did the honors as we all held hands. I felt my mother's hand in mine, limp at first—then stiff, agitated. As my little brother spoke, I let the words wander through me as if they were alive and indeed, they did seem to come alive. A fuzziness washed over me, warm and assuring. It was a strange sensation, yet instinctively familiar. If there remained an element that science had yet to explore or explain, this was it.

With the food properly blessed, Nicky turned to me, eyes twinkling, and clapped me on the back. "Feel that, don't you?" he said. My mother sighed with irritation. Nicky rolled his eyes, covering his mouth conspiratorially. "Know what that is?" he whispered.

I shrugged noncommittally. "Happiness, I guess."

"No, not just happiness," he hissed. "That's the Holy Spirit, Link."

Though I knew he wasn't joking, I cocked my head quizzically, just in case I was wrong. My mother slapped a dollop of mashed potatoes onto Nicky's plate, eyes narrowed in warning. He reached out to touch her arm.

"Love you, mom," he whispered. "You know that?"

My mother stared for a moment, motionless, with the serving spoon poised in midair. Honestly, I thought she might smack him with it but she didn't. All signs of irritation melted slowly away, revealing a smile that only a mother can produce—and only then with a boy like Nicky at the other end of it.

With a worried half-smile, Cass glanced around the table, undoubtedly waiting for one of us to speak in tongues, or perhaps to fetch a fistful of venomous snakes.

My mother waved a playful hand at the man. "Don't you mind us, Cass," she laughed. "It's been a long while since we had company; guess we've all forgotten our manners."

This was all Cass needed to hear. He dug in and didn't mutter an intelligible word throughout the entire meal. He ate with the relish of a man who had never known that food could be so good. My mother doted over him, heaping seconds and thirds onto his plate until his stomach could hold no more.

Hands down, best dinner ever.

THIRTY THREE

Since there is really no appropriate time to introduce a person like my senior English teacher—considering that pure evil has no discernible beginning or end—I suppose that now is as good a time as any. I have known many teachers in my life, as it happens; few were as memorable as Ms. Bollinger—and in case I've been too subtle with my lead-in, this should not be mistaken for a compliment.

We didn't hit it off well, Ms. Bollinger and I. From day one, when she drilled me with a glare that could curdle motor oil, I knew that I was in for a rough semester. To her mind I had the unmistakable hallmarks of a troublemaker. And I suppose that—on paper, anyway—she might've been right.

Family history of criminal behavior? Check.

A reputation—however exaggerated—for violence? Check.

An erratic record of attendance? Check.

The wardrobe of a nonconformist? Um, in a manner of speaking.

Well, let me tell you, Ms. Bollinger wasn't having any of it, and she was only too eager to make good on that promise. When a pencil rolled off my desk one day and clattered to the floor—with as much clatter as a pencil could manage, considering that one end was made of rubber—she banished me to the principal's office for causing a disturbance. Just like that. I was stupefied. Not even Mr. Donovan knew how to handle it, so he let me spend the rest of the period in the library.

From that day on, it was always something with Ms. Bollinger.

"What's that, Mr. Chase? You've run out of paper? Well, perhaps my pen will run out of ink when the time comes to award passing marks."

Good grief.

Eventually, her pettiness wore me down to her level. In my recollection, I was never overtly disrespectful; yet I did take my sweet time to respond when called on. And I may have raised my hand once or twice to ask questions that I already knew the answers to. Okay, fine—you got me; I may have let that darn pencil get away from me now and then.

Before long, Mr. Donovan didn't even bother asking; he just waved me on to the library and rubbed at his temples, which had become more salt than pepper lately.

Ms. Bollinger grew up in North London and was unmarried—shocking, I know. She favored wool sweaters and shoes that could easily be confused for clogs. Other than these tantalizing tidbits, I knew nothing about the old Brit except that she openly detested everything about this protestant cesspool that we called home. In her bitter opinion, we Americans had taken great pains to bastardize the language we so blithely referred to as English. Nay, we didn't speak English!

We spoke American.

Therefore, only those who were truly committed to the revival of proper English rhetoric could possibly hope to win her favor—kind of a tall order for a bunch of high school Okies. For the many who fell short, Ms. Bollinger was not to be counted on for sympathy much less the encouraging words that struggling students often craved.

She was brutal, spiteful and ... I suppose that I should admit quite brilliant.

Ms. Bollinger took us through a litany of published works, breaking down choice selections to expose the triumphs and failures of word usage, symbolism, painterly dialogue and much more. I didn't always agree with her conclusions; neither did I always understand them. Nevertheless, their insightfulness never ceased to amaze me.

Sadly, her intellect was overshadowed by everything else that made her who she was. What could possess a woman who loathed this country with such fervor to settle smack dab in the middle of it? It was confounding, to say the least.

Unlike her predecessors, who had allowed me to skate by on the celebrity of a single writing contest, Ms. Bollinger didn't give a rat's behind what I or anyone else had accomplished in the past, and this disinterest extended well into the realm of school policy. As a matter of fact, the woman threw precedence out the window with the implementation of Shawnee High School's first pass or fail grading system—outside of music and athletics, that is. It wouldn't stand the test of time, of course, but it didn't need to stick around for long to turn a few lives upside down.

As for the day-to-day horrors of her company, Ms. Bollinger was in the habit of condemning unsatisfactory work to the trash without explanation. Feedback was redundant, she maintained; we either met her requirements or we didn't. And, as she was fond of reminding us, there was really no sense in bothering with her assignments unless we were prepared to put everything we had into them—which when you think about it, spared nothing for our other nightly homework. As a result, the entire class floundered—not only in the vacuum of her tutelage, but in a state of sheer exhaustion for trying so hard.

If this bothered Ms. Bollinger at all, she managed to channel her disappointment into pure snideness.

As my own frustrations mounted, the temptation to needle her became irresistible. And in my defense, the woman's mile-long list of pet peeves cried out for mischief, all on its own. Don't worry, I was careful to keep things above the belt—I did want to graduate, after all. But that's not to say that I pulled any punches.

I went out of my way to split infinitives—a habit that lingers today, born out of jestful repetition; "... [so-and-so] was the first *to courageously abandon* long-standing traditions ..."

I bombarded her with pervasive alliteration; clouds were *billowing bales of balloons*, the sea *gray like the Gaussian gales of Galway*.

Whenever possible, I ended perfectly good sentences on a dreadful preposition—yet another of the peeves that I've been referring to.

See what I did there?

In short, I shamelessly picked away at that woman's wavering sanity and I'd be surprised if she didn't at least consider the plausibility of running me over with her car. Of course, she *did* start it.

Just saying.

Despite the amusement of our feuding, I was frightened to death that she would flunk me. My future as a high school graduate hung on a single stroke of her pen; therefore, as often as I quipped with her, I also busted my hump to turn in quality work. And for the most part, I managed to squeak by. Still, she rarely acknowledged my efforts with more than the indifferent return of my papers. Don't get me wrong—I knew better than to expect an outpouring of praise; but her cold silence did have me worried.

And as it turned out, I had good reason to be worried.

There came a day in early February when things took a dangerous turn for yours truly. Ms. Bollinger didn't return my assignment that morning and while it was hardly the first time my writing had failed to impress her, I was taken aback on this particular occasion. The assignment in question—a short story which was supposed to demonstrate allegory—happened to be some of my best work. For once, I had even tabled my needling for the greater good of the piece.

Empty-handed and fairly bewildered, I gave Ms. Bollinger a questioning glance. In reply, she affixed me with a blank stare on the way to her desk. It occurred to me that I must've forgotten to turn in my assignment; however unlikely, this seemed to make more sense than any alternative I could imagine. Alas, even if I had merely forgotten, there was no such thing as late work in her class. I was simply out of luck.

Only, it didn't end there.

At the end of class, Ms. Bollinger stepped briskly toward my aisle, granting my classmates a stale *good day* as they passed. When only I remained, Ms. Bollinger positioned herself at the mouth of the aisle, barring me from a polite exit.

"A word, Mr. Chase," she said. The unpleasant bend of a smirk distorted her mouth, which after many years of frowning had shriveled into a faint slit. Her eyes were glacial—pale blue with a mysterious streak of cobalt seeping up from the depths. Appropriately cold, too, though I detected in them what I perceived to be an abandoned longing for warmth. Her hands were at her hips, one clamped tightly around a sheaf of rolled up papers that could only be my story.

"Planning to be a big shot writer one day?" she asked—or remarked. Hard to say, really. Her accent, which tended to inflect every statement with a hint of interrogatory, sometimes made it difficult to determine when a question was really a question. Worse, she was both obscenely fond of rhetorical questions and easily agitated by responses to them. This put me between a rock and a hard place, so I—perhaps wisely—held my tongue.

Ms. Bollinger shook her head as if I had just failed a test of some sort and asked me to sit down. I slipped off my backpack and obeyed, returning to the desk I had only just departed.

"This story of yours," she said. "Perhaps you can tell me more about it." Even as I watched, a bank of clouds spilled across her eyes, smothering the blues in drab shadow. "What inspired it, perhaps?" A smile—for lack of a better word—appeared on her face but it held nothing of the goodwill a smile was supposed to impart.

My eyes darted to the clock on the wall; I had four minutes to get to my next class. If I left at that moment, I might just beat the bell. Yet when I considered the fallout of my tardiness, I realized that I feared Ms. Bollinger more than my next instructor. "Well, it's kind of personal," I confessed. "You didn't like it?"

"You insolent child," she spat. "How *dare* you."

I felt my mouth go dry.

Ms. Bollinger made a visible effort to collect herself and then smiled again. "This little game you've been playing—it hasn't been completely without its charms, you know. I should've known you'd take it too far, though. Can't say I'm surprised."

My cheeks burned. What in God's name was going on here?

"You know what I think, Mr. Chase?" I sincerely did not. In fact, I couldn't remember the last time I had been so lost in a conversation.

"I think you're a bitter little boy with a chip on his shoulder. You have some talent, as I'm sure you know, and I imagine you're rather accustomed to being given a free pass because of it. Or perhaps you've simply learned to milk that unfortunate disfigurement of yours in a time like this. Well let me assure you that *this* little stunt—" She slapped her hand against the paper on my desk for emphasis. "—will not go unpunished. There will be grave consequences, young man. You'll see that soon enough."

My blood was beginning a slow boil. I didn't have the slightest idea what stunt she was referring to and there was absolutely no call for a personal attack, in any case. In anger, I wanted to lash out, to point out that if either of us was an expert on bitterness, it was most certainly her. That I hadn't been given a free pass in my entire life and if she had bothered to get to know me at all, she would know that perfectly well. These words—and many more—were on the tip of my tongue, but I bit them all back. This was obviously some kind of misunderstanding; I just needed to keep my cool long enough to help clear it up.

"Ms. Bollinger, you're obviously upset," I noted. "Maybe if you could explain what the problem is, I might be able to help." Ah, crap. I was going for a reasonable tone but even to my ear it sounded patronizing.

Sure enough, the older woman laughed humorously, shaking her head in disbelief. "Oh, Mr. Chase. I refuse to play this little game of yours." Her eyes squinted, now hot with indignation. "We both know what the problem is."

A screw was clearly loose in this woman; to allow our conversation to continue, particularly in her current state, would only invite more of her misguided abuse. I motioned to the clock. "I'm gonna be late."

Ms. Bollinger crossed her arms with an indifferent shrug, and if such a gesture could speak aloud, I'm guessing that it might've said something along the lines of: *that's the least of your problems, you little twit.* "Very well," she agreed in a growl. "I think we're done, for now. But this isn't over, Lincoln Chase. Not by a long shot."

Dizzy with trepidation, I reached for my coat and backpack and stood, eyes never leaving hers. When she didn't move aside, I stepped around her and bolted for the door, more than half expecting an attack from behind.

As I shuffled down the hall a moment later, mind boggled, skin still tingling with resentment, I heard something that caused me to stop. It was a whimper or perhaps a stifled sob, echoing through the nearly-empty hallway. There was nothing angry or even exasperated about the sounds; likewise for the soft moan that followed. Only sadness. Yet I was pretty sure they had come from Ms. Bollinger's classroom.

Before I could ponder this any further, the tardy bell rang.

I arrived three minutes late to Chemistry. Thankfully, Mr. Shrum—stickler for punctuality, friend to the paddle—was too busy toiling over a dying overhead projector to look up as I walked in. I slipped into my seat and let out a long, seething breath.

What in the world had I gotten into?

That night during dinner, the phone rang. It could easily have been a telemarketer or one of Nicky's many girlfriends—young ladies he described as *friends who were girls, not girlfriends*. But I knew. Even before my mother picked up the phone, I knew exactly who was on the other end. And I knew that things were about to get ugly.

I scrutinized my mother as she answered, "Hello?" into the receiver. Her face paled, then tightened as she held the receiver tightly against her ear. "Is that right," she muttered. Glancing at me, she frowned and padded into the living room for privacy, stretching the slinky phone wire to its full fifteen feet.

My poor mother. I didn't envy the task of deciding when to trust the knee-jerk instincts that must come with being a parent. The inner voice that insists, *My child would never do that!* despite a mountain of incontrovertible evidence. After all, the public school system owned us for the better part of the day, subjecting us to all manner of social experiments; when you think about it in those terms it's a little hard to believe that any mother could honestly say what her child was capable of in her absence, and my mother was no exception. Even if she happened to be right on this occasion.

Despite her attempts at privacy, her hushed voice cut through the stillness like gunshots.

"Lincoln would never do that," I heard her whisper. Groaning under my breath, I squeezed my eyes shut. I had no doubt that my mother's trite assurance would only reaffirm to Ms. Bollinger that all mothers were hopelessly deluded.

"No, he isn't perfect," my mother said and though her words seemed agreeable enough, there was no mistaking the irritation in her tone. "But I know my son. He would never intentionally—" Cut off, she was quiet for a second. Nearby, the refrigerator compressor kicked on and the floor began to vibrate; as if any help was needed, the effect seemed to draw even more attention to the awkwardness of the situation.

"Ms. Bollinger!" my mother suddenly barked. "Do not call me at my home and speak to me like that!" A brief silence, followed by, "Yes, well, I'll be speaking with Mr. Donovan in the morning, too. And you can bet your [Scooby Snacks] I'll be mentioning your rude behavior!"

Nicky covered his mouth to stifle a guffaw.

A second later, my mother returned abruptly to slap the phone back into its cradle. Dropping back into her seat, she unleashed a small growl. She looked at me with deadpan eyes, cheeks aglow.

"Wrong number?" Nicky teased.

My mother sighed between her teeth and then giggled. "Pass the salt, would you Mr. Smart Alec?"

THIRTY FOUR

Funny how you can see something coming from a mile away and still let it catch you by surprise. I'm certainly guilty of it, anyway. Barely fifteen minutes into first period, an office aid popped in to fetch me and for a few frightening seconds, I honestly couldn't make sense of why. To my credit though, I put on my best poker face and managed to comply without crying or losing consciousness.

Not that I was disappointed to miss out on all that hot Algebra II action, but I did have the feeling that every step toward the office was more like a step toward the gallows. It didn't help that the stupid office aid—a freckle-faced girl that couldn't possibly have been old enough for high school—performed an original song along the way, which went something like:

You're so busted, yeah!
You're so busted, oh yeah!
Nowhere to run, nowhere to hide,
'Cause you're so busted, yeah!

Soon enough, she paraded me past the receptionist to Principal Donovan's door, depositing me there with a *sucks to be you* smirk. "Go right in, please," the receptionist commanded. "They're waiting for you."

Inside, my mother was already seated, as was Ms. Bollinger. By their heavy breathing and blustering scowls I surmised that some heated discussion had already taken place. Mr. Donovan stood by with a neutral expression, one so convincing that I couldn't help but envision him practicing it before a mirror. The principal motioned toward an empty chair next to my mother.

"Have a seat, Lincoln," he said. "Sounds like we have quite a situation here." Ms. Bollinger *humph*ed in assent, or perhaps in protest of what she might have considered an understatement. Mr. Donovan shot her a cautionary glance but stopped short of any actual reprimand. "I understand you've written something rather, um … inflammatory, Lincoln. Ms. Bollinger is understandably troubled—enough so that she has recommended a three week suspension."

My mouth dropped open. Three weeks? Good Lord—had that cretin even read my story or had she confused it with something else? One of those neo-Nazi manifestos, perhaps? A satanic prayer book, bound in human skin?

Before I could frame a response, my mother leapt to my defense. "That's ridiculous. We aren't talking about grand theft auto, guys. A suspension like that would jeopardize Lincoln's chances of graduating, and I very much doubt that—"

"Doubt very much," Ms. Bollinger grunted.

My mother stiffened. "Ex*cuse* me?"

"Doubt. Very. Much." The older woman's gaze flicked to me and she grinned. "Mr. Chase, I dare say we've unraveled the mystery surrounding your penchant for silly phrasing!"

Eyes bugged, I glanced at Mr. Donovan who grimaced, then shook his head in warning. "Ladies, please," he soothed. "Let's try to stay on point, alright?"

My mother licked her lips. "Maybe it's time we saw this little *inflammatory* assignment for ourselves?"

Ms. Bollinger, glowering with troll-like dexterity, snatched a stack of papers from a satchel at her feet. "By all means," she tittered and handed them over with a bit more zest than my mother might have preferred. My mother rewarded this with a sickly sweet smile.

The telephone on Mr. Donovan's desk rang and he pushed a button to silence it; the button began to blink. Watching my mother read, it suddenly dawned on the principal that he ought to see the evidence for himself. "Do you have a copy for me?" he asked Ms. Bollinger, finally settling into his chair.

At this, my English teacher frowned. "No, I'm afraid I only have the original," she muttered. "The copy machine is ..." A timid chuckle. "Well, you know how stubborn that thing can be."

Mr. Donovan hunched forward over his desk, lowering his voice as if there was any chance of being heard by one of us and not us all. "Gilda, I've shown you several times how to work the machine. Just punch in how many copies you—"

Distracted from her reading, my mother suddenly couldn't suppress the urge to interrupt. "Wait a second, are you saying you haven't even read this thing?"

The phone rang again and was once again silenced. Groaning deep in his chest, Mr. Donovan leaned back into the springs of his chair. "No, Mrs. Chase," he grumbled. "I have not. The first I learned about any of this was when the two of you barged into my office. As in—" He made a show of consulting his wrist watch, which was buried in a kinky nest of dark arm hair. "—all of twenty minutes ago. When exactly was I supposed to read it?"

This, of course, was exactly the sort of response my mother had been fishing for. "Well," she sighed, flashing a pretty smile. "I just assumed Ms. Bollinger would've at least run it by you before calling to harass me in the middle of dinner."

Eyes darkening, Mr. Donovan turned on the aging Brit. "One would think."

"Be all that as it may," Ms. Bollinger responded, cheeks flaming red. "We are all here, and we can all read. The two of you can take turns—unless of course you'd rather Mr. Chase read it aloud for your amusement?"

Mr. Donovan waved this off. "Forget it, I'll wait. But in the future—"

"It's fine," I chimed in. "I don't mind. If it'll help, I mean."

My mother opened her mouth to protest but seeing something halting in my expression, closed it without a word. She handed me the stack of papers, which was now curling at the edges from careless handling.

The room slipped into silence and I now felt the burden of six heavy eyes on me. Clearing my throat, I began to read.

I shared the story of a young French woman named Sophia, who spent the better part of her adult life consumed with caring for her older sister, a withering woman skirting the end of a debilitating disease. Sophia worked long hours cleaning houses and waiting tables to pay for medical specialists, nurses and bottles of expensive pills; her every waking moment came and went in devotion to her dying sister. When she wasn't working and the day nurse was off, Sophia was no less busy—cooking and cleaning, changing bed pans, treating bedsores.

Sophia loved her sister dearly, yet she dreamed of a normal life—to sleep a full eight hours rather than the three or four she was lucky to manage as her sister slipped in and out of painful consciousness at night; to live in Paris and fall in love. To have a child. So strong were these yearnings that she considered putting her sister in a home. Such facilities were costly but just manageable, if she was willing to live on a tight budget. And when she was bluntly honest with herself, Sophia realized that she was willing.

She made a few phone calls, toured a nearby facility. She spoke with members of the staff, even a few of the residents. Still on the fence, she decided to sleep on it.

As it turned out, Sophia's misgivings were left untested; her beloved sister died unexpectedly that very night. Stricken with grief, yet suddenly untethered for the first time in years, Sophia fled the town she had known since birth for the seclusion of a strange, faraway city. It was no Paris, but certainly distant enough to cloud her guilt. And at least she could afford to live there in comfort for a while, whereas Paris might spare a broom closet at best.

In time, Sophia met an up-and-coming entrepreneur and fell in love. His business soon thrived and the two were married. They bought a modest home in the suburbs and had three children, back to back. They took family vacations every spring; Versailles, Provence, and of course: Paris. Sophia was happier than she had ever been.

She would always miss her sister, naturally, yet in those rare moments of weakness when guilt wormed its way in, Sophia took solace in the knowledge that her sister truly was in a better place—free of bedpans and soiled sheets, of needles and feverish delirium. Sophia wisely resolved to train her eyes forward, realizing that the best things in life had yet to come.

Perhaps to satisfy my juvenile adherence to cliché, Sophia's tale concluded with a predictable *happily ever after*. And because I thought that she honestly deserved such an ending, I didn't feel the least bit cliché for indulging it.

When I was finished, I let the papers fall into my lap. The story was loosely allegorical of the time I spent with my grandfather and therefore close to my heart; but it mostly came from nowhere. Probably not the best time to notice, with a jury looking on and all, but what the heck? There really is something about reading a piece aloud that draws its finer details to the surface; I was quite pleased with this one.

With hands clasped, I faced my English teacher. I was vindicated and under the circumstances, there was no stopping the victorious smile that reached my lips—I had earned the right, after all. Yet in the very moment I let it shine, a terrible thought hit me and I felt that stupid grin flicker off like a popped filament.

All at once I got it, what the fuss was really about. And I had to admit that if I was right, the truth was pretty appalling.

"Very well done, Lincoln," Mr. Donovan finally intoned. "You have quite a way with words."

Disregarding the principal, whose flippancy had officially worn out its welcome, my mother threw up her hands. "I must be missing something, guys. I won't pretend to be well-read but that seemed like a beautiful story to me. And I can tell you that Lincoln spent a great deal of time writing it. I watched him sit under a tree for two hours working on it. In the freezing cold, mind you. He takes his writing very seriously."

Two hours? Try an entire Saturday.

Immediately, Mr. Donovan piled on. "Actually Ms. Bollinger, I'm afraid I'm a little confused as well. You did say *inflammatory*, right? That was the word you used? Because I have to be honest—I didn't hear anything like that."

Poor Ms. Bollinger lost it then. Her face wrenched with emotion, eyes suddenly wild and darting. She pivoted in her seat to level a finger at me with jowls quivering like jelly. "You are a cruel child," she hissed, and as she spoke her voice took on the wavering quality of a dying flame. "You have no heart in you at all. Only stone."

My eyes filled with tears—not for me but for Ms. Bollinger. Because I now understood where her bitterness came from and I could easily imagine how she must be feeling.

In the meantime, this sort of talk was proving too much for my mother. She launched to her feet and I suspect that if not for my presence, she might've knocked the older woman silly. "Now hold on just a second, lady!" she spat. "My son has more heart than you could possibly understand. I don't know what your problem is but I've had just about enough—"

"Sophia was like you, wasn't she?" I interjected, and in that near blind spot where you sense movement more than you actually see it, my mother fell silent to look at me. Eyes glued to Ms.

Bollinger, I continued, "You lost someone, too. This—" I laid a hand over the papers in my lap. "It happened to you, didn't it?"

It took a second for my mother to catch up; she got there with an audible gasp, covering her mouth with both hands and dropping back into her seat. Ms. Bollinger looked away with a slow shake of the head. Not in denial, to be clear; chagrin maybe.

"Wait, it can't all fit, though," I muttered. "I mean, Sophia was French, and—" I paused to catch my breath even as a new revelation hit home. "And the ending … the ending wasn't right at all, was it?" In fact, when I thought about it, the ending couldn't have been more wrong. Because there had been no *happily ever after* for Ms. Bollinger. For her, the dream must've lived on. Or worse, it died altogether.

The woman crumpled in a way that seemed to add decades to her middle age and began to weep. "How can you know all this?" she demanded. No, I realized; though firm, she wasn't demanding anything—she was pleading. Begging even. Indeed, the rage within her had simmered down to a state of pure sorrow and I'd be lying if I said that it didn't break my heart to have played a part in it. "Who have you been speaking to?" she cried. "Please tell me."

"Nobody, I swear. I—I mean, it was just a story." Unaware of it, I had risen to my feet. "I made it up. I didn't know …" I approached her slowly, half expecting Mr. Donovan to step between us, but he did not. A quick glance found him riveted in place, mouth hanging wide open like that of a mounted fish. "I'm so sorry," I whispered. "I really had no idea."

At once, Ms. Bollinger cried out and with fresh rage, she leapt at me. A funny thought occurred to me then, as she flapped against me with those impotent little fists; I thought about the wandering tree—the endless ideas, the moments of sweet eureka that seemed to come from its midst—and I wondered.

If I expected a friendship to rise from the ashes of this unfortunate misunderstanding—and I must confess that I really was that naïve—my optimism was sorely misplaced. The Brit was perhaps a tad less zealous with her daily tongue lashings but in all other respects, she remained as cantankerous as ever. Still, that isn't to say that I walked away empty-handed.

You see, in the grand scheme of adolescence, I had met my quota of buddies. I had suffered hardship and learned to persevere. I had slowly come to grips with who I was and—perhaps more importantly—who I would never be. What I continued to lack, on the other hand, was the guidance of a gifted teacher—one with the wherewithal to push me toward new heights.

Given what I had been through with Ms. Bollinger, I suppose that it was only natural to see her in a different light. No longer the devil's minion, she now appeared as a perfectly rational human being whose outer shell was perhaps a bit thicker than most. Like me, she had weathered the injustice of great loss, even if she wore her scars a little differently than me. One thing was now plain to see: I could learn a lot from Ms. Bollinger, if I would only meet her halfway. She was, after all, a highly educated instructor with a commanding grasp on the mechanics of her craft. Too, she knew how to embrace vulnerability—on paper, anyway; to harness it in such a way that the written word could be made more beautiful, more powerful even.

I was done fighting.

With only a few months left of high school, I finally put my childish feud with Ms. Bollinger to bed and committed to learning everything that I possibly could from her. And in return, Ms. Bollinger opened the floodgates.

Across the years, her teachings have never left me, even if I fail to do them justice. What's more, her willingness to invest so much energy in me—despite an enduring dislike for all things *Lincoln Chase*—has inspired me on more than one occasion to look for the good in people, particularly when first impressions alone fail to endear them.

So here's to Ms. Bollinger; may she live out her retirement in peace. And for my own peace-of-mind, may she never hear what I'm about to tell you.

It's a well-known fact that men are aroused by the sight of women fighting. Or so I've been told. I'm not sure if it's merely the primitive writhing of female bodies or if there's supposed to be something more Freudian at work. Whatever the case, this flimsy generalization fell apart for me the moment I stumbled upon Ms. Winters and Ms. Bollinger mud-wrestling in the library parking lot.

Well okay—technically speaking there wasn't any mud; but there was no shortage of dirt and gravel, along with cigarette butts and what might have been a piece of hamburger bun.

Witnessing them tussle in such a way—slapping and pulling hair like angry toddlers—the whole universe seemed to have fallen out of kilter. Not only was there the paradoxical entanglement of parallel tangents in my life, there was the behavioral conflict of these women rolling around on the ground in spite of their reputations for sophistication. The whole thing struck me as so bizarre, in fact, that I honestly couldn't decide who to root for.

Aside from shocking, the ineffectual grappling of these women left neither one any worse for the wear. Honestly, it might've been one of the funniest things I had ever seen.

If that shirt hadn't torn open.

In vain, I have stared at white walls for periods of hours in effort to bleach that image from my memory. And since I wouldn't wish a similar fate on my worst enemy, I will spare you the details. But if you're wondering who it was that bared all, let's just say that she would've described this confrontation as a *row* rather than a fight.

Turning away—too late, of course—I discovered that I wasn't the only bystander; patrons had begun to gather, along with several members of the library staff. They—we—looked on in horror, unsure of how to process what we had just witnessed.

It was then that Clyde Hampton plowed into our midst. "Good Lord," he barked, rushing into the fray. *Never fear, ladies and gentlemen—The Custodian is here!* In a split second, the older man had wrenched the two women apart, yanking them to their feet with startling strength. "Stop this nonsense right now!" he shouted. Noticing the state of the Brit's ruined blouse, Clyde shrugged off his jacket and wrapped it about her shoulders.

"Oh for Pete's sake," he grumbled. "Just look what you've done to her shirt, Irene."

Ms. Winters turned up her nose with an audible scoff. "Nothing under there but pale blubber and a couple of old buttons anyway," she snipped.

God help me, if only I could deny the accuracy of this description …

With teeth gnashing, Ms. Bollinger made a lunge for the librarian but Clyde easily held her stationary.

"Now, now, Gilda," he soothed. "That's enough of that."

The police arrived and soon began to shoo away the bystanders, including me. Still in shock, I trudged inside the library to check out the book I had come for, though I must've known that nothing in its pages would ever offset the emotional cost of fetching it that day.

So what, might you ask, would drive these matronly pillars of society to such impropriety, and in such a public venue?

Ah, 'twas love, of course.

Neither Ms. Winters nor Ms. Bollinger had ever married and though one could propose a number of arguments to explain why, I'm of the opinion that no man had ever lived up to their lofty standards.

Until now. *Clyde Hampton, you old dog!*

You see, while Shawnee wasn't the smallest town around—please reference nearby Meeker for that coveted title—it offered a pretty narrow selection of eligible bachelors, narrower still for women of refined tastes. Further, Valentine's Day had recently come and gone—you know, the international disenfranchisement of the lonely, a holiday that never fails to usher in hopelessness and self-loathing? Yeah, that one. Under the circumstances, a kind-hearted widower like Clyde Hampton must've set knees to wobbling for miles in every direction.

Nevertheless, these were grandparental if not asexual figures in my youthful perspective; it was impossible to imagine them in any other form without cringing—or gagging, if such thoughts were permitted to venture too far. Yet here was proof that the same hormones coursing through the veins of teenagers with such animalistic vigor remained potent in senior citizens.

Alas, I could've done without that information.

In the days that followed, it became increasingly evident that the pursuit of Clyde had resolved with Ms. Bollinger no closer to finding happiness. Too depressed to care anymore, in fact, she overlooked countless opportunities to belittle my word usage in class; even her lectures fell into ill-prepared disarray, which—given her outspoken distaste for laziness and procrastination—spoke volumes.

I felt terrible for her. Not that I begrudged Ms. Winters in any way, to be clear. But I could identify with Ms. Bollinger to such an extent that a rejection of her affections felt like an affront to me as well.

Because if the whole truth must be known, Ms. Bollinger wasn't the only one dying of loneliness.

THIRTY FIVE

It should come as no surprise that when my senior prom came along, I went solo. Unless you're surprised that I went at all, in which case I can only point to Philip, who remained incapable of taking no for an answer. Technically speaking though, I didn't actually go alone—just dateless.

Speaking of Philip, he and Jeremy had joined forces to rent a limo for the night, which seemed like a tragic waste of money at the time, considering they both owned cars. But it was their dime, not mine. Funny thing, though—as I watched that sleek sedan crawl around the bend of Lakeview Park, I realized how quick to judge I had been. Long and black, polished to a high sheen—I had never seen anything like it, except on television. Not only was it a magnificent sight, it was a free ride to an alternate reality—if only for the night. I'd have paid anything for the feeling it evoked in me, if only I had known it existed.

This dreamy spectacle lost a bit of charm as the driver tried and failed repeatedly to maneuver the vehicle into my narrow driveway. I was out the door and halfway to the car when he finally gave up. Seeing me, he stepped out and, with a sheepish grin, opened the back door.

Of all the people I expected to see inside, Ivy was not on the shortlist. Yet there she was—linked at the hip with Jeremy, who looked happier than I had ever seen him. Startled, I froze in the doorway and then backed out. There was a strangling sensation in my chest and I honestly wasn't sure that I'd be able to get in that car. I could barely breathe, much less put on a happy face.

Dropping to my knees, I pretended to fuss over my shoe, sucking in half a dozen breaths as quickly as they would come.

I can do this, I insisted. *I* need *to do this.*

"Get in here, weirdo!" came a voice from within, followed by a spattering of unruly chortling. Gritting my teeth, I took the plunge. Inside, Philip clapped me on the back and adjusted my cheap boutonniere. His date—a cute redhead named Crystal, whom I sat behind in Biology as a sophomore—snickered, remarking, "Jeez, Phil. You gonna take him out for a romantic dinner later, too?"

Laughs all around.

I stole a glance at Ivy and found that she was looking at me too. She smiled and mouthed an uncomfortable *hi*. More than ever—dressed to the nines and primped to absolute perfection—her beauty was a physical force to be reckoned with. Dismayed, dazed, I plopped into an empty seat, angling my body toward the window.

The car vibrated as our driver ground a gear—once, twice, then a satisfying *thunk*—and suddenly we were off.

The night wasn't complete torture but neither was it as advertised. Jeremy looked at Ivy with the same adoration that I myself had felt for so long. And worse, Ivy seemed just as smitten with him.

This crap was not in the brochure.

Jeremy deserved happiness as much as anyone, of course. More than most, when I thought about it. And let's be honest: Jeremy was far better suited for Ivy than I would ever be. But knowing all that didn't make things hurt any less.

After months of saving up for what Philip had promised to be the best night of my life, all I wanted to do was get as far away from there as possible. Jeremy cornered me at one point, concerned, but it didn't take much to mollify him; he was a little too bedazzled by the gorgeous girl at his side to use that enormous brain of his.

Philip was oblivious or merely disinterested. As for his date? Crystal was nobody's fool. When she saw that I wasn't dancing, she sat down next to me and took my hand, giving it a sympathetic squeeze. "You okay? It's Ivy, isn't it?"

I looked away, cheeks ablaze.

"Nothing to be embarrassed about, Link. Pretty much every guy she meets goes a little coo-coo over her."

I nodded, shoulders sagging. "You think she knows?"

"About you or everyone else?" Crystal laughed at her own wit—a musical sound, like little bells on a wind chime—and took a moment to consider her words. "I don't want to give the impression that Ivy likes to flaunt her super powers, but she is very aware of the affect she has on guys." The redhead sighed, adjusting her corsage with manicured fingernails. "Anyway, my guess is she's known about you for a while."

"Lovely," I brooded. "I'm afraid to even ask what that means."

"Just saying, when she saw you earlier, she went rigid as a board."

I slumped in my seat, even more deflated. It took very little effort to imagine what must've gone through Ivy's head.

"Oh goody ... it's Frankenstalker. Again."

I could certainly understand Ivy thinking such thoughts, considering that—until recently—I had done my part to provoke them. But that isn't to say that I actually felt deserving of them.

"Why are they even here together?" I whined. "I mean, they aren't even students at this school!" Not to split hairs, but Jeremy was in college and Ivy attended a private school; why in God's name hadn't they gone to her prom instead of spoiling mine?

Crystal giggled. "Well, it did take a little doing to get the Fabulous Four together. According to our tickets, Ivy's with Philip; I'm with Jeremy."

"The *Fabulous Four*?"

"Oh, that? Ivy and I have been best friends since we were toddlers, and of course she and Philip are 'friends-who-used-to-be-more-than-friends'. Well, you probably know that part, right? Anyway, Jeremy's been hanging out with Phil a lot lately, who spends a lot of time with me."

"Okay ..."

"Well, we're each pretty normal on our own. But when you put us all together, we're ..."

"Fabulous. Got it."

Crystal blushed. "Yeah, I know it's lame. Phil teases me about it, too. Anyway, as for Jeremy and Ivy: when you hang out with someone a lot, one thing tends to lead to another, you know? It was just a matter of time before they hooked up."

Grimacing, I released a forlorn sigh. "Okay, I think I've heard enough."

Crystal gave me a glossy pout, patting me on the knee. "I'm sorry, Link. If it's any consolation, Ivy is pretty fickle. Chances are, she won't be with Jeremy for long." She glanced at the happy couple, who was chatting with a group of kids that I didn't recognize—probably more foreign invaders with nothing better to do than exploit the prom's honor code. "In the meantime," Crystal warned, "you should probably keep your distance."

I turned to her warily. "Um, what?"

Crystal's expression grew serious. "Listen, I know Ivy pretty well and believe me: that girl either hates you or she has a fierce crush on you. Either way, she's dating your friend. Best to let things run their course naturally, know what I mean?"

I nodded.

Crystal leaned forward to cup her mouth, whispering secretively in my ear, "But if it makes you feel any better, my bet is on the crush."

I rolled my eyes, belying a stab of pathetic hope. "Oh, please."

"Seriously! Trust me, I hear all about the people who rub her the wrong way. But the crushes? Not a word. She keeps those all to herself."

I took a moment to look at Crystal—I mean, really look at her. Her eyes were dark green, the color of cut jade, framed by long, curvy lashes. The copper sheen of her hair was accentuated by a faint band of freckles that spanned the bridge of a mildly hooked nose, resolving into rosy cheeks. She was adorable. Way too adorable to be wasting away her senior prom with the likes of me.

"Thanks Crystal. You're a very kind person. Philip's lucky to have you."

Her sweet smile dimmed. "Me? Yeah, right." She laughed but there was little merriment in it. Her gaze turned to Philip and for the first time I caught a glimpse of discontentment in her face. The star quarterback was standing by the punchbowl, watching over Ivy and Jeremy with a nebulous expression.

Ignoring his date.

"If you haven't figured it out yet, Link, Philip only wants what he can't have."

Though I sensed a deeper meaning in this, I decided to take it at face value. Philip could be a stupid punk; I knew that as much as anyone. Nevertheless, thanks to my big mouth, Crystal was now down in the dumps with me. This struck me as an insult to chivalry, so I really had no choice but to table my own drama for the moment. One of my better decisions, if you're keeping track.

"Crystal, have you ever seen what a cat does when you put scotch tape on it?"

Her eyes narrowed. "Huh?"

"They sort of spaz out, you know what I mean? Like, kind of lope around in a circle, shaking their paws."

Crystal looked at me as if I had just shown her a collection of shrunken heads—which was ridiculous, of course; I mean, how would I even carry something like that around, wearing a tuxedo with false pockets?

"Tell you what," I tried again. "Give me a few minutes on the dance floor and I'll show you exactly what it looks like. Fair warning, though—it won't be pretty."

Crystal giggled, eyes now sparkling. "Lincoln Chase, are you seriously asking me to dance?"

We got jiggy with it. We shooped. We did the humpty hump. We walked 500 miles. Crystal and I danced like spastic fools until the music abruptly slowed tempo; for two such newly-bonded friends, slow dancing ushered in a period of terrible awkwardness. Fortunately, by then Philip had snapped out of his brooding funk; he coaxed his lovely date off the dance floor with a cup of punch and whispered something in her ear. Grinning, Crystal snuck away to powder her nose. Melissa Ethridge bellowed through the loudspeakers, something about walking across the fire or changing her boss's tire.

To me, Philip awarded a crooked smile. "Thanks for keeping her company, bro."

"Yeah, well. Next time I'm pulling out all the stops, so you better keep her close."

Philip snickered absently, attention already wandering. "I hate this stupid song."

Sometimes you gotta quit while you're ahead.

It was a quarter to ten when I ducked out and I'd be surprised if anyone noticed my absence. Through unfamiliar neighborhoods

I strode, wingtips snapping in a determined clip. At one point, an elderly woman gasped as I barreled down her side street; to my amusement, she shuffled into her house with the gait of an emperor penguin and soon thereafter could be heard screeching inside about the best-dressed hoodlum she'd ever seen.

It wasn't until Lakeview Park appeared around the bend that I finally let my pace flag. My trailer was easy to pick out, even from a distance; one had but to count the porch lights. In the prevailing darkness, the glow of my television flickered in the living room window, bringing me to a halt. I wasn't ready to face my family just yet.

With no real forethought, I turned on my heels and plodded onto Pruitt Field, toward the wandering tree. The ground was soft from a recent rain yet I pushed on, undeterred. At the foot of the tree, I slumped to the ground and gazed up into the whispering canopy. It occurred to me that I was probably ruining my tuxedo and that my deposit was on the line. But I didn't care.

The future, which had seemed like a wide open frontier just hours earlier, was now collapsing in on me, crushing what little remained of my weary spirit. It dawned on me then that I might always be a prisoner here. Like Brutus, I had become a fixture of Lakeview Park; only, when the time came for me to leave this world, fewer would mourn the loss of me than that old dog, the hero.

Across the years, Brigham cried out to me. *"Someday, Link. Someday things are gonna be different. You just have to believe it's gonna happen, otherwise it never will."*

Hadn't I believed? Hadn't I given myself completely to that promise?

The final days of high school practically whipped by from there. The campus had taken on a different light and though the change itself must've been gradual, the extent of it managed to hit me all at once. The linoleum-tiled halls and painted lockers, the nondescript wall clocks, the gymnasium bleachers—everything around me triggered a nostalgic response, flooding me with an exaggerated fondness for this place. The sight of kids I had grown up with—or alongside, at the very least—engendered feelings of camaraderie that I knew weren't quite rational. Occasionally, Mr. Donovan smiled at me in the halls or slapped me on the back in passing and though I grinned, I knew without a doubt that he was looking forward to my graduating even more than I was.

Still, even if I wasn't completely blind to the illusion, I'd be lying if I said that it didn't feel good. I had dreaded this school as a freshman yet it now filled me with pride. A sense of accomplishment even.

I have often wondered how my memory came to be so distinctly selective yet I realize now that the answer was simple: I gave myself permission to be an idiot. Perhaps if I had been more honest with myself I might've seen things as they actually were. And I might've been less destroyed by what was about to happen.

Though he had narrowly escaped death just a month earlier, Philip's survival only seemed to embolden his alcohol consumption. He wore it like a badge, proof that he was dauntless, invincible. Sadly, the weekend before he was supposed to don a cap and gown, Philip's drinking caught up to him again at a house party.

Apparently, he was already tipsy on arrival and in a hurry to seal the deal. Ever the life of the party, Philip quickly—and predictably—got out of hand; before long, a hole had been kicked through a bathroom door and the kid on the other side had threatened to call the cops. This must've been quite a shock to the girl dumb enough to host a senior party while her parents were out of town, like there was any real possibility of hiding such a destructive event from them.

Anyway, Philip soon got the boot. He was, of course, in no condition to drive, yet neither was anyone else sober enough to care.

And where, you might ask, was I during all this? To my chagrin, I must confess to hiding out in my bedroom under the guise of doing homework, scared to death that a venture into public might cross paths with Jeremy and Ivy.

My mother drove me to the hospital every evening after work. For the first few visits, Philip's prognosis hung in the air like a question mark. One side of his head was shaved to the scalp, stitched together in a crooked half-moon. He stared out the window with a blank expression, unable or unwilling to acknowledge my presence. His other visitors received similar treatment, and soon enough they stopped coming by altogether. Jeremy hung in there longer than most, but even he had his limits.

The truth is that I might've given up as well, except that Philip's silent treatment translated as the sort of shoving match I was too stubborn to lose. And I suppose that my nervous inability to eat or sleep might've played a role. Whatever the reason, it seemed imperative that I be there when Philip was ready to talk. And I had to believe that he would, eventually.

His doctors weren't completely convinced. "Head injuries are tricky things," one explained. "The tiniest amount of damage has the potential to dramatically affect a person's behavior, as well as their basic motor functions." Thank you, Dr. Buzzkill, for taking the time to crush a boy's hope.

Philip's father spent a lot of time at the hospital, bemoaning their administrative policies and nitpicking the nursing staff half to death. Yet if Mr. Hampton stepped foot in Philip's room for even a second, I never saw it.

The man's wife, on the other hand, couldn't stay away. She hovered over Philip constantly, running her fingers through his remaining hair, fussing over his blankets. Worrying over his blood pressure cuff. Philip's only reaction was to close his eyes.

Mrs. Hampton spoke very little with me around, though she had the simian eyes of a person with a lot to say. Perhaps it was only my guilty conscience at work, but I got the sickening feeling that this lady blamed me for her son's rebellious streak, that she honestly mistook me for the bad influence in the room.

Philip's mother cried a lot, too. I tried once to comfort her but her gruff reaction sent me scampering from the room like a wounded dog. Thereafter, I took to waiting in the hallway during her visits, flipping pages in a paperback to mask the sounds of her crying.

Ah, good times.

On the rare occasion when I had Philip to myself, I must confess to torturing the guy. But hey—that's what friends are for, right? Incessant humming, arrhythmic foot-tapping. Some toe-tickling. Once, in a particularly devilish mood, I hijacked the television with a Charles in Charge marathon until I could literally see tears gathering in his eyes.

Poor Philip, he didn't stand a chance.

Accordingly, I take full credit for breaking him on day four. I was singing a Spice Girls song—for the fifth time in a row—when Philip suddenly turned to me and groaned. I swear, the weight of the whole world lifted off my shoulders at that moment; over the course of days, hope had been narrowing into a tiny thread, stretching thinner and thinner until there was really nothing left but for it to snap. So great was my relief that I honestly couldn't decide if I should smack Philip upside the head or crush him in a bear hug.

"You don't take hints well, do you?" he croaked. "And for God's sake, Link—the Spice Girls?"

Grinning profusely, I agreed. "What can I say? Someday I'm gonna make a woman very unhappy."

We both laughed, then fidgeted in silence. I wasn't sure what to say; in my rush to be at Philip's side that day, I must've run off without my *What To Say When Your Friend Snaps Out of a Pretend Coma* handbook. So I did the best I could to be encouraging.

"I guess you'll be going home soon, huh? A few more days?"

He lifted a shoulder indifferently.

"C'mon, man. Cheer up. At least you'll be out in time to graduate."

Philip looked away. "Yeah, right."

"Listen, Phil," I soothed in what I hoped was a reasonable tone. "They'll let you make up any work you missed." A thought occurred to me then, drawing a lazy chuckle. "Actually, they're practically making stuff up to keep us busy. I can't even remember the last assignment I turned in for credit."

Philip pushed his head deep into his pillow, as if with enough effort he might disappear into its protective folds. His stitches rasped against the fabric like tiny claws. "I was already failing, Link."

"You mean—"

"Yeah, as in *before* this."

Appraising him warily, I determined that he was in fact serious. "I don't get it, Phil—you've always had better grades than me."

"C'mon, Link. You're smarter than that." Frowning sharply, Philip raised his arms to stretch, stopping short at the end of his IV leash. A jagged ribbon of stitches peeked from the underside of his throwing arm. His hands plopped back onto the bed. They began to fumble with the seam of a thin, blue blanket that was draped across his lap. My eyes teared up. I couldn't help it; my friend just looked so helpless.

"What about academic probation?" I wanted to know. "I mean, you haven't missed a single game all year. I thought if you were failing a class—"

Philip scoffed with a hint of contempt, though I sensed that it wasn't necessarily directed at me. "Most of my teachers are coaches, Link. They'll pass me just like they always do." His face wrinkled then, as if he'd just remembered the smell of an old fart. Turns out, he had. "But not that hag, Bollinger. No way she's gonna let me through."

The situation couldn't have been more futile, I realized; one of the brightest futures imaginable snuffed out in the blink of an eye. The totality of it was suddenly too much to take standing up. I plopped into the only chair in the room and scooted it over to the bed. "Do your parents know?"

Philip shrugged and began to pick at the tail of his hospital ID bracelet, gaze fixed somewhere beyond the ceiling. I thought I might've lost him again at that point but he spoke up soon enough.

"My mom's probably clueless," he decided, "but you know my dad." Actually, I didn't; and based on my impressions thus far, I wasn't in a hurry to change that. "I'm sure he's got eyes and ears all over this town," Philip was saying. "My dad makes a living digging up secrets and selling lies; for some reason people respect him for it." In disapproval, Philip rolled his eyes, which triggered a pained grimace. "Guess that's why they pay him the big bucks."

He thought for a second longer, then added: "Probably thought he could grease me through at the last second."

A surge of hope—however shameless—took the bow out of my back. "Is that still a possibility?" I had to ask. It certainly wasn't an option to be proud of, but under the circumstances, what else was there?

"After this?" Philip snorted. "No way, man. That bridge went down in flames."

I clicked my tongue. "Technically, it was a telephone pole." Philip laughed, but then his face dimmed and I wanted to kick myself. "I'm sorry, Phil. That was stupid of me."

"No, no. It's fine," he mumbled. "Just realized my car's gotta be totaled." His expression hardened, then went abruptly slack. "You know, my dad started this." His eyes darted to mine, then away again. "The drinking, I mean. Poured us both some twenty-year-old scotch after the team took state sophomore year. Said it was what men did." Philip fell silent for a several seconds, eyes slowly filling with tears. "Like the constant reminders are supposed to change anything."

My mouth parted as it dawned on me what he was actually saying—what seemed to be buried in the subtext—yet before I could think it through, Philip plowed forward.

"Left the bottle on my dresser that night. He didn't even say a word when it was empty the next day; just brought another home like it was a gallon of milk or something. Like drinking until you puke in bed is a rite of passage."

Hearing this, my own father didn't seem so bad. Come to think of it, there was a part of me that wished he was around to give Mr. Hampton the business end of a work boot.

Don't get me wrong; Philip wasn't innocent—far from it— but it was disgusting that a kid should find himself in these circumstances under the direction of his father. And when I thought about it at length, I realized that Philip's innocence had never stood a chance against that kind of misguided parenting. It was a wonder that he wasn't in worse shape. And considering how hard it was to believe what I was hearing, I knew that no one else in his right mind would believe it either.

"Phil, have you told anyone else about this?"

He looked at his hands, which were trembling slightly. "Nah," he whispered. "What would be the point?" His eyes shot over my shoulder and at once his features tensed. I didn't need to turn around to know that his father was there.

"Well, would you look at that, folks," drawled the lawyer, dripping with filthy sarcasm. "We got ourselves a bona fide healing on the third floor!"

THIRTY SIX

Graduation was both surreal and a profoundly lonely experience. Considering how much time and energy was spent in reaching such a significant milestone, I had given surprisingly little thought to the ceremony itself. With that said, there were certain things that I had always thought of as a given; the possibility, for example, that my family might not show up never even crossed my mind.

For many of us, influenza has the ring of a wintertime affliction, yet it abounded that spring and didn't fizzle out until mid-summer. Many of my classmates fell upon the mercy of Nyquil and chicken soup during those final days of high school. Such was the case for Nicky on graduation day, except that neither Nyquil nor brotherly love could talk down a hundred and three degree fever.

As for my mother, she wound up stuck at work. The flu had made an appearance there as well, stealing bones from the usual skeletal crew. In a tight pinch, my mother's butthead boss had strong-armed her into a double shift. Given the choice between overtime pay or the threat of losing her job—and knowing that her boss didn't make idle threats—my mother relented. This was a decision that she would always regret, though I have never held it against her. To be honest, I'm not sure if there's really a right or wrong decision in a situation like that. Not when you're a Chase, anyway.

A stage had been erected on the football field, along with rows and rows of chairs. I won't bore you with a blow-by-blow of the ceremony itself, which could be summed up as an hour and forty-five minutes of mind-numbing ritual and rhetoric. It is worth mentioning, however, that when my name was called, I managed to cross the platform without tripping; considering all that could go wrong for a person like me, this was about the best I could hope for.

One of the more joyous moments was finding Philip in the stands, bandaged up and all smiles. It was bittersweet, of course; he should've been right there with me, where he belonged. Still, it warmed my heart to see him grin with such abandon. Mr. and Mrs. Hampton accompanied him—grudgingly, based on their stony expressions.

Looking around a bit more, I spied Jeremy. If my initial reaction was to smile, it quickly curdled when I saw Ivy at his side. I gave them a quick thumbs up and was careful to look elsewhere from that point on.

When the babbling finally ceased, one hundred and forty graduates threw their caps into the air, just as the wind issued a huge gust, which carried my cap somewhere beyond the stage. I never recovered it and frankly I've never missed it.

We began to disassemble at once. From nowhere, while cameras were still twinkling in every direction, something bizarre happened. Bizarre enough, in fact, that it capsized my sense of melancholy. Exiting the field, I was confronted by a face that I immediately recognized, yet couldn't begin to make sense of.

"Congratulations, Lincoln Chase," a man said. "You did a good job. I'm very proud of you." His eyes were slightly crossed, his head bobbing to one side in a strange, rhythmic tic. When he reached his hand out to shake mine, I couldn't help but hesitate; in another universe, this man could've passed for my father.

Entranced, I accepted his handshake. His fingers gripped mine in weak spasms, each quaking independently as if driven by tiny, humming motors. When we parted seconds later, a crisply folded ten dollar bill was left in my palm.

I was bewildered, but even as I stuttered some words of thanks, the strange man was already walking away. I tracked him in a daze, unable to tear my eyes from the sight of him. He was bigger than my father, I realized, and he traveled in an unruly gait, as if one leg had a mind of its own. A kind-faced woman met him beyond the forty yard line and with a patient smile, steered him toward the parking lot.

Unsure of what else to do, I crammed the bill into my pocket and let out a nervous laugh. For a brief self-indulgent moment, I allowed myself to pretend that the impossible had happened—that my father had leapt mountains and wrestled the sun to see me graduate. This was ridiculous, of course, and the fantasy fled as quickly as it came. Naturally, a much more depressing thought moved in to take its place.

It occurred to me then that a stranger from some distant branch of the Chase family tree had found the means to honor my accomplishment, while the banalities of daily life had proven sufficient to sideline the people who should've been there. I suppose there's no harm in admitting that it hurt deeply, even if no one was truly to blame. Once in a while, irony administers a wound that never really heals, perhaps because we can't keep from picking at it. This remains one of those for me.

A fat tear had gathered in one eye and at the precise moment when I noticed it, I felt the stupid thing broke loose. I wiped it from my cheek just in time to greet Philip, who—despite his still-healing injuries—lifted me from the ground in an obnoxious bear-hug before running off to congratulate his teammates. Not a bitter bone in that guy's body.

The ceremony was followed by a school-sanctioned party at a nearby hotel. Nearly every graduate made a brief appearance—all but the flu-ridden, as far as I could tell. We showed up en masse because a new computer was to be raffled off; we left shortly thereafter when the party turned out to be a special kind of lame. Not to be ungrateful, but seriously—the chaperones had us playing Scrabble and Trivial Pursuit on graduation night.

The vast majority of my peers wandered off to private parties in which kegs would take the place of punch bowls—and who could blame them? As for me, while I felt compelled to join the fun in some way, whatever tolerance I might've held for the drinking scene was long gone.

I looked for Philip, hoping to diffuse any temptation to hop off the wagon, but he was nowhere to be found. He might've gone home with his parents, I knew, but I had a sinking feeling that he was up to no good.

Crossing the hotel parking lot, I heard my name called out. I turned, half expecting to see my father's doppelganger again, but instead I found Jeremy and Ivy trotting in my direction, squeezing between cars and dodging other pedestrians. I met them in the middle.

With a hello, I shook Jeremy's hand. Funny how that stiff sense of ceremony managed to linger long after my cap and gown were shed. It caught my notice that Jeremy's palm—once calloused by the friction of a baseball bat—was now soft as a baby's bottom. He looked relaxed—at peace even—and he laughed at the silliness of shaking my hand when a shot to the arm had always sufficed.

I glanced nervously at Ivy and tried to smile. God, she was beautiful. So beautiful that I couldn't look her dead on without my eyes losing focus. She offered her congratulations and when I learned that she had graduated the week before, I returned the sentiment. Then we all stood there without a word as five seconds ticked by, my heart keeping time with throb after aching throb. Jeremy cleared his throat and then abruptly perked up.

"Oh, yeah!" he screeched. "Almost forgot."

He led the way to his car and while I followed dutifully, my flesh cried out to make a run for it. From the back seat, Jeremy retrieved a package wrapped in thick butcher paper.

"To inspire future works," he explained and handed it over.

Tearing away the paper, I gasped. Inside was a leather-bound writing journal, along with a sleek writing pen. "Wow, this is amazing," I breathed.

"It's engraved, too. The pen, I mean."

Sure enough, there it was: my name scripted in gold lettering down the hardwood shaft. This was possibly the most thoughtful gift I had ever received and on another day I would've gushed with gratitude. But I was out of sorts and in no shape to hide it. Worse, something about the journal was dragging me back through time, to a moment when a single lily grew in the shade of the wandering tree. Though no good could possibly come of it, I thought about the poem given to me by the old tree on that day. Words close to my heart; an ode to the girl standing so close right now that I could touch her if I was to simply reach out my hand. Yet despite everything, all I could think about in that moment was her with Jeremy.

I began to tremble.

"Okay there, Link?" Jeremy asked. His expression verged on crestfallen. "You don't like it?"

"What? Of course I do, man."

"You sure? You look a little pale. Not coming down with anything, are you? There's some flu going around."

Maybe he wasn't far off; I did indeed feel nauseous. "Nah, I'm fine. Really. It's just—kind of an emotional day, you know?"

Jeremy smiled wistfully, perhaps reflecting back on his own graduation experience. "Yeah, I know what you mean." He cleared his throat, eyes darting to Ivy. "Listen, we're headed out for coffee or ice cream or something. Wanna come along?"

I thought about all the times Jeremy had been there for me. Since early childhood, this guy had tolerated the stigma of my friendship with little or no return on his investment. With sadness, I remembered last fall—how empty he had been upon return from baseball camp; how I had wished that I could do something—anything—to help him. And finally, as if I needed further motivation, I considered Crystal's warning to keep my distance.

"Thanks, Jeremy," I said with the brightest smile I could muster. "Really, this is perfect." I ran my fingertips across the leather of the journal. "But you guys go ahead. I should probably get home to check on my brother."

It was very dark when I reached Lakeview Park. The lights were off in my trailer, as were others near the middle of the horseshoe. Stepping up to my front porch, I heard footfalls and came to a halt. The ember of a cigarette flared, illuminating Cass's scraggly face, some ten feet away.

"That you, Link?" he asked.

"Hey, Cass."

"Didn't scare ya, did I? Looks like yer porch light's out." He noticed the journal in my hand and gestured toward it with his cigarette. "Y'win an award or somethin'?"

"Nah," I sighed. "Just something a friend gave me today." I needed to be alone but I knew that Cass would be hard-pressed to pick up on this in broad daylight, much less under the obscurity of pitch darkness. Not that I'm one to talk.

Cass reached into his back pocket to produce a folded envelope. "Got somethin for ya, myself," he said with pride. Stepping forward, he slapped the envelope against my chest; I reached for it just as he let it go. "Don't spend it all in one place now, hear?" he said, and with a wink, the bachelor headed for his trailer. "Catch ya later, Link."

Inside, Nicky was dead to the world, snoring with such medicated enthusiasm that the whole house seemed to rumble with each sour breath. His forehead was still hot to the touch yet it seemed less alarming now. A grocery store bag hung from one bedpost, overflowing with crumpled tissues.

Poor kid.

My mother was still at work. I sat down to watch some television, desperate to settle my restless mind. The only thing on other than infomercials was one of those late night religious programs. This one showcased a woman whose makeup was so garishly applied that her features bordered on clownish. And her hair … good Lord, her hair. She was sitting in what looked like a throne borrowed from some low-budget fantasy movie set, eyes scrunched shut in fervent prayer. Blinking text on the lower third of the screen invited me to call—operators were standing by—to make my donation. I lay on the couch for awhile, marveling that somewhere in the Four State Area, someone was literally watching this on purpose. I turned off the TV and listened to Nicky saw logs, staring at the popcorn ceiling for a minute.

Followed by another.

Then, quite abruptly, I rose and bounded out the door.

I found myself moseying into town with no particular destination in mind. Anywhere but home would suffice, I supposed, though I knew it wasn't really home that bothered me as much as the idea of being motionless. Eventually, I heard voices in the distance and headed toward them. As I got closer, the voices became more intelligible and I realized that it was a house party.

And while there were probably many such parties going on that night, a familiar voice rose above all others at this one.

Bizarre coincidence, you might wonder? Meh, not really. That's just life in a Podunk town.

It was standing room only inside, where Philip was downing whiskey straight from the bottle and slurping beer chasers. Sneaking tokes off joints as they made their rounds. Stitched up and covered in bandages, the absurdity of his inebriation was unbearable. If not for his head wound, I might have thumped his ear.

It wasn't easy to break Philip away from the festivities; considering the fit he threw, you'd think it was an unforgiveable breach of protocol to depart such a function without first wearing out his welcome. Unfortunately for Philip, he'd forfeited any say in the matter with his recent mission to rid the world of telephone poles—at least, as far as I was concerned. So I dragged him out the front door and across the porch, glancing toward the side street where partiers were coming and going.

I was about to ask how in the world Philip had even gotten there when Crystal stumbled out the door and grabbed me from behind.

"Link!" she squealed, hands clasping across my chest.

I'm not gonna lie—it felt good. With the exception of my mother, no girl had ever—

Crystal spun me around and planted a wet kiss on the cheek—also nice, though demeaned a little by her party stink; you know, not so much the smell of beer itself but the signature odor of a person who has had one too many? And it didn't help that she and Philip used to be an item, even if they didn't so much as acknowledge each other now.

"You can't leave," she pouted. "You just got here!" Her huge green eyes batted and I almost forgot why leaving was so important. I mean, the night was still young and—

It dawned on me with a start that I had let go of Philip, and that I had precious little time before he realized it, too.

Crystal leaned in again. "'Cause I was kinda thinking we could—"

It was then that Philip lunged for the steps. Bumping Crystal aside, I got a handful of shirt and tried to haul him back. Not that I minded him leaving, to be clear—that was the whole point, after all—but I couldn't trust him do it responsibly on his own. We wrestled for a few seconds over control and I nearly lost my grip again when Philip slapped me in the saddle bag; somewhere in the middle of all this, Crystal stomped off, and I can't say that I blamed her.

If we had left even a moment earlier, there's a good chance I might've missed Jeremy and Ivy pull up to the curb. But what can I say? Even after all those years, the universe still had it in for me. And unless I've just become paranoid in my old age, I realize now that Crystal might've been in on it, too.

Anyway, just as we cleared the steps, Philip made a mad dash for a car—his father's, I surmised—with keys wielded in front of him like a weapon. Thank God Jeremy was there to head him off in the middle of the yard. Logically, there must've been sounds of good-natured scuffling but I honestly can't recall any; I was consumed by the vision of Ivy as she walked slowly toward me, eyes locked on mine as if we were the only two people in the world.

With just a few feet between us, she stopped. She looked at me intensely and opened her mouth to speak, but nothing came out. *"Please ravage me right here on this lawn!"* did seem a little improbable, yet there was no doubt that something was on her mind. Alas, just as she was gearing up to give it another try, Philip bumbled to the ground at my feet.

And then—because nothing is quite done until it's overdone with Philip—my good friend introduced my shoes to the wonder that was his stomach contents. There were laughs and groans all around, even a sympathetic retch or two. It seemed that everyone had a reaction, in fact; everyone but me and Ivy. I, for one, barely registered the bile soaking into my socks, though it would certainly get my attention later. You see, a thought was emerging from the back of my brain, pushing everything else out of focus.

This was it, I realized. My last chance.

After tonight, I was unlikely to stand this close to Ivy ever again. She would undoubtedly flee to some faraway university for promising young goddesses; I'd spend the remainder of my days in the shadow of what might have been—what *should* have been. This was my mindset as lips began to part and a last-ditch declaration of undying love formed on my tongue.

But then, I thought about Jeremy. Kind, selfless Jeremy. A guy with heart and brains and talent galore; an open book who— not only more than *me* but more than *any* of us—was truly worthy of Ivy's attentions.

"Be good to him, okay?" I whispered. "He deserves you."

To this, Ivy closed her mouth and swallowed visibly. I pulled Philip to his feet and plucked the keys from his hand.

"C'mon, Phil," I said. "Let's call it a night."

Mrs. Hampton met us at the front door, face hooded in the stark porch light. Philip was perhaps only marginally aware of his surroundings, yet he had the presence of mind to understand that he was in trouble, for what little that was worth.

"Uh-oh," he bellowed. "Whuss wrong this'ime? Dy forgedda clean my room?"

Mrs. Hampton was seething. "For God's sake, Philip—look at you! If your father was here to see this, he'd—"

Philip guffawed. "You kiddin? Dad slip' me coupla fiffies'n the keys ta th'beamer. On gra'jation nigh—like, th'mother'fall parry nize, mom. Fill'n th'blanes, unkay?"

This remark seemed to knock the wind from Mrs. Hampton and I immediately felt sorry for her. For Philip, too, if there was any truth to the implications. Well respected or not, Mr. Hampton was rapidly overtaking Coach Briggs on my list of Shawnee's most despicable.

Philip snorted. "Where'see hidin an'way?"

His mother crossed her arms as bitterness crept slowly up her face like the tide. "He took the Mercedes to the office," she mumbled. "Something came up."

"Gossha. Puddin in s'overtime with'new sec'shary, huh?" He winked conspiratorially and I wanted very much to smack him. I mean, who talks to their mother like that?

Mrs. Hampton covered her mouth, eyes stricken, forehead wrinkled in dismay.

"C'mon, Phil," I muttered. "Ease up."

He scoffed. "Oops! F'gah we're sposa, like, preten ever'thin's fruity. Peashy. Ever'thin's peashy, righ?"

Mrs. Hampton was shaking her head sadly. "You can't keep doing this, son," she said. "You're killing yourself—don't you see that?"

Philip plopped to the porch stairs with a grunt. "Yeah, well. 'Fad whole lossa help wiffatt." Mrs. Hampton seemed about to reply, but caught herself when Philip suddenly nodded off. She glanced at me as if I had something to do with the timing of this, but I could only shrug.

It took both of us to wrangle Philip upstairs to his bedroom. He didn't make it easy, either. Over and over, he came to with a start and tried to pull away, only to ragdoll in our arms as he dropped back out of consciousness. All this up a flight of stairs, mind you.

Still, as tough as that was, rolling him into bed proved to be a far more precarious affair. Confused or perhaps even angry, Philip began to flail at us, throwing wild punches as if we were assailing him rather than gently laying him down. My necklace was ripped off in the process as was a clump of my hair. Not to mention that I took a pretty healthy blow to the ribs.

Mrs. Hampton fared better down by his feet, though she yelped and cried throughout. By the time she got Philip's shoes off, he was out again—this time for good. She perched on the edge of his mattress to comb fingers through his hair, much as she had done at the hospital. When she began to hum faintly—*Hush Little Baby*, I think—Philip's breathing turned to snores that easily rivaled Nicky's.

It seemed rude to sneak off, yet I felt like a peeping Tom there, bearing witness to an intimate moment that ought to have been private. Too, my puke-soaked feet were chafing, which didn't bode well for the long walk home. I cleared my throat. "Is there, um, anything I can help with?"

Mrs. Hampton snapped erect as if she had forgotten all about me, then impaled me with a glare. "Don't you think you've done enough?" she demanded, cheeks glistening in the lamplight.

Taken aback, I gaped.

"Why can't you kids just let my son alone for once? Stop dragging him down to your level?"

"Um, my level?" My cheeks were burning now. "Mrs. Hampton, I think there's been a misunderstanding. You may not remember me from the hospital, but—"

"Oh, I know exactly who you are. And what's more, I know *what* you are. You're a taker. You see something you want and figure you're entitled to it because life has been unfair to you, right? You don't care who it might hurt, you just take it. And as long as my son's too generous to say no, you'll just keep on taking and taking until he's all used up."

It was hard to bite my tongue at this because it had always been Philip who consumed people in such a way; his friends were mostly content to vie for his good graces. Yet there was no sense in throwing Philip under the bus—certainly not for the sake of proving a point, at that.

I tried to keep my voice calm and reasonable, though I felt far from it. "I haven't taken anything from Philip. He's my friend and I'm trying to help him."

"Oh? Well, congratulations— you've done a bang-up job so far."

Sigh.

This was an argument that couldn't be won, I knew, because it wasn't rooted in rational thought. And try as we may, no one can out-argue emotion. This woman was incapable of seeing the truth—that much was clear—and little peasant Lincoln Chase wasn't about to change her mind.

"I'm sorry to have upset you," I grumbled, followed by a nod to the door. "I'll show myself out." At the last second, I remembered my necklace, which hung off the bed, still tangled in Philips fingers. I reached for it and immediately recoiled as Mrs. Hampton slapped my hand away.

"Now wait a second, that's my—"

"Get out!"

THIRTY SEVEN

The tinkling of keys against Formica roused me from a light doze. Nicky's snoring had lost steam by then, thank God, which allowed me to more or less string thoughts together, at last. Several years before the wall clock had died at ten after five; funny how I looked at it now as if it ought to do a bit of good. The Sherlock Holmes in me deduced that it was probably around two-thirty, considering that my mother was just now getting home from work. All this to say that I was too lazy to consult a working clock; such a commitment would require me to stand up while a perfectly good broken one was staring me conveniently in the face.

When my mother spotted me in the living room, she dragged her feet to the couch and plopped down beside me, eyes tired and puffy, ponytail slack after a sixteen hour shift. She patted my knee and put on a flimsy smile.

"I'm so sorry, honey," she said, and the smile instantly fell apart. "I should've been there." Her breath hitched and she leaned into her hands. "What kind of mother misses her son's graduation?"

"It's okay, Mom. Really."

She shook her head, eyes squeezed shut. "No, it's not okay." From her apron pocket, she teased a pathetically thin wad of tip bills and dropped it into her lap. "I should've quit that stupid job a long time ago." She began to cry bitterly into her hands.

Too tired to summon words of encouragement, the best I could manage was to pull her close and hold her until the tears subsided.

"Did you throw up?" she sniffled. "It smells in here."

"New cologne—you like?" My socks and shoes were airing out on the back porch, yet their smell would linger inside for days. Such was the disparity between odor and aroma, it seemed. I mean, bake some fresh cookies and the aroma fades almost before they're cool enough to eat; cut the cheese, however, and you'll smell that in the drapes a week later.

Ah, the things a mind will stop to ponder when deprived of a little sleep.

Snuggling into me, my mother asked about the ceremony; I indulged her with a few highlights, drawing particular attention to the mysterious brush with my father's doppelganger. I must've been expecting some kind of revelation from her—a theory, at the very least—yet my mother offered nothing more than a half-hearted, "Huh," before closing her eyes.

Minutes later she was snoozing, face streaked with mascara, apron infused with the permanent stench of burnt coffee and cooking grease.

My own exhaustion was at its peak, as well; pushed to the edge, no doubt, by a month's worth of unpleasant odors crammed into a single evening. I shook my mother awake—gently, despite my frustration—and ushered her to bed. Thankfully, she didn't beat me for the courtesy, because I was far enough out of sorts that I might've hit back out of reflex.

Nicky barely stirred as I emptied my pockets onto the dresser. First the ten dollar bill; then a mini Swiss army knife. Three fifths of a pack of Big Red gum, a few loose coins. Lastly, Cass's envelope.

Inside was a hundred dollar bill.

I couldn't believe it. Alas, I had reached a level of weariness that effectively disarmed excitement; I was lucky to squeak out a smile then when I might've peed my pants a few hours earlier.

Slipping into bed, it occurred to me that I hadn't eaten anything since lunch. Anxiety alone had suppressed my appetite for most of the day, yet now that things had calmed, my stomach seemed to be collapsing in on itself. However starved I might have been now, though, I was too worn out to do anything about it. So I lay there in the darkness, reflecting on the day. Listening to the rumbling in my tummy. Feeling sorry for myself.

Sulking.

Had I really been so naive to think that today was actually going to be about *me*?

At once, I felt the absence of my necklace; the skin around my neck tingled, as if to bemoan the loss of a dear neighbor. Though it also filled me with wonder, the presence of that meteorite fragment had never failed to ground me in reality, even when reality was the last place I wanted to be. Tonight I felt untethered, in danger of blowing away.

I glanced out the window at Cass's porch. I wondered how the old man could possibly tolerate a life of such overwhelming solitude. How he could continue to go through the motions, day in and day—

Just like that, it hit me. I knew exactly what to do with that hundred dollar bill. The idea brought a much needed smile to my face, as well as some closure to what felt like the longest day ever. I closed my eyes and released a sigh that seemed to bury me deeper into the sheets.

And then finally—*finally*—I slept.

Paws-N-Claws wasn't the only pet store in town but it was definitely the closest. Even still, we're talking about a forty minute walk on the heels of a very short and unsatisfying night of sleep. The temptation to put it off for another day was almost unbearable and if procrastinating might've promised something more than a day lost to Nicky blowing his nose every other minute, I might have given in.

Anyway, I persevered. Only once I got there, I learned that the store didn't even carry Pit Bulls—none of them did—though the owner denied any prejudice toward the breed. They were just a little harder to sell, he explained. Perhaps a Dachshund would do? No? Hmmm. How about a nice poodle?

As usual, I couldn't catch a break.

With a little legwork, I might've found a Pit in the classifieds, or through the grapevine, for that matter. Who knows—at that very moment, a family might've been giving away Pit Bull puppies in the Walmart parking lot. But I was tired. And frankly, I barely had the legwork left in me for the trip home.

So I walked out with a black Labrador Retriever, barely six weeks old.

It was a bad gamble and I knew it. The canines of Lakeview Park didn't tend to be fighting breeds by pure coincidence; only the toughest survived and a Lab didn't stand much of a chance against a peer group of Pit Bulls and Rottweilers and Bull Mastiffs. Worse, this sweet little girl was the runt of a litter.

In her favor though, she did have a small patch of white fur just below one eye—a blemish to her pedigree, some might say, yet an endearment to me.

When the store owner saw which way I was leaning, he offered to throw in a leash and collar, as well as a ten pound bag of puppy kibble to sweeten the pot. I won't pretend the effort was wasted on me, though the kibble didn't exactly appeal to the long walk home; but it's worth noting that it was sheer cuteness that ultimately closed the deal.

You see, when I first spied her in the back and ventured over for a closer look, the Lab's ears shot up and her tail began to wag with such vigor that she lost control over her own rear end; that little tail of hers dang near took flight like a helicopter rotor, slapping her siblings silly along the way. I bent down to scratch her head and while the other puppies went more or less berserk— as puppies are prone to do—this one sat on her haunches and waited. Actually sat and waited!

And oh my goodness, don't even get me started on those sparkling brown eyes and floppy ears.

Now, I'm not suggesting that a Pit would've been any less adorable—I had no frame of reference, since there were none on site—but the point became quite moot beyond my first exchange with that sweet little Lab. She was exactly the puppy I would've chosen for myself; I could only hope that Cass would feel that same connection.

Actually, I kind of figured that if he didn't, Nicky and I would go ahead and take her off his hands. You know, just to, um—harrumph—help out.

I left the pet store with my new friend bounding at the end of her leash. A quarter mile in, though, she began to whine and drag her paws, so I scooped her up and draped her over one shoulder. She fell asleep immediately and slept the rest of the way home.

I won't lie—it was hard to part with her. The decision was made even more difficult at home, when Nicky came shuffling into the living room and squealed with delight at the sight of her. The way his eyes lit up, I could swear he was a little kid again, and for a short while I remembered what things had been like so long ago, back when my family was still whole.

With Nicky's help, I tied a loose bow around the squirming animal and crept out the back door. I tiptoed up Cass's porch stairs and, before I could over-think it, set her down on his doorstep; she sniffed and then sneezed but otherwise remained remarkably still. With a sharp knock, I hightailed it back to my trailer, hoping to God the puppy wasn't in hot pursuit.

Thankfully, she was momentarily distracted by the discovery of a dead bug on the porch.

Nicky and I watched from the living room window as the Lab rolled around, pawing at the bug until it fell between the planks. Then she remembered the ribbon around her midriff and went to work on that. Her little tail thumped happily against the floor boards and from my vantage, the sound might've been the distant rap of knuckles on a door, softened by winter mittens.

Soon enough, Cass erupted onto the porch with an unlit cigarette bobbing in his mouth, head snapping around irritably. The bundle of fur at his feet must've whined or something because Cass suddenly leapt backward, hands clawing at the doorframe to break his fall. For a moment, while he pulled himself upright, the old man grimaced as if disgusted and my stomach lurched in dismay.

But then, the puppy abandoned her ribbon to engage Cass's slippered feet. I chuckled at the sight and so did Cass, though his expression reflected uncertainty as much as amusement. He looked around once more and as his gaze hinged toward us, Nicky and I were obliged to dive away from the window. We returned seconds later to find the bachelor on his knees, lifting the puppy into the air by the armpits. He drew her close for inspection and a pink tongue darted out to dislodge the cigarette from his lips. Cass's mouth stretched into a grin that was so profoundly joyful that it somehow fluttered through the window to alight on my own lips.

Best hundred bucks I've ever spent, by far.

That evening after dinner, while Nicky was taking a much needed shower and my mother was snoozing on the couch with a romance novel tented on her chest, I sat on my bunk, fondling a certain ten dollar bill. My imagination ran wild, desperate to make sense of the stranger who looked so much like my father. Of course, the problem with a rampant imagination is that it doesn't necessarily take cues from reality. Unless there actually was a portal to an alternate universe buried under the football stadium. Frustrated, I folded the bill neatly in half and slipped it into my sock drawer for safe keeping.

I suppose that's when it happened.

Something welled up within me as I stood there, deep in my bones like the gathering of a great shiver; begging me to come *now*—quickly, *quickly!*—before it was too late.

And so, I came running.

The sky was already dimming when I arrived at the wandering tree, backpack slung hastily over my shoulder. At half a dozen steps out, I felt the magic swarm on me and my heart began to race all the more. I couldn't unpack my gear fast enough, it seemed; even before I was settled in, my new pen practically jumped to flourish across the paper and unless I'm mistaken, my hand went along for the ride rather than leading the charge. The words flowed from me, true, yet the thoughts that inspired them came too quickly to call my own. And they had nothing to do with the stranger, or his ten dollar bill.

They were all about a boy named Denny.

Denny was a well-to-do kid with a terrible secret. It wasn't that he preferred poetry over sports, or that muscle cars bored him as a rule. The problem was that he didn't dwell on girls the way his friends did at school. He wanted to—even pretended to when he could stomach it—but the truth was that he liked boys. He liked them in the way that he knew boys were supposed to like girls. And try as he might, there was nothing he could do to stop it.

As far as secrets went, his was frightening enough all on its own; boys who liked boys were said to be depraved, after all—abominations in the eyes of the Lord—though Denny didn't feel particularly depraved or abominable. Yet the gravity of this secret was made all the more unbearable by an overbearing father. The man couldn't stand the sight of weakness and Denny's peculiarities brought out the worst of his loathing. He didn't often raise a hand against his son but the man didn't need to; his tongue was destructive enough.

Denny's mother had her suspicions too, of course, but she preferred to look the other way. Just a phase, she told herself, though deep down she knew better.

Intentionally or otherwise, Denny's parents killed him a little at a time—glances of disgust, snide comments, all reinforced by a calculated regimen of indifference and conditional affection—until the Denny who loved Frost and Dickenson, who cleaned his room without asking, finally died.

Only, he didn't die in the flesh; rather, a new Denny was born.

Into the world, a strapping young athlete emerged; the kind of son a father could brag about and show off to his friends at the country club. The kind a mother hated to punish because—well, boys will be boys.

Denny put all he had into becoming this character, at first for the sake of his parents and later for everyone else's. The whole town had fallen in love with his persona, you see. They sensed greatness in him, though Denny couldn't bring himself to share their enthusiasm. Similarly, his schoolmates adored him because he was handsome, with a knack for all the things that boys aspire to do well—trivial things that Denny would have gladly traded for a walk in their mundane shoes.

He tried to be grateful because he had accomplished much as an imposter; yet even if it was he who had sold the illusion, Denny found that he resented those with the gullibility to buy it.

It didn't take long for Denny's spirit to erode, hollowed out by the scouring of a million white lies. By the steadfast ache of loneliness. The part of him that had once delighted in so many things was dead; there was no delight anymore. Only the compulsion to pretend remained and though it had once seemed like the path to salvation, Denny was now captive to it.

So as men were supposed to do, he drowned his sorrows.

A drunken Denny felt excused—if not free—to be imperfect. And even if he never revealed his secret to another soul, Denny could at least treat others with the same contempt that he held for himself. He could tear them down, piece by little piece, just as his parents had torn him down.

Or better yet, he could tear it *all* down. He could—

Hands shaking, I let the pen drop from my fingers, refusing to write another word. The story tugged at my insides, pleading for me to finish it—quickly, *quickly!*—but I was done. I didn't have it in me to write what could only be a vile ending. Not to this tragic story.

Because I knew perfectly well that it wasn't just a story.

THIRTY EIGHT

I'm not sure what held me together during the return home; what pulled me apart, on the other hand, was easy enough to define. It went beyond the disturbing revelation that my friend had lived a life of such suffering, though the filthy injustice of this alone was indeed a skewer through the heart. The coup de grâce was an overwhelming sense that all hell was about to break loose; and perhaps worse, that it was up to me to stop it, somehow—whatever *it* was.

Past my mother and Nicky I surged, into the kitchen toward the only ray of hope I could envision. The telephone. Philip's number fell off my fingers by the grace of God and muscle memory alone, as far as I could tell. When the line began to ring, I screwed my eyes shut and held my breath, trembling like a pot of boiling water.

Please answer, Philip.

Five rings.

C'mon, Phil. Let it be all in my head—just the musings of a lunatic.

Ten rings.

For the love of God, pick up!

No answer.

Just to be sure, I let the line ring fifteen more times before hanging up and trying again. And then, once more to be sure that I was sure. What little remained of my frazzled composure quickly unraveled from there; by the time I thought to call Jeremy, I'm afraid that I truly was raving like a lunatic.

Funny thing, though: instead of the walls closing in on me—which, however unpleasant, had become a familiar sensation in times of despair—everything seemed to fly outward this time. Much as a mouse retreats into a hole in the wall, I shrank back into myself—a journey that would measure inches at most, if it was even physically possible, but seemed to span a hundred miles. My edges began to fall away, exposing me as the island I had always felt that I was at heart. The crushing weight of the seas bore down on me, driving me under with one indifferent wave at a time.

The feeling of isolation was unbearable, yet it couldn't have been more than a taste of what Philip had long endured. I simply couldn't wrap my mind around the enormity—the unfailing persistence—of his daily burden, nor would I ever really understand.

Still, whether or not it was within my means, I couldn't shake the need to empathize with Philip. So I tried to imagine what it must be like: every moment of every single day, pickled by the fear of discovery; suffocated by the knowledge that, as much as I craved to be loved for who I really was, the world had decreed that I was unlovable and therefore unworthy of happiness.

The image proved too much in that moment, as it does even now.

Burying my face in my hands, a wail rose up within me. I clamped down to stifle it, perhaps just to know that I could, but it wrenched free, emerging in a strangled moan. I felt like I was losing my mind.

Then, as if stretching across a vast plain, a hand reached out to give my arm a squeeze. It was my mother, I realized. Well, sort of. Face rippling in and out of focus, she was more like a projection of the woman, an echo. I needed the real person, but she was just so far away. I wanted to tell her everything—to let it all out before it consumed me like the fires of hell—yet I knew that she'd never hear me from such a distance; she couldn't possibly understand.

Nobody could.

"Come here, baby," my mother crooned, and though it felt as if I might fall through empty space, I leaned into the barren chasm between us, toward the comfort of her outstretched arms. "Everything's fine," came her faraway whisper. But it wasn't true. Nothing was fine.

Beneath all the noise and turmoil, you see, the wandering tree was still calling out to me—*finish it quickly, quickly!*—as if life and death should have any business relying on me. This alone nearly broke me, I'm convinced, because I simply wasn't built to shoulder that kind of responsibility.

No man was.

But then, all at once, the tree let go. The world drew in again, gathering around me like an old, familiar blanket. Yet even while I embraced it, sagging with relief, I wailed even harder because I knew—

Well, frankly I wasn't sure what I knew. Philip had done something—that much seemed clear, even if I couldn't bring myself to consider the possibilities. One thing I did feel certain about: it was too late.

Jeremy pulled into my driveway much sooner than the speed limit could possibly have allowed, bless him. By then a calm had settled over me. I wasn't at peace exactly; merely adrift as shock carried me along, whispering in my ear that it was okay to check out for a while. Forever, if it suited me.

"Let's go," Jeremy said, and I followed him to the car in a daze.

Buckling in out of habit, I let my eyes flutter closed.

"Snap out of it, okay?" Jeremy pleaded. "I need you."

For what it's worth, I tried. And blessedly, the farther we got from the wandering tree, the more human I felt. Before long the whole situation felt so dreamlike that I had to question the resilience of my sanity.

There was a car in Philip's driveway and the house windows were aglow. Hope surged through me. Maybe he was in there right now, eating dinner or watching TV with his mom. Hustling up the walkway, a flicker of movement in one of the windows caught my attention; yet for whatever reason, no one answered the door.

Jeremy had to drag me back to the car by my shirt sleeve.

The football stadium across town, where the people of Shawnee had first swooned over Philip's superhuman abilities, was empty. As was the baseball field. We tried every party house we could think of, called or visited his most recent girlfriends.

Nobody had heard from Philip.

Out of ideas for the moment, we pulled into the lot of a strip mall and parked facing the main drag. Cars swooshed by for a full minute before Jeremy finally spoke.

"What is all this, Link? I mean, what exactly did Philip say?"

I chewed my lip. Honestly, how was I supposed to respond? I hadn't heard from Philip in days, and our last interaction could be summed up as the unauthorized trade of a dear necklace for the sickly bruise on my ribs.

"Fine," Jeremy snapped. He reached for the gear stick but then changed his mind, sighing irritably through his nose. "Listen, I'm trying to help here, but you're gonna have to level with me."

He was right, of course; I wasn't being fair. But if I had learned one thing about Jeremy over the years, it was that he had little patience for anything that seemed to betray scientific explanation; the truth would only push him farther away. So I played dumb, presenting my palms in a show of bafflement—quick thinking, I know.

"C'mon, Link," Jeremy urged. "What are you not telling me?" His voice was tightening, I couldn't help but notice, taking on the quality of a braided cable that was beginning to unravel under great stress. Not that I blamed him; if we were approaching the end of his patience, it was my own stupid fault. Regardless, a change of tactics was clearly in order.

The truth was bound to come out anyway, I reminded myself. And if anyone could be trusted to keep a secret in the meantime, it was Jeremy. So I decided to loosen the purse strings, just a smidge. "Okay, okay," I relented. "I found out earlier today that—" At once, my nerve faltered. It took a moment to muscle it back into line, a task made more difficult by Jeremy's impatient glare. I swallowed with difficulty. "Philip is, um … he's a homosexual."

There. I'd said it. Yet I hated myself for the way the words had come out, thick with superstition and even a hint of revulsion. This was Philip we were talking about, dang it, and of all the detestable things the guy had probably done in his life, being gay wasn't one of them. His sexual preference wasn't even the tragedy, anyway. At least, it shouldn't have been.

Jeremy swiveled back toward me just as a slice of headlights illuminated a surprisingly indignant frown. "Wait, he actually told you that?"

I shrugged noncommittally, which at the time seemed more palatable than an outright lie.

"Wow," he breathed. "What else did he tell you?"

"What, like that isn't enough?"

Shaking his head, Jeremy began to pick at the steering wheel cover.

My cheeks burned. "How long have you known?"

He smiled sadly, dodging the question expertly, without so much as a shrug or a glance in my direction.

"Nice. So were you guys ever planning on telling me?"

A police cruiser flew past with strobes on and we tracked it from one end of the windshield to the other. For a while thereafter, neither of us had anything to say. But then, just as I began to think that my friend had forgotten all about me, Jeremy spoke up.

"Remember how much I used to obsess over baseball?" he said, and though he offered a wistful smile, his voice sounded smaller than I had ever heard it. "Man, seems like so long ago." He chuckled at the memory, though it failed to strike me as silly.

"Don't change the subject," I growled.

Jeremy looked at me for a long moment, tapping the steering wheel with his thumbs. Tick-tock, tick-tock, tick-tock.

I slouched in surrender. "Fine. You were a prodigy. I never got why you bailed on it."

"Yeah, well. Baseball camp pretty much ruined the game for me." He stole a glance at me, expression now creeping with expectancy. He was trying to throw me a bone, I realized.

"Seriously? We're finally gonna talk about that?"

He nodded.

"Okay, so did something happen? Something that involved Philip?"

Jeremy exhaled sharply and I saw the first twinkle of emotion collecting in his eyes. "It's not a pretty story, Link."

"They rarely are."

Jeremy smiled humorlessly, fingers raking through his hair. "Okay, then. There were a lot of coaches running the camp; a few league celebrities but mostly they were local. There was one who rode us way harder than the rest—called us filthy names, had us running laps every time someone messed up. I always felt like he was watching me too and it really bothered me because I couldn't figure out what his problem was." Jeremy's eyes hardened as he took a deep breath, remembering things that were perhaps better left forgotten. "Anyway, one night the guy sent for me after dinner. Said I needed some extra motivating because I wasn't giving a hundred percent. It was BS but I didn't have much choice but to go along with it. Figured I was in for laps until lights out or whatever."

"Did he do something to you?" I whispered.

Jeremy paused to close his eyes, striations of muscle shimmering along his jaw. "He kind of forced himself on me— tried to kiss me, wanted me to touch him. Said if I didn't cooperate, he'd send me packing. He'd tell everyone he caught me peeking in the showers like some kind of perv. Said no one would take my word over his—I was just another low-rent Indian, and no one gave a crap about people like me."

My hands curled into white-knuckled fists. I was almost afraid to hear the answer, but I had to ask. "So did you, um ... you know?"

A smirk teased the corners of his mouth as Jeremy's eyebrows bounced suggestively. "Oh I touched him, alright. Punched him in the gut."

"You *what*?"

"Put everything I had into it and he went down hard. Threw up all over the floor, too. I told him to steer clear of me and we'd both forget the whole thing. But if he started slinging mud, all bets were off."

"Oh my God! What did he do?"

The smirk deepened. "Nothing. Didn't have much of a choice, when you think about it. I mean, like he said: I'm just a low-rent Indian. He had a whole lot more to lose than me."

"Holy crap, man." I stared at my hands, which had weaved themselves into a single, trembling fist. "Wait—what about Philip? How was he involved?"

Jeremy glanced away and when he looked back again, the smirk was history. "Well, the next night it was Philip who disappeared after dinner. Nobody drew any attention to it but I knew exactly where he was. Sometime after midnight, he snuck back into the dorm and got in bed." Jeremy cleared his throat, eyes flashing angrily. "It happened pretty much every night, after that."

A rock had formed in the pit of my stomach, festering in pure anxiety. "And no one else knew?"

"Oh, I'm sure a few of the guys noticed him coming and going, but I doubt they had any idea what was going on. And besides, Philip didn't seem particularly bothered by what was happening. I mean, it didn't affect his performance on the field at all. He was still the same old smart-mouthed diva, you know?"

Hearing this, the rock in my stomach began to smolder angrily. "What's that supposed to mean?" I demanded. "It was okay because he liked it?"

Jeremy looked like he wanted to clock me but he kept his cool. "I'm explaining why no one suspected anything, Link. Don't put words in my mouth."

Crap. "Sorry man. I shouldn't have said that."

"It's fine," he muttered. "Trust me, there's nothing you can say that I haven't already thought a few hundred times. It's hard not to feel responsible, looking back, you know?" When his eyes darted to mine, I saw just how haunted he remained by the whole affair. "I mean, instead of stopping the guy for good, I let him become someone else's problem. Philip's problem."

"Have you told anyone else?"

"Sort of," he muttered. "I mean, I wrote an anonymous letter to the school board when I got home. As far as I can tell, they didn't do anything about it. Truth is, I've been waiting for him to come after me ever since, you know? A guy like that, he's a ticking time bomb."

He was referring to the coach, of course, but it seemed to me that Philip fit the description just as accurately.

"Anyway," he sighed, flashing a tired smile. "Eventually, this kid came along and whipped Philip's butt. Not really sure how, but somehow that got things moving in the right direction."

The implication hit me like a freight train. "Wait a second," I gasped. "Are you talking about—"

"Yup. Good old Coach Briggs."

We burned through a full tank of gas the next day, zipping around town in search of Philip. The police encouraged us to file a report until they realized that Jeremy and I weren't actually related to Philip; likewise, the hospital could tell us nothing. Once again, we tried the Hampton home and, as before, no one answered the door.

Philip seemed to have fallen off the face of the earth.

I should've finished that story at the wandering tree. I mean, what if the ending had led me right to Philip? What if by refusing to cooperate, I had turned my back on the only real chance anyone had of helping him? The possibilities had me fighting tears all day, yet I still couldn't bring myself to confide them in Jeremy. He wouldn't understand. And worse, if by some miracle Jeremy believed even a word of the strange truth, he would undoubtedly despise me for failing Philip, just as I had begun to despise myself.

It was early evening when Jeremy dropped me off at home, careworn and drained of all hope. From the porch, I heard my mother bustling around inside with pots and pans; the prosaic familiarity of the routine beckoned me, yet something caused me to hesitate with my hand on the doorknob. A black Mercedes was parked in the middle of Pruitt Field. From where I was standing, I could just make out the form of a woman staring up at the wandering tree, hair blowing in the wind.

"Lincoln, is that you?" came my mother's voice. "Come and give me a hand, would you?"

Sitting down at the dinner table ten or fifteen minutes later, I glanced out the window to find the mystery woman standing within a stone's throw of the back porch. And she was squinting through the very window she was framed in, mouth slack, eyes unblinking. I knew her, I realized.

"Who is that?" Nicky wanted to know.

When I turned back to the window, Mrs. Hampton was hurrying away. I rushed out the back door and called out to her but the wind must've swallowed my voice. From the foot of the steps, I watched her trudge back to her car, knowing that I was too exhausted to catch up.

"Do you know her?" Nicky asked from the doorway. Glancing back in his direction, my heart skipped a beat. There it was—my beloved necklace—hanging from the doorknob like some kind of talisman.

It was then that sirens whined to life in the distance and the phone began to ring.

THIRTY NINE

Mr. Hampton answered the door. At well over six feet tall he had the abiding physique of a man whose fascination with debauchery still permitted a daily run and the occasional game of squash. He was a slightly blown-up facsimile of his son—he being the copy in my estimation, because his features were both smudged and perhaps a little harsher than an original probably ought to be—except that unlike Philip, Mr. Hampton had eyes that could drill holes through steel. By all appearances, he was precisely the ruffian that his son had tried so often to portray.

This was my first glimpse of the attorney close-up and I had to admit that he was a commanding presence. It was easy to see how Philip might've been intimidated by his father. Given what I had learned about the man, the price of his respect was well outside my means; fortunately for me, I didn't have any desire for his approval. I'd sooner kick him in the nuts than kiss his butt.

"Can I help you?" he drawled, though the disdain in his eyes assured that he wasn't the least bit interested in helping me. A crystal glass of something brown dangled in one hand and I had no reason to believe that it was his first of the day. But hey—who's counting? I mean, it was well after ten in the morning; had to be five o'clock somewhere.

"I'm here to see—"

"Come right in, Lincoln," interjected a voice from beyond the entryway. Mr. Hampton's eyes flickered to one side but he remained in place, barring the doorway.

"You're the Chase boy," he grunted with a disgusted frown. This took me aback, though in retrospect, of course he would know who I was; an acclaimed attorney wasn't likely to forget a brutal murder that took place in his own stomping grounds.

Before I could respond, Mrs. Hampton appeared at his side. Probably a good thing, too, because I was feeling uncharacteristically combative. "Thank you, Bill," she said through clenched teeth. "I'll take it from here."

Glowering over me with that crooked smirk, Mr. Hampton suddenly looked so much like his son that my brain stalled. Yet the resemblance vanished almost instantly, and when I tried to bring it back into focus, I discovered that I could no longer juxtapose Philip against this pompous turd—facsimile or not. Sure, Philip could be a punk; but it had mostly been an act with him. His father was the real deal.

I gave the lawyer my best deadpan stare, silently daring him to push my buttons. And with a knowing chuckle, he obliged. Leaning to one side, he created an opening that would scarcely permit a book to pass through. I can't even tell you how close I came to calling his bluff; to this day, I sometimes fantasize that I had. But Mrs. Hampton had no patience for such nonsense.

She squeezed into the gap, placing a firm hand on his arm. "Bill, *please*." With angry splotches blooming on her neck, she gently steered her husband out of the way to beckon me inside.

Hesitating on the doorstep, I cringed. "I brought someone," I confessed. "He's my ride. And one of Philip's best friends, too."

Mrs. Hampton peered over my shoulder to get a look at Jeremy, who had gone unnoticed up to this point. The weird splotches on her neck grew more pronounced, joined by a splash of pink across her cheeks. "Oh my goodness, Lincoln. How rude of me. It never occurred to me that transportation might be a problem."

"It's no problem," I assured her. "Jeremy isn't just a friend, he's also my personal chauffeur. He lives to serve."

Jeremy snickered. "You wish."

"Seriously, Mrs. Hampton—you need a ride somewhere? Just say the word." This I delivered with an exaggerated wink. What can I say? I was nervous.

With a polite titter, Mrs. Hampton led the way to her home office, which was nestled in the back of the home; her husband, in the meantime, grumbled up the stairwell for all to hear.

Once we were seated, and Mr. Hampton was comfortably out of earshot, she sighed. "Please forgive my husband. He's having a hard time—we're *both* having a hard time with this, as I'm sure you can imagine."

I nodded and so did Jeremy. For my part though, this was merely an acknowledgment of their tragic circumstances; it was in no way a commitment to pardon the dirt bag with whom she shared living space. One day, there would be a reckoning.

Mrs. Hampton opened her mouth, perhaps to expand on her previous sentiment, but a gust of emotion seemed to suck the wind right out of her. I knew the feeling well and—fair or not— whatever anger I held toward her went limp; that or it simply tip-toed over to her husband's side of the ledger.

"I'm so sorry for your loss," I said, blushing at the frog in my throat. There was a stinging in my eyes and I don't mind telling you that I was more than a little surprised by the sensation; one can only cry so much, you know, and by rights I should've been dried up like an old corn cob by then.

"Thank you," she replied in a hoarse whisper. "I still can't believe he's gone. That he would—" Her voice faltered, but there was no need to complete the thought. We were all thinking it, after all.

Next to me, Jeremy harrumphed and for a moment I was afraid that he intended to pinch the elephant in the room; this had always been his custom with me, anyway—

"Hey, what's with the huge zit on your nose?"

Or, *"Dude, are you wearing girl's pants?"*

—but I underestimated his restraint. "The service was beautiful," he said. "Philip would've liked it."

Mrs. Hampton nodded with a wan smile. "Yes, it really was lovely, wasn't it? Thank you both for being a part of it." She appraised Jeremy for a moment, one eye squinting slightly. "You played baseball with my son, am I right?"

Jeremy smiled.

"I thought you looked familiar. Quite a pitching arm, as I recall."

Her eyes clouded, meandering over the wall behind us. Twisting in my seat, I found dozens of family photographs peering down at me.

Philip as a toddler with an ice cream cone.

The whole family at an amusement park.

An eight- or nine-year-old Philip grinning up at his father.

Perhaps it was selfish of me, but I couldn't resist the urge to take advantage of the lull in conversation. Maybe it was the nostalgia brought on by those pictures, or maybe I was merely flirting with Obsessive Compulsive Disorder; in either case, it felt more important than ever to understand everything that I possibly could about Philip's final days.

"Mrs. Hampton, would it be okay if I asked you a question?"

She blinked, squeezing off a fat tear. "Of course."

"I was just wondering if you could tell us where Philip went before, um ... before everything happened? I mean, we looked everywhere for him, including—" Stealing a glance at Jeremy for moral support, I licked my lips. "Including here. We came by a couple of times actually, but no one answered the door. Only, I'm pretty sure someone was here."

As Mrs. Hampton frowned, her eyebrows smeared into a contemplative ridge. "I see," she muttered, tapping her desk with a long fingernail. "Lincoln, are you familiar with the phrase *quid pro quo*? It's a legal term." Cocking her head in thought, she snickered. "Frankly, everything in this house can be summed up in legal terms."

I nodded.

"Perhaps we can help each other, then. *Tit for tat* as they say?"

I shrugged. I know, I know—you don't even have to say it; my fondness for words was proving useless.

"That night, when you brought Philip home drunk? It was the last straw, I'm afraid. His behavior was simply out of control. I worried that it was only a matter of time before he got drunk and crashed into some poor family on their way home from Grandma's. He needed help. So the next morning Bill and I drove him to the city,"—*the city* being Oklahoma City, some thirty miles away—"and checked him into a rehabilitation facility."

So far, my suspicions weren't far off the mark.

"We hired a house sitter and relocated to the city for the week. She was instructed not to answer the door for anyone, by the way. The house sitter, I mean—so I wouldn't take that personally. Anyway, Bill had other business in the city and of course I wanted to be as close to Philip as possible. But eventually, Bill and I had to come home."

Her eyes wandered back to a picture on the wall, where they lingered for several seconds.

"It wasn't easy to leave my son behind," she whispered, and it seemed to me that her voice had changed pitch, taking on a faraway quality. "You can't imagine how hard that was. I don't care how big he was, Philip was my baby. My pride and joy." She smiled bitterly. "We didn't learn that he had run off from the facility until … until it was too late."

My lips pressed together like a vice, trying to press down on sorrow as if complex emotions could possibly be contained in such a way. "Thank you," I squeaked, clamping down even harder.

Mrs. Hampton wiped the tears from her cheeks and at once—quicker than should've been humanly possible—she was composed again.

"Now then, boys. Perhaps you'll indulge *my* curiosity?" Philip's mother lifted her eyebrows. The expression implied that she was awaiting our approval but I got the distinct impression that she was actually bracing herself. Though for what, I could only guess. "I wonder," she said, "did either of you know the man? The one he … ?"

At a loss for words, I might've offered a sober nod had Jeremy not beaten me to the punch.

"I thought as much," she confided, trailing into a long withering sigh. She took a breath so deep that it barely stopped short of a gasp just as a tear streaked down her cheek. The woman was barely holding it together. "Why'd he do it, boys? Why would my baby want to … to *kill* someone like that? I just … I can't make sense of it."

Jeremy paled and I knew that he was at least considering the merits of sharing the awful truth. But again, I needn't have worried; Jeremy was a model of propriety.

"Mrs. Hampton, what Philip did—I'm not sure anyone will ever really understand it. But regarding Coach Briggs? There's only one thing you need to know about him." My friend's gaze became piercing—angry even, though his voice retained a gentle timbre. "That man was a despicable person. A predator. Some might argue he didn't deserve to die the way he did, but that's not to say he deserved to live either."

Mrs. Hampton covered her gaping mouth, eyes swollen and fluttering. Over the coming months, eleven young men would step forward with allegations of sexual abuse against the former coach. But for the moment, the community was content to laud the late and great Coach Briggs, none the wiser. And while the Hamptons were perhaps more familiar than most with the coach's aggressive tendencies, not even they would've guessed just how depraved the man had actually been in life.

When Philip's mother opened her mouth to speak, I could barely breathe because I thought for sure that she was about to ask for clarification. Details that would only cut her deeper, if not destroy her altogether.

Rarely have I been so thankful to be wrong.

"Is it horrible that I should believe that so easily?" she pleaded. "That my son did the world a favor? It seems so ... callous. Cavalier, even."

"Of course not," Jeremy and I assured her almost in unison. And thankfully, our reassurance seemed to settle her nerves considerably. As a matter of fact, she appeared to be recharging in a way, steeling herself to put the whole matter out of her mind. I can't speak for Jeremy but my own relief was nothing short of dizzying.

"Well thank you for your candor," she said. "Probably best that we leave it at that for now." And then, with the practiced wave of a hand, the subject was dismissed from conversation. Mrs. Hampton straightened in her seat, lifting her chin with a regal grace that—in my limited experience—only the affluent ever pull off with conviction. "I suppose you must be wondering why I asked you to come here today."

I nodded; the thought had indeed crossed my mind.

"First of all Lincoln, I feel that I owe you an apology. The way I treated you—I presumed to know something about you based purely on your affiliation with my son. A terrible thing to say, I know. To explain, though: Philip attracted all sorts of unsavory kids, as you must know. They followed him around like beggars, like he was their personal Daddy Warbucks. Some even went so far as to steal from him, though Philip didn't seem to care.

Naturally I assumed that you were one of them. I know better now."

"What changed your mind?"

Flashing a cryptic smile, Mrs. Hampton looked quickly away. "Wish I had a simple explanation for that."

Strangely, I felt that I might know the answer, even if she was reluctant to share it. So I took a baby step in that direction. "I saw you in Pruitt Field, you know. That day, I mean."

She stiffened noticeably, though my comment couldn't have been much of a revelation; she had left my necklace behind, after all.

"Is that so?" she whispered. "Do you have it with you, then?"

I felt an eyebrow hike up. "Uh, excuse me?" It was like she was reading my mind and the feeling was just a wee bit disconcerting.

Abruptly, her mouth had begun to quiver as if a wild animal was bucking for freedom behind her lips. *Whoa,* I thought. *What is this?* "The necklace," she said. "Are you wearing it now?"

"Yes. Always."

Cradling her face in spindly fingers, Philip's mother began to laugh—deliriously it seemed, given that her eyes were more stricken than amused. I didn't have the slightest idea how to react, and I wasn't alone in my dismay.

Seeking out my gaze, Jeremy frowned with worry of his own. "Uh, maybe we should come back some other time?" he suggested.

The woman turned to him in surprise, as if she had forgotten all about Jeremy in the brief time since he had last spoken. The sight of him, however, seemed to ground her, calming her visibly. "Please, that won't be necessary," she said. "Forgive me—my nerves are a little frayed, that's all."

Dubious, Jeremy allowed his gaze to settle on her desk where a slew of documents was splayed. The air seemed to thicken around us and I knew that I should let sleeping dogs lie. Alas, I couldn't help myself.

My knees began to bounce, powered by pure anticipation. "So you were saying? About the necklace …?"

Jeremy skewered me with a glare of rebuke. "Dude—leave it alone, would you?"

But Mrs. Hampton had other plans. "Jeremy, I wonder if you could give us the room for a few minutes?" She asked this sweetly, wiping her nose with a tissue that seemed to spawn from the air itself. "There's a rather private matter that I need to discuss with Lincoln."

Jeremy's eyes drained of expression, a sure sign that he was offended. A slit-eyed, sidelong glance removed all doubt, yet what could I do but shrug? "Sure," he replied—somewhat curtly, I might add. "No problem."

"Please, make yourself at home," Mrs. Hampton encouraged him. "There are snacks in the kitchen, or you can wait in the den if you prefer. There's a television in there with cable."

Much in the same way a good friend will laugh at you when you step in dog crap, I couldn't help but be amused at this situation. So I gave Jeremy a smirk that might've said: *Yeah, have some Doritos and hang out with good old Bill.*

When we were alone, Mrs. Hampton swallowed audibly. "Could you show me?" she asked. "The necklace?"

Warily, I did. Her hands began to shake when she saw it; mildly at first, then so fiercely that she had to clasp them together to keep from knocking something over.

"My Lord," she whispered, then gulped. "Lincoln, I don't know how to ask you this without sounding like I've lost my mind. And who knows, maybe I have—it feels like that lately, with all that's happened." She dabbed at her eyes and tried to smile. "Anyway, I have to ask. Has the tree in that field ever … I don't know, spoken to you? Not in words really. More like … impressions, maybe?"

My chest was suddenly heaving, eyes bulging in their sockets. I nodded.

"Has it ever … *shown* you anything? I mean, something that turned out to be true?"

Again, I nodded.

Mrs. Hampton sighed and began to wring her hands. "Honestly, now that I'm sitting here with you, talking about it out loud like this? The whole idea sounds ridiculous!" she exclaimed with a laugh. "If not for that necklace of yours, I'd be on the phone with my shrink about now."

My eyes narrowed. "What does my necklace have to do with anything?"

"I'm sorry, Lincoln. I know I'm not making much sense. Please just bear with me, okay?"

I shrugged.

"I suppose there's no harm in admitting that I don't normally put much stock in the supernatural. Haven't since I was a little girl. But that day, I felt like the tree was calling out to me. Bill and I had just returned from the city and I was sitting right here—" She opened her arms above the expanse of her desk. "—and out of nowhere, I just *had* to get in the car and drive out there that very minute." She leaned forward. "And as soon as I got out of the car, that tree seemed to pour out this … this *story*." She wiped her eyes again. "*Your* story, as it turns out."

I felt faint.

"Don't get me wrong, it could've been about anyone. But when the story ended, I was drawn to this little mobile home on the edge of the field, and I was compelled to bring that necklace of yours. Only, when it came time to knock on the door, I couldn't get up the nerve. So I hung it on the doorknob and left." She cringed. "Cowardly of me, I know. Anyway, I had a hunch it might be you, but I wasn't sure until now."

"What kind of hunch?"

"Well, you had the necklace on when you took Philip home, so there was certainly that. But mostly, I think it was the scars. In the story ... you know, there was this accident? I thought of you immediately but then I second guessed myself because—well, the scars seemed so much worse in the story than they actually are."

My cheeks felt like they might actually ignite.

"Where did you get it, anyway?" she asked gently. "That part of the story was ... vague. Did Philip give it to you?"

"Philip? No, of course not. Why would you think that?"

"Well, it isn't much of a stretch, when you think about it. Pruitt Rock is a bit of a family obsession, after all. The truth is that I kept the necklace from you because I thought that you'd stolen it from my son."

My lips skewed to one side in a rather indignant frown. Irritated, I allowed my gaze to travel the room, taking in the little details that defined what it must mean to be a Hampton. There were old photos in walnut frames, shadow boxes full of little rocks. A vintage gumball machine filled with candy. Some kind of weird sculpture carved from burled elm. One of Philip's many football trophies.

My eyes flicked back to the shadow boxes, just as something clicked in my head. My frown softened. "Oh my God ... you're a Pruitt, aren't you?"

Philip's mother cocked her head to one side, eyebrows slanting with amusement. "Well, of course I am," she laughed, and for a second I could only stare in amazement. "Sadly, I'm the only one left."

"So that field behind Lakeview Park—Pruitt Field—it belongs to you, then?"

She smiled.

Thank goodness I was sitting because if I had been standing as this all came to light, I would surely have collapsed. I wheezed for a few seconds, trying to decide if and how this changed anything. The whole situation was simply too much to process, so I circled back to one of her earlier points. "So you thought I stole one of your meteorites."

Folding her arms across her chest, Mrs. Hampton took a moment to carefully frame her words. "Yes, I'm afraid I did." Her smile hardened and then went crooked, just like her late son's. "But Lincoln, let's be honest, okay? We both know it wouldn't have been your first time stealing from us."

Already out of sorts, this nearly pushed me over the edge. "Mrs. Hampton, I'm not sure what the wandering tree showed you, but I can assure you that I have never stolen anything from Philip."

With a neutral expression, Mrs. Hampton reached into her desk drawer and delicately withdrew a sheet of notebook paper. "Maybe not knowingly," she said and slid it across the desk to me.

As I read the first line, the bottom of the world must've dropped away, because suddenly, I was in a freefall through an abyss of bottomless guilt. The words written on that paper were all too familiar. *My* words, though penned neatly in someone else's hand.

Only ... not. Because when I thought about it—I mean, when I *really* dug through my memory—I realized that it was a lie. A little white lie that had gone unquestioned for so long that it was allowed to grow into an absolute monster.

These beautiful words had never been mine at all, you see; irrespective of their rightful owner, I had claimed them as my own, just as men had once claimed the land I now called home. A gift from the wandering tree—that was how I justified it. Had that been mere wishful thinking or was it yet another lie? In my fragile state, I honestly couldn't say for sure. Yet there was no denying that I had stolen, plain and simple.

"Where did you get this?" I was moved to ask, holding the paper before me with the reverence of a lost sea scroll.

The woman who had once ejected me from her home in anger now smiled enigmatically. "You found this poem written on a roll of paper, didn't you? Hidden in one of the knotholes of that tree?"

I sagged in my chair. "Not exactly," I muttered. "It was sort of blowing along the ground."

Mrs. Hampton leaned forward on her elbows, eyes twinkling with mischief. "Yes, well. It must've blown free. The point is, who do you think put it there?"

As I followed her down this strange path, one that she had clearly mapped out for this very discussion, the air around me seemed to retreat. I was completely at this woman's mercy and the realization put a hitch in my breath. "Um, you did?"

"Yes, that's right," she chuckled. "I did a lot of that when I was young, leaving trinkets and notes with the tree. Many of the children from my generation did. The tree—what'd you call it, *the wandering tree*? I like that—it's covered with hiding places, you know; knotholes and crevices and such. Have you ever noticed?"

I had.

"It may sound like superstitious voodoo nowadays, but as a kid, I never had any doubt that the tree was magical. I grew up believing it could fix things, broken things that were otherwise beyond repair."

Feeling broken myself, I tried and failed to connect the dots. "So you left your poem there to … to fix something?"

Mrs. Hampton frowned. "I'm afraid you misunderstand, Lincoln. *I* didn't write the poem, don't you see? Philip did."

FORTY

My entire body went numb.

"My son wrote that in the seventh grade. For me, it was the first tangible proof that there was something different about Philip. He felt too deeply for his age. He understood too much about the nature of love. He was wise well beyond his years, and if I'm being completely honest, it scared Bill and me to death."

In my shock, this piece of information fell flat. I mean, the subject of the poem was clearly a young lady. And that simply didn't fit with what I knew to be true about Philip.

Once again, Mrs. Hampton appeared to read my mind. "It isn't about a girl, Lincoln. Surely you've figured that out by now?"

The disbelief in my eyes must've betrayed that I had not.

"It isn't about romantic love at all, in fact. To Philip, I think the bond between mother and child was the closest he could come to imagining love requited." The poor woman's face crumpled as she explained this. "Because the love of a mother is … it's supposed to be unconditional."

I read the poem again, this time with brand new eyes, and I saw at once that she was right. The girl was a symbol, a font of boundless beauty and affection. Somehow, the words were even more beautiful now than ever before.

Philip's mother was crying now, bitterly, and I suspect that it was shock alone that prevented me from joining her.

"I am so sorry, Mrs. Hampton. There is no excuse for what I did."

She shook her head emphatically, laughing through her tears. "No, Lincoln. I'm not angry with you." She dabbed at her tears and reached across the desk for my hand.

Without hesitation I gave it to her.

"The tree showed me more than just your story, you know. It gave me a glimpse into your heart. Obviously, you've made some mistakes. But even in your worst moments, Lincoln, you're still a kinder person than any I've known in a long while. You loved my son for who he was."

Giving my hand a firm squeeze, she swallowed a moan.

"It's me I'm angry at, not you. Because I failed my son. When I took that poem of his to the tree, I was so desperate to heal him. I prayed at church too, but nothing worked. It was the only time I ever acknowledged that Philip was going through something more substantial than a phase, you know? And in my arrogance, I really thought that he needed fixing."

A sob was creeping into her voice, but she pressed on.

"The thing is, though? It was me and my husband, all along. It's so clear to me now—*we* were the broken ones. We killed the most beautiful thing that ever happened to us."

I was in a pretty fragile state when Jeremy dropped me off at home. So fragile, in fact, that a week droned by before I could bring myself to face the world again. I stared out my window for most of that time, watching the wandering tree wave hello—or goodbye, depending on which way the wind was blowing. It stood mere feet from the rubble stone property line, now. Over the course of my life, the giant had crawled from the middle of my window to the very edge of view. Which, according to my very scientific calculations, meant that the wandering tree had literally accomplished more in my lifetime than I had.

I would later learn that the pasture abutting Pruitt Field—the same bur-patch, you may recall, where I nearly died years before—sold that very week. The property had been on the market for longer than I had been alive, so it was a pretty big deal. I'm sure the transaction was intended to be kept on the down-low; naturally it was the talk of the town. Yet even if the new owner remained a mystery, it didn't take a genius to figure out what he had in mind. And there was nothing I could do to stop him.

On some level, I had come to resent the old elm. I understood that it hadn't caused Philip's demise any more than it had caused mine—even if I didn't completely understand the scope of its mystical properties, I got that much. But still, the sight of it filled me with unease. I suppose my resentment stemmed from selfishness as much as anything; I had come to the tree for answers, you see, and left with the sky falling.

Shuffling out of the bedroom, I found the house empty. There was a note on the fridge.

Doing laundry. Back by noon. EAT SOMETHING!

I poured a glass of orange juice and trudged to the kitchen table, gaze drawn unconsciously to the window. Looking at the tree now, I was tempted to pay it a visit; there remained the mystery of the stranger at my graduation, after all. But when I considered the possibilities, I had to admit that I wasn't ready.

Then again, neither was I any less determined to get answers. If my mother wasn't talking and the wandering tree couldn't be trusted to give me what I needed, there was really only one option left.

So I made up my mind and picked up the phone.

Checking in with security, I emptied my pockets into a plastic bin. It wasn't until a laminated visitor badge was clipped to my shirt that I suddenly began to question the wisdom of my intentions. Oddly, despite the long drive to McAlester—a hair under two hours, factoring in a couple of wrong turns—not once had I second-guessed what I was doing. Now, with the parking lot far behind me, the idea of my coming here seemed idiotic.

I should've just written a letter, I realized; in my impatience, I had borrowed Jeremy's car and set off toward instant gratification, as if there would be anything gratifying about visiting my father in prison. Nevertheless, it was too late to turn back now.

Speaking of the old man, after a ten minute wait, he approached the security glass divider with a dumbfounded grin. He looked incredibly small, like a miniature of the giant I had once looked up to. Like my grandfather, my father's hairline remained intact, yet it was mostly gray now—shaggy but thinning so that his scalp could be seen beneath, smooth and shiny like a polished egg.

I stood at his arrival. Just so you know, it wasn't good manners that drove me to my feet; truth be told, I think I was about to make a run for the door. But I managed to swallow down the impulse, knowing that if I hastily indulged it, I might never learn the truth. We sat in our plastic chairs and took a few seconds to appraise each other. When he was satisfied, my father nodded toward the phone and we both put them to our ears.

"It doesn't look so bad now, does it?" he said, beaming at me. His voice was scarcely above a whisper, so faint that I had to squash the phone against my ear to understand him.

"What's that?" I asked.

He drew an invisible circle in front of his face, gesturing toward mine with his chin. "Your face," he said, a little louder this time. "Looks pretty good."

"The magic of plastic surgery," I lied.

"It's been, what—three, four years?"

I shrugged. "Something like that."

His grin dimmed a little and he cleared his throat. "I didn't think you were ever coming back."

"Neither did I."

To this, my father nodded sagely, draping a pale arm across his miniature pot belly. "Fair enough," he said. He wanted to know about me and Nicky and I told him what little I could think to share. Yet when he asked about my mother next, I felt my hackles rise.

"She's lonely," I snapped. "And worn out after raising two kids on her own."

Eyes piercing, the old man nodded.

"Sorry, Dad—I mean—" Ugh. I hated to use that word, to call this man my dad. As if he was around to do the things that dads were supposed to do. As if he had any claim to the title now, given what he had done to my family. To me.

His eyelids fluttered, but he managed a tight smile.

I tried again. "I came to ask you something."

Eyes narrowing, my father stiffened. "Well, okay then. What's on your mind?"

I reached for my wallet and remembered at the very last second that it wasn't there. Honestly, I'm not sure what producing that ten-dollar bill was supposed to accomplish; it was a worthless visual aid, even if it proved to me that the stranger wasn't a figment of my imagination. Nevertheless, for whatever reason, I felt less prepared without it.

Tilting my head to one side, I tried to get my head together. "What can you tell me about Benjamin?"

"Franklin?" he chuckled—uncomfortably, I noted. "Not much." He began to pick at a spot on the tabletop.

"Not that Benjamin," I corrected, laying on a little heat. "Tell me about Benjamin Chase."

The old man stopped picking and looked sharply up at me, raking a thin clump of hair away from his eyes. All traces of a smile were gone now. Guarded yet raw like exposed nerves, his gaze darted about my face, probing. Digging.

"What do you know about Benjamin?" he demanded. His tone was unapologetically brusque, and a younger me might've cowered in fear. As it was though, I grinned. Because I knew in that moment that my long-held suspicions were well founded. And that the exhausting trip here would be worth it, after all.

"Only that he exists," I scoffed. Scooting to the edge of my seat, I drilled the man with a cool glare. "And that you and Mom have done your best to keep him a secret."

Leaning back, my father made a sound that might have been a grunt of frustration or merely the inevitable creaking of an old man. He looked thoughtfully at the ceiling for a long time.

I waited him out.

"We were trying to protect you kids," he said finally. "But it turns out it was really me you needed protection from." His eyes flicked to me and then fell away.

I said nothing, though my mind abounded with choice words of assent. This close to uncovering the truth, I refused to be baited by such low-hanging fruit; I would not dignify his pity party.

"He was your uncle," my father said with a gruff sigh, picking at the table once again. "*Is* your uncle, as far as I know."

"*Aaaa*nd?" I drawled, a hint of exasperation in my tone.

He shrugged like a child who has just been asked if he wants to go to his room.

"Come on, *Dad*." I spat out the words with some sarcasm, but the truth is that my heart was only half in it. "No more secrets, okay?"

The old man looked at me, and then he was looking through me, remembering.

"Benjamin is my older brother. Everyone called him Ben, except my daddy. I was always Fin to my daddy, never Finton. But for some reason, Ben was Benjamin—like he was the good son, you know? The one Daddy was proud of." Frowning, he squinted a little, as if to refine his focus through the murk of decades. "Anyway, Ben was barely a year older than me but he was a lot bigger. Almost as big as your grandpa, if you can believe it. I can remember—"

Abruptly, the narrative came to a halt; my father leaned forward, face crestfallen. I could see the musculature of his mandibles flex. "Hold on a second, Link. You gotta promise me something before I go on."

"This isn't a negotiation, Dad." Funny, the more I called him that the less it bothered me. "I'm not asking for a favor here. I'm asking for the truth with no strings attached because it's the right thing to do."

"I know, I know," he chided, clawing at the scruff of his neck. "I'm not tying on any strings. But you gotta try real hard to remember this was a very long time ago, okay? A completely different age when folks had a different way of thinking about things. That's my condition."

"Fine."

He chewed his lower lip and I noticed for the first time that he was missing a tooth. "Listen, Link, I just don't want you getting so hung up on who your grandpa used to be that you forget who he became, okay? The truth gets pretty ugly sometimes."

I felt my blood pressure rise at his implication, but I wasn't about to back out now. "I accept your condition."

"Well okay then," my father sighed. He twisted his head to the side, which generated a tiny pop in his neck, and then took a grand preparatory breath. When he looked at me again, there was so much sadness in those eyes, so much regret that my heart ached. Before I could pinch myself for caring, the man began to speak.

"The thing about your grandpa is that he used to have a serious temper. You know how big he was—you didn't want to cross him, ever."

No argument so far.

"Anyhow, one day Daddy got angry about something my momma said and he smacked her upside the head. Before anyone could think to stop him, my brother Ben was on him like a Pit Bull." As my father squeezed his hands together, hissing between his teeth, it became apparent just how difficult this was, reliving such a painful memory. I felt grateful to him, but only a little; this was his rightful penance, after all.

He looked at me and blinked. "Did I already mention that Ben was big?"

I nodded.

"Oh. Anyhow, he wasn't just huge, he was strong. I took after my momma, I guess, so I've always been pretty small."

Had he really? Had my father been this diminutive man all along? How small I must have been for his shadow to swallow me whole.

"But Ben?" my father was saying. "He was just like Daddy, temper and all." He paused, at a momentary loss for words.

"Go on," I prodded. With the truth so close, my agitation mounted almost as quickly as my patience wore thin.

"Well, they had a pretty good scuffle, only neither of 'em was winning. So Daddy reared back and popped him one." My father shook his head, eyes suddenly wet. "Ben went out like a light." He laughed bitterly and shrugged his shoulders. "That's the way things were done back then—no such thing as time-outs or grounding, no loss of television privileges."

I nodded, though it was hard to imagine—so hard, in fact, that I harbored a tiny hope that it wasn't true. Could this be the fictional ramblings of a bored prisoner? The possibility seemed marginal at best. For the moment, I'd take what I could get.

"Anyhow, we figured Ben was just unconscious, but he wouldn't wake up. Turned out to be in some kind of a coma. He spent a couple of days in the hospital before he finally snapped out of it, but ..." He bit his lip, swaying his head from side to side.

"Sorry," he whispered, tears now damming up against his baggy eyelids. "Ain't easy to talk about, you know?"

I nodded calmly, though inside I was boiling, churning with disgust.

"Anyhow, Ben woke up with brain damage. He was … well, I guess you could say he just wasn't right. Didn't talk right anymore, couldn't do things like normal kids."

My body was shaking now, victim to a relentless swell of emotion. "So you're telling me that Grandpa … he—" I was forced to abandon the words as they piled up at the back of my throat.

No, this simply couldn't be true. Not *my* grandfather. Not the man who had written love poems to my grandmother, the gentleman who had mowed a widow's yard for two summers in a row, without accepting a penny in return. "You're lying," I seethed. "I don't believe you."

"Son, you got to understand—"

"Stop!" I was out of my seat, stretching the phone cord to its puny three feet. The urge to rip it free and smash it to bits against the Plexiglas was almost unbearable.

My father's eyes went wide with alarm.

A guard peeked around the corner, glaring first at me and then at my father. "Don't make me regret this, Fin," he barked. I glanced at my father, who was nodding apologetically. The guard disappeared.

"Gotta keep it down, Link. Thing is, we don't normally get this long with visitors."

I flushed, embarrassed less by my outburst than by my failure to appreciate the limitations of prison life. Ashamed, I returned to my seat and sulked quietly.

"I know this is hard to hear, Link. Believe me."

"If any of this was true Grandpa, would've gone to prison," I insisted. "Just like you."

My father closed his eyes and took it on the chin. "I told you, son. Things were pretty different back then. The law considered it an accident, so that was the end of it."

As hard as this was to swallow, and despite my show of staunch disbelief, I must've known deep down that my father was telling the truth. The man was many things but I had never known him to be a bald-faced liar. Nevertheless, the story was an ugly blight on Grandpa's memory, one that might never fade. I wanted to hate my father for that. I wanted to hate him for keeping me in the dark for so long, too, yet it was I who had set out with such determination to dredge the familial tar pit. And when you go digging for bones, you gotta be ready to find some.

So there it was. As if the Chase family tree wasn't already diseased enough, burled and choking on its own twisted branches, here was a flame that might well burn it to the ground. Maybe that wouldn't be such a terrible thing; maybe we deserved to go up in flames.

"What happened next?" I croaked, crying profusely now, though I couldn't be pressed to say when the first tear fell.

My father looked at me with uncertainty, probably wondering if I was worth all the effort; that or he was trying to decide if I was even capable of handling what remained of the story. Eventually, he set his jaw and moved on.

"Well, my momma was never the same after that, for one," he confided. "She got real quiet, kinda distant. To all of us, not just Daddy. When she died, it was all I could hope for that she was finally out of her misery."

"What about Ben? What happened to him?"

"My daddy put him up in a little town outside Amarillo. There's a special hospital there for people with brain injuries. Ben needed special care, understand? He couldn't take care of himself, couldn't even wipe his own butt without making a mess. Couldn't leave him alone—not even for a second—because he had a knack for hurting himself; truth is, he hurt other people too, when he got real mad." My father snorted. "Kid was just so dang big."

Very little of this jived with the man I had encountered and I said as much.

My father shrugged, wide-eyed. "I can't explain that, son. Haven't seen Ben since I was fifteen years old. Glad to hear he's improved, though—can't even tell you how happy that makes me." He laughed suddenly, choked off a sob, and then laughed again. "He came all the way out to your graduation? Sounds like your mother's still a busy bee."

My mouth fell open. I fancied myself a reasonably intelligent guy yet it had never occurred to me that my mother might have orchestrated Ben's presence at my graduation. At some point, I needed to quit taking her word at face value. Well intended or not, a lie was a lie. And though I was as guilty as anyone, I was done with deception.

Lost in his own thoughts, the smile on my father's face grew and soon began to twitch. Happy tears pin-balled down the scraggle of his gaunt cheeks. The good news that his brother was alive and well might've been the best thing to happen to my father in years, I realized. And I had to admit that, as taxing as this visit had become, I was secretly glad to be there with him. To share not only the joy, but the heartache with someone who could truly appreciate the difference.

"How'd he look?" my father mewled.

"He looked really good, Dad. Happy too."

When I confronted my mother about Ben early the next morning, she stormed into her bedroom and shut the door. I was about to follow after her—angrily, I might add—when she abruptly reemerged, smiling broadly. She handed me a dated brochure for a place called the Four Leaf, located in Wayside, Texas. According to the brochure, which had gone yellow and brittle with age, the facility specialized in long-term care for victims of brain injuries. In my excitement, I barely registered my mother slipping the truck keys into my back pocket. A minute later, I looked up to find her sitting at the kitchen table, wearing a smug little grin.

That self-aggrandizing look of hers—like everything had gone precisely as planned, like all the deception had been not only worth it but necessary—would normally have irritated me. But not today; I was too emotionally sapped to take offense. Then again, maybe I was just tired of being angry all the time, of holding grudges. Of expecting perfection from others when I myself was far from perfect.

"Just have it back by morning, okay?" she said. "You got cash for gas and tolls?"

FORTY ONE

"You ready?" Nicky whispered.

I was not. After a five hour drive with an air conditioner that blew more hot air than cold, all I wanted was a shower and a very long nap. But I nodded anyway because what else was I supposed to do? I mean, we were there.

A big-haired woman at the information desk made a phone call on our behalf, whispering unintelligibly with a hand cupped over the receiver. For a few irrational minutes, I expected a S.W.A.T. team to descend on us. Two out-of-towners dressed like vagabonds, sweating nervously like they're primed to rob the place? I'm pretty sure I'd have called for backup myself.

But then, oh my God ... there he was. Uncle Ben, standing at the end of the hallway, wearing Big Smith overalls and brown slippers. Face lit up, hands splayed across his cheeks like he'd just found a golden ticket in his Wonka bar.

"Lincoln!" he exclaimed, and my heart soared.

"Uncle Ben! Come meet your other nephew."

With a giddy squeal, he rushed toward us, which—though sweet—wasn't unlike a rhino running us down. We met him halfway and when we all collided, my long lost uncle scooped me and Nicky into the mother of all bear hugs—seriously, I think one of my ribs actually popped out of joint for a second. He smelled of

Old Spice and bananas and ... oh my goodness—that smile! I swear, that smile could've powered the whole building for a month.

As much as I wanted to push the thought from my head, I wished my father could've been there with us. What a relief it would've been for him to see his brother face to face after all these years. Maybe I'd bring him someday. Maybe someday we could all start over.

We took Ben to lunch at what I will affectionately refer to as a geriatric buffet; not only were we the only patrons below the age of fifty-five, I didn't find a single food option that required teeth to get down. Not to mention a bathroom sign that advertised an assortment of adult diapers, available upon request for those pesky emergencies.

We talked for close to an hour about nothing of any real consequence—our favorite crafts, a book on amphibians that Ben was reading, what mashed potatoes were made of—just enjoying the man's curious nature. His resemblance to my father—and especially my grandfather—was nothing short of dazzling; it was like God had taken the best bits of each and mixed them all together to make Ben. He was perfect.

Honestly, there were moments when it seemed to defy common sense that he was holed away here, in a secluded town perhaps known best for its production of ketchup packets or something. But then, Ben's childlike grasp of the world would resurface and I felt profoundly grateful that Ben was at home in a place so devoted to his happiness.

Nicky had convinced me—perhaps wisely—that no good could possibly come from talking about Grandpa and we painstakingly stuck to this plan. It was more difficult than you might think because Ben couldn't stop talking about the man.

"Is he in the truck? Tell him to come inside, guys," he begged at one point. And later, "Where's my daddy? I'm supposed to make him coffee. I always make him coffee." Nicky thought this was cute, but me? I nearly broke down over that one.

Upon return to the Four Leaf, we were greeted at the door by the care director. Mrs. Nance was a plump, bright-faced woman whom I immediately recognized as Ben's tagalong on graduation day. She gave us the dime-tour of the facility, which was clean and cozy, and not at all the depressing madhouse I had been unconsciously bracing for.

"You're not thinking of stealing my Benny away are you?" she half-joked when the tour was over. "We'd plumb lose our minds without him here to keep us entertained." Though kind, her gaze seemed to develop a serrated edge and I got the message.

Don't you dare even think about it.

Well, I'm not gonna lie; I was already entertaining the possibility because it made sense to me that Ben should be closer to his family. But even if we could somehow provide the kind of care that Ben needed on our paltry budget, and if Mrs. Nance wasn't standing by to give me the stink eye, Ben was clearly traumatized by the very mention of leaving. This had been his home for many years and he didn't want to leave.

"Don't worry, big guy," I assured him with a gentle clap on the back. "We're not gonna take you away. We're just here to get to know our uncle Ben."

Like a window shade, relief wiped across his face, scraping away the terror. His trademark grin returned in full force. "Okay!" he bellowed, and we all laughed. At once, though, Ben's smile turned sour. "I think I have to poop now."

Some encounter the divine in holy places or at the very least in nature. I have certainly found evidence of a higher power in those situations, and on occasion I can even remember feeling that

I was undoubtedly in the presence of something much, much greater than myself. Yet as a young man, I had never experienced the personal touch of God. I grew up going through the motions of church without really understanding what we were doing, much less why we were doing it. These were simply things that one did at church, just as raising one's hand and thumbing through textbooks were things that one did at school.

Over time, I soaked up bits and pieces of Christian ritual, snippets of scripture and Southern Baptist doctrine; these I allowed to coalesce into an overtly stylized image of God, one that I accepted as an accurate depiction, however unflattering. He was a paradoxical if not bipolar being in my estimation; from one side of His mouth, He decreed that man should not kill; from the other, He commanded men to wipe out entire cities—to slaughter men, women and children alike. It's no wonder that I was so profoundly affected when God suddenly reached out to me; I was terrified of Him.

As it turned out, the Lord chose to reveal Himself as I lazed about the house, fully-dressed after several days on the road. Though travel weary, I was otherwise of sound mind. No, I was not binging on religious television, nor had I given in to the wiles of experimental music. No cold medicine or Jolt cola; nothing that might have enhanced my vulnerability to external influences.

It was simply my time.

I wish that I could offer up some poignant explanation—perhaps a convenient vision packed with grand symbolism or revelation; a testimony so inspiring that it would instantly validate my faith to anyone who heard it. But the truth is that, while I did indeed experience a vision—or rather a vivid dream—I suspect that it will fall flat in the telling. It was meant for me after all, even if I'm compelled to share it with you now for the sake of continuity.

When I closed my eyes to doze late that morning, I knew immediately that God was there, even if I couldn't see Him. I couldn't see much of anything, in fact. I was suspended in thick, soupy darkness; my hands and feet flurried through meaningless tasks and while they accomplished nothing, the importance of these tasks weighed heavily on me.

"Don't stop now," the darkness seemed to hiss. "Just a little more, just a little longer." Only, the harder I tried, the more I wasted away, the more desperate I became to comply. I think I was dying and I had the resigned heart of a person who knew how to do nothing else. I felt God looking on, yet I didn't cry out for help because I was more afraid of Him than the darkness.

It was then that, from nowhere—and yet from everywhere— Jesus spoke to me. Not in a human voice, really; it was more like the air itself breathed my name, sending a great shudder through the darkness. Immense relief—joy even—flooded through me as the black void retreated, scattering like shadowy rodents. Suddenly, I was free, drifting into a light—one that I had been blind to until that very moment. This was where I belonged, I realized; I could feel its warmth on my face—literally *feel* it tingling on my skin. It was beautiful and—and …

Well actually, that was pretty much it.

When I awoke, my first thought was that I must've imagined the whole thing. Actually, if I'm being completely honest, I went so far as to hope that I had imagined it because believing in Jesus Christ was sure to make a mess of things.

But I knew.

Deep down in the nuclei of my cells, I felt it. With the same confidence that I would always know my earthly father's voice, I recognized my creator's. The question was, what did I intend to do about it?

My necklace was just shy of scalding hot, the bit of space rock stinging like a brand against my skin, but I couldn't get the dang thing off; the best I could manage was to fish it from under my shirt collar to let it hang loosely against the fabric. Trembling now, I padded barefoot to the bathroom, where I splashed cold water on my face. Stalling. The water felt good, soothing my burning cheeks and cleansing the fog from my mind. I dried my face with a towel that—by the smell of it—was a week overdue for washing, still avoiding the mirror. By the time I got up the nerve to steal even a furtive glance, my heart was all but pounding out of control. And rightly so, because to this day when I think about what I saw in my reflection, the little hairs on the back of my neck still stand on end.

My scars were healing right before my eyes—not merely fading, as if that wouldn't be enough, but literally narrowing, folding in on themselves. They didn't disappear altogether, yet I almost had to look for one to find it. Even more bizarre, I somehow looked unchanged. I mean, when compared to the me I had been only minutes before, I looked the same. Honestly, if I hadn't been watching the transition as it happened, I might never have noticed the difference, though it truly was dramatic.

With unsteady hands, I yanked the wallet from my back pocket, snatching out my driver's license. I looked at the little picture there and back to the mirror, again and again.

God help me, this wasn't a dream—it was *happening*. And if this was real, then … oh, crap—so must be the rest of it.

Sharing this part of the story with you now, I can imagine how it must sound—and believe me, I was tempted to keep it to myself. Nevertheless, it's important that I be transparent on this subject because it shaped how I saw things from that day forward. You see, I knew in my heart that with a single whisper, Jesus Christ had claimed me. And if I needed physical proof, I had but to look in the mirror. To deny the truth would be to choose the same path that Philip had walked—to live a lie that would eventually destroy me.

All of this to explain why, in a moment of absolute awkwardness, I dropped to my knees on that cold linoleum floor and called out to Jesus.

Definitely not my typical morning routine.

The first thing I did as a new believer—aside from giving my knees a thorough wipe down—was visit Clyde Hampton. I might've shared the news with Nicky first if he wasn't out on a lunch date. Again. Seriously, Romeo had nothing on this kid. Anyway, as strongly as I now believed that Jesus Christ was the real deal, I needed some perspective on things. I mean, where exactly did something like the wandering tree fit into the blueprint of Christianity? What about evolution? What about dinosaurs, the Big Bang? The list went on and on because I was a guy who needed to understand things, who disliked loose ends.

The church office was open and once inside, I didn't have to look hard to find Clyde. The older man was leaning against the welcome counter in the foyer, chatting with Ms. Winters and a woman who might've been the receptionist. An array of Chinese takeout cartons was splayed across the counter and the air smelled of fried cuisine.

When Clyde saw me approaching, his face lit up. "Well, look what the cat dragged in!"

"Just following my nose," I chuckled. "Am I interrupting?"

"Lincoln!" Ms. Winters cried, rushing over to embrace me. "I haven't seen you for weeks," she complained, though she beamed like a spotlight. "I'm worried about that beautiful little brain of yours, you know; it's going to shrivel up like a raisin, the way you've been neglecting it lately. When was the last time you read a book?"

I laughed. "Things have been a little crazy lately."

Stealing a glance at Clyde, her smile pitched to one side and she winked. "Ah, but you have no idea."

This was precisely the sort of comment that would normally pique my curiosity; but I had ventured all this way with a single purpose in mind and I refused to be distracted now.

"Why don't you join us, Lincoln?" Clyde tempted, gesturing toward the open food cartons. "It appears that our eyes were bigger than our stomachs." The two women giggled.

My stomach growled. "Oh, no thanks. Not really hungry," I lied.

Clyde shrugged. "Suit yourself. So what brings you by, my good friend? Not that you ever need an excuse."

"Well, I was hoping we could chat for a few minutes." Eyes flicking to Ms. Winters, then to the receptionist, I offered a nervous smile. "Something kind of, um, personal. If you have time, that is. I can always come back."

The old man straightened. "Nonsense," he chuckled. "You're here now. Would you ladies please excuse me?"

Patting Ms. Winters affectionately on the hand, Clyde smiled in a way that I had never seen him smile before. My heart warmed at the sight of them together, two beautiful souls who had been alone for far too long. Until that moment, the ring on the librarian's finger had escaped my notice and despite my rush to get Clyde alone, I almost asked if they had a date picked out. But the man was already striding down the hall and I was too socially awkward to backpedal now.

With the help of the custodian's enormous key ring, we commandeered an empty Sunday school classroom and sat in folding chairs. My nerves were crackling with such insistence by then that I could barely contain myself; even before we were settled in, I was already pouring out the details of my dream, the supernatural healing of my face. Clyde listened with a half smile, yet there were times when his eyebrows furrowed and I couldn't decide if he believed me or not. It would've been too much to ask of a stranger, I know—to believe such a farfetched tale, that is— but Clyde was no stranger. He was my friend and I desperately needed him to believe me.

When I was finished, Clyde nodded in hearty approval. "That's wonderful news, Lincoln," he laughed, slapping his thigh for emphasis. "I'm so happy for you."

I couldn't help but grin, though it stemmed more from relief than enthusiasm. "You don't think I'm crazy—about my face, I mean?"

"No, Lincoln, I do not." The custodian leaned forward to examine me, plucking a pair of reading glasses from his shirt pocket. "I'm always amazed at how far the Lord is willing to go to call one of His own." He cocked his head and leaned a little closer. "And now that you mention it," he whispered, "the difference is quite astounding. I can't imagine how I missed it before."

It felt weird, letting him scrutinize my face like that, but I refrained from backing up. "The thing is, I have some questions, Clyde."

The old man nodded, mouth slightly agape. "Fire at will, my friend."

I intended to ease in with something facetious—*How exactly did Noah keep the animals from eating each other on the ark?* for example—but a much more salient thought gripped me, as it often had since Philip died, and began to dig its claws in. "I've been thinking about Philip," I confided. "About what it means that he … you know. How he died."

The fate of the world seemed to hang on this one issue for me, though I couldn't put my finger on why. I mean, chances were that I'd find a way to stomach the breakdown between science and religion. But *this*? Good or bad, I needed to understand.

Off came the glasses, and as Clyde's arms folded across his chest, an immense sigh rattled between his teeth. "Well Lincoln, that's a sore subject indeed," he muttered. His eyelids drooped slightly and I wanted to punch myself in the face for putting him through this. Yet if there was anyone I could trust to give it to me straight, it was Clyde. Of course, he might just change the subject; or worse, flat out refuse to discuss the matter. And if he did, I certainly wouldn't hold it against him. The way his tongue touched his upper lip, though, I knew that he was gathering his thoughts rather than declining to answer.

So I waited.

"I'm afraid that God's word isn't very clear on that subject," he finally explained. "There are plenty who believe Philip committed an unforgiveable sin by taking his own life. Others believe that once a person is saved by grace, only the persistent resistance of the Holy Spirit is unforgiveable. And I suppose you could support either argument, depending on how you chose to connect the dots between scriptures."

"What do you believe?"

Clyde rubbed his eyes, whose whites were rapidly turning pink at the corners. "To be perfectly candid, Lincoln, I'm not sure that Philip ever accepted Jesus as his savior to begin with. His parents kept him away from church for his whole life, you know. And me by extension." He laughed humorlessly, head wagging from side to side. "Bill always detested our beliefs; he thought of the Lord as some scaled-up version of the tooth fairy. He just ... he just never understood."

My back went rigid to the point of discomfort. "So what're you saying—Philip went to hell?" My lower lip trembled as I forced out the words; I hated the way they felt on my tongue.

Clyde's mouth stretched into a white-lipped grimace and though he opened it as if to speak, he resolved instead to nod. A tear streaked down his cheek and perched on his chin.

"I don't understand," I confessed, and while I couldn't blame Clyde for the ugliness of the truth, anger rippled through me, honing a distinct edge on my voice. "How could God make Philip the way he was and then punish him for it?"

Collecting himself, Clyde wiped his chin. "Lincoln, God didn't make Philip into a homosexual; it's just something that happens. All over the world, throughout time. Even in the animal kingdom, if you weren't aware of it." He shrugged with a frown.

"But you have to remember, this world?" He slashed a hand vaguely toward a bank of windows. "This is the devil's domain. God intervenes when it serves His purposes but make no mistake about it—until Jesus returns, life is supposed to be hard. We have Adam and Eve to thank for that. Bad things happen to good people. They get sick or hurt, killed for no good reason. They're born with deformities, mental disabilities, unnatural desires. The devil is much busier than we give him credit for."

"You make it sound like Philip was some kind of mutation." I couldn't help the bitterness in my tone.

"Homosexuality isn't part of God's design, Lincoln— scripture couldn't be any clearer on that point. And by the way, a four leaf clover is a mutation. So are twins. Being unnatural alone doesn't make something deplorable, and certainly not unforgiveable. But there's an element of immorality tied to homosexuality that simply can't be resolved—short of blatantly ignoring God's word, that is."

"Sounds like an impossible situation."

"On the surface, yes. But let me ask you something, Lincoln: have you ever had lustful thoughts?"

"Of course I have," I grumbled. "Who hasn't?"

"Exactly; we all do. But the mere fantasy of committing a sin is sinful in God's eyes, which is why forgiveness is so crucial. When you think about it in those terms, we're no different than Philip. We're all the same."

I considered this for a few seconds before rebutting. "Not to be rude," I said, "but that seems like a tidy oversimplification."

Infinitely patient, the custodian leaned back to appraise me. "How's that?"

"We're all sinners, I get that. But when the time is right, the two of us will be able to act on our desires without sin, right? I mean, we can get married so we have an end in sight."

Clyde nodded, eyes dropping to his lap. He knew exactly where I was going yet he was kind enough to hear me out.

"What did Philip have to look forward to?" I continued. "He spent his whole life knowing that he'd never be free to love or be loved on his own terms. That's something we've never had to suffer through."

The custodian showed me his palms. "That's a fair point," he said. Leaning forward, he patted me on the knee. "But just so there's no confusion, Philip's sexuality didn't doom him to hell." He paused to chew his cheek for a moment. "Between you and me, I didn't have any idea that my grandson was gay until after he was gone, so I can't say if he ever acted on his feelings. But you know what? It wouldn't have mattered. Jesus paid the price for Philip's sins, just as He paid for yours and mine."

"Still doesn't seem fair," I brooded, barely holding tears at bay.

"Fair? No, there's nothing fair about what Philip went through. But since when is life fair? You of all people ought to recognize to that. The Lord never promised fairness, Lincoln; he promised justice. And there's a world of difference between fairness and justice."

The distinction went over my head then just as is does today, whenever my emotions are allowed to take over. It would take many years to wrap my mind around the concepts that Clyde seemed to navigate with such clarity. And in a manner of speaking, this was only day one for me; I couldn't very well expect all the secrets of the universe to be revealed in a single sitting. And yet, given my disappointment, I must've been hoping for exactly that. Nevertheless, lacking any retort for the moment, I could only wipe my eyes and concentrate on keeping it together.

Clyde placed a fatherly hand on my shoulder, giving it a gentle squeeze. "Lincoln, I wish I had easy answers to your questions but the truth is you've got to dig into the word to find them. And sometimes, all you can do is pray for understanding because not everything is black and white."

I was afraid of this very response and I must admit that it pushed me back on the fence a little, confirming my suspicion that life was about to get pretty complicated.

Clyde offered to pray for me, and though I was frustrated and out of sorts—and somewhat weirded out by everything—I agreed. Wrapping his hands around mine, Philip's grandfather asked the Lord to reveal things to me—if not understanding, then acceptance. Afterward, he hugged me fiercely.

"I can't tell you how proud I am that you've responded to the Holy Spirit," he said with his trademark, toothy grin. "Too many push it away these days."

I smiled in response, but I was cringing inside. I didn't have the heart to tell this dear man that I might not be up to the challenge.

I mean, what if I wasn't ready?

FORTY TWO

When you stop to think about it, forgiveness is truly one of the most bizarre things a person can do. I mean, to let go of the past—the empirical evidence of what has happened and what is therefore likely to happen again—and to consciously move forward as if it never happened at all. I know, I know—we like to think that to forgive doesn't necessarily mean to forget, right? But the truth is, to forgive—and I mean to *really* forgive—one must completely scour away the past to begin anew. Forgiveness by any other definition is only a sketch of the real thing, one that can easily be smudged out of existence in the heat of the moment or worn like a badge for the sake of keeping score. I suppose that's why forgiving is so hard. And why my own forgiveness will always be precious to me.

Many years before, Ms. Winters had warned that we should never define a person by a single mistake. She was right of course. It was time to break free of bitterness, to be vulnerable again to the people whom I was so determined to forgive. If not for their sake, then for my own.

Still, I won't pretend to have looked forward to the day when my father finally walked away from prison. By then, the man had become more of a household legend than a living creature. I hadn't seen him in years and though bittersweet, our last meeting failed to linger in my mind as a fond memory.

My mother insisted on being there to meet him when he walked through the gate and while it surprised me, I didn't argue. "You may never understand, Lincoln," she explained. "But the heart wants what the heart wants. No sense in fighting it."

I did understand, though. Because it was a sickness we shared. More than a decade before, I had pinned my heart on a ghost and fooled myself into believing that I'd get it back someday. Likewise, my mother had never made an effort to move on from my father, despite his long absence. Given the choice between solitude and substitution, you see, neither of us could bring ourselves to settle.

My father had beaten my mother, yet she had abused him in an entirely different fashion. Each had left a permanent mark on the other. I could only hope they were mature enough to do things right this time. Strange that it took my father's incarceration for my mother to fully appreciate the value of fidelity, but there's no denying that the heart has a mind of its own.

My father paroled twelve years into his eighteen year sentence. Upon his release he was placed in a halfway house on the outskirts of nearby Dripping Springs. The rules there were stricter than any of us might've expected and as a result, we saw very little of him for the first several months. He found a job digging ditches on a road crew and, despite the stigma of his criminal record, his work ethic soon prevailed. He was promoted to crew foreman; within a year, he was taking home more than he probably ever had.

Though my father had filled out a bit since leaving prison, he remained smaller than me by a fair margin. Clean-shaven with a decent haircut, he looked pretty good for a man his age—all things considered. Still, prison is kind to no one.

It wasn't until my father moved back in that I saw just how profoundly the system had changed him. No, I'm not referring to the missing tooth or even the menagerie of crude tattoos on his forearms. The man was harder now, coiled to react. Wary of every movement around him as if his own family might be conspiring against him. Too, his eyes darted to the door almost constantly. He slept on the couch for the first week and I'm betting it was for the sole purpose of keeping that door within line of sight. Knowing that he could open it and leave at a moment's notice, and that no one would hunt him down for trying—that must've been an amazing feeling. Maybe even an overwhelming one.

Incidentally, it was around this time that Mrs. Hampton spearheaded the construction of a community park in Pruitt Field, complete with swings, a jungle gym, a baseball diamond and a pond stocked with perch and small-mouthed bass. This she commemorated Lily Park, a nod to her beloved son.

Nicky had long since married and moved out by then, but he and his wife Renee—a sweet Cherokee girl he met at church— came by regularly with their two-year-old, Bella. We grilled hotdogs and played in the new park. Nicky and I played catch with my dad while the ladies entertained Bella and talked about … I don't know—whatever it is that ladies talk about when men step outside of earshot.

There was a feeling of restlessness in the air during those days, like something of great significance was building up and would one day discharge. Yet if growing up in Lakeview Park had taught me anything, it was to live in the moment. To not be held captive by what may or may not happen.

Even if this was a painful lesson to learn, I'm glad to have learned it. Because these were some of the happiest days of my life, in part because I refused to live in fear anymore. A period of restoration—of deep healing—was desperately needed in my family, and despite the crazy trajectories this life had thrown each of us into, we all managed to converge here again, on Lakeview Park. To finally be a family again, rebuilding what we had spent a lifetime tearing down.

Maybe I really was naïve. I lived in an apartment that could easily be mistaken for a crack house. I drove a ten year old Honda Civic that burned as much oil as it did gas. I had been on a handful of dates in my entire life and, though none had ended in disaster, neither had they amounted to much. Yet despite all that, I would pit my happiness against anyone's.

Life was good.

EPILOGUE

In September of 2002, lightning finally struck. The wandering tree was estimated to be more than a thousand years old when it breached the Pruitt property line, where it entered the legal ownership of Mr. Hampton. Specialized lumberjacks and their oversized chainsaws were flown in from northern states to do what the locals had failed to do, time and time again.

As the national media immortalized the terrible act of destruction, the largest tree in Oklahoma came crashing to the ground. I felt the impact deep in my bones, yet there was more to it than that; something magical was ripped from me in that moment—a steadfast presence that had gone unnoticed for my entire life; until now, when it was suddenly gone. The abruptness of the loss affected me like the passing of a dear friend and I couldn't help but cry out.

I have never hated a human being as I hated Mr. Hampton on that day.

The great elm was reduced to a pile of rubble in a matter of hours and soon after, an excavator creaked into position. The machine nibbled away at the stump with such vigor that the ground vibrated under my feet even a hundred yards away. Long after, I stumbled to my parents' trailer, awash in helplessness, the clattering of that diesel engine still rang in my ears.

I didn't sleep a wink that night, though I doubt I would've fared any better at my apartment. Even my parents were distressed, though neither could pinpoint exactly what was so horrible about cutting down a tree; the wandering tree had never been more than unclaimed firewood to them, you see; yet even they had the sense that a great injustice had befallen us all.

The next morning, I stomped out to Pruitt Field and watched what was left of the carnage. It wasn't morbid curiosity that drew me, to be clear. Actually, there wasn't much to see by then. Accordingly, the media had lost all interest, as had the townies. Even the historical society had abandoned ship. The only spectators remaining were residents of Lakeview Park, a downtrodden lot that looked on in somber silence.

I'm not sure why I felt so duty bound to stick around; I mean, the tree was gone. Nevertheless, I looked on as the largest bulldozer I had ever seen heaved the stump from the ground. It came up in pieces, some the size of cars.

Mr. Hampton paced excitedly around the site with a bounce in his step. When he recognized me, his face darkened—but only for a moment. The aging lawyer glanced at the crater on his property and then back to me with the snidest of grins, which he accentuated with a sarcastic thumbs up. The expense of removing the wandering tree must've been enormous, maybe even more than the legendary Pruitt Rock could hope to offset. No, there had to be something much more primal than money driving that man. Something vile, detestable even.

My mind ventured back a decade to that poor Indian man, mutilated and abandoned off a rural back road; I wondered if anyone would notice if Mr. Hampton was to disappear. Of course, he was white. And considering his prominence, which had only compounded with the controversial death of his son, I was pretty sure that his absence would raise some eyebrows. Under the circumstances though, it seemed worth the gamble.

Before my primal impulses could win over common sense, I retreated to nearby Lily Park, where I plopped onto a bench that overlooked the pond. Broken, slumped in defeat.

"Don't go blaming yourself," came a sullen voice from behind me. "There's nothing any of us could've done, least of all you, Lincoln."

I glanced over my shoulder at Mrs. Hampton, who continued to approach in remarkable silence. "Can't figure it out, Mrs. Hampton," I sulked. "Why would he do this?"

"Actually, it's Ms. Pruitt these days. And believe me—there's no figuring Bill out. He's well beyond reason."

I smiled weakly.

Mrs. Hampton—um, Ms. Pruitt, that is—sat beside me on the bench. "He wasn't always like this, you know," she muttered. "Not that it counts for much now."

"He bought the Peterson's farm right after Philip died," I pointed out. "He's had this in the works for quite some time."

I was fishing for her take on the subject, but Mrs. Pruitt ignored the bait. "That day, when you and Jeremy came to see me?" she reminisced. "That was the day I knew my marriage was over." She sighed, brushing a wisp of hair from her eyes. "I suppose there were other moments when I thought we might be in trouble but I always pushed those thoughts aside."

"I'm sorry to hear that."

"Don't be," she laughed. "I can't imagine what took me so long." Her gaze fell to the cross hanging on my neck—a gift from Nicky after I was baptized a few years back—and a look of disdain washed over her face. "Don't tell me you've been drinking the Jesus Kool-Aid, Lincoln."

The spite behind this statement struck me like a slap to the face; I swallowed.

Ms. Pruitt grimaced just as a hand fluttered to her mouth. "I'm sorry, Lincoln. That was incredibly rude of me."

Speechless, I could only chew my lip.

"It's just that Christians have always rubbed me the wrong way. I grew up in church, you know."

The last thing I wanted was to indulge a religious debate with this woman—with anyone, for that matter—yet it felt important to at least try to understand her anger. So I dared a probing question. "Forgetting about Christians for a second, do you believe in God?"

Ms. Pruitt leveled a frown at me. "That would be a long conversation indeed, Lincoln. But let me sum up the paradox of Christianity with this: my son—your friend—was a homosexual. I can't say if he was born that way or not but he certainly wasn't brought up to be gay. How can you believe in a God who creates homosexuals and then condemns them to hell?"

That she felt fit to bring Philip into the discussion ruffled my feathers, but only for a second. Though gone, Philip would always be at the center of her life, I realized. Still, in my lingering indignation, my first instinct was to pick her statement apart; it conflicted with what I knew to be true on several levels, after all. Yet when I thought about it, I realized that winning an argument would accomplish nothing; at best it would spawn another.

The thing is, you can't really argue spiritual matters with someone who has rejected the Spirit, because the spiritual realm doesn't bow to logic any more than it abides by the laws of physics.

"Believing in God isn't like joining a political party, Ms. Pruitt," I pointed out. "You either believe or you don't. Acting on what you believe—well, I guess that's a different story."

With a sidelong glance, Ms. Pruitt pursed her lips. "I'm afraid that sounds a bit naïve, Lincoln. And you're dodging the question."

"Maybe I am," I admitted. "The truth is, I have plenty of unanswered questions myself. The only thing I can say with certainty is that Jesus is real. And despite what other Christians might profess, the Bible says that Jesus came to save people from their sin, not to persecute them for it."

A grudging shrug. "I'm afraid the church may have a more destructive perspective on such things than you realize."

I wanted to point out that it wasn't the church that destroyed Philip, it was his parents. But I bit this back, knowing that such an inflammatory jab would only push her away. And to be honest, I didn't wholeheartedly disagree with her assessment of the church.

"Ms. Pruitt, life has been incredibly cruel to you. You have every right to be angry."

I reached nervously for her hand, afraid that she might smack mine away, yet she snatched it greedily. We sat like that for a while, hand in hand, while the bulldozer revved and smoked, defiling what was left of the wandering tree.

I turned away, choosing instead to behold the beauty of Lily Park.

"You did a wonderful thing here," I told her. "Philip would've loved it. Especially that." With my chin, I motioned toward the ball field, where a few kids had a game going. Two women sat in the bleachers, chatting in the sun. I couldn't help but smile at the sight. It was a dream come true for the kids of Lakeview Park. And for me.

Without a word, we rose and approached the chain link fence. A kid in his early teens popped a foul ball and I watched it arc into the safety net and roll back to the ground. Mrs. Pruitt took the lead, strolling past the ball diamond toward the southernmost point of the field.

"When I was a little girl, the wandering tree was right about here," she declared, marking the ground with the toe of her flat. I felt an eyebrow sneak dubiously out of bounds; we were easily thirty yards upstream from where the tree had resided in my childhood.

A sharp cry reached out from beyond Pruitt Field and though I knew full well what it must have meant, I turned to look anyway.

Mr. Hampton was barking at the excavator operator, lurching in a wild tantrum. The operator volleyed a retort and tossed his hard hat to the lawyer's feet. The exhaust stack stopped billowing smoke and the man left in a huff.

It might've taken a few seconds for me to interpret the meaning of all this but Ms. Pruitt interrupted my flow of thought with a gasp; snatching a fistful of my sleeve, she began to laugh.

I followed her gaze to the ground, where a lump of rusty stone protruded from the ground. Ms. Pruitt dropped to her knees—panty hose and all—and began to claw the dirt away in dainty clumps. Mystified and sufficiently intrigued, I joined her. Within minutes, an area the size of a dinner plate was visible; a few minutes more widened it to a serving platter. The bit of space rock around my neck was getting hot, yet as it tinkled against my cross, the stinging heat somehow comforted me. My pulse thundered in my ears, and it had nothing to do with exertion.

Ms. Pruitt clambered to her feet with a shout of victory, though her cheeks were streaked with dust and tears. She turned toward her ex-husband, who was watching intently from afar, and shook her fist. Sobs overtook the woman as she collapsed to her knees.

"He cut it down for nothing," she hiccupped, trembling and smeared with filth. "It was all for nothing."

I cried with her because the wastefulness truly was unfathomable. Perhaps the most beautiful part of my childhood— often the only thing worth remembering—had died in vain.

When she had calmed, Ms. Pruitt regarded me with a hint of a smile, and I imagined that I could read her thoughts. Who knows, maybe I actually had; it's hard to explain such a thing in retrospect, especially when it was the furthest thing from my mind as it happened.

In tacit agreement, we began to rebury Pruitt Rock. A last second addition, I unchained the meteorite from my neck and dropped it in the hole. The wandering tree was gone, true; yet this cosmic relic had survived. I would protect it from that day forward, no matter the cost. No one would disturb it again, I vowed.

Not on my watch.

When the dirty work was done, we retraced our steps past the ball field in the direction of the pond. Glancing toward the old Peterson farm, I noticed that Mr. Hampton was gone; only the excavator remained, skirted by disorderly mounds of limbs and branches.

"Lincoln," Ms. Pruitt said as she pulled me to an abrupt stop. With a look that was neither alarm nor curiosity alone, but certainly both, she squinted into my face.

"Have you always looked like this?" She wiped her eyes with the tips of her fingers and leaned back to appraise me from a different angle, lips opening in wonder. "Seems like you used to be horribly scarred. Did I … *imagine* that?"

My hands shot unconsciously to the terrain of my cheeks, which was now smooth as silk.

Covering her mouth, Ms. Pruitt looked at me for a long time, eyes wide and sparkling with disbelief. "My God," she laughed. "Look at you, Lincoln! You're beautiful!"

But I didn't need to look; I knew exactly what I would see. And frankly, something of greater interest was vying for my attention. One of the women in the bleachers was now peering intently at me under the visor of a flattened hand, and it seemed to me that …

Well, the mind plays tricks, doesn't it?

Except that when I returned her gaze, the woman slowly rose to wave at me. My heart began to pound so hard that the whole world seemed to tremble. A fifth chamber of the organ—a long forgotten one that had fallen still—filled with warmth for the first time in many years, swelling with wonderful intensity.

Mrs. Pruitt squeezed my arm and I turned to look at her. "Who is that, dear?" she whispered but then caught her breath. "Oh … she's—it's *her*, isn't it?"

Ivy was moving toward me now and though the wandering tree lay scattered in pieces, I could swear that I heard it whisper a story. The most beautiful story I had ever heard, about—

ACKNOWLEDGMENTS

This was a very difficult book to write. If not for the help of some very patient friends, I honestly might've thrown in the towel. I would like to express my heartfelt thanks to Nancy Zavodny and Connie Garrett, whose encouragement has never failed to come precisely when I need it. Likewise, thanks to Pastor John-David Meissner for his friendship and steadfast guidance. I am also indebted to several fellow authors who were kind enough to lend their ideas and constructive criticism (Ken Oder, Claire Fogel, Aaron Smith, Gary Jonas). And finally, a HUGE thank you to my wife and kids for tolerating my writing, despite the many hardships that accompany it.

ABOUT THE AUTHOR

Daniel Wimberley is a professional web developer, moonlighting writer and self-proclaimed voice of the dork. Well, the voice of *a* dork, anyway. He isn't smart enough for the fraternity of nerdhood yet he is helplessly drawn to it like an ewok to the *Starship Enterprise*.

Daniel lives with his wife and children in northeastern Oklahoma. He enjoys website programming and integration, audio and video production and a host of similar pastimes that are sure to lull you to sleep.

For more useless trivia about the author, visit danielwimberley.com, or you may email him directly at geek@danielwimberley.com.

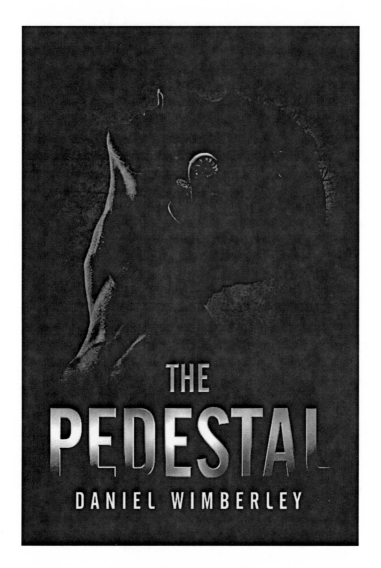

THE
PEDESTAL

DANIEL WIMBERLEY

"It grabs you by the throat and won't let go!"
-Ken Oder, author of the Whippoorwill Hollow series

Order yours from Amazon today!

CPSIA information can be obtained
at www.ICGtesting.com
Printed in the USA
LVOW11s1352291116

514933LV00002B/359/P